SPLINTER EFFECT

SPLINTER EFFECT

A NOVEL

ANDREW LUDINGTON

MINOTAUR BOOKS
NEW YORK

First published in the United States by Minotaur Books, an imprint of St. Martin's Publishing Group

www.minotaurbooks.com

Library of Congress Cataloging-in-Publication Data

Names: Ludington, Andrew, author.
Title: Splinter effect : a novel / Andrew Ludington.
Description: First edition. | New York : Minotaur Books, 2025. |
   Series: A splinter effect book ; 1
Identifiers: LCCN 2024031161 | ISBN 9781250349309 (hardcover) |
   ISBN 9781250349316 (ebook)
Subjects: LCGFT: Time-travel fiction. | Action and adventure fiction. |
   Thrillers (Fiction) | Novels.
Classification: LCC PS3612.U269 S65 2025
LC record available at https://lccn.loc.gov/2024031161

Our books may be purchased in bulk for promotional, educational, or business use. Please contact your local bookseller or the Macmillan Corporate and Premium Sales Department at 1-800-221-7945, extension 5442, or by email at MacmillanSpecialMarkets@macmillan.com.

First Edition: 2025

10 9 8 7 6 5 4 3 2 1

For Tess, who taught me to believe.
And for Charlie. I'm sorry I was too slow to get this in
your hands, big guy.

SPLINTER EFFECT

ALEXANDRIA, EGYPT

2018 CE

Rabbit Ward crashed into the protective glass cylinder as the time machine jerked him back to the present. Reflexively, he looked over his shoulder for pharaoh's soldiers, but they were gone, left behind in the desert two thousand years ago. He'd pushed it too close this time. A moment later and he would have spent the rest of his life in Roman-occupied Egypt.

She'd gotten him again.

"Welcome back, Rabbit. You look terrible."

The cylinder depressurized with a hiss, rose from its recess in the floor, and retracted into the ceiling.

The snark belonged to Ian March, the team's technical lead. He grinned at Rabbit from behind the raised semicircle of control consoles. Rabbit returned the smile and saluted him with his middle finger.

"In your dreams." Ian laughed and resumed his work with the two junior techs who ran the equipment with him.

Rabbit straightened as the cramp in his side subsided and scrubbed his short hair with one hand. It was as clean as it had been when he left twenty days ago. The first rule of time travel: nothing returns to the present that didn't start there. That included the grime that had caked his body in 48 BCE when he sprinted into the circle of stones he left to mark his spot. He envisioned a Rabbit-shaped cloud of dirt and undigested food slopping to the ground in the remote palm grove. Must have scared the hell out of his pursuers.

The Egyptian national time dilator in Alexandria looked like something from a sci-fi film, but it was functionally identical to more utilitarian models. Everything on the platform went back in time. Everything that made it back to the same patch of ground twenty days later came back home. Everything else was superficial. But what the hell, time machines were incredibly expensive to own and operate. If Egypt wanted to trick theirs out in stainless steel and glass, who was Rabbit to judge?

A physician stepped onto the platform and began to examine him. Rabbit complied without concern. Apart from fatigue and a few bruises, he knew he was fine. While Rabbit's appearance wouldn't turn any heads (he was middle weight, middle height, ethnically hard to pin down, all of which helped him blend in across eras) he had the kind of practical, workhorse body that seemed to be designed to take abuse. And it had taken far worse over the years.

He stuck out his tongue for the doctor's inspection as a fashionably dressed woman approached from behind the control console.

"How did it go?"

"It was . . . interesting." Rabbit raised his arms at the silent behest of the doctor.

"I like interesting men. I like interesting books. But, honey, I am far less fond of interesting time travel. What happened?" Neither her quip nor her Tennessee twang could hide the anxiety in her voice. Patty-Jo West, PJ to her friends, had been the collections curator for the National History Museum in DC for three decades. She had been Rabbit's boss and friend for two of those. He had seen her through two divorces and the untimely death of her eldest daughter. He knew her tone as well as anyone.

Rabbit lowered his arms and turned his head to let the doctor look in his ears. "Maybe we should discuss this on the way to the excavation."

Two hours later, PJ and Rabbit were sitting in the back of a white SUV, traveling south on Wadi Al Natrun-El Alamein Road. The sun shone brightly outside, but the tan interior was a steady sixty-eight degrees. Through the window, the farmlands at the outskirts of the Nile Valley were giving way to desert.

Rabbit glanced at the driver. He appeared to be fixated on the road, which was exactly what it would look like if he were eavesdropping.

PJ saw his glance. "Medo, honey, would you put on some music?"

With a nod, the driver flipped on the radio. Egyptian pop filled the cabin. PJ turned to Rabbit. "Well?"

"She was there again," he said softly.

PJ scowled. "How do you know?"

"She practically introduced herself."

"Looking for these, handsome?" a woman's voice called through the din of the fire consuming the roof of the Alexandrian book repository over their heads. The inferno Caesar had started had driven everyone else from the library. They were alone.

Rabbit wheeled around, his heart sinking at the sound of Modern English.

The petite woman facing him was dressed in Hellenic white and blue, her dark brown hair braided and arranged around her head like a crown. Despite the cinders drifting in through the open door, she was smiling broadly and looked as though she couldn't think of anywhere she would rather be.

She had her hand on a stack of scrolls piled on a clerk's desk. "Daedalus of Athens? That's your pseudonym? Really? It's like you want me to find you."

"*What do you want?*"

"*Half.*"

"*Fine,*" he said.

"*Don't be so hasty. I don't mean half of your piddling payment; I mean half the space in that fancy container.*" She pointed to the crate hanging at his side. Rabbit reflexively laid a hand on the masterwork glass scroll case he had commissioned for the job.

A cloud of smoke passed between them. Fire kindled to life on the clerk's desk next to her. She waved the scrolls over the flames.

"*The choice is yours.*"

Rabbit jerked his sword from its sheath, its steel edge glinting dully in the smoke. "*I could leave you here.*"

"*You won't though.*"

He wiped sooty sweat from his brow, hesitated, then jammed the blade back into its sheath. "*Dammit. Fine. Ptolemy threw his whole force at the Sun Gate. We're clear to the west. I have a horse waiting outside the walls.*"

"*I know.*" She grinned and produced a set of saddlebags from a nearby chair. "*I parked mine next to yours.*"

"PJ, she knew my whole plan down to the location of the dig. That's why I didn't want to tell you in the facility."

PJ rifled through her stylish little handbag and pulled out a lipstick. "Once is a coincidence." She applied some fresh crimson and smacked her lips. "Twice is a conspiracy."

"That's what I thought. Do you suspect somebody on the team?"

"Honey, I suspect everybody." She glared at the lipstick as if it had insulted her, tossed it back into her purse, and sighed. "I'll have to start an official inquest. I'm damn disappointed, Rabbit." She cracked that last phrase like a whip. The driver looked in the rearview mirror.

"I know," Rabbit replied.

"These people are like family."

"I know."

She rolled her eyes. "Well, you're awfully sanguine about it."

"I haven't slept in two days. Maybe it'll catch up to me." As she harrumphed at this, his attention was drawn to a gathering of vehicles on the side of the road ahead. "That it?"

PJ nodded.

"What's the story?" Rabbit asked.

"Oh, you know, a new filling station planned a few miles south of St. Moses Monastery found something out of the ordinary while digging for the fuel tanks."

Rabbit yawned. "Funny how often that happens."

The SUV crossed the opposing lane and crunched to a halt on the sandy side of the road. Rabbit stepped out into the heat of the afternoon while the driver opened PJ's door for her.

"Thank you, honey," she said and followed that with something in Masri that made the driver smile as he climbed back into the SUV.

PJ and Rabbit walked over to the large white tent that sheltered the excavation from the weather. A uniformed guard stood at the entry. He wore a pistol on his hip, but he smiled at them as they approached and held open the tent flap to admit them.

"Doctors."

"Well, thank you, honey. What's your name?"

"Nasir, ma'am."

"Thank you, Nasir. Don't stand directly in the sun, now. Do you need a water or anything?"

"No ma'am," he said and smiled.

She led Rabbit inside. PJ would remember the man's name and use it every time she saw him going forward. It was a talent Rabbit admired.

The moment they entered the shade of the tent, Elliott Hemmings, an archaeologist from New Zealand, rushed to intercept them.

"PJ, it wasn't my fault."

"What wasn't?" growled Rabbit.

Hemmings shot him a quick scowl but addressed PJ. "I came

straight here from the hotel the moment the report came through from the diggers, but the excavation crew said someone had already been here from the museum to collect what they found."

Rabbit bristled. "You were in Alexandria? When you knew they were digging today? Dammit!"

The Kiwi's cheeks flared red. "It would look pretty suspicious if I showed up ten minutes after they reported . . ."

"Apparently that didn't occur to the person who did your job! Let me guess—American woman, dark hair, about this tall?" Rabbit said, holding his hand at his chin.

Hemmings looked surprised. "How did you know that?"

Rabbit marched toward the hole in the ground.

Hemmings called after him, "Maybe you're working with her!"

Rabbit heard PJ's honey voice calming the archaeologist behind him as he looked into the six-foot hole scooped up by the excavator. It had taken Rabbit and the thief hours to dig it. At the bottom of the hole was a slab of sandstone he had placed over the magnificent scroll case to protect the glass and tip off the diggers that something was worth slowing down for. He had commissioned the slab as well; some meaningless Greek phrases were etched into the stone. Just enough to send up red flags to anyone who happened upon it in antiquities-happy modern Egypt.

He jumped into the hole, bringing a trickle of sand with him that slipped into his low boots. Hemmings's whining objection trailed after him, but Rabbit ignored it.

Standing on the slab, he could see where someone had dug out beneath it. He slipped his hand into the cavity under the rock. It was empty.

Rabbit was taciturn on the drive back to Alexandria. The stone slab could be sold off to some foolish collector. A community of people followed Rabbit and his peers and gladly bought up any items they used to do their jobs. The sale would cover the costs of the dig but fall far short of the expedition expenses.

"The jump, props, costumes, airfare, lodging . . ." PJ was tearing herself up about the loss.

"I'll explain it to the museum secretary," offered Rabbit.

"Marty is the least of my worries. It's the sponsors I have to explain it to."

"I can—"

She cut him off. "No, you can't. You have many skills, Dr. Ward, but diplomacy isn't one of them."

A horn blare caught their attention. The SUV slowed to a stop amid a sudden snarl of traffic. PJ craned her neck to look out the front windshield, then settled back into her seat in irritation. "Another protest. We'll be here a while."

Someone passed the side of the car waving a red flag and chanting. Rabbit looked behind them. Protesters appeared to be passing around the car on all sides. PJ had pulled out her phone. "What is this about?"

The driver, Medo, looked in the rearview mirror and replied in excellent English, "Your president declared unilateral American support for Israel."

She read from her phone, ". . . *recognized Jerusalem as the capital of Israel.* It's clumsy, but I wouldn't call it unilateral support."

Medo gestured to the crowd growing denser around them. "Does it matter?"

PJ scanned more stories. Rabbit scanned the crowd. The chants weren't in unison, the signs were scrawled with marker. This wasn't the protest of an organization; it had all the hallmarks of a social media feeding frenzy. If the police didn't come quickly, the crowd would turn their attention on . . .

A rock hit the car's windshield. Medo swore loudly in Masri.

"Do you have a scarf?" Rabbit hissed.

"A what?" PJ asked, looking around them, suddenly realizing their precarious position.

Rabbit grabbed the colorful edge of cloth poking out of her pocket. The square of flower-printed silk snapped open, and Rabbit wrapped it over her head. "We have to get out of here."

He popped open the first two buttons on his shirt and pulled it up over his head. The last thing they needed was to be singled out in all this anger.

Ignoring Medo's protests, Rabbit slipped out of the car and hauled PJ after him. The trickle of protesters was turning into a river, the chants getting louder and more coordinated by the moment. Rabbit steered PJ to the sidewalk through the shoving, shouting crowd and onto a calmer side street. Glass shattered behind them. PJ lowered her scarf as she straightened up to see what was going on. Rabbit put it back in place and took her hand. "Keep moving."

Ten minutes later, the disheveled pair trudged up the steps of the Alexandria National Museum. The National was their partner in the scroll expedition; the staff had worked with PJ and Rabbit off and on for years. Rabbit had never been so relieved to see the Italianate mansion.

Inside, the National staff fretted over their state. Two kind employees took them to the administrative office, made them tea, and settled PJ in a chair. Her breathing settled, but her makeup was smeared, and her hair was wild. A porter approached them.

"Doctor, a package was delivered for you."

"A package? From whom?" asked PJ.

"Respectfully, it is addressed to Dr. Ward."

The admin handed a long rectangular cardboard box to Rabbit. The label simply read:

Dr. Robert Ward
c/o the Alexandria National Museum

Confused, he pulled out a penknife, slit the packing tape across the top, and folded back the flaps.

"Well, thank god for small mercies," PJ breathed.

The scroll case lay nestled in a bed of Styrofoam packing in the box. Rabbit lifted it out, holding his breath. He wasn't willing to relax until he saw what was inside.

The outer sheath of copper was green and pitted from two thousand years in the sand. It almost matched the glass tube inside.

Rabbit gently rotated the lid back and forth to release it from the tube. The interleaved layers gave way with resistance, and the lid separated with a gentle pop.

"It's beautiful," PJ said.

"The old man does good work," he agreed, thinking of Meriiti, the venerable first-century glassmaker from whom Rabbit had commissioned the piece. The twelve thin leaves of glass that ringed the mouth of the scroll case slotted together so perfectly with the corresponding leaves on the lid that a speck of dust would have interfered with their closure.

He held the green glass tube up to the light. Roll upon roll of buff parchment lay within. Rabbit sagged with relief. The thief had kept her word and given him his scrolls after all. Up to that point, he hadn't admitted to himself how nervous he really was. You couldn't lose very often in his line of work before they found someone to replace you. The stakes were just too high.

A flash of pink in the center of the scroll case caught his attention. He reached for the interior.

"Rabbit, don't touch them!" PJ warned.

Rabbit delicately slid a small square of fresh pink paper out with his index finger. It read, in flowing script:

A favor for a favor. Stop in to see Dr. Ashish Agrawal at the British Museum on your way home. You're welcome.

LONDON, UK

2018 CE

The Victorians were mad about Egypt, of course. Unwrapping mummies was the in-vogue dinner party activity of the period. I'd like to think it ceased because British society realized how grotesquely they were treating the deceased, but it's more likely they just got bored of it. Let's take the stairs . . ."

On the layover in London, Rabbit begrudgingly followed the thief's tip and stopped to visit Dr. Ashish Agrawal at the British Museum. Over their handshake, the young archaeologist started talking about mummies. He led a bemused Rabbit through the museum and down into the working levels of the facility on an unbroken stream of words. Rabbit hadn't even introduced himself.

"Animal mummification is less well known but much more common. Millions of animal mummies have been discovered over the years, and a lot of them ended up in England as souvenirs as well. With the decline of Egyptomania, a lot of inheritors donated their family embarrassments to the museum where they just choked the stores." Agrawal's voice danced through pitch changes like a bell choir, ringing through the long, quiet hall.

The archaeologist opened a heavy door, and British punk music spilled out of the brightly lit lab. A handful of young scientists working in the lab ignored them as Agrawal ushered him to a work-station with dual oversized monitors. A dusty balsa wood box sat on the counter beside the computer.

"We have a ton of them, just lying in boxes. Most of them haven't been touched since they were first cataloged. At any rate, I was trolling the reserves looking for a sample to try out the micro-CT scanner, and this one was sticking halfway out of its cubby. It was like it was calling to me and—"

Rabbit raised his hand like a school kid, cutting off Agrawal mid-sentence.

"Yes?"

"Why am I here?"

Agrawal knitted his brow. "Your assistant said you would be interested in my findings."

"My assistant. Right." Rabbit pictured the woman waving good-bye as he stood peeing in the sand. "Only she didn't give me a lot of information. I've been meaning to fire her. Maybe you could help me out with some context."

"Of course." He nodded. "You see, it's the bandages that are of interest. Animal mummies vary greatly in quality. Some of them were used as offerings in temples, others were cheap fakes filled with sticks. In human mummies, the wrappings were made of linen. But linen was expensive, so many of the animal equivalents were wrapped in whatever was at hand: old clothing, used parchment, papyrus. Some of those wrappings contain writing which can be read using a micro-CT scanner."

"I've heard about that."

"I am putting together a proposal for a large-scale investigation of the museum's holdings. To make the case, I wanted to find some-thing of historical significance in a sample."

"And did you?"

He grinned. "Yes, I did."

Agrawal tapped his computer keyboard and the monitor lit up, displaying white, handwritten Greek characters on a black background. "This is from a sheet of papyrus in one of the layers wrapping this little fellow." He patted the wooden box. "It's a shipping manifest for boats delivering spoils of war to Constantinople in 535 CE."

Rabbit's stomach began to sink.

"535?"

"The year after General Belisarius defeated the Vandals at Carthage. He returned to Constantinople with a vast treasure to the new capital of the empire. Some of that treasure had been taken from Rome itself eighty years before, when the Vandals sacked the city."

"I know the story."

"I thought you would. And you might even be able to guess what I found." He scrolled down and read, "*The treasures of the Jews, including a seven-pointed candelabra.*"

"The menorah of the Second Temple," Rabbit muttered. He felt nauseous.

"It's the first tangible proof that it survived the sack of Rome!" exclaimed Dr. Agrawal. "Do you think you might try to retrieve it? If you did, would you be willing to write a letter of support for my proposal?"

Rabbit wasn't listening. His mind was back in Rome, 455 CE, twenty years ago in Rabbit's lifetime. *He was staggering under the awkward weight of the menorah. Storm clouds raged above the Aelian Bridge, his sweaty hands slipping on the beaten gold.*

"Dr. Ward?"

Rabbit snapped back to the present.

Agrawal continued, "There is one other curious thing about the mummy that you might find entertaining." He slid the box closer to the edge of the counter and worked the lid free. "In the museum's collection, we have crocodiles, dogs, donkeys, cats. Lots of cats. We even have two mummified elephants, if you can believe that. But to the best of my knowledge, this is the only example on record . . ."

He opened the box like he was performing a magic trick.

Rabbit stared at the contents.

". . . of a rabbit."

WASHINGTON, DC

2018 CE

Have a seat, Robert."

Martin Friedman, secretary for the Smithsonian, pointed at a Sheraton armchair across from his rosewood desk. Rabbit and PJ had received his summons when they landed in DC. Friedman was a solid administrator with good credentials. Undergrad from Spellman, PhD from Yale, MBA from Kellogg. It was his seventh year as secretary. He was bull-necked and as solid as a brick wall. He apologized for it with delicate, frameless glasses and tweed suits.

He glanced down at his papers. "*Epigoni, Odysseus Acanthoplex,* and *Triptolemos.* Three of the lost plays of Sophocles." His brows arched above his eyewear. "Unfortunately, the Bloch Family Foundation sponsored a mission to get six."

"I was robbed, sir."

He filed the papers into their manila folder. "I know. And unfortunately, so does everyone else. This town does love its gossip."

Rabbit ground his teeth. "I have a plan for Macedonia to ensure it doesn't . . ."

"Macedonia's off."

Rabbit stared.

"I'm sorry," Friedman continued. "The sponsors lost confidence after Alexandria. Pulled their funding last night."

PJ had been getting redder with every word, and now she exploded. "With all due respect, sir, it's the sponsors who keep the stringers in business. They pay a damn sight more to get personal trophies than they do for historical preservation, I'll tell you that!"

"I am aware . . ."

"I mean, if nobody's going to enforce the Adams-Cortez Act, what's the point in having it?"

Friedman put up both oversized palms like a referee. "I said the same thing to Homeland Security last week. The problem is that the people who fund illegal operators also fund us. And political campaigns. Fine them, jail them, our resources dry up as well. The appropriations committee has made it clear that the Feds will fund time dilation infrastructure but not missions. We are stuck with private sponsorship, which means the stringers are here to stay. We have no choice but to outcompete them."

"How am I supposed to beat this woman if I don't have a mission?" Rabbit protested.

Rabbit had spent twenty years traveling through time. He had always imagined his career ending when he got too old to swing a sword. Or dodge one. He had taken his favor with sponsors for granted.

"I was pondering that myself. Assuming you don't know anything about this woman that could lead to her arrest, then your best course of action might be to walk through the door she led you to."

Rabbit shook his head in confusion.

"The menorah."

Rabbit started to protest, but Friedman cut him off. "Hear me out. Before these recent thefts, the menorah was the only artifact you ever failed to retrieve. It's high profile, everyone associates it with you. Securing it would signal to everyone that you still have what it takes."

Rabbit stood up and went to the window. Friedman's office in the Smithsonian Castle had a view of the Moongate Garden. It reminded him of Alexandria.

Eighty expeditions. More than half his adult life spent adventuring through the past and he still couldn't outrun that goddamn menorah. Lost on a bridge in Rome.

Along with Aaron.

"You have funders lined up?"

Friedman cleared his throat. "I've spoken with the Israeli Historical Authority. They suggested we contact the Kahan family. They funded the first expedition, yes? They may still be interested."

"Marty," PJ warned.

"I can't go to the Kahans," said Rabbit.

"PJ would do the outreach, of course."

"The Kahans won't fund me."

"What makes you so sure?"

"David and Sarah Kahan won't fund me because I killed their son."

Friedman's mouth hung open for a moment before a delayed "oh" escaped.

"You didn't kill Aaron," PJ said softly.

"I can't go to the Kahans." Rabbit came back and sat. "What other options do I have?"

The secretary took a deep breath and let it out slowly. "You'll always have a place at the Institution. You could do research for younger archaeologists, write your memoirs."

"What if I get my own funding for Macedonia?"

Everyone knew it was PJ who cultivated the sponsors. She was a master of the deal, had brought in hundreds of millions in expedition funding. She was comfortable in the world of privilege. If her partners were withdrawing support from Rabbit, his chances were slim.

"You're welcome to try."

Which is how Rabbit ended up at the Kennedy Center Hall of Nations the following evening amid an affable display of American wealth mingling beneath the vivid drape of multinational flags. He plucked a champagne glass from the tray of a circulating waiter, drained it, and took another.

The evening's event was celebrating the lifetime achievement of a prominent theater composer. Rabbit had scored a ticket from PJ in hopes of rubbing elbows with some of the nation's privileged class.

He had certainly chosen the right event. One glance around the hall confirmed that many of the attendees had fortunes that started with a *b*. Those were his targets. Sponsoring his work was expensive; it made a nice write-off.

Breathe. Shelve the cynicism for another day.

The Bloch Foundation was hosting the event, and pharma-blue signage guided people through the facility. Eleanor Bloch, the matriarch of the family, had sponsored Rabbit's ill-fated trip to Alexandria. If he did nothing else, Rabbit had to convince her to defend his reputation in her community. He had completed seven missions for the Blochs over the years. She would understand that these thefts were nothing but a blip on the radar. He hoped.

Rabbit relaxed his grip on his champagne flute before he snapped the stem. Jesus, he really wished he had attended a few more things like this over the years. PJ had given up trying to get him to schmooze years ago. He'd never seen any point in it. Rabbit offered a service that these people wanted badly. He didn't need to befriend them.

And he hadn't. As Rabbit walked through the crowd, he spotted the faces of nine of his former sponsors. None of them looked at him with the faintest recognition. He was beginning to panic when he heard the drawn-out vowels of a familiar voice and tied it to the pinkish head and palm tree–print tuxedo of Mark Peach, director of the arts wing of the Bloch Foundation.

"Mark," Rabbit said, feeling like a loner at a high school dance.

Peach's round face split into a grin. "Robert Ward. You are the very last person I expected to see here."

Rabbit shifted awkwardly in his rented shoes. "Yeah, me too."

"Shame about Alexandria."

"Not a total loss though. Three plays."

Peach turned to his companion, a tall, gaunt woman dressed from head to toe in black. "Is five hundred a good batting average?" The woman looked offended to be asked. Tapping an index finger the color of an eraser against his chin, Peach answered his own question. "I think it is." He turned back to Rabbit and popped out his bottom lip. "Too bad this isn't baseball."

Anger welled up hot in Rabbit's chest. He fought to hold it back. "Listen, Mark, I know I haven't always been the most collegial . . ."

"What? You mean when you called me an officious tick?"

Rabbit winced at the memory. "I mean, you were defending organized crime."

Peach cut him off. "Did you need something?"

Rabbit wanted to slap the smug look off Peach's face. *Suck up your pride.* "Would you be willing to put in a good word for me to the other foundations? It would mean a lot to me."

Peach softened. "In that case . . ." He glanced at his companion, then back at Rabbit. "No."

Rabbit stalked away from Peach, fuming. Realizing he had better get to Eleanor before her officious tick did, he darted through the crowd until he spotted her.

She was standing near the Millennium stage, embroiled in a conversation with a vaguely familiar young couple who looked almost like twins.

"Dr. Ward! Nice to see you. Ethan, Anne, this is Dr. Robert Ward. Dr. Ward is an actual time-traveling archaeologist." She said it as though he were a two-headed cat.

Eleanor Bloch was in her early seventies, thin and stylish with a pile of hair so smooth and grey it looked like steel.

"Really? That's . . . so cool," the young man said. He was a good-looking kid with blond curls. "I'd love to pick your brain about that sometime. I've been workshopping a script about treasure hunters and . . ." He paused. "Sorry. I'm such a fanboy." Rabbit realized where he'd seen the young man. His face had been plastered all over the Metro recently on action movie posters.

"Dr. Ward just returned from an expedition to the Library at Alexandria."

Ethan looked like he might explode with excitement. His companion scanned the crowd, searching for someone more interesting.

"Since we're on the topic," Rabbit said, "could I have two minutes with you, Mrs. Bloch?"

The young woman caught the hint. "It was very nice meeting you," she said with a charming smile and dragged the young man away.

Rabbit turned to the event sponsor. "I want to apologize."

"Whatever for?" she replied, looking genuinely shocked.

"The expedition . . ."

"But you did marvelously. Alan and I were so pleased."

And so it went. Rabbit was contrite, while his sponsor claimed she couldn't have been happier with the outcome. Only once did she admit that she had always hoped to read *Philoctetes in Troy*, adding, "Are you sure no one can return to the fire a second time?"

He shook his head. "The Adams-Cortez Act prohibits going to the same place and time twice."

"Like life, I suppose." She sighed. "Speaking of that, tell me, what does Rabbit's next chapter hold? You really should talk to Ethan. Your stories would make a riveting series."

"I spend too much of my time on the road for that, I'm afraid."

She nodded slowly. "I had heard ... Well, never mind, I hope you enjoy the rest of the event."

Dismissed.

Rabbit melded back into the crowd, taking away the only words of consequence from his interaction with Eleanor. *What does Rabbit's next chapter hold?* It was as bad as Friedman had said. Eleanor was gentler about it than Peach, but she had also written him off as a retiree. A has-been.

What the hell was he going to do with himself? As far as Rabbit was concerned, he was at the top of his game. Fit, sharp, experienced. The only reason this was even an issue is because that goddamn woman had targeted him. The next time he saw her, he'd ...

"Dr. Ward?" A booming bass shocked him out of his thoughts. Rabbit turned to see a bulky figure with a red bow tie and waistcoat striding toward him. He looked vaguely familiar, but Rabbit couldn't place him. With surprising dexterity, the man caught Rabbit by the hand and gave it a firm, moist shake.

"Pat Reardon, NOGWHISTO. I've been trying to reach you through the museum."

"I've been out of town ..." he said absently.

"It's just, you see, we're having our network meeting here in DC later this week and I'd be most appreciative if you would participate in a panel talk."

"Who?"

"NOGWHISTO. Network of Global and World History Organizations. Our regional is here at George Washington University. Saturday at five p.m. with cocktails after."

"Saturday tomorrow?"

Reardon nodded. "The panel is on the role of chrono archaeology in the historian's discipline. It would be quite a coup to get the legendary Rabbit Ward."

This was exactly the kind of request Rabbit usually ignored. He was a busy man; he didn't have time for public appearances. Today, the flattery was like balm on a burn. "It's a little short notice." He was ashamed of himself for playing hard to get but, hell, he needed this.

"I assure you; we reached out as soon as we had the venue set. I mean . . ." He spread his arms as though framing Rabbit in a portrait. "Rabbit Ward."

"What time again?"

"Five o'clock. You'd make a lot of people very happy."

"What the hell," Rabbit replied. "Send me the details in an email?"

"Gladly! And thank you again. You won't regret it." He pumped Rabbit's hand again.

Rabbit walked away feeling like he could breathe once more. Who knows, maybe he could talk to one or two potential sponsors. On his way to see Eleanor, he had spotted a young tech luminary. Rabbit was pretty sure PJ had told him the guy was obsessed with King Arthur. Might be something there.

Rabbit was rounding the corner back into the Hall of Nations when he collided with someone coming out of it. He and the tall man apologized in unison while trying to defend their tuxedoes from their dripping champagne flutes.

Rabbit froze.

David Kahan.

Aaron's father.

David was looking good-humored, then confused, then his face fell sharply as he recognized Rabbit. His bushy grey brows knitted together. His fleshy mouth solidified into a hard line. He had aged since Rabbit had seen him last, since he had screamed in Rabbit's face, since he had dissolved into tears and nearly collapsed in his wife's arms. Since Rabbit had ruined his life.

Kahan opened his mouth to say something, then closed it again. He looked around sharply, then leaned in close.

"Stay away from my family," he whispered. Rabbit could smell the champagne and salmon on his breath. "Come on," he said, taking the arm of the woman next to him who was just turning away from their previous conversation. Sarah, his wife.

"You go ahead," she said, more composed than he. "I'll be right with you."

David snorted, reminding Rabbit of a frustrated bull, and stalked away.

She smiled at Rabbit. It was a cordial smile, the same one he had basked in when he was younger. The Kahans had been his first and most generous sponsors. The power couple behind one of the most successful investment firms in the world, David and Sarah had treated him like family. They had trusted him with their own son, after all.

"If someone told me when I woke up, I would be talking to Rabbit Ward before the end of the day, I would have laughed in their face."

"Hello, Mrs. Kahan."

"Mrs. Kahan? It used to be Sarah." She sipped her champagne.

"Fifteen years ago, maybe." Those years were barely evident on her. She still had that vivacious energy, the same wildly colorful style. She was the California version of Eleanor Bloch.

"Suit yourself. You're looking good, young man."

"Not so young anymore."

"You'll always be the same amount younger than me. That's a gift of time."

Even in Rabbit's peculiar line of work that was true. Whatever time Rabbit spent in the past also passed here in the present. If he was gone for a week, he would return a week later. He assumed they could bring him back a moment after his departure, but that would have aged him unnaturally compared to his friends and family. A gift of time, indeed.

"To what do I owe this unexpected encounter, Dr. Ward?"

He hadn't expect to see her here. Truthfully, he hadn't expected to ever see her again. But here she was, glasses pushed back up her forehead propping up her excellent dye job. The same warm smile on her face. Had she really forgiven him? Had Rabbit been clinging to his guilt long after he had been absolved? The words spilled out of his mouth before he could catch them. "The menorah."

"I see."

"A scientist at the British Museum found new evidence. Turns out, it wasn't lost in the Vandal sack of Rome."

"This seems like something the Smithsonian could have approached the foundation about."

"You would have said no."

"Did you want to hear it from me directly?"

"I wanted to make my case."

"All right," she said, "so make it."

He had thought about this a lot since returning from Alexandria. "With everything going on in the Middle East, Israel must feel very isolated right now. America has shown its support, but America is a long way away. The country is surrounded by enemies, and this might get a lot worse before it gets better. Isn't this the perfect time to shed some light on all that darkness?"

Sarah walked a few paces in silence. Handed her flute to a passing waiter. Just when Rabbit was about to say something, she spoke.

"You were like a son to David, you know," she mused. "It broke his heart a second time that you didn't attend the funeral."

Rabbit felt the air leave his body like he'd been punched in the gut.

"I didn't think it was right. It was my fault."

"David is a Jewish man. Full of fire. When Aaron died, he was upset and looking for someone to blame. You could have helped him through that if you'd had the courage to face it. You could have helped him heal. He would have forgiven you, but you never gave him the chance. You abandoned us."

"Sarah, I'm sorry, I . . ."

She cut him off. "I'm not finished. You walked away from him and let him burn because you were too much of a coward to face him. He has slowly burned up inside. I lost my son, and then I lost my husband because of you."

"Sarah, I'm . . ."

"The British Museum called us right about the time they must have called you."

The non sequitur caught Rabbit off guard again. He felt like he was boxing Ali.

She continued, "The foundation has agreed to sponsor a mission to Constantinople. Yeshua Nazarian from the Israel Museum will be the archaeologist. He's here tonight, if you want to say hello." She pointed across the room to a solid-looking man with a full, jet-black beard. He nodded back at them.

"We've met," Rabbit said hollowly. Nazarian was good. A cold-hearted prick, as far as Rabbit could tell, but good.

Sarah took his hand. Rabbit was taken aback by the gesture.

"You misjudged us, Dr. Ward. David is full of fire, but my heart is stone. Live with what you did. And what you didn't do. That's your punishment."

And she was gone.

Rabbit's hands were shaking. A waiter passed by with a tray, collecting glasses, and he handed off his, more than half-full. He bobbled and nearly dropped it.

Whatever equanimity he had recovered was shattered. He was no longer just Rabbit Ward, wash-up. He was Aaron's failed defender. *"I'm counting on you to protect my boy!"* David had joked when they had embarked on Aaron's first mission. But it wasn't a joke, really. Aaron was a boy. Sent to do a grown-up job.

Rabbit could still hear him screaming for help.

WASHINGTON, DC

2018 CE

Are you going to send us back with diapers?" Rabbit growled.

"I know he's young." PJ was talking him down after Rabbit's first meeting with the twenty-year-old partner being forced on him.

He was pacing in the garden outside the Smithsonian Castle back and forth past PJ, who sat on a stone bench like a gravity well regulating his orbit.

"This is a dangerous job."

"I know."

"Those overindulgent parents of his—"

"I know. But if we want their funding, this was their condition."

"The kid should be, I don't know, partying with models, whatever privileged brats do after they skate through college."

PJ gently corrected him. "I don't know about skating. He graduated summa cum laude from Harvard. A year early."

"Why does he even want to do this?"

"Well, honey, I can hypothesize, if you actually care about the answer."

That caught his attention. He stopped and glared, not at her but certainly in her direction.

"Imagine you were a smart, ambitious kid like Aaron. You come from *intergenerational wealth at a scale most people can only fantasize about. You can take over the family business, go into politics maybe. But whatever you do, you know what they'll say. You only got where you did because Mommy and Daddy paid for it."*

"They did pay for this. Literally. In cash."

"They paid for him to go, sure. But what he does when he gets there is all up to him." She rose, smoothed her jacket lapels. *"Sixteen hundred years puts a lot of distance between him and his privilege. I suspect that young man wants to make his mark in the world, same as anyone. Same as you."*

Rabbit landed on his back with a grunt. Ian, the lead tech from Rabbit's team, offered him a hand and helped him to his feet.

"What's up with you today?" Ian asked.

"What do you mean?" Rabbit asked, softening his knees and raising his guard. He knew exactly what Ian meant. He couldn't seem to keep his mind present today. It was too busy replaying Sarah's last words to him. What ate at his stomach was not so much surprise or disappointment but a grim satisfaction that he had been right. They hated him, as they should.

"Oh, I'm just referring," continued Ian with mock innocence, feinting at Rabbit's face and following up with a jab to the gut, "to your general suckage."

They were partnered for some Krav Maga free sparring, and Ian had been dominant for the last ten minutes. Rabbit had been practicing the discipline longer and was normally able to handle Ian with ease. He had gotten his friend and coworker into Krav Maga about two years ago after an altercation with some yahoo tourists in a bar had almost gotten violent. Ian had taken to it well, but he didn't have the opportunities Rabbit did to put it into practice in the real world. Despite that, he was kicking Rabbit's ass today.

"You want to do some knife defense?" Rabbit asked. It was Ian's weakness.

"Hell, yeah. Today? I would keeeel you."

"I've got another class coming in here in five minutes, guys." Colleen, one of the owners of the hole-in-the-wall gym, was rearranging pads in preparation for the next group.

"Thanks, Col," said Ian, dropping his guard and heading for the informal changing room. Rabbit followed suit. Before they'd even left the mat, Ian spun and aimed an elbow strike at Rabbit's face, letting out a clipped yell. Had he not stopped short, he would have landed it perfectly.

"Seriously though," Ian said earnestly as they left the mat, "you really suck today."

Rabbit hadn't told Ian about his meeting with Friedman or the disastrous gala. Talking to his friend about it would have made it too real. He'd thought that sparring would take the edge off his nerves, but he'd been wrong. He was still wound up like a clock.

"Something up with Karyn?" Ian asked as they entered the tiny changing room.

Rabbit gave him a blank look.

"Oh my god, you don't even know who I'm talking about. Did you end it? You must have ended it. Tell me you weren't shitty."

"Oh, Karyn. She said she didn't feel the connection."

Ian glared.

Rabbit stripped off his sweaty clothes. "Okay, she said she didn't think I was capable of connection."

"And this was when?"

"I don't know, a little before the library jump." Rabbit fished his towel out of his duffel.

"That was weeks ago! You could have told me."

"Why?"

"She's Devon's boss."

"So?"

"So, what if he mentions you and upsets her? It could be bad for him."

Rabbit shook his head. "She's very mature. Besides, Devon . . ." He stopped, but it was too late. Ian stared.

"Devon what?"

"Nothing. Forget it."

"No, I'm intrigued to hear your thoughts on my personal life."

"I just think you might be taking things more seriously than he is." A grim silence followed. "It's none of my business."

"That's one thing we agree on," Ian responded coolly as Rabbit escaped into the shower.

Ian was a romantic. He was always trying to set Rabbit up with someone "of substance" despite the overwhelming evidence that women of substance uniformly deemed Rabbit insubstantial. Meanwhile, Ian himself was always trying to reform some good-looking playboy into a one-man man. Rabbit put it out of his mind by the time he turned the water off.

When he returned, Ian was staring at his phone.

"Everything okay?"

"Check your email."

The subject line caught Rabbit's attention. FBI INQUEST IN-TERVIEW. So, PJ had kicked off a formal investigation after all.

"Is this about the stringer?" Ian asked.

"I assume so." The lie hurt. Rabbit knew they weren't looking for the stringer. They were looking for whoever sold her information.

"Why are they dicking around with us? You don't think they're trying to pin something on you, do you? Because that's just bullshit."

Ian continued his defense, but Rabbit didn't hear it. His attention was caught by the next email in his inbox, subject line NOG-WHISTO.

Dr. Ward,

It was a pleasure talking with you at the gala. On behalf of the NOGWHISTO bureau, I am delighted to welcome you to this Saturday's panel discussion. Details follow. The title of the panel is "The Role of Time Travel in Academic Historical Research." If there is anything you need in advance of the event, please do not hesitate to contact me.

Sincerely,

Pat Reardon

"Shit," Rabbit swore under his breath.

Three hours later and totally unprepared, Rabbit was sweating bullets in a stairwell in the Elliott School of International Affairs on the George Washington campus, awaiting his doom. Rabbit hated public speaking. He would rather face down a Marian legion single-handedly than sit in front of a room and answer questions. His sports jacket felt itchy. He took it off. Then he was cold. He put it back on again.

"Dr. Ward?" A voice behind him made him jump. The administrator of the event (Susan? Cheryl?) held the door open to the hall for him. "They're ready for you."

"Okay." Rabbit thought he would be sick.

He followed her to the door where she held him back as he was being introduced.

"Our second panel member is an extremely accomplished chrono-archaeologist headquartered with the Smithsonian Institution. Specializing in the ancient Hellenic and classical Mediterranean, he has participated in over eighty expeditions in his twenty-year career. His most recent work took him to 48 BCE to retrieve several of the lost plays of Sophocles. It is my pleasure to introduce to you, Dr. Robert Ward."

Susan or Cheryl urged him into the auditorium to the polite applause of the assembled historians. His vision swam as he took in the crowd. The room couldn't have held more than a hundred people in its stadium-style seating, but it might as well have been the world population to Rabbit. The lights over the audience were dimmed and the shades were drawn, but he could still see clearly to the back row. He gave them a bilious smile and turned to the head of the room where a short, draped table awaited him. There, grinning at him, was a face he had not seen in a long time.

"Sonofabitch," Rabbit whispered and smiled.

Daichi put his hand over his own tabletop microphone as Rabbit sat down next to him. "How the hell did they get you to agree to this?" His California accent sounded exactly as Rabbit remembered it from their days together at Stanford, but his cropped black hair was speckled with grey now. He wore a close-fitting black jacket and a tall-collared shirt. If Rabbit looked like a 1960s academic, Daichi looked like an anime hero.

The audience had stopped clapping. Rabbit once again looked out at them and felt his abdomen tighten up.

"Drs. Ono and Ward, thank you both very much for joining us today," the moderator intoned from a podium next to their table. "We're going to open it up to the floor in a few minutes, but let's get started with a pre-submitted question." He consulted his notes. "Dr. Eloise Baird from Tufts University asks, 'Since time travel was legally sanctioned twenty-seven years ago, its use has heavily favored the location and reclamation of artifacts over pure research. What is your perspective on this?'"

Daichi laughed. "No softballs, huh?" The crowd chuckled. "Seriously though, I think the question might reflect a Western bias. The government of Japan strictly prohibits private funding of time travel expeditions and enforces a ratio of fifty percent pure research, so yeah, we're just ... better over there." He delivered the closing line with just the right tone to crack up the audience.

"Dr. Ward?"

"Well"—Rabbit's mouth was dry, and his voice sounded constricted as he spoke—"it's true that private sponsorship pays for virtually all time travel in the United States. A single jump requires as much energy as a nuclear explosion, so it's . . . expensive. Fact is, corporate sponsors aren't willing to pay that price tag unless they get something out of it that they can attach their name to."

He saw a lot of nodding heads in the audience.

"I'm not trying to bite the hand that feeds me but, yeah, I do wish there was more funding for pure research. I don't think it's going to come from the private sector, so where does that leave us?"

He was starting to relax. He could tell the audience, all of them historians, were with him.

The moderator smoothly picked up the cue. "Again, an open question to you both. Dr. Hollis Mayfield from Oxford University asks, 'Have you ever seen anything in your work that makes you doubt the Krishnamurthy-Chang Effect, also known as the Splinter Effect?'"

Daichi turned to Rabbit and pointed back and forth between them. Rabbit gladly passed the baton back to his old friend, who smiled at the audience. "If I did, would I know it?"

That got a big laugh and applause that took a moment to settle down.

"Okay, okay, I'll stop being glib. The real answer is I don't know. The Splinter Effect states that history cannot be *materially* altered. If I go back in time and change something enough, reality splinters"—he drew a V with his hands—"creating a parallel reality in which the change I made took place. Since I come from this reality, I will always return to it and, in this reality, the impacting incident never happened. That's why I never tried to kill Hitler."

Another laugh.

The moderator jumped in. "But how do you know that your actions didn't alter your memory of the reality that created you?"

The Japanese time traveler jokingly examined his name tag. "Network of Global and World History Organizations. No physicists in the crowd to check my work. Okay, the theory as I understand it is that my memory of my own reality, which would cause me to select the change, ensures that I can't change it. Or something like that."

"Chang wanted to call it the 'Observer Effect,'" volunteered Rabbit.

"Really?" Daichi turned to him.

Rabbit nodded. "The whole idea was to disprove the fear that Lorenz's Butterfly Effect could apply retroactively. Krishnamurthy thought it was better PR to name it after what happens, not what doesn't happen."

"That's pretty good for an archaeology major," Daichi joked.

"I can go one better," Rabbit offered. He looked at the moderator. "Do you have a marker for this?" He jerked his thumb at the well-lit whiteboard behind them.

"Blue or red?" he asked, holding them up.

"Both." He accepted the erasable markers and went to the board. "Okay, here's how it goes. There is only one rule. You can have red lines and blue lines, but you can't have purple lines. Got it?" He looked to the audience, who was nodding.

"This is our timeline," Rabbit continued, drawing a red line on the board. "And this is when we are." He concluded the line with an X. Next, he drew a circle on the line to the left of the X. "The circle represents a major historical event. Let's call it . . ."

"The eruption of Mount Vesuvius," someone interjected from the crowd.

"Perfect. The eruption of Mount Vesuvius. That was what? 80 CE?" he asked.

"Seventy-nine," the volunteer offered.

"Yeah, dummy," jibed Daichi.

Rabbit ignored him and wrote the number 79 in the little circle. "Okay, say I go back to Pompeii a week before the eruption." He drew a dotted arc under the red line from the X to the circle, also in red. "Before the eruption, I swipe a bunch of jewelry from the rich Romans on vacation and I bury it in a deep hole. Then I decay back to the present." He followed the red line again in red, reemphasizing it. "We can go to the place where I buried it and, provided no one dug it up between then and now, it will still be there. In fact, if only we'd known where to look, it would have already been there before I left. I didn't change history when I went back. I learned about how my choices in the past have already affected the present. Now," he continued, "say I have the power to stop Vesuvius from erupting. I go back and plug up the volcano or whatever. That means I altered something that we know to be true in our history. It no longer fits within our history." He dramatically uncapped the blue marker. "Now, what was our first rule?"

"No purple," someone called back.

"No purple," Rabbit confirmed. "So, from the moment I created that significant change, history has no choice but to diverge into two parallel histories." He drew a blue line angling up and away from the red circle. "Two universes. And even though I might spend a couple of hours traveling in this timeline"—Rabbit traced the blue line with the marker—"I will still decay to my own history, here." He jabbed the red X. "I can stop the volcano from erupting, but not for me, and not for you."

"What happened if you buried the jewels in the blue timeline after you stopped the eruption?" Daichi asked, teeing him up.

"Somebody in this history might find them." Rabbit drew a blue X at the end of the blue line, parallel with the X on the red line. "But we"—he pointed to the red X—"won't, because it happened after the splinter."

"Lucky bastards got your jewels, Rabbit."

A hand went up from the front row.

"So, what counts as a 'significant' change in history?"

"Nobody knows that for sure," said Daichi.

Rabbit continued, "That's why we spend as much time as we do trying to find the last known location for artifacts. If you can find it right when it dropped out of human observation, you can sneak in and set it aside for later. We didn't change it. In our reality, that's the way it's always been. We just didn't know it."

"Could you give me an example of that?"

"Sure. Last week I was in Alexandria for the famous burning of the book repository. Before the whole place went up in smoke, I extracted some scrolls and buried them in the desert. If I hadn't taken them, it seems likely that they would have been destroyed with the building. But in our reality, they've always been buried in the desert. Now, to lift from Dr. Ono's example, if I had decided to kill Julius Caesar while I was there, that would have altered the set of circumstances that sent me back to retrieve the scrolls in the first place, rendering it impossible." Rabbit made a V with his hands. "That might be the clearest way to think about it. When we go back in time, we're just trying to make sure we don't change history so much it would have prevented us from leaving on the trip in the first place."

The questioner didn't seem satisfied. "So, time is self-healing?"

"That's not exactly right, but it's close enough practically to be useful. You could say that on our timeline"—he pointed at the board—"the red line is malleable enough that, so long as I don't alter anything we *know* to be true then my actions won't create a splinter. The physics of that aren't quite right, but the outcomes are close enough. Of course, there is a lot of guesswork here. Really, the best we can do is know the history and try our best not to change anything in the written record. Is that enough?"

Nods from the audience.

"Let's take another question." The moderator gestured to the side of the stadium seats, where three people were lined up at a microphone stand.

"Where did you get your nickname, Dr. Ward?" The woman asking looked like someone had dared her to ask.

"My kid brother couldn't pronounce Robert," he responded, the line practiced and delivered by reflex.

"Let's keep the questions on theme if we could," the moderator said, encouraging the next person to speak.

"This is a question for either of you," said the young man at the mic. "This is going back to the original question. Two people usually go through the time dilator at once. Why not have one of them be a historian?"

Daichi smiled, but Rabbit knew him well enough to see how much the insinuation irritated him. "I consider myself to be a historian," he said simply, the smile fixed on his face.

"Okay, but you are focused on an objective, which is going to make you less objective." That got a couple of chuckles. The young man looked pleased with himself. "What if the other person was just there to observe?"

Daichi's face formed an expression most people would interpret as a smile. Rabbit knew better. It was the look he had right before he ripped you a new one. "Do you know the Honjo Masamune?"

"It's a sword, right?"

"It's a sword," Daichi confirmed. "It went missing after World War II when Japanese nobles were required to turn over their weapons to Allied forces. Tokugawa Iemasa decided to set a good example and turn over his sword collection to a nonexistent sergeant with the unlikely name Coldy Bimore, at which point Honjo Masamune disappeared. I went there to see if I could intercept it. Well, it turns out 'Bimore' and his people who showed up to collect the swords were profiteers, not officials. Don't forget, the war was over, but I was shot trying to get the sword and would have died if my partner hadn't gotten me back to the decay point."

The young man was slowly sinking into his shoes.

"Don't let the media coverage fool you. We live in the safest time in human history right now. No, I'm sorry, but it doesn't make sense to send an academic in place of a chrono-archaeologist. Next question."

A woman stepped up to the mic. "Thank you for coming today." She cleared her throat and read her question from an index card. "I understand that time travelers need to return to the exact location from which they traveled in order to return to the present. What happens if they aren't there at the right time?"

Rabbit could tell Daichi was still worked up, so he leaned toward his mic. "There is a lot of conjecture about this. The assumption is that any traveler who isn't in place at what we call the 'decay point' at the right time would remain in the past. And since the Adams-Cortez Act prohibits multiple trips to the same time-space, that means you'd be stuck there for the rest of your life."

She nodded and asked a follow-up. "Has that ever happened before?"

Rabbit took a deep breath. "Yes." The audience went very quiet, allowing Rabbit to fully hear the screaming in his head.

Daichi and Rabbit stayed at the NOGWHISTO happy hour for the minimum polite interval and then retreated to a quiet hotel tavern on 16th. They sipped cocktails for an hour amid the inescapable DC Americana at a wood bar so polished it looked like glass. Rabbit learned that his classmate was now married, had two children, lived in Tokyo, and, like Rabbit, spent much of his life roaming the past. Daichi waited until halfway through his second margarita before he casually asked, "What's this I hear about you hanging it up?"

Rabbit groaned. Daichi had even heard about his problems? Reluctantly, he explained everything—the stringer, the thefts, the menorah and the Kahans funding Nazarian to find it, and Rabbit looking down the barrel of a forced early retirement.

He sighed into his cocktail. "Everything went south after I let Aaron die."

Daichi didn't correct him as PJ always did. He just gestured for another drink and looked Rabbit square in the face.

"Want some free advice?"

Rabbit shrugged.

"Whatever you did or didn't do, leave it in the past."

Rabbit smiled ruefully. "Not exactly our MO, is it?"

"I'm serious. This weird-ass business we're in messes with the head. We go back in time. We change things."

"We don't."

"It seems like we change things. And that can get you thinking that you have some kind of superpower to make things right. But that's all bullshit."

Rabbit stared into his drink.

Daichi thought for a moment and then said, "Do you ever play video games?"

Rabbit shook his head.

"Well, I play with my son. There are these narrative games, right? Story games. When we started playing, any time something went badly, he would want to restart the game from the last save so he could fix his mistake. It just really bugged him to move on from that point knowing there was a better choice he could have made. It took a while, but I finally convinced him there is no 'right' path, there's just the one you put your feet on."

"I feel like I should be offended that you're offering me recycled life lessons you taught your kid."

"To be fair, I'm a really fucking great father."

"I take it the moral is about learning to live with regret or something."

"Not regret. Acceptance. You're really good at what you do, Rabbit. Almost as good as me." He swigged his drink.

"So, I should accept that the stringer beat me."

"Accept that she beat you. Accept that Aaron died. Accept that the Kahans don't forgive you. You can't change any of it. And the more you dwell on what-ifs, the less you focus on what you can control— what direction to hop next."

Rabbit's phone buzzed in his pocket.

"What is it?" Daichi asked.

Rabbit stared at the message from PJ then handed it to Daichi, who read it aloud. "An anonymous donor came forward this evening and offered terms for the menorah . . ." Daichi's face split into a grin, and he slapped Rabbit's shoulder. "Holy shit! You got a sponsor!" He clinked his glass against Rabbit's. "Time to hop."

GREECE

2018 CE

PJ had come by his apartment the next morning in the middle of his hangover. "I don't like it."

"Why not?" Rabbit asked her.

"Because it's damn peculiar is why not. In thirty years I've never heard of an anonymous sponsor. You know these people, they all want to monogram everything they do."

Her Appalachian twang thwacked his eardrums like a rubber band. "Friedman doesn't seem to mind. I suppose he doesn't want to be beaten by another museum."

"Marty wants to give you a shot at clearing your reputation."

"Good, that's what I want, too."

The argument continued, but PJ's defeat was a foregone conclusion. If Friedman was on board, it was going to happen. Was Rabbit curious about the funding? Sure. But he wasn't about to inspect that horse's teeth when he had a mission to perform. The terms were acceptable; the menorah would be owned by Israel with periodic tours to the Smithsonian guaranteed. Everybody wins.

Now, as he sat across from her in a military van bumping over an ill-maintained lane in a little Greek town, Rabbit realized how concerned PJ really was. Oh, she had asked the lead soldier his name

(Sergeant Henry Ames) and had charmed everyone around her, but Rabbit could see the set of her lips. She was angry because she was worried. "You all right?" Rabbit asked her.

She didn't deign to respond.

The CIA and FBI had sided with PJ. They didn't care about Rabbit's safety, but they cared very much about a portable fuel source being brought inside Turkish borders.

"Isn't it true that one of these portable power sources is, essentially, a nuclear warhead?" the CIA agent, Randall, had asked.

Friedman protested. "The power sources we operate on use plutonium . . ."

Randall spoke over him, "Enriched plutonium."

"But that's where the resemblance ends," Friedman continued. "They are extremely safe, and one hundred percent shielded to prevent radiation leakage."

"In the wrong hands, could that device be used as a deadly weapon?"

Friedman picked up his pen. "In the wrong hands, this could be used as a deadly weapon."

"Not a nuclear weapon, Secretary."

Rabbit watched this exchange silently. His authority issues would be no help to the team, so he kept his mouth shut.

Secretary Friedman shifted tactics. "Why are we talking about this now? We have been using the same equipment for years."

"Turkish protestors have been swarming the streets ever since POTUS said he was going to move the US embassy to Jerusalem." She imitated a protestor in complete deadpan that would have been funny if she had a sense of humor. "Death to America. It's not the time."

"It's precisely the time," PJ interjected, winding up. "Ever since that little speech, tensions in the Middle East have been heating up."

"Which is why . . ." Randall started.

PJ cut her off. "Let me finish, please. Protestors may be chanting 'death to America,' but it's the Israelis and Palestinians who are counting bodies. And what support have we given them since touching off that powder keg, hmm? Not too damn much. Our sponsors believe that the retrieval of the menorah will send a real signal that Israel is not alone."

"With all due respect, Dr. West, the menorah isn't going anywhere. Why not wait a year, get it then?"

The smug look on the CIA agent's face was too much for Rabbit. "Because of the Internet," he interjected. Everyone in the room turned and looked at him in surprise. "If we know the menorah turned up in Constantinople, so do others. What's to stop a hostile actor from sending someone back to retrieve it first? Say that country, or terrorist organization, claims one of the holiest relics of Israel? What do you think they might do with it? You think you have problems now?"

"None of those actors have time travel capability. The Adams-Cortez Act..."

"Has done precisely nothing to stop freelancers from operating internationally," completed Rabbit.

"We understand you've been having some trouble with that lately," Cook, the FBI agent, said out of the blue. To Rabbit's surprise, she looked like Rabbit had just handed her a present. "You have a leak in your organization, Doctors."

Rabbit nodded. "This all suddenly makes sense. I thought you guys hated each other," he continued, indicating the two agents.

He could feel PJ urging him to be quiet.

Cook continued, "A leak in your organization is a matter of national and international significance. The bureau and the agency work together hand in glove in these matters."

"We appear to be at an impasse," said Friedman. "Can we at least agree that there is a pressing need to conduct this mission now?"

Reluctantly, Randall and Cook nodded.

"But you won't let us use a portable power source on Turkish soil."

"Correct."

"So, what do you propose?"

"Bulgaria," Randall said without hesitation.

"You've got to be joking," Rabbit spat, while PJ rolled her eyes, head, and shoulders at the idiocy.

"What? The Kozloduy plant produces all the mega wattage you need to operate." The CIA agent seemed to think they were being prima donnas.

"That's in Sofia?" Rabbit said. "That's hundreds of miles from Istanbul!"

"Three hundred and fifty," the CIA agent specified, sounding like Rabbit was exaggerating.

"That's a fifteen-day walk under optimal conditions," said Rabbit.

"It's inconvenient, I understand."

PJ jumped in. "No, you don't. Time travel has limitations. Rabbit can't go back for longer than twenty days at a time."

"Then find someone else to . . ." Cook replied, but PJ cut her off.

"The machine can't send someone back longer than that," she corrected. "If we drop Rabbit in Sofia, he'd have to turn around before he even reached the site."

"What about Greece?" suggested Rabbit, pulling out his phone and consulting it. "We go portable, but just over the border. You can assign a detail to watch over the device, maybe get cooperation from the Greek military. That would give me"—he looked up from the phone—"nine travel days each way and two days in Constantinople to work."

"Two days isn't enough to . . ." Secretary Friedman protested.

"We could agree to that," Randall nodded.

"But it's not enough time," reiterated the secretary.

"Rabbit," PJ asked, "can you do it?"

He thought about it for a moment. "No, but it sounds like I don't have any choice."

So, for the next week, the team scrambled. Wardrobe prepared a worn, wine-colored wool tunic, a shorter mantle decorated with traditional Byzantine embroidery, and brocade trousers made of raw silk. Props had created a batch of Roman solidus coins in a leather pouch and a curved Persian dagger to wear on his belt. Facilities arranged for the loan of Germany's time dilator, which was on the way to Greece by high-speed rail. Under the uncharacteristically visible presence of the CIA, two portable power sources were created, one for the jump, one for the return.

He and his team were swept up from the little Greek airport by an efficient and extremely intimidating convoy of US Special Forces operators who shuttled them into an unmarked van and whisked them off to the border.

"The signal here is nonexistent," grumbled Claire, looking at her phone. Rabbit didn't say anything, but he glanced at the dashboard. Among a few other devices mounted to the dash was a plain black rectangle the size of a deck of cards with a short antenna. He had to assume it was a cell jammer. No one in the car would be able to report their whereabouts while they were in transit. Smart.

Rabbit still couldn't believe anyone from this team would turn against them. PJ predated Rabbit on the team and was the one who had called the FBI in the first place. Ian had joined the team as a junior tech eleven years ago and was one of Rabbit's best friends. He would never do anything to put Rabbit in jeopardy. Claire joined five years ago. From what she had said and what he'd seen in virtual meetings, she lived alone, had a cat, and spent most of her time and attention outside of work on the Magic Kingdom. Trey was the newest to the team at three years. He was quiet and private and never got anyone's jokes. Of the group, he was certainly the one Rabbit knew the least. It just seemed unlikely that this reserved young man would take such a huge risk with his future. Or maybe

Rabbit just didn't want to believe the worst of anyone on whom he had rested so much faith.

So much faith.

Aaron was constantly ogling the architecture and the flow of life in the city he had grown up reading about. In the year of their arrival, 455 CE, Rome was on the brink of political irrelevancy. The vibrant city Rabbit had visited under the rules of Augustus, Trajan, and Septimius Severus had declined into a quaint, old-money city for the out-of-touch. Within a few days, it would decline into much worse.

"Do you think the menorah's in there?" he asked Rabbit as they stared up at the shuttered Temple of Peace. *Four hundred years before, it had been the grandest building in Rome. Since then, it had been burned, restored, remodeled, and finally closed during the Christian persecution of the pagans. In 455, it was twice as old as Rabbit's America.*

"Probably not anymore." Rabbit shook his head. "It's more likely they moved it to the Imperial Palace or stowed it in a warehouse somewhere."

"How are we supposed to find it?"

A bored soldier was posted at the barred main entrance to the temple. He was leaning against the wall in the shade of one of its many columns.

"Let's ask," said Rabbit with a grin.

Aaron trailed him up the steps to where the guard was standing.

"Excuse me," asked Rabbit politely. "We're visiting the city and were hoping to see Titus' treasure." *Happily, tourism wasn't a new concept.*

The guard laughed harshly. "Get lost, Jews."

"If you could just tell us where they were moved . . ." *Rabbit continued humbly, wringing his hands in supplication.*

The guard lunged forward a step, hand on the hilt of his sword. Rabbit fell back and tumbled on his ass. He raised his hands pitifully to shield himself, but the guard didn't continue his attack. Instead, he just laughed that grating laugh again and retreated to the shade. "All of that old crap is in storage now, you can't see it, you stupid Hebrews."

"Thank you, thank you," *muttered Rabbit, nodding his head repeatedly as they escaped the scene. The moment they were out of the guard's* sight, Rabbit dropped the act like a hat. "Score. Warehouse makes sense. Too valuable to melt down, not Jesus-y enough to put on display. What's the matter?" he asked, noticing Aaron's silence.

"Nothing," Aaron grumbled like a teenager. Well, truthfully, he was barely older than a teen. Just out of undergrad.

He sulked for the entire walk across the forum district before he finally erupted.

"How can you do that!"

Rabbit was shocked at the outburst. "Do what?"

"Scrape and fawn to that fucking bigot. It's humiliating!"

People around them were starting to stare at the young man shouting in the gibberish language. He had slipped into Modern English in his rage.

"Latin," Rabbit whispered commandingly. He steered Aaron away from the onlookers. "What's the problem?" He pointed back in the direction of the temple. "That was my shot at the Oscar." No response. "Hey, listen, we got the information we needed, right? It's a win."

"I know but . . . Why do they hate us so much?" He said the last quietly. They both knew the "us" referred to the Jewish people, not to Aaron and Rabbit.

"I mean, I can tell why I hate you," Rabbit said in mock sincerity. Aaron cracked a tiny smile at that, but it didn't last. Rabbit could see how hard his mentee was taking this. He pulled him aside at a wine stall and bought them a couple of glasses. "Drink," he said. The wine was heavily watered, and Aaron took a big swig. "Look, I know it's a hard pill to swallow, but sometimes you have to play the part to get what you need in this job."

"That's what we've always done, isn't it? Play the part, bury your pride, make someone else feel big so you don't scare them." He drank again and seemed to be cooling down. "You know my family has money."

"I think I remember hearing that."

"It doesn't stop the bigotry, you know. And I'm not just talking about the Jews. Middle Easterners, Latin Americans, Black people. Any nail *that sticks up gets a whack. The color of your skin and the god you pray to. That's what people kill and die for. It's always been that way, hasn't it?"*

Rabbit leaned against the counter of the wine stall, wondering if he had underestimated his young companion. "Ancient Rome would be a great place to live if it weren't for all the Romans."

"Some things never change," Aaron muttered into his ceramic cup.

Rabbit shook his head, coming back to the present and thinking about how he would soon be going nine days out of his way to avoid giving terrorists a dirty bomb to use against Israel. "Some things never change," he muttered under his breath.

"What'd you say?" asked Ian, next to him.

"Nothing."

"Humph. Any chance we could stop for a coffee on the way?" Ian asked the soldiers in front.

The driver of the van glanced in the rearview mirror with a smirk. "Too late. We're here."

Indeed, they were pulling off the road already into a border station. The highway narrowed into a checkpoint for cars and trucks passing between Greece and Turkey. Although it was still early, a line of vehicles was already waiting for review. The vans pulled into the median and passed them, earning a few irritated honks from the waiting cars. A few hundred yards closer to the station, they pulled off into a lot shielded by nondescript cinder block buildings and parked between two semis.

One of the soldiers opened the door for them. The second van pulled in behind them as they clambered out.

"This way, folks," he said, sounding like a tour guide. He led them past the second van. Its sliding door was open. Four soldiers sat inside wearing full combat gear.

Ames went to the back of one of the semis and slid a short ladder out of the recess below the box. Climbing up it, he entered a code on a discreet keypad that unlocked and opened a person-sized door in the metal sheeting. He hopped off the ladder. "After you."

One by one, the team climbed into the trailer. Inside, the boxy space was outfitted similarly to other portable dilators. At one end was the round jump pad, this one ringed with a permanent plexiglass housing with a small door. At the other end were the control consoles with chairs. The space was dimly lit, mostly over the consoles. Ian immediately began inspecting the controls. "Very German," he concluded.

Before they'd even settled in, Ames returned carrying a steel briefcase, which Ian accepted from him.

"We'll be right outside," the sergeant said and left, closing the door behind him.

"Weirdest day ever," concluded Claire.

As they always did, the techs chattered to each other as they prepared. This was partially for themselves and partially for Rabbit. The traveling time dilator had no changing space (there wasn't room with all the equipment), and their banter was an indirect way of telling Rabbit they weren't paying attention to him getting naked fifteen feet away. He stripped down and stepped into his new clothes, which didn't feel new. He didn't know what kind of wizardry those costumers employed, but the trousers, tunic, and overshirt were as broken-in and comfortable as anything in his closet at home. The traditional Byzantine designs on the cloth were embroidered, which marked him as a man with money; poorer clothing would have had the designs stamped with dye. He cinched up the leather belt, knotted it through the iron ring that served as the buckle, and let the tail hang in front. He slipped on his sandals, knife sheath, and purse, and packed all of his modern clothing into the duffel bag that had contained his costume.

Tossing an additional wool short cloak over his shoulder, he handed PJ the bag. It was the same routine at the beginning of every jump but, of course, this wasn't just any jump. He knew she disapproved of him going and was biting her tongue. But she still uttered the phrase she always sent him off with. "Good hunting."

The chatter of the tech team abruptly pivoted from talk about some TV series Ian and Claire were raving about into the detailed set of prep talk that preceded a jump.

"We have power lock."

"Gunning."

"Spinning up in three."

Rabbit walked over to the plexiglass cylinder, opened the door, and stepped onto the metal disk of the dilator. Closing the door muffled the team's voices.

"Two."

He softened his knees. He knew from experience that he sometimes appeared in the past a few inches off the ground and dropped. Never belowground, thankfully.

"One."

Rabbit breathed in the smell of the plexiglass, the truck, the parking lot exhaust.

"Jump."

GREECE

535 CE

The truck disappeared, and Rabbit squinted in the full sun. He looked around quickly for threats, hand on his knife, but he was alone in a stand of olive trees. No, not a stand, they were too regularly spaced. A farm, then. Made sense, the nearby Maritsa River irrigated farms in modern-day as well. Now that he thought about it, he could hear the river. In 2018, road noise hid the sound of it tumbling over its rocky bed, but not in 535. The air was clean and cool, too, and the sky overhead was a shade of blue he never saw in his time. He took a deep breath, appreciating the scent of the trees and grass, slowly let it out, and then got to work.

The first task in any jump was to ensure that he could find the decay point that would take him back to his own time at the end of the dilation. He dug around with his sandal heel to mark the spot in the scrubby grass then hunted around until he turned up a sizable flat rock, which he laid over the divot. Next, he made X-shaped cuts in the bark of the four trees surrounding the rock for good measure.

The next step was to find the Via Egnatia, the Roman road that spanned from Dyrrachium on the Mediterranean across Greece to Constantinople. It shouldn't be hard. E-90, the road the soldiers had used to take them to the customs and immigration checkpoint, followed closely the path of the Via Egnatia, which was a major reason for choosing the jump spot. This was true all over Europe. Modern highway engineers borrowed from the Romans, who had paved paths trodden by earlier tribes, who had followed the paths of the animals. *All culture is built on other culture.* Rabbit walked north through the idyllic little olive grove for less than three minutes before he saw a clearing ahead. He sped up his pace in nervous anticipation.

Back when Constantinople was called Byzantium, Via Egnatia was well-used and maintained. By the fourth century, however, violent instability in Greece had kept both travelers and engineers away, and it had fallen into disrepair. It had been described as impassable until it was rebuilt at the order of Emperor Justinian I in the sixth century. Rabbit was now in 535 CE, eight years into Justinian's thirty-eight-year reign. He sincerely hoped the highly efficient emperor had already done this much-needed job.

As he approached the clearing, he saw a mile marker, a stone obelisk the height of his knee, tilting crookedly from the soil. *Good fortune and bad,* he thought. The obelisk would be the perfect marker to guide him back to the decay point, but its condition didn't spell good things for the quality of the road. A few more steps confirmed his fears. The "road" was little more than a collection of paving stones half-buried or jutting awkwardly from the ground. Rabbit growled. Jogging on that would be worse than nothing. He'd turn an ankle in the first mile.

Rabbit took a moment to mark the path of olive trees from the mile marker to the decay point and then resigned himself to a very challenging slog from here to the city.

A half mile on he reached the bridge over the Maritsa, which was thankfully sound. Its graceful double arch made it look like a sea serpent spanning the crevasse.

At the top of the first arch, Rabbit heard something in the distance that faded as he descended into the low middle of the bridge. When he climbed the second arch it was clearer. Sharp, high-pitched, and rhythmic, it was coming from some distance ahead of him. He tried to stave off his hope for the next two miles but, once its source came into sight, a smile split his face. In the distance, a Roman road crew was working on the Via Egnatia.

A mile away from the men he was spotted. A figure from the gathering mounted a horse and walked it toward him. It was a Roman soldier, no doubt on detachment to guard the crew. Like Rabbit, his horse picked its way carefully across the rough ground at the side of the broken road, leaving the rider free to study Rabbit, his bow drawn and nocked. The legionnaire was outfitted quite differently from the late republican mode made famous in sword-and-sandal movies. Trousers, boots, and a light mail cuirass. He was armed with a short recurve bow and longsword. The Roman legions had faced Goths and Huns for centuries by this time and had adopted their strongest qualities. Too bad for Rome that its politicians lacked that adaptive spirit. Over the empire's long life, generations of egotistic, partisan squabblers did more to damage it than the scattered moments of genuine competence could overcome. *Some things never change*, Rabbit thought.

"State your business, traveler," the soldier genially demanded in Greek.

"I'm bound for Constantinople," replied Rabbit. "Antigonus of Rome, I'm a spice trader." He spoke in Latin just to reinforce the image.

The soldier was talking to him, but his eyes roved the road and trees behind Rabbit, wary of a surprise attack. "Are you telling me you walked from Rome?" he asked incredulously. He was a solid young man with a wide, tan face and dark hair. His beard was trimmed short to hide its patchiness.

Rabbit adopted a "you're not going to believe my bad luck" face and said, "My mare broke her leg twenty miles past Traianopolis. I thought to buy another from a local villager, but I've seen no one since who didn't run from me."

"They're afraid of bandits. This damn road," the soldier spat. "Once it's rebuilt and we can move troops, we'll get it cleaned up. Don't you have any bodyguards?"

"I could afford guards or a new horse, but not both. It appears I broke that news to them prematurely." Rabbit shrugged. "I don't suppose you . . ." He eyed the soldier's mount.

The young soldier smiled. "There's not enough gold in your purse for this beauty"—he patted the horse's neck, and it blew through its nose—"or for the hell I'd catch for selling her." He seemed to decide Rabbit was no threat. "I'll walk with you for a bit, though."

"A little company would be welcome," said Rabbit, switching to Greek. He crossed to the other side of the road and began to walk toward the workers. The soldier slowly walked the horse parallel on the other side.

"I barely had time to think when I passed through the last town," said Rabbit. "What's the news of the world?"

"All anyone is talking about is the Vandals. You heard that at least, yes?"

"They were defeated?"

"Defeated? They were destroyed. Belisarius reclaimed the city and drove the last of the cowards into Numidia. They won't get a warm welcome there, I can tell you."

"May the devil take them," Rabbit said, which seemed to please the soldier. "Did this just happen?"

He nodded, "Last month. The news spread like fire, though. They say Belisarius killed that cur Gelimer in single combat but that's probably just talk. He's due back in town any day." He looked patriotically wistful. "I saw him once when he came back from Persia. Great man."

"How goes the roadwork?"

That snapped him out of his reverie. "Slowly," he groused.

Rabbit heard stories in the young man's tone. He didn't want to be here. And if he didn't want to be here, there might be an opportunity for Rabbit to exploit.

"I take it this isn't your preferred post."

"It's important work. The region's been a mess since my grandfather's days. Once the road's done, we can move troops again, clean up the bandit problem, get trade moving again. The olive oil alone would pay for this road."

"That does sound important."

He sighed and kept his horse walking. The mare was an especially fine animal, lean and tall with a dappled grey coat. *Arabian*, Rabbit thought. *Expensive*.

Sensing the young man's temptation to say more, Rabbit baited him. "I mean somebody has to keep the road crew safe . . ."

"Exactly! It's important work!"

Time to prod a few things and see what's sore.

"Not everyone's cut out for the battlefield."

The young man glowered at the broken road, stewing. They were approaching the road workers, none of whom looked up from their labors. A noise behind them caught Rabbit's attention but, before he could even turn to investigate it, the young soldier had rotated smoothly in his saddle, drawn and fired his bow. Rabbit followed the arrow to its destination. Seventy-five yards away a goat took two stumbling steps and fell in the tall grass, dead.

"Shit," swore the young man, "I hope she didn't belong to a farmer." He shrugged. "Well, it beats mush for dinner again."

He dismounted and tied his horse to a nearby tree. When he began to walk toward the fallen goat, Rabbit followed.

"That was a hell of a shot."

"That?" he said with false modesty. "Ignis wasn't even running."

"Ignis? That's your horse?"

He nodded.

"She really is a beautiful creature."

"Fearless, too. Doesn't shy at blood or even thunder."

"Where'd you get her?"

"My uncle," he said sourly. "Trying to make up for getting me assigned to this shit detail, probably. You're free to go, you know. Seemed like you were in a hurry."

"I am."

They reached the goat. It was lying on its side with the arrow sticking straight up from the side of its head. Rabbit whistled in appreciation at the young man's skill.

"Your talents are wasted out here playing guard."

He jerked the arrow free from the dead animal. "You think I don't know that? Here, take its back legs." The two of them picked up the limp animal between them. "I was supposed to go to Carthage, but my uncle pulled some strings and got me reassigned."

"Why?" They awkwardly carried the animal between them, trying to keep their feet clean. One end was leaking blood, the other leaking urine.

"He's a worrier. My father died on the battlefield, and he took me and my sister in. He wants me to go into the church."

"This doesn't look like a cloister," Rabbit joked.

"I was an ass about it. Made such a stink he finally allowed me to take one tour of service 'to get it out of my system,' then promptly got me assigned here. He probably thinks I'll just get bored. Anyway, what does it matter now? The war's over."

Poor kid. Just waiting for the hook. Rabbit gave the line a tug.

"One war is."

"What do you mean?" he asked.

"Italy's next. Justinian will declare against the Goths."

"Bullshit. Queen Amalasuintha and the emperor are allies."

"Sure, but you know she appointed her cousin to rule with her?"

"Theodahad, yeah."

"He turned on her. Had her imprisoned at Martana. Hold on a

second." Rabbit set the goat's rump down and readjusted his grip. "Idiotic, if you ask me. It'll give the emperor all the reason he needs to invade."

The young man was thinking hard. "How old is this news?"

"Fresh enough. I heard it in Dyrrachium."

They walked the last dozen yards in silence.

The road crew was steadily working. An engineer was obviously in charge, making sure the road was built to spec, while fifty-odd masons and strong backs leveled the ground and set the stones. Four soldiers in addition to the young archer were in the camp, placidly playing dice and relaxing. They were all grey-haired and bore the scars and world-weariness of veterans. Unlike Rabbit's companion, they seemed perfectly content to play out the rest of their service away from active combat.

When Rabbit and the young soldier carried in the goat, the vets excitedly set about cleaning it. There was some chiding about stealing from the local citizenry, but it was perfunctory; they were clearly eager for richer fare than the road generally offered.

Rabbit watched the young man carefully. He seemed to be on the verge of making a decision. While the other soldiers cleaned the goat, he loitered by his horse, stroking her neck.

"Best of luck to you," Rabbit said to the soldier. "I'm off. Perhaps I can pick up a horse in Heraclea." He started off gratefully on the newly laid road that stretched ahead of him like a smooth ribbon of stone.

Fifteen minutes later, he heard hooves on the stone road behind him. He had to keep the grin off his face as, a moment later, the young man rode up alongside.

"I'll take you."

"To Heraclea?"

"To Constantinople."

"Are you sure?" Rabbit asked. "Your post . . ."

"Those old farts don't care if I go. All I do is annoy them with my griping. Besides," he said, "when you tell the emperor what you know, he'll see why I had to bring you as quickly as possible."

He offered his hand to Rabbit.

"I can't argue with that," Rabbit said, took his hand, and swung up behind him on the tall horse. The young soldier urged Ignis into a gentle trot.

"What's your name again?" the soldier asked.

"Antigonus," Rabbit said.

"I'm Andor."

Rabbit was able to buy a horse for himself about four days into the trip. It was a short, knobby-kneed old roan who looked humorous beside Andor's regal mount. Despite the nag's limitations, the men made much better time on the two mounts. Ignis, who was an exceptionally trained warhorse, seemed relieved to be rid of Rabbit's unbalancing weight behind the saddle; her tail was high, and she broke into a floating trot at the slightest urging.

In the hour of riding after they left the village, the young soldier was pensive. Rabbit left him to his silence, assuming that he would say what was on his mind when he was ready. The coast road was beautiful, and Rabbit didn't mind enjoying it from the back of his stolid little horse. The Mediterranean winter was mild, and the sun was shining. For a few hours, the time traveler didn't have to do anything other than enjoy the crisp air off the sea.

"You carry a lot of gold in your purse for a foot traveler," Andor finally said, ending his long silence.

"I wasn't always on foot," Rabbit replied.

"You didn't encounter any bandits on the road?"

"No, must have just been lucky." Andor went silent again, and Rabbit saw him chewing on his lip as he pondered something. "What's on your mind?"

"I was just thinking if you made it all the way from the coast without seeing trouble, well then, maybe the road isn't as dangerous as everyone thinks."

"Could be," Rabbit allowed.

"And if the road isn't quite so dangerous, maybe the repair crew doesn't need quite so many guards."

"You're wondering if you could get reassigned."

"Well, if what you say is true, General Belisarius is going to need good men in Italy."

Rabbit was struck by a sudden pang of guilt. Not only was he luring this glory-hungry kid onto a dangerous battlefield, now he might be leaving open a host of laborers with less protection than they deserved. "I think I just got lucky, Andor," he said. "Villagers along the road were as surprised as you at my good fortune."

The soldier looked disappointed but attempted to recover. "What's your business in the capital, anyway?"

"Eh, trade. Nothing too exciting."

"What do you trade in? My uncle buys and sells all sorts of things. Has his own warehouses, too. Maybe he could help you."

"It sounds like your uncle is very successful. I doubt any of my ventures would be lucrative enough to interest him."

"I'll introduce you all the same. You never know where you'll find opportunity."

Rabbit smiled, liking the generous young man. "No, I suppose you never do."

CONSTANTINOPLE

535 CE

Rabbit and Andor reached Constantinople a day and a half ahead of Rabbit's schedule. The last day included a detour around a large, brackish lake or inlet that frustrated Rabbit to no end. Once they rounded that, however, they entered onto a straight stretch of road through farms. At the end of that road, looming above it all, stood the capital of the Eastern Empire. Call it Byzantium or Constantinople or Istanbul, it was breathtaking by any name. At half a million inhabitants, it was the largest city in the Mediterranean and would remain the focal point of wealth, culture, and knowledge in this part of the world for a thousand years.

Guarding it against generations of attackers stood the Theodosian Walls, a marvel of engineering that would repel armies until 1453 when the Ottoman Empire would put a nail in the coffin of Rome. What looked like a single, albeit impressive, stone wall from a mile away was actually a system of ingenious defenses. At the front was a deep, brick-walled moat filled with water that served as a barrier for infantry and cavalry, but also dissuaded anyone from trying to tunnel below, lest it collapse and drown the sappers. Anyone getting across the moat would face a short wall arrayed with narrow openings through which defending soldiers could ram spears while remaining protected from enemy arrows. Behind that stood the pa-rateichion, a stretch of flat earth on which to array soldiers in defensive formation, should it come to that. They wouldn't be alone of course, because behind them stood what was called the outer wall. Twenty feet high, it was dotted with towers that allowed defending archers to fire down at nearly any angle. On the extremely unlikely chance that forces summited the outer wall, they would have to do it all over again because behind that stood the inner wall, which was higher and thicker than the first; its towers were massive enough to mount artillery as well as bowmen. Even when Constantinople was weak, the walls remained strong.

Rabbit had been to the city when it was called Istanbul, but never when it was Constantinople. The ruins were impressive but touring those had not prepared him for the awe he felt at seeing the city's defenses in their prime.

The ground was cleared for hundreds of yards outside the wall. Rabbit and Andor rode toward it among a stream of travelers and tradespeople, carts and horses and livestock. They all queued up for admittance at the Golden Gate. The line extended across a stone bridge that spanned the moat. Wide enough to admit two wagons pulled by oxen, the bridge looked like it could survive the ages. As they crossed it, Rabbit looked over the edge at the moat. He knew it was over thirty feet deep, but it could have extended to the center of the earth for all he could see; the water was completely reflective and black.

"Antigonus," Andor said, pulling Rabbit's attention away from the moat. The line had moved on without him. He urged the horse forward.

The Golden Gate wasn't just a gate. It was a fortress built into the walls. Its entry was a single, wide opening in the outer wall, flanked by tall, crenellated towers. Behind the towers of the outer wall were the building-sized towers of the inner wall. On one tower stood a massive bronze cross, on the other a statue of the goddess of victory.

Topping the gate wall in the center was a giant statue of a man in a chariot being pulled by four elephants. Theodosius I, Rabbit knew. He wondered how hard it would be to get them down from those walls.

The pair rode ploddingly through the outer gate and into a courtyard. Here, transverse walls had been built between the outer and inner, making the Golden Gate a formidable defensive position, should the inner wall ever be breached.

War wasn't on anyone's mind at the moment though. The line of travelers just wanted to get past customs and enter the city.

The gate on the inner wall was made up of three arched entrances. The line Rabbit and Andor rode in went through the door on the right. Occasionally, someone would exit through the left door. The center was closed with solid bronze doors. Above it, an inscription in bronze lettering read:

Haec loca Theudosius decorat post fata tyranni.
Aurea saecla gerit qui portam construit auro.

"Theodosius adorned these places after the downfall of the tyrant. He who brought a golden age built the gate from gold," Rabbit read.

Andor looked at him curiously. "Haven't you ever been here before?"

Rabbit shook his head. "No, what made you think that?"

He shrugged. "I don't know. I suppose you just seem very . . . worldly?" He went on rapidly, clearly worried he had offended. "The center gate is ceremonial. It's only opened for triumphs."

"Will the general ride through there?" asked Rabbit. He was pleased to have a change in topic; this young man was too clever and suspicious for Rabbit's liking.

Andor shook his head. "It's for the emperor himself." Rabbit had a little thrill of superior knowledge. Andor would be so excited when he learned that Belisarius was to be honored with a triumph in his name, not the emperor's. No general in the empire had received that honor in five hundred years.

They were approaching the entry gate, finally. It was twelve feet wide at least with an arch thirty feet overhead. The central entrance was twice as big. Stepping into the shade of the arch, the air felt chilly and damp.

"Are the crowds always this bad?" Rabbit asked.

"This is worse than usual. A lot of people are coming for the parade, I bet."

They finally reached the customs house a few minutes later. It was just a little stone hut in which a bookkeeper sat, scribing notes. Two additional customs agents were outside the hut and would occasionally confirm the reported contents of a merchant's cart.

"Name," the seated agent demanded of Andor, who was in the lead.

"Andor Psellos, cavalry, Legio Macedonia." If the young soldier expected to impress the customs officer, he was disappointed. The man just grunted and took a note.

"What's your business?"

"I am bringing this man with news for the emperor."

That got his attention. The man glanced up at Rabbit and looked over his horse doubtfully. "What news?"

"That's for the emperor's ears," said Andor, a little too haughtily.

The customs agent looked sour. "And who are you?"

"Antigonus of Rome." There was nothing to be gained from drawing out this interaction, and Rabbit had found that the most quickly dismissed personalities were not the abrasive, but the very dull. He slouched his shoulders slightly and looked not at the customs agent's eyes but at his cheekbones. Sure enough, the man quickly jotted down his name and urged them along.

Once past the checkpoint, the road opened up onto a spacious stretch of hilly farmland from the Theodosian Walls to the Constantinian Walls where the city began in earnest. Only a few monasteries broke up the pastoral landscape.

From the road, Rabbit could see the vast defenses at his back, the not-insubstantial walls ahead, and the seawall to his right, built to block a naval landing. He couldn't see it from here, but he knew that the city boasted yet a third set of walls that protected the imperial district from invasion or civil unrest. The city was the most heavily fortified in history for one reason. Money.

Constantinople was uniquely situated for trade between the East and West. Built on a peninsula jutting into the Bosporus Strait, a deep natural waterway connecting the Black Sea to the Mediterranean, it dominated both the sea passage and the narrow strip of land between Anatolia and Thrace. Materials and goods from Mesopotamia, Persia, India, and even China flowed west, while corresponding goods from Britain, Gaul, Germania, Spain, and Rome flowed east. Almost all of this vast current of trade flowed through the new capital of the Roman Empire, enriching it and making it a juicy target for attack. The emperors of Rome had no intention of having their new center of power fall prey to barbarians as the Eternal City had.

The two men on horseback rode pleasantly to the Old Golden Gate set in the Constantinian Walls where they passed through without fanfare. The Old Gate was constructed of large marble blocks and showed even more Greek influence than the Theodosian Walls. The decorative stonework and covered, pillared walkway crowning it made it look almost like a temple rather than a defensive barrier. As he passed into the sunlight on the other side of the wall, Rabbit was treated to his first real view of 535 Constantinople.

If the streets of Alexandria of 48 BCE were a study in order, Constantinople of 535 CE was all about decorative excess. From his vantage on the slopes of the Seventh Hill, the land fell away to a valley, only to rise again to the Third Hill in the distance. What lay before him looked like a gaudy quilt of architectural color. The air was redolent with spice and sea and sewage, and everywhere the sounds of human and animal voices, construction, and music vied for attention. It was the sort of city one could lose oneself in without even trying.

He glanced over at Andor, who grinned back at him, clearly proud to be showing off his hometown.

Rabbit was at a decision point. The young soldier had done him a tremendous service bringing him across Thrace. In doing so, Andor had gifted Rabbit with an additional day to acquire the menorah and considerably more energy to spend doing it. He felt compelled to keep his half of the bargain and go to the Imperial Palace with him.

If he was successful, Andor might go to war, where his dreams of glory would run up against a harsh reality. What did this boy know about war? Yes, he was a gifted shot, but that wouldn't save him from becoming grist for the mill when the armies came together. It wouldn't save him from getting one of the innumerable fatal diseases that claimed the lives of so many glory-hunting boys.

Rabbit could give him the slip. Without Rabbit's testimony, he wouldn't even approach the palace. The worst that would happen is a rebuke for leaving his post on the Via Egnatia. He'd live.

He gently eased his mount into a slower walk. It wasn't difficult, the gangly little roan was always struggling to keep pace with her taller traveling companion.

He waited until they approached a side street that was comparatively less crowded. Andor seemed fixed on navigating a crowd gathered around a puppet show being enacted. It was a parody of the defeat of Carthage that both celebrated and lampooned Belisarius. The perfect distraction.

Rabbit turned the roan into the side street and picked up the pace down the cobbled street. He put a block between him and the intersection. No hoofbeats followed him. At the next corner, he turned onto another street. No pursuit. He breathed deeply.

Dismounting, he led the horse on a winding path through the circuitous city, sometimes taking crowded main streets, other times insanely narrow alleys. He found a small, shabby stable where he boarded the roan and paid for three weeks of food. He hoped he would be able to find it again when it was time to go but, if not, he would simply buy another mount.

Afternoon turned to evening. Across the city, olive oil lamps were lit in front of dwellings and public buildings creating pools of warm, flickering light amid the hazy darkness. He would need to find a public house to rent a room for the night. Most of them also offered a tavern at ground level, which stood out bright and loud as the rest of the city shut down, so it shouldn't be hard to pick one out.

He was following his ears toward one of them when three dark figures crossed the mouth of the alley in front of him. They were talking loudly, and for a moment he thought they might not notice him. Then one of them nudged another, and they all quickly drew a bead on him.

Crap.

A kind of postural shift happens when a group of young men encounters prey that says a lot about their intentions. Men intent on killing, for example, will attempt to reduce their perceived threat, if they must be seen at all, thereby reducing resistance. These three young dandies did the opposite. They puffed up like turkeys and began to swagger toward him, blocking the alley. They wanted the thrill of power, not the risk of true violence. Rabbit considered obliging them with a show of terror, but that also introduced the risk they might want to up the game by hurting him. They would also certainly take his gold, which he needed for his mission.

"Good evening," he said, imbuing his voice with a quaver of bravado-covered fear.

His Latin inspired a chorus of laughter from the toughs. Greek had become the principal street language of Rome since the power center of the empire had migrated east, and his language marked him as a country rube.

"Good evening!" one of them mocked in a high-pitched bumpkin accent. They were enjoying this.

Rabbit's heart was hammering, and he could feel his pulse in the veins of his forearms. Intellectually, he might have sized these boys up, but a deeper part of his brain was afraid. That part was begging him to run. If he did, though, they would be on him before he left the alley. They looked young and fit. Suddenly, Rabbit felt old.

Breathe deep, breathe slow, he told himself.

"Are you lost, little Red?" said the leader. Rabbit realized with a start that these three toughs were Blues, chariot-racing hooligans who supported a particular team, much like British football supporters. Excitement suddenly washed away his fear. These were real Blues! Their feud with the Greens had caused a fire that ravaged the city only a few years before. The Reds had long ago been subsumed by the Greens, so these boys had marked him as an adversary because of the color of his tunic. Or at least that was their excuse.

"Can I ask you a question?" Rabbit asked, switching to flawless Greek.

The language shift stunned them, and they stopped in their tracks.

"How many people were actually killed in the Nika Riots? Were you there? I'm asking for purely academic reasons."

As the leader opened his mouth, Rabbit leaned back slightly and kicked him in the balls with the force of an NFL punter. He felt bad, not for the thug's sack but because Rabbit truly did want to know the answer. The leader dropped to his knees clutching his groin.

The two toughs behind him advanced. Now that Rabbit had struck the first blow, their demeanor shifted. Their shoulders came forward, and they went silent. He had made killers of them after all. Worse, both of them drew long daggers from sheaths at their belts.

Rabbit drew his own knife and held it in a downward stabbing grip. He softened his knees and waited for them to build up the nerve to advance.

One of them suddenly yelled in shock and pain as a tuft of hair puffed away from his head like a dandelion in the breeze. He looked around in terror, blood already running down his face. His companion was staring at him in confusion.

Rabbit took a step forward, planted his right foot, and pivoted his torso, rotating on the spot in a low round kick he had practiced a thousand times. His left shin whipped around like an iron bar and slammed into the side of the bleeding tough's knee. The boy dropped like a stone, clutching his leg and howling in pain.

The unhurt thug backed away, his eyes darting everywhere. He was obviously torn between helping his friends and getting himself to safety. As it usually does, self-preservation won out, and the young man ran from the alley the way he had come, swearing to bring reinforcements.

Rabbit crouched low and looked behind him.

The clop of horse hooves brought Andor into sight. He had another arrow nocked in his bow. Rabbit heaved a sigh of relief.

The young soldier gracefully slid out of the saddle without releasing his drawn bow. He gestured to Rabbit with a tilt of his head to follow.

Within a minute, they were back to the calm of a wide main street, where a few wagons were delivering goods or carrying waste away.

Andor sheathed his arrow and slung the bow behind his saddle. He turned to Rabbit, his face set and hard. Rabbit prepared himself.

"I am so sorry," the young soldier blurted.

Rabbit was stunned.

"One minute I'm walking down the Mese and the next you were just ... gone! I got distracted and I didn't keep an eye on you, and you had just told me you were new to the city! I feel terrible." He looked close to tears. "Will you forgive me, Antigonus?"

"Please don't apologize," stammered Rabbit, a heavy weight of guilt settling in his stomach.

"I understand." He hung his head.

"No, I . . ." He felt sick saying it, but Rabbit could see how badly Andor needed this. "I forgive you. Truly," he added.

The soldier immediately brightened up. He took Rabbit's hand and kissed the back of it. "Then we are repaired. Thank you." Something suddenly occurred to Andor. "Where's your nag?"

"I boarded her. I was just looking for a public house when . . ."

"The Blues, I know." He spat. "If anything, they've gotten worse since the riot. With the Greens down, they act like they run the city."

"Thank you," Rabbit said earnestly. "You saved my life."

The young man wagged a finger at him knowingly. "You can't fool me, Antigonus. You dispatched two of them without wetting your knife. Where did you learn to fight like that?"

"Gymnasium," Rabbit said casually. Athletic culture, including grappling, was a cultural norm in Rome, but not in Constantinople where Christian modesty frowned on sport that was commonly performed naked. He hoped Andor's knowledge of wrestling was limited.

"If a spice trader can do that, I can't imagine how the Eternal City ever fell." Andor meant it as a compliment, but Rabbit couldn't help picturing the Vandals pillaging that same city decades ago. It fell all right.

Rabbit cleared his throat. "Well, save me you did, and now that you have, do you think you could direct me to a decent inn?"

"An inn?" Andor exclaimed. "Don't be ridiculous. You'll stay at my uncle's house, of course."

"Won't he be shocked to see you? I mean, you're supposed to be in Thrace learning how boring the army is."

"Don't worry. My uncle spends most of his time at his country home; he won't be there. Probably."

Andor and Rabbit approached the house as quietly as they could. The young man hadn't exaggerated, his uncle was rich indeed. Although he lived outside the Byzantium Wall that protected the imperial quarter, his neighborhood was populated by large houses of three to four stories modeled on the traditional Roman style. From the street, one could see only the upper stories, as every property was surrounded by high walls that shielded their courtyard gardens. A warm glow from ample oil lamps set in the walls showed off colorful frescoes and mosaics splashed across the outsides of the garden enclosures.

Andor knocked on the wood and bronze door of a house in the middle of the block. A moment later, a little window opened in the door.

"Young master Andor!" exclaimed the voice within. The bolts were unfastened with a clatter.

"Thank you, Phraates," Andor said and handed the reins of his horse to the gawping servant. Andor led Rabbit through a courtyard garden complete with a gently tinkling fountain. Like the rest of the street, the garden was quiet to the point of feeling abandoned. Rabbit was surprised, therefore, when Andor opened the front door, and they were greeted with raucous laughter from inside.

Andor led them through the entryway to what would have been the triclinium in a traditional Greek or Roman home, a room reserved for men only. Instead, the two of them entered the combination living and dining space dancing with lamplight and populated with several young men and women eating and drinking around a low table.

One of the women looked up, spotted Andor, and hopped up from the cushioned couch on which she sat. She ran over to him with a squeal.

"Brother!" She hugged him and then stood back to take him in. As she did, her smile faltered. "What are you doing here?"

"When I heard my baby sister was having an unsanctioned party, I beat the man who suggested it. I'll have to atone to him later," he said, grinning.

She punched him in the stomach playfully. "Aren't you going to introduce me to your companion?"

"Antigonus, this is my sister, Portia. Portia, Antigonus."

She inclined her head in a pious little gesture of greeting.

"Antigonus was traveling the road alone, so I accompanied him back to the city."

"Alone?" she said in amazement. "You must be very brave."

"Or very foolish," Rabbit replied with a smile.

She gestured to the dining room. "Either way, you'll be in good company at our table. Join us, won't you?"

Rabbit thought of protesting, but the smell of the food was making his mouth water. It also wasn't every day he was able to experience a meal in the sixth century.

"Uncle is in the country," she said to Andor as they walked into the room. "He won't be back for a few days, so I thought it would be nice to get together . . . with my fiancée!"

"What? When did this happen?" Andor was beaming.

"The families agreed last week."

The dinner party guests had ceased their conversations at the newcomers' approach. Andor turned to a short man with a halo of flyaway hair and dark, simple clothes. "Welcome to the family, brother!" he said, embracing the spluttering man.

"Don't be an ass," his sister laughed along with the other guests. She explained the joke to Rabbit. "That's Brother Bautista, our family doctor."

The doctor smiled tipsily to Rabbit; his round cheeks flushed.

Andor dropped the joke and was now embracing a thin, handsome young man, clapping him on the back. "Be good to her, Cyril."

His voice cracked with sudden emotion that would have embarrassed Rabbit. But Andor grinned and blinked away the mist in his eyes unapologetically.

Another couch was produced for Rabbit and Andor, and they settled in around the table with the other guests. In addition to Brother Bautista, Portia, and Cyril, there were also Vallast, an animal dealer from Dalmatia, and his wife, Freni, who avidly collected poetry from her native Persia.

"What brings you east, friend?" asked Brother Bautista, his eyes soft with wine.

"I'm hoping to find a supplier of peppercorns."

Vallast shook his head. "In Rome? What for? Those Goths don't spice anything. It's nothing but bread and meat, bread and meat."

"That's all you eat," his wife pointed out.

"Nonsense. I ate a turnip yesterday."

"Well, I have a feeling Greek food may be making a comeback in Rome before long," Rabbit said and popped an olive in his mouth to emphasize the point.

"That sounds like more than just a feeling," said Portia, eager for the gossip.

"Amalasuintha's been locked up," Rabbit said. "On an island."

"Who's that?" asked the doctor.

"The queen of the Ostrogoths," Freni answered with ill-concealed contempt for his lack of worldliness.

"The gothic nobles can't stand her," Vallast explained and put his nose in the air. "Too Roman, too intellectual, too political."

"For a woman," completed his wife.

"You can take a Goth out of the forest, but you can't take the forest out of the Goth," Rabbit said. It was easy to sound pithy with a few thousand years of literature behind him.

"Oh, that's good," said Portia. "I like him better than most of your friends, Andor. Stolid soldiers or pious priests, most of them. No offense," she said to the physician/monk. He shrugged it off.

"Get back to the point," Vallast said. "Do you think Justinian will invade over a little exile?"

Rabbit shook his head. "No, but a little murder might do it. Think about it. As long as she lives, power rests with her, exiled or not. Dead, she leaves behind a marriageable daughter for some aspiring Gothic leader."

"What about her son? What's his name?"

"Athalaric. He drank himself to death last year," Rabbit said.

Vallast whistled through his teeth, which made his wife cringe. "So, Justinian sends the general back to Italy."

"And, God willing, the price of pepper goes up," said Rabbit, spreading his hands like a magician who has just performed his best trick.

"Speaking of which," Andor said. "I'm glad you're here, Cyril. Cyril's in the civil service," he explained to Rabbit. "Do you think you could get us an audience with the emperor?"

Cyril nearly spat his wine. He glanced desperately at his fiancée for support. She just looked at him, wide-eyed.

"Uh, I could try. When?" the poor young man offered. Rabbit felt for him, so obviously caught between wanting to make a good impression on his soon-to-be in-laws and his naturally withdrawn nature. It was the first thing he'd said all evening.

"Tomorrow morning," Andor said.

Cyril looked queasy but nodded his assent. Portia patted his knee.

"When does Belisarius arrive from Carthage?" Rabbit asked.

"Within the week, apparently," said Cyril, looking glad for the change of topic. "That's all anyone is talking about in the palace."

"I for one will be glad to have some military presence back in town," said Vallast.

"Short on customers?" teased Portia.

"No. Well, yes, but that's not what I mean," he continued, apparently unaware she was playing with him. "The demes are getting out of control."

"The Blues, you mean," said Freni.

"They strut around like they run the place," he agreed.

"A few of them accosted Antigonus tonight," Andor said.

"Are you hurt?" slurred Brother Bautista. Rabbit wouldn't have admitted it if he was. The good doctor looked like he could blunder into plenty of harm right now, Hippocrates be damned.

Andor laughed. "Hardly! I can't say as much for his abusers, though. He fights like a cornered cat, this one!"

Portia sneered. "Boys. Why must it always come down to fighting? Cyril's never been in a fight in his life, have you dear?" Her fiancée mumbled his response.

"They teach it in Rome, Antigonus says."

"But why?" Portia insisted. "You seem like a civilized man, Antigonus."

"Truthfully? I lost someone when I was younger. I made it a point to be ready, in case it should ever come to that again."

She flushed. "I'm sorry. I didn't mean . . ."

"It's fine. I don't much care for it myself if I can avoid it."

There was a moment of silence during which they all heard the front door close. A moment later, a man appeared in the entry. His thin lips were set in a sneer as he took in the dinner party. The whole assembly had gone deathly still, and Rabbit instantly reinterpreted his surroundings. What had appeared to be a quaint historical salon was actually an illicit house party.

"I'm so glad you're all enjoying the hospitality of my home." The man dripped the words with sarcasm. He was balding, with skinny limbs and a round, distended belly. His fine clothes were rumpled. "The party's over. Go home."

The dinner guests rose at once, looking ashamed of themselves. They mumbled their goodbyes under their breath and exited hastily under the arch glare of the newcomer.

The door had barely closed before Portia excused herself. To his credit, Andor stood his ground. He introduced Rabbit and requested a room for him in the house, a wish that was granted with a sullen nod. When he tried to lead Rabbit from the room, however, his uncle stopped him.

"Melitta can show him to the guest room. I want a word with you."

CONSTANTINOPLE

535 CE

THREE DAYS REMAINING

The muffled argument between uncle and nephew was still in Rabbit's ears when he fell asleep in a guest room that night. He woke with the sun coming through his window and heard the sounds of the household already in motion. It occurred to him that, of all the things he knew about the ancient world, he had never really mastered the protocol of being a good guest in any era. Should he get up and wander around until he found Andor? Should he wait in his room for someone to come get him?

He got out of bed and was hit by the cold. These winter days had been in the sixties, but the night was near freezing. His breath was misty in the air. Shivering, he slipped on his clothes.

A soft knock sounded at the door.

"Come in," Rabbit said.

The door opened and Andor was there. "You're up," he said, looking surprisingly fresh and cheerful for a man who had been locked in verbal battle well into the night. "Come on, I want you to meet my uncle under better terms. It's freezing in here!" he said, shivering. "Sorry, I should have had a brazier brought up."

Rabbit thought of how many people had died in domestic fires throughout antiquity and shook his head. "I sleep better in the cold."

Andor led him downstairs to the kitchen, where two elderly women and a young boy were preparing food. It was much warmer here; the bread oven was already firing. Two bowls of dough sat rising on the counter beside it.

One of the women was whisking something in another bowl, and Andor walked over to peek into it.

"Anything for me in there?" he teased.

She shoved him away. "Andor Psellos, I have quite enough to do without you standing on my skirt hem. Go meet with your uncle where you belong."

He looked plaintively at her like an overgrown puppy.

"Ugh, there's fruit and nuts in the jar there." She indicated a shelf across the room.

He darted in and kissed her on the head.

"Get off!" she scolded but looked pleased all the same.

Andor fetched a ceramic jar from the shelf and poured two cups of dried fruit and nuts. He handed one to Rabbit.

"This is my friend, Antigonus. He's very important, so be nice to him."

"Go!" the two ladies demanded.

Rabbit followed him into the triclinium. A fire was set in a bronze brazier in the corner, but it struggled to warm the large room. He had been too engrossed by the social engagement the night before to notice but, now that he saw the room in daylight, it struck him as both grand and shabby. Everything in the room was of high quality, but none of it went together, and there was too much of everything. Rabbit marked Andor's uncle as a bachelor of humble beginnings who had amassed wealth but no taste.

The man sat at a little desk by a window, going over paperwork.

"Good morning, uncle," Andor said.

The merchant waved absently over his shoulder for them to sit down while he completed his task. They parked themselves on a couple of couches.

After a moment, the man turned in his chair and grimaced when he saw Rabbit. He fixed his gaze on Andor. "You should have told me our guest was with you. I apologize," he said to Rabbit, "for my rudeness."

"Not at all," Rabbit replied in Greek. "I'm the one who should be apologizing to you for turning up in your home uninvited."

The man looked satisfied with that. He came over and sat opposite Rabbit, carrying a steaming cup of something that smelled of herbs. "My nephew tells me you're a spice trader."

Rabbit shrugged. "More of a backer. I've financed some trips to and from the east."

"Antigonus, was it? It's not a name I'm familiar with. No offense."

"None taken," Rabbit said. "My scale is humble. I doubt it would have come to your attention." He glanced around the grand house to emphasize the point.

Andor jumped in. "I thought if Antigonus had shipments coming through the city, he might rent your warehouses and carters."

"My warehouses are full," his uncle said simply. As he said it, however, Rabbit noticed that his eyes strayed to the paperwork he had left on his desk. "Nephew, I think it's best you get about your business so you can return to your post. You can't wear that to the palace. Go put on something more appropriate. I want to speak to your friend a moment."

Andor seemed reluctant to leave, like a kid being excluded from the grown-ups' table. But he did as he was bid, and Rabbit heard his feet ascend the stairs before his uncle turned his attention back on Rabbit.

"My nephew is an innocent young man. His heart is with God."

"I can see that. He was extremely generous to bring me safely to the city."

"Innocence gets young men killed."

Rabbit said nothing in return.

"I noticed his piety when he first came to live under my roof. It was the only thing that rivaled his foolishness. Bishop Victor has offered him a life in Africa where he can study the mysteries. That is where he will be going, to the open arms of the church."

"Victor? Victor Vitensis?" Rabbit asked, surprised. Victor had written copiously of the trials of Catholic Christians in Carthage at the hands of the Vandal Aryan Christians. Some credited him with inspiring the invasion that Belisarius just completed.

Andor's uncle nodded. "He is a great man."

"I have no desire to change Andor's fate," Rabbit said and meant it. He wasn't sure, but he had the feeling that Victor Vitensis would have to be exceedingly old at this point. Andor would be lucky to see that offer fulfilled.

"Then why is he now talking about Italy?"

"Oh. Well, that may have been my fault. I shared some gossip about the Gothic Kingdom. I'm sorry if it inspired something in him that you don't approve of. It didn't occur to me."

"Didn't it?" The man's eyes bored into Rabbit uncomfortably. "Thirty years in business teaches a man to trust his instincts about people. All of mine are telling me the opposite. I'll tell you what I think. I think you used Andor to give you safe passage and lodging. I think you'll keep using him until his utility is done. And then you'll discard him to whatever fate should befall him. So, I'm going to warn you, once. You do what you have to do to send my nephew back to his post where he can work this military fervor out of his system safely. If you don't, well, you ought to know I am a close personal associate of Germanius Thrax." He dropped that name like it was a grenade. It meant nothing to Rabbit, however, and his lack of reaction clearly disappointed the man. The stairs creaked in the distance and Andor's uncle abruptly shifted his tone. "Now, as to the matter of warehouse space, I'm sorry to repeat that my facilities are overfilled." Andor entered the room brightly.

"Ready?"

Rabbit stood, nodding. The man's words about Rabbit's callous nature had stung him. He wanted to retort but knew that urge was all about him and not about the mission.

"You might try the Sycae," said Andor's uncle.

Andor was leading him out now, but Rabbit was thrown by that comment. Sycae was a Constantinople suburb across the Golden Horn inlet. It was reserved for foreigners. Was he just being insulting? Or did he know something? Rabbit had to shake off this feeling. The man had really gotten under his skin.

Andor led him around the couches and past the desk and windows on the east side.

The garden outside was cold but warming as the morning sun rose over the wall. Andor was dressed in white layers with colorful embroidered patterns down the front and back. He breathed in the chilly morning air.

"Let's walk," he said.

They went out into the street, which was busier than the night before, but still afforded space enough for a private conversation.

"I trust you," said Andor.

Rabbit looked at him in confusion.

"My uncle thinks because he has misjudged people in the past, it gives him special insight. Personally, I think he wrongly identifies experience as wisdom."

"You were listening?" Rabbit asked wryly.

"Of course!" He smiled. "Now, I have a question for you. Who is Germanius Thrax?"

Rabbit shook his head. "I've never heard the name before, but your uncle was using it to try to scare me."

"Well, I happened to get a glance at my uncle's books as we left. This Germanius fellow is currently renting all of my uncle's warehouses so he must be very rich."

"Andor, just how many warehouses does your uncle own?"

Andor looked at him meaningfully. "Many."

The walk from Andor's home to the imperial district was riveting. There was construction everywhere, of course. Justinian was rebuilding a city ravaged by the fires of the Nika Riots. Still, many buildings along the Mese were complete, and they were spectacular. The road itself was as wide as a modern expressway and dotted at regular intervals by even more expansive, stone-paved fora, the ancient forerunner of the town square.

As they passed through a round forum, Rabbit paused. In the foreground stood the Column of Constantine. A bronze statue of the emperor stood at its top holding a spear and crowned with what looked to Rabbit like an angelic halo. Beyond that he could see the massive Hippodrome, the chariot-racing track, said to seat 150,000 fans. To its left, the monumental Hagia Sophia church crowned the highest hill in the eastern city. Workers crawled over its massive dome, rushing to complete the structure on Justinian's schedule.

Rabbit was struck by the timelessness of the church. *I'll tour you in fifteen hundred years,* he thought. *Four nations and two changes of religious practice and you still stand.*

"Tourist," said Andor, breaking him out of his reverie. He was smiling though, proud of his city.

They passed the Palace of Antiochus with its hexagonal hall in front that would one day become a church and outlive the rest of the structure. Behind it lay the burned rubble that had been the Palace of Lausos. Weeds grew up between the fallen stones and blackened timber.

"They'll clean that up," Andor assured him with embarrassment. "Come on." He put a hand on Rabbit's shoulder and led him past the wall of the Hippodrome. During their walk, the general appearance of the crowd had slanted increasingly toward the well-to-do.

As Rabbit spied the Chalke Gate, the entry to the great palace complex, he was struck by the color and energy of this square. On the left side of the gate was the Augustaion, a covered marketplace for the city's upper classes. This morning it was filled with wealthy patrons or their servants buying food and goods. To the right stood the unfinished Baths of Zeuxippus. Its white marble walls were clad in scaffolding across which artisans crawled, implementing the elaborate decorations that would complete the façade.

Maybe that professor at George Washington was right, thought Rabbit. Maybe we should send more people back who can simply record these things. Rabbit was catching fleeting glances everywhere he looked of ancient splendor, but he had no time to focus on it.

This time when Andor took Rabbit's elbow to urge him back into motion, he was looking off nervously toward the shade of the marketplace canopy. Rabbit followed his eyes and saw a small gathering of brightly dressed women staring back at him. One eyed Rabbit invitingly over her veil. "Ignore them," the soldier said uncomfortably. "They think you're a tourist."

It took him a moment to understand Andor's discomfort, and then it dawned on him. They were prostitutes. Rabbit had read that Empress Theodora had all but eliminated the profession during her reign, but the three women trying to entice gold out of his purse told a different story.

"Fascinating," he said.

"Come on." Andor anxiously pulled him toward the palace.

Rabbit glanced back at the sex workers, but he didn't see the one who had made eyes at him. There was something about her that had caught his attention, but he didn't know why.

At the Chalke Gate, they got into a line so long that Rabbit wondered if it was possible to ever reach the palace within the day. Within half an hour, however, their names had been taken and they were shuttled into a wide courtyard to mill around with hundreds of other petitioners waiting to be called.

Despite the name, the palace was not a building. It was a city within the city, complete with its own defensive walls, churches, residences, and offices. It even had polo fields. Between the buildings were garden terraces from which the many high-ranking members of the government could take in the sea while conducting the business of state. There was hardly an undecorated surface in the entire massive complex. Even here in this outdoor waiting room, the walls were frescoed and crenellated. Rabbit was gazing around at it all when Andor's soon-to-be brother-in-law appeared at their side.

"Cyril!" said Andor.

The young administrator looked exhausted.

"I can't guarantee you an audience, Andor. I pulled some strings to get you to the front of the line and speed things up for you, though."

Andor embraced him, much to the young man's discomfort. "Thank you, Cyril."

"Andor Psellos?" a high, clear voice called.

Rabbit's heart jumped. This was the moment he had been waiting for. As he was lying in bed the night before, he had debated whether he should go through with this audience. As a rule, chrono-archaeologists preferred to stay out of the public eye. Too much influence on major decision-makers could lead to a splinter and undo everything they had worked for in the mission. Rabbit knew that Queen Amalasuintha's imprisonment would soon meet the ears of the emperor. History said that Petrus Liberius would convey the news of Amalasuintha's fate in April, which would afford Justinian justification for reconquering Italy for the Roman Empire. Rabbit worried that spilling the beans early might derail the noteworthy career Liberius had enjoyed after rolling over on his Ostrogothic masters. On the other hand, direct access to the court, even for a few minutes, might give Rabbit crucial information about the menorah that might help him in his mission. He finally decided that he could minimize the risk in two ways. If he told the news that the queen of the Italian Goths had been imprisoned only, it would still allow

Liberius to drop the other shoe. Also, he reasoned, there was no chance that a lowly merchant would be granted access to the throne room, no matter what news he carried. No, at best, he might give his testimony to the urban prefect, the head administrator of the city, who would convey it to Justinian himself. Rabbit had gone to sleep resolved in his plan to say as little as he must and learn as much as he might.

Andor and Rabbit thanked Cyril once more and followed the bureaucrat into the Daphne Palace, down a hall, and into a small administrative room.

The clerk sat behind a small desk on the only seat in the room. He pulled out a quill and dipped its tip in a jar of ink.

"State your business." He didn't look up.

Andor looked at Rabbit, a little helpless. He was struck by the boy's youth again. He might have the ambition and energy to get them here but, when it came to working within the bureaucracy, he looked to the adult in the room.

"I am Antigonus of Rome," Rabbit began.

The man cut him off with a labored sigh. "Are you filing a legal claim, asking for a boon . . ."

"I have news that may interest the emperor."

At this, the man looked up and pursed his lips. "And what is this vital news? Is the price of salt rising in the Eternal City?"

Officious prick, thought Rabbit. *All right, two can play at that game.*

Rabbit smiled and nodded gently. "Come on, Andor. I told you no one cared about Ostrogothic court intrigue. Let's go."

He strode out, not looking back. He made it a full ten strides back toward the exit when the high voice of the administrator chased after him. "Did you say court intrigue?"

Over the next few hours, Rabbit learned why the word *byzantine* had come to be synonymous with complexity.

The arrogant administrator had turned them over to a minor spymaster, who had turned them over to a senior spymaster, who had turned them over to the chief spymaster, who had finally turned them over to the Master of Offices. It was to him that Rabbit gave his testimony. Several hours lost for what after all was no more than a few sentences of revelation. Rabbit was prepared to walk out the door, his job done, when the Master of Offices shook his head.

"Come with me," he said brusquely.

Rabbit and Andor exchanged equally nervous glances as they rose and followed him.

He led them out of the pavilion and across a terrace, where the master's insistent pace drew attention from the people waiting there for an audience.

From there they proceeded through the grand door of another palace, where they walked on a richly patterned carpet down a hall festooned with frescoes. Recessed niches set in the wall held statues Rabbit wanted desperately to pilfer before they were lost to time.

"Stay," the officer ordered, pointing to the floor as though they were dogs. Rabbit bit back a snarky comment.

After what seemed like an eternity, the door to the inner chamber opened and the master returned to guide them in.

If the rest of the palace complex was rich, it paled by comparison to this room. Rugs and tapestries, gold and marble alike were all designed to draw the eye to the far end of the room where, sitting atop a gilded throne and lit from a window above as though by the rays of God himself, sat the Emperor Justinian the Great.

CONSTANTINOPLE

535 CE

The artist who had crafted Justinian's likeness in mosaic in the Basilica of San Vitale had done him justice, if flatteringly. He looked older now at fifty-three than he would in the mosaic, which wouldn't be crafted for another decade. Still, the fundamentals were there. The large dark eyes and oval face. A narrow, disapproving mouth, thick arched brows, and a prominent chin.

His clothes were the same cut as everyone else in the city, but his were brighter, more elaborately embroidered, and inset with jewels. The toes of his red boots, a distinctive accessory worn only by the emperor, stuck out from beneath his robes. But the most notable item of clothing he wore was the crown on his head. The days of the old Roman Republic were a distant memory; the leaders of the Byzantine Empire were considered to have special authority vested by God. It was the model that would dominate Europe for the next thousand years.

Rabbit saw the emperor through fleeting glances only, of course. On the reverent walk to the throne, he kept his eyes on the floor until he reached an elaborate circular design in the carpet where the pile was crushed. Here he prostrated himself beside Andor, kneeling and putting his forehead on the rug. It smelled like feet.

"Rise," the emperor said in a surprisingly casual tone.

Rabbit and Andor got to their feet.

"I hear you have news about our friend, Queen Amalasuintha?"

Now that he was free to look around, Rabbit saw two additional people in the room other than the silent guards. A stunningly beautiful woman stood behind a second throne with her hands on its high gilt back. She was dressed in finery as rich as the emperor's, cosmetics enhancing her dramatic almond eyes and full lips. That had to be Theodora, one of the most influential empresses in the history of Rome. The other was a wizened old man. His face was a mass of blue-veined wrinkles, and he leaned heavily on a walking stick. A leather cap was forced down over the back of his dusty grey hair, and the rest of it rebelled into unruly curls that matched his beard. But it was his eyes that drew Rabbit's attention. They were almost black and burned with fierce intensity for a man so old.

Rabbit pulled his eyes off the old man and cleared his throat. "King Theodahad imprisoned the queen. A few weeks ago, on Lake Bolsena."

"How do you know?" Justinian, for all the pomp of his appearance, spoke surprisingly simply.

"It's no secret, the Gothic nobles are ecstatic. They always thought she was too Roman." Rabbit shrugged.

"She is your ally," the old man spoke to the emperor. His voice croaked with age but, at the same time, it was filled with energy and excitement that surprised Rabbit. "It's justification to march."

The empress shot the old man a look of disbelief, probably for giving private counsel to her husband in front of a couple of nobodies.

She took charge, slowly turning her eyes from the old man to the two guests. "We are aggrieved to hear of it," she said to Rabbit. Unlike her husband, Theodora's voice was trained and pitched to sound imperious. She had been an actress after all. "She has not been otherwise harmed, I take it?"

"Not when I left the city."

"Which was when?" she pushed, sounding suspicious.

Rabbit had prepared for this question the night before and was glad he did. He pretended to think it over briefly then said, "Five weeks? Something like that. I sailed from Brundisium."

"Whatever for? The sea route around Sicily is safer and faster."

Rabbit patted his stomach. "Ships and I don't get along well. I try to minimize my time at sea."

"You picked a strange profession then."

Rabbit smiled. "Perhaps that's why I'm not more successful."

"Why should we believe you?" She persisted. "You could be luring the Empire into a trap."

Andor spoke, his voice tight with tension. "Begging your pardon, but it was my idea to bring Antigonus to you, not his."

"Clever men can often make you think something was your idea, young man," said the empress, and Rabbit saw her eyes flick almost imperceptibly toward the old man. She didn't seem to like his influence over her husband. Rabbit wondered again at the old advisor's role in court.

Justinian shrugged. "The Master of Offices will confirm or deny it soon enough. Was there any other news you had from Rome, Antigonus?" The emperor, famed in history as being hyperproductive and impatient, was done with the interview.

This was the moment he truly dreaded. Andor had asked for a good word from Rabbit to help get him a posting with the general. It was all the repayment the young man wanted for his generosity. But would Rabbit truly be doing him a favor by sending him to war? Would it be kinder to say nothing, to disappoint the soldier and further solidify his path as a religious scholar? He thought of Helias Psellos, Andor's uncle, and his cutting words. He thought of his own younger days and the people who supported his insane dream of traveling to the past. How could he deny Andor the same support?

"No more news, lord, just an impertinent observation."

Justinian's eyes widened. "Go on."

"This young man saved my life. He shoots an arrow as true as any Hun. In my opinion, he's wasted guarding a construction crew."

The emperor considered Andor. "What's your name?"

"Andor Psellos."

"His uncle is Helias Psellos," said the old man. "The boy is detached to protect the team repairing the Via Egnatia."

"Your family is rich, young man. What makes you want to go to war?" the emperor asked.

"I wish to expand the greatness of the empire for God."

Justinian's face softened. "That's a good answer. I'll take your observation under advisement, spice trader."

Rabbit made a short bow.

"My lord?" creaked the voice of the old man. "Might I suggest we keep our Roman visitor close by, in case anything else should come to mind?"

"You mean imprison him? Whatever for?" replied the empress sweetly.

"I did not necessarily mean imprisonment . . ."

"No? Isn't that your answer for everything? Our jails are so swollen with the Jews you keep naming as rebels that I wonder if we shall not be outnumbered in the palace before long."

"As I've said, once the treasures of the Temple are . . ." he began, but she cut him off again.

"You have said. In the meantime, half of the imperial loaves are disappearing into the dungeons."

The emperor, looking weary of the bickering, intervened. "Where are you staying while in the city, Antigonus, should we require anything more of you?"

Andor spoke up first. "He's staying at my uncle's home."

"Very good. You see? If we require the man again, we will know where to find him. Does that satisfy you, Joseph?"

The old man looked sour but didn't seem eager to push this any further. "Of course, that's very wise."

The emperor gestured, and a guard led them from the room without another word. Once they exited onto the terrace, Rabbit asked Andor quietly, "Who was the old man?"

"Joseph ben Levi. They say he's a sorcerer."

"What do you know about all these arrests they mentioned?"

"Not a thing. But then, I've been laboring down in the hinterlands all season."

Rabbit chewed the news over in his head. Justinian was staunchly anti-Semitic, but there was an unattributed story that said a Jewish advisor would convince Justinian that the menorah was bad luck and should be sent back to Israel. That advisor was never named, and there was no more evidence that the menorah had ever been removed from Constantinople than that it had arrived in the first place. Still, it was one hypothesis. Rabbit had assumed it was wishful thinking by later historians. Now he wondered if Joseph ben Levi was that advisor.

"How long has he been in Constantinople?"

"I don't know, forever, by the looks of him. Antigonus." Andor got very serious. "I want to thank you for what you said. Those were very generous words."

"I hope I didn't oversell your skill," Rabbit joked.

Andor puffed up proudly. "Test me against a Hun any day."

Rabbit smiled. He was about to respond, but he was distracted by the other people occupying the terrace. They had all ceased their conversations and had turned their attention to the sea.

Rabbit followed their gaze. In the distance, a flotilla of large, tall-masted ships was sailing toward Constantinople. On the flanks of the formation were a few protective dromon warships, their churning oars barely visible in the distance.

Andor swelled with national pride. "The general is back."

Rabbit was also feeling emotional, but for a different reason. He gazed hungrily at the flotilla. On one of those boats was a treasure that had been pillaged over five hundred years before, displayed in Rome for generations, stolen again and taken to Carthage, and was now returning to its first plunderers. Its value was more than its weight in gold, although that was considerable. To the early empire, it was a tangible symbol of what happened to nations who rose up against Rome. To the Byzantines, it symbolized the ascendance of Christianity. To Rabbit, it was a mark of his fatal failure and his chance for redemption.

This time, he would not let the menorah slip out of his grasp.

By the time they left the palace, the whole town was buzzing about the return of General Belisarius. It would take an hour or more for the ships to arrive in port, and already people were streaming south to greet them. Justinian had offered the general a choice, assume the lucrative governorship of North Africa or return to Constantinople and march in the first triumph awarded to a non-emperor in five hundred years. The general had chosen the latter, which seemed to satisfy the emperor that Belisarius was more interested in glory than in power. Glory Justinian could share, power he would not.

Rabbit pondered this as he followed Andor in search of something to eat. This was a crucial juncture in his planning. The menorah was not specifically mentioned in the history books describing the triumph. Procopius simply wrote of "the treasures of the Jews" being on display, which could refer to any of the artifacts of the Second Temple. To Rabbit, this spelled flexibility. He could take it before or after the triumph and probably have no greater risk of a splinter one way or the other. From here on, his top priority would be to know where it was and what was planned for it at all times. A weakness in its protection would present itself.

Andor, for his part, must have been continuing the conversation in his head that they had been having on the terrace. He picked it up again out loud as they paid for their food, a few vegetables seasoned and wrapped in flatbread.

"I know I should start learning about my uncle's business at some point. It's not like I have the connections for a command post. I just want to help, you know? I feel like I can make a difference. Anyway, I have time. My uncle will outlive us all," he concluded lightly.

"Well," said Rabbit, "you never know what the future will bring."

Rabbit did, of course. The next few years under Justinian would be tumultuous indeed. Belisarius would be dispatched to Italy with too few men and end up besieged in Rome. The army of Illyricum would split to provide aid to him. Persia would sack Syria and the Bulgars would attack Thrace. There were plenty of opportunities for Andor to find the military service he so desired. As for his uncle's long life, well, in six years the black plague would arrive on Justinian's doorstep, killing forty percent of the population. His uncle would be very lucky indeed if he survived that.

"All I'm saying is, don't be afraid that you won't be needed," Rabbit concluded.

Leveraging his military position and the natural entitlement of the wealthy, Andor led the way to a spot on top of the defensive wall overlooking the Harbor of Julian. The two of them perched on the crenellation thirty feet above the wharf and watched the crowd jostling for position on the hilly streets overlooking the sea. Rabbit pitied the porters charged with transporting the treasures through that mob . . .

Something occurred to him. Where were they transporting it all?

"You said you'd never heard of Germanius Thrax, right?"

Andor shook his head as he chewed and swallowed some of his loaf.

"Maybe that's because he's not real." In answer to Andor's confused look, he explained. "What if your uncle's warehouses are reserved for the loot from Carthage but your uncle wanted to keep it quiet?"

"Why would he do that? He loves boasting about his importance."

"Fair point. It just seems strange that he would rent out all of his space to someone and miss out on the valuable government contract."

"I see what you mean," Andor admitted. "If it is true, then, whatever Thrax is storing there must be extremely valuable."

Rabbit watched the first ship enter the mouth of the harbor. Even at this distance, he could see crates on the deck. The ship was so full that treasure had spilled out of its hold. And a line of similarly overloaded ships stretched into the distance.

"It certainly must be."

CONSTANTINOPLE

535 CE

The ocean currents around the peninsular city of Constantinople were notoriously treacherous. Only experienced sailors familiar with the approach could land a fleet of large ships successfully. If an enemy penetrated those swirls and eddies without being dashed on the rocks, they would face high walls that defended every shore and ringed each of the five great harbors. The Theodosian Walls famously kept out land invaders for hundreds of years, but no one ever took the city by sea.

Though smaller than the Harbors of Theodosius or Prosphorion, the Julian Harbor was the closest to the palace. That would be where the general's ship would land. Rabbit had no idea where the menorah would enter the city, and there was no point trying to guess.

Andor was taking in the scene like a kid. Rabbit had a great view and a good companion. It was sunny and beautiful, and he was watching the victors who avenged the Roman Empire sail into Constantinople. If Andor, who lived in this era, could be so swept up in the moment, maybe Rabbit could follow his cue and just enjoy it.

The lead ship moored at the long dock. Sailors and longshoremen worked together to secure the big dromon to the piers and, a few minutes later, the gangplank was lowered and the man himself walked down it alone. The sound seemed to hit Rabbit physically in the back as the crowd went berserk with excitement. He turned around. Every street up the surrounding hills was packed. People were on the roofs of the nearby buildings. They were cheering, singing, weeping, waving homemade banners.

The general had a sense of drama. He had donned a gleaming scale-mail shirt and a waist-length crimson cape for the debarkation. A large black cross stood out against the shine of his mail. He stood on the dock and waved to the crowd for a moment. A chant began in the crowd that quickly spread. "Victor! Victor! Victor!"

A horse was brought to him on the dock, and he left the harbor accompanied by a small company of palace guards. No doubt his first stop would be to check in with Justinian.

As the horses disappeared into a crowd that parted like the Red Sea, longshoremen began unloading crates and chests one by one down the gangplank. They settled in a geometric drift. Gold, statuary, idols, ceramics, and countless other treasures were enclosed in those packing crates. Each one would need to be recorded to ensure that nothing got "lost" along the way. Of course, John the Cappadocian, Justinian's famously corrupt financial manager, would manage to line his pockets from this landing; that was simply part of doing business in Constantinople. Rabbit briefly entertained the idea of pinning the disappearance of the menorah on John but dismissed it just as quickly. He was a notable public figure; if he was believed to have stolen such a priceless treasure, it would make history and splinter the timeline for sure.

What Rabbit needed was an opportunity for the menorah to be lost due to accident, catastrophe, or simple oversight. He had engineered such things before. The problem, of course, was time. According to Procopius, Belisarius would first celebrate a groundbreaking "Christian" triumph in which he would walk from his home to the emperor's private box in the Hippodrome where he would present the dethroned King Gelimer. That would happen soon, perhaps as early as tomorrow morning. "Later," for Procopius was vague about the interval, he would also celebrate a traditional triumph, in which the captured treasures would be paraded through the streets along with fifteen thousand vandal captives and a small cohort of victorious Roman soldiers. This would be a glamorous affair that required planning and work to orchestrate. It seemed like the sweet spot for retrieving the menorah would be between the two triumphs. In that interval, there would be a flurry of work executed by a lot of people. It would be disorganized, and people would be harried. The perfect time for mischief.

"What are your plans for the rest of the day, Andor?" Rabbit asked.

"Lunch with my sister. Other than that, I was hoping to just kill some time here in town and see if . . ." He trailed off, embarrassed.

"See if the general seeks you out?"

"Something like that," he admitted.

"If you're looking for occupation, would you mind doing me a favor? My curiosity is piqued about this Thrax fellow. If he's so rich, he might be a good contact for me. Would you be willing to talk to a few people and see if he's the real thing?"

"I'd be happy to. What are your plans?"

Rabbit lied casually. "I'll ferry across the Horn to Sycae. I assume that's where I'm likely to find most of the eastern traders?"

Andor nodded.

"Thanks for your help," Rabbit said honestly.

He smiled. "Beats sitting on a horse all day watching bricklayers."

Rabbit loitered by the docks after Andor left. The dense crowd filtered away as the allure of watching boxes pile up waned. Carters had begun to arrive partway through the unloading of the ships, accompanied by a host of guard troops sent to ensure the safe transport of the bounty.

By early evening, the wharf was groaning under the weight of the treasure. To make way for the ships still waiting to unload their cargo, a force of laborers began to move the boxes and chests onto carts under the watchful eyes of the guards. Rabbit hoped it was all going to the same place for short-term storage because he had no idea which crate held the menorah.

As the carters left the harbor, Rabbit fell into the wake of the parade. The city guards brushed him off when he got too close, so he took a side street one block north and followed the path of the wagon train as it traveled west through the city. He wanted to be at the front, where he could tell if the carters split up to go to different destinations.

At each intersection, he glanced south and saw the wagons trundling slowly along. A block before the Forum of the Ox, he finally outpaced the parade. Cutting south, he sped up, planning to walk in front of the lead cart where he could keep an eye on it.

Just before he reached the Mese, however, he heard a commotion of shouting that increased in volume as he rounded the corner onto the main street. The front of the wagon procession had gotten tangled up with a comparatively small caravan of carts being led by what looked like Bedouins. The animals of both factions had panicked and were rearing and kicking as the carters shouted and tried to disentangle the mess. The city guards were cursing the Bedouins in Greek, while the Bedouins cursed them back in Arabic.

The whole thing would have been quaintly amusing if it wasn't so familiar. Rabbit had orchestrated situations exactly like this to recover artifacts from other time periods. Instantly, he thought of Nazarian.

As the nomads clashed with the Romans, Rabbit paid attention to their carts. Most of them were wrapped in cloth, but on one, the cloth was flapped open. Impulsively, he ran to that cart and scrambled up the wagon wheel onto the bed. One of the Bedouins was tugging at the cloth covering, but Rabbit spotted a large crate tucked in among numerous rolled carpets. He began to shout in Greek to the city guards. The Bedouin shouted at him and lashed at him with a little leather quirt, but Rabbit kept up the alarm until at last, a few guards came over to see what the fuss was about. The moment they spied the wooden box, things escalated quickly. Rabbit leaped from the wagon to avoid being shoved off by one of the guards as they drew swords. The Bedouins scattered, some on horseback and others on foot, leaving their caravan clogging the road.

The guards called over some of the carters, who lifted the crate out of the Bedouin wagon and opened the lid. Rabbit climbed back onto the wagon to see that the inside of the crate was filled with straw. The carter lifted out a handful, revealing two of what Rabbit knew were seven tines of the enormous gold candelabra. His heart leapt. That was it. That was the menorah.

As they carried it back to the wagon train, Rabbit quickly and desperately assessed the situation. Could he grab it and run? No, of course not. The front of the wagon train was crowded with workers and armed guards. He'd be cut down before he laid hands on it.

He climbed down from the wagon, suddenly wondering if he had just made a huge mistake. It might have been easier to steal the menorah from the small group of thieves than it would be from the Roman army. The Bedouins had to be Nazarian's. Who else would target that one item among all the other treasures?

Of course there was one other. Her. The stringer knew it was here, too.

Rabbit was used to competition, of course, but a three-way fight in two days was going to make this a hell of a lot harder.

But at least he knew the menorah was really here. He even knew which wagon it was in. He could see the crate, perched proudly on top of a neatly organized load of goods.

For the next half hour or so, he followed that wagon as the train headed west along the Mese, through the walls of Constantinian, through the farms and arbors of the outer city back to the Theodosian Walls. It stopped at the Second Military Gate, north of and in sight of the Golden Gate. Here the procession came to a halt and began to unload.

Rabbit spotted a harried-looking administrator carrying what looked like a forerunner of a clipboard. He sauntered in the clerk's direction.

"Miraculous," said Rabbit, assuming a wide-eyed wonder.

"It'll help the treasury; Lord knows we need it," he said absently, trying to slough Rabbit off.

Rabbit pressed on. "Why put it here?"

"For the triumph. They'll set it up to pass through the Golden Gate for the parade. Until then, it'll be under heavy guard," he said, as though warning Rabbit not to try anything. "Excuse me," he said and walked away into the crowd.

Unlike the Golden Gate, which was a fort unto itself, the Second Military Gate was, well, just a gate. Still, a detachment of soldiers and the gate towers overlooking it all would make the site secure enough. This wouldn't be an easy snatch-and-grab job.

He waited until he had a good sense of the disposition of the temporary camp and then walked back toward the inner city, thinking through his options. In the best scenarios, Rabbit would enter history close to the point when an object was actually destroyed or lost forever. The Library of Alexandria was an excellent example. There were several popular stories about how the menorah disappeared. One said it had been dropped into the Tiber back in Rome. Another claimed it had been melted down and ransomed to the Visigoths as coins during their sack of the Eternal City or lost at sea by the Vandals after theirs. Now that he knew for certain it was here, he could dismiss all of those. Another story said that the "treasures of the Jews," perhaps including the menorah, were shipped back to Jerusalem to protect Constantinople from their curse. That one might be useful.

He was so absorbed in his thoughts that he didn't notice the clip-clop of trotting hooves approaching him from behind until the rider was almost upon him. Rabbit moved to one side of the road to let the rider pass. Night was settling, and it was dark in the fields of the outer city. The carters and dray animals were long since back in the city limits, so Rabbit was curious about the latecomer. To his surprise, he saw the bald pate and skinny frame of the customs official riding a mule.

Mule and rider passed him without a glance and continued down the Mese. Rabbit resumed his walk, watching the receding mule for lack of anything else to draw his attention. A few hundred yards away, the mule abruptly turned off the road.

Interesting.

Above the tops of tall grape arbors that lined the road, he could see the dark shape of a building with a dome and a cross rising above the crops. He knew that monasteries were dotted through the outer city and the monks often made wine. The man had turned into the yard of this one.

If there was one thing Rabbit had learned early in his career, it was to notice things that didn't fit. Doing what he did required more than just making a plan and executing it. He had to know what was truly going on in a place to navigate it successfully. Or so he told himself. It was also possible that he was just too curious for his own good. Whichever motivation it was, Rabbit sensed something amiss. The customs official had been hard at work all day and night. He should be exhausted. So why would he stop at a monastery before going home for the night? And why was he trotting his mule in the dark when a wrong step could break its leg?

Instead of proceeding to the churchyard, Rabbit stepped off the road, walked between the grape arbors, and approached the building through the cover of their vines. When he was close to the building, he squatted down and peered through the leaves.

The official's mule was there among several other animals, all of them placidly tied to hitching posts.

A few flickering slivers of light peeked out from small windows set close to the ground. There were lamps lit in the half basement, and someone didn't want them to be seen.

Okay, he thought, *if you don't want to be discovered, what other security do you have in place?*

He didn't have to wait long for an answer. Only a moment later, something passed in front of those twinkling lights. Rabbit focused on the movement and resolved the shape in the shadows. There was a dog, about knee height, wandering the grounds. It was ignoring the mounts as they were ignoring it, but he suspected it wouldn't take kindly to a strange human in its territory. Rabbit was suddenly conscious that the gentle sea breeze was blowing from his right. If that shifted, his scent would alert the dog to his whereabouts. He had no idea if the animal was dangerous but, even if it wasn't, its bark would alert everyone inside about the uninvited visitor.

He racked his brain for ways to trick the dog and came up blank. Maybe if he had a steak, he could distract it but, of course, he didn't. So, Rabbit turned his attention to tricking the people instead. He felt around on the ground and picked up a couple of small rocks. He wound up and threw them hard toward the back of the church, where they clattered quietly. Sure enough, the dog erupted in barking.

Within a moment, the front door opened, and a man came out. He looked around the building and out at the road, then went back inside.

Rabbit repeated the action three more times. Each time the dog launched into its warning, each time the lookout perused the grounds. Each time the search was less thorough and accompanied by more irritated mumbling. Finally, the man didn't come out at all when the dog set off the alarm.

Satisfied, Rabbit unsheathed his knife and wove through the grapevines toward the church. The moment the dog scented him, it erupted in furious barking, but the lookout ignored it as another false alarm. Luckily for Rabbit, the dog pulled up short of him by about five paces to bark rather than attack. He was also wagging his tail. "Fearsome," Rabbit commented under his breath.

He ignored the yapping and walked quietly toward the building. By the time he reached the window, the animal reverted to a quiet growl that it gave up after a minute or two.

Rabbit knelt by the window and put his eye to the chink in the glass where light was coming out.

Inside were a few dozen men sitting, rocking gently in their seats as they spoke in quiet unison. Their heads were covered in voluminous white scarves with fringes at the ends. Rabbit may not have been a religious man, but he knew at a glance what he was seeing: a Jewish prayer service.

He sat up. The little dog mimicked his change of position, staring at him. Rabbit scratched him behind the ears.

Why would Jews meet in the basement of a monastery? He knew Justinian's Rome was cruel to the Jewish people, but observing the Sabbath in private wasn't punishable like a pagan ceremony would be. Why take the additional risk of meeting in a church of all places?

He put his eye back to the glass. The men appeared to have completed the service. They were uncovering their heads and slowly began to talk to one another. If the prayers had seemed secretive, this was even more so. The men huddled close, speaking in hushed but intense tones. Rabbit couldn't make out the words. They were in disagreement about something.

He moved down the wall toward a light peeking out from another window. He put his eye to it.

The customs official was sitting at a little table writing furiously. His prayer shawl was folded neatly and sat on the table next to his work. What was he writing that was important enough to make him stop on the way home at this hour?

The man finished his task and went into the adjoining room, leaving the pages on the desk to dry. Rabbit stared through the glass, dying to see the pages, but the tiny peephole didn't give him the angle he needed. He was tempted to open the window, but it appeared to be solidly cemented into the frame. There was, however, one small hole in the glass. Rabbit took the point of his knife and pushed it through the hole. It met almost no resistance but, as he pushed, it revealed a line of light at the top of the frame. He pulled the knife back and the line disappeared. The window wasn't painted dark, someone had placed a piece of card or wood or something in front of it to block access. He stuck his knife in the hole again and this time shoved it through in a short but forceful poke. Light flooded out of the window as the screen tipped away from the glass and fell to the floor. Luckily it didn't appear to make much noise. No one came in.

Through the unobstructed window, Rabbit had a much better view of the pages. On the left side of the table was a pile of pages attached to a board. That would be the shipping manifest he had recorded that afternoon of the Carthage treasures. On the right side was a single page, its ink still drying. Rabbit scanned the page until he spied what he was looking for. "The treasures of the Jews claimed by Titus including . . ." A list followed that included the menorah. He recognized the handwriting and the blotch of ink he remembered from the rabbit mummy. That was the page he had seen scanned at the London Museum.

The sound of voices coming from the other room was growing louder.

He squinted, searching the page atop the clipboard for the matching text. "The treasures of the Jews claimed by Titus including . . ." He read down the list. No menorah. The list included censers, oil decanters, and a table, but no menorah.

A shadow fell across the doorway. Rabbit jerked himself out of the light and threw himself to one side of the glass.

A shadow the shape of a head appeared in the patch of light cast through the window. Obligingly, the little dog walked up to the glass, attempting to sniff the person on the other side. A moment passed and the blocking screen was reinserted in the frame, darkening the night again.

Rabbit got to his feet quietly, prepared to move quickly if someone came out to check the grounds. He circled around the back of the church and pushed his way into the arbor on the other side of the churchyard. Squatting down, he got a clear view of the mule tied up in front and waited.

Within a few minutes, the official exited the building carrying his clipboard. He slid it into a neat little saddlebag and mounted the beast, kicking it into a brisk walk.

Rabbit jogged down the arbor line and waited until mule and rider passed him by. Then, as casually as he could, he resumed his walk on the road, now pursuing man and mount down the Mese.

Nothing Rabbit had ever read had given him the impression that Judaism had gone underground like this in 535. He had always pictured scattered families practicing in their homes as they had in many times and places. The risk these people were taking to practice their religion together hinted at a larger population of the faithful right here in the heart of the Christian Empire than he had ever imagined. And a bolder one.

Fine, he admitted, a historical writer should come back too.

Luckily for Rabbit, the customs official didn't seem to be in quite as much of a hurry as he had been prior to scribing the copy of the manifest. Or perhaps he was just worried about the animal's surefootedness in the dark. Either way, the mule didn't move too quickly for him to keep up.

The official passed through the inner Constantinian Wall, which, happily, was open and unguarded during times of peace. At several points, the man looked around him nervously, but Rabbit had stayed far enough back that he was confident he wasn't seen.

Curious as he was about the conditions of the Jewish community in the city, what kept him on the man's trail was the manifest.

Why stop and make a copy of it? And why in such a strange location?

At the Forum of the Ox, which was well lit with oil lamps, man and mule turned right. The flat paving stones of this forum were pale grey slate that grew steadily darker from the edges to the center, where it was nearly black. This was the site of Constantinople's executions and torture. Its stones were stained with fire and blood.

Leaving the ominous sight behind him, Rabbit followed the man down a side street that descended gently to the Harbor of Theodosius. He could still see the mule clopping downhill ahead of him. The flickering lights of the oil lamps lining the road outlined him in gold against the black of the harbor. Just as Rabbit began his own descent, however, the man and mule turned off the road to the left.

Rabbit walked briskly down the hill, balancing speed against silence. At the intersection where the man had vanished were two windowless warehouses with rough stone bases and tall wooden facades. He plastered his back against the nearest of them and held his breath, listening for the sound of hooves. Everything was quiet on the side street, however, so he ventured a glance around the corner. The alley was wide enough for a sizable horse-drawn cart to turn into the large loading doors on either side. The door on the left was open enough to let a sliver of lamplight fall across the alley stones and creep up the opposite warehouse wall where it illuminated the first few Greek letters of a painted sign. Psi-epsilon-lamda. *Psellos.* These were part of Andor's uncle's storage empire.

Rabbit crept closer to the open door.

There were voices inside, becoming more audible as he approached.

"Good job done. The Thracian sends his thanks."

Rabbit ventured close enough to see the customs official standing in a ring of men all notably wearing blue elements to their clothing. "The Thracian" had to be Germanius Thrax.

"You can keep his thanks. I'll take the price we agreed to," said the administrator coldly.

The other man offered a tight-lipped smile along with a small cloth purse. "Don't you worry about that. Thrax always pays out." The man was middle-aged and of average stature, but he gave the impression of being extremely dangerous, nonetheless.

The official opened the purse strings and checked the contents. When he was satisfied, he cinched it shut again and secreted it away under his cloak. "Whatever does he want it for, anyway?"

"That's none of your concern."

"I could lose my job for this. I just want to make sure ..." His words trailed off as the man took a step toward him. The customs official had just realized what Rabbit had taken in at a glance. This was not a man you wanted to irritate.

"You're testing me. Do you want to test me?"

The customs official blanched and shook his head.

"Good." Now he attempted to sound lighthearted. "Go home, diddle your wife, pretend this never happened. Tomorrow you'll be a little richer and you'll never have to think about this again."

This was about to wrap up faster than Rabbit had planned for.

He backed away from the tall door quickly and ran into something. An arm snapped around his neck and pressed his Adam's apple like a steel bar.

Reflexively, Rabbit grabbed the arm to fight the choke hold as the man called out. The door swung wide, bathing the alley in firelight as the crew from inside poured out. Their leader strode up to Rabbit.

"Who's this?" He turned and glared at the official. "Did you bring him along with you?"

"No. I swear! I've never seen the man."

"Wait ..." The leader stared hard at Rabbit. "Bring a candle 'round, Magnus."

He held the flame uncomfortably close to Rabbit's face. "I know who you are." He grinned. "From the picture! It's our lucky day, lads. Did you know there's a bounty on your head, friend? No, I suppose if you did, you wouldn't have come snooping around here, would you?" He turned. "Get some rope. Thrax wants him alive."

Before he could turn back, Rabbit gripped the arm holding him with both hands, lifted his feet off the ground, and kicked out at the leader. Both heels connected with the man's sternum and drove him into his mates.

Rabbit planted his feet on the ground and bent over forcefully. As his assailant bent over with him, he chopped backward with his left arm and hit the man in the groin, twice in quick succession. The armbar loosened around his neck and he broke free. For good measure, he shoved the doubled-over guard onto his ass and took two steps toward the road he had come from.

Another lookout was standing in the mouth of the alley. Rabbit reversed and ran in the opposite direction.

The first man to recover from the tangle at the warehouse door reached for him, but Rabbit stiff-armed him like a running back and sprinted past.

There were no oil lamps lit in this direction, and his eyes weren't adjusted to the moonlight, but Rabbit had no choice and ran full speed into the dark.

As if on cue, he stubbed his toe on a crooked paving stone and nearly went down. He managed to keep his feet, but his right foot had gone numb and was like a club at the end of his leg. Still, he kept up the pace as best he could. He cut right at the intersection, his sandals skidding on the stone. He dodged around some barrels, then realized that the ground underfoot had changed to wood plank. Worse, the road to his left was falling away while he was running on the flat. He swore to himself as he realized he had veered onto a narrow balcony attached to the side of the warehouse. With every step, the ground was getting farther away; better to jump back to street level now than get trapped at the end of the balcony. He planted his left hand on a railing just visible in the gloom and vaulted over it. He dropped five feet to the stones, softening his knees to absorb the shock. As he did, another of his pursuers collided with him and flipped over Rabbit's low pose.

He launched back into a run, but his legs were leaden from the drop. Only adrenaline kept his reckless speed up. His pinwheeling feet were close to tripping over one another.

He broke past the edge of the warehouse. Dammit, another pursuer was coming from the right; they must have circled around to cut off his escape. His feet were still spinning as something hit the ground behind him and splattered him with liquid and splinters. It smelled like a urinal. Seriously, had they just thrown a chamber pot at him?

A few more steps. He tried to cut left. There couldn't be anyone that way. But finally, his fatigue caught up with him. One foot crossed in front of the other and he tripped spectacularly, not just falling, but launching himself from the force of his momentum. He braced for impact, but instead fell and fell farther than made sense until, with a shock, he hit a cold floor of water and plunged beneath the black surface of the Theodosian Harbor.

CONSTANTINOPLE

535 CE

The shock of cold gripped him like a vise. His lungs contracted involuntarily, fighting against the compelling instinct to hold his breath. He didn't know which way was up; the world was completely black. His lungs had been heaving from the adrenaline of the sprint, and he hadn't even gotten a moment to draw breath. Every animal impulse screamed for him to get to the surface. One lone human impulse screamed the opposite in reply.

Something hit the water above him, sending shards of moonlight lancing through the water with its sloshing boom.

Surface now and they'll bash your head in from the dock.

Wrestling his mad panic, Rabbit turned his face away from the surface and willed his shaking limbs to swim. He pulled his arms tight to stroke but, wait, no. He was already in motion. His brain giddily fought to make sense of what he was feeling. It was as though he was being propelled by a strong hand away from the dock.

He kicked once, twice, going with the water.

His lungs demanded air so violently it was all he could do to keep his lips clamped shut against the sea. *Just follow the current. Current!* He realized. He was in a current. Now it was pulling him to the left. He followed the strength of the water.

His body slid against something slimy and he recoiled.

His mind was fading, insisting that he felt air on his face.

He blinked. No, it was air. The unmistakable quality of sound had changed, too. Fighting the urge to gasp, he slowly let the burning carbon dioxide out of his lungs and replaced it with salty-sweet air.

There were thudding footsteps above him. And voices.

He rubbed his eyes, the salt water stinging. He was under something. The dark ceiling above him resolved into boards separated by slits of moonlight. He was up against the stone seawall under the wooden pier that extended off into the distance in both directions. Above him, the Blues were still searching the surface for him.

He opened his mouth wide to let the air refresh his addled brain.

The water was still bumping him against the slimy stone. What had saved him? Of course! He was in the Harbor of Theodosius where the Lycus River poured from its underground passage into the sea. He must have fallen directly into its current. Its eddy had carried him in a semicircle back under the pier. That was a bit of luck.

Now that the adrenaline was passing, he realized he was cold. Very cold. He couldn't stay here much longer.

The walls of the harbor were sheer stone. Unclimbable. The wood-plank pier extended the quay out over the water. He couldn't climb its slick posts and, even if he could, he wouldn't want to expose himself to the waiting Blues.

That meant he had to put distance between himself and them before searching for a way up. There had to be an emergency ladder or a stray rope somewhere. They couldn't write off every longshoreman who happened to fall into the water. He was shaking so badly that it was obscuring his vision. For instance, a distant oil lamp, far around the bend of the harbor looked like it was blinking. No, hold on. It was blinking. Not just blinking, it appeared to be blinking in a very regular pattern. Three short blinks. Three long blinks. Three short. Three long.

SOS. That was Morse code for SOS. He almost laughed at the ridiculous notion and had to bite it back. Forget it. All that mattered now was that it was a guide. He would swim toward the light, far enough that the Blues wouldn't see him surface. Swimming would keep him warm. Warmer anyway.

He kicked his feet and began to stroke toward the light, staying close to the harbor wall under the cover of the planks. Every few strokes he would check the light. Dammit, it wasn't his imagination. That light was blinking. His progress was infuriatingly slow, however. The long tunic and cloak dragged at his every stroke, slowing. His limbs were getting heavy. He couldn't feel his face. On the next stroke, his head almost didn't surface; when he took his gulp of air, it was accompanied by rivulets of water.

He had to lighten his load.

With trembling hands, he untied his belt and slipped off his cloak. Next, he slithered out of his tunic. It made him feel lighter, but also colder. The only thing he held onto was the belt, to which his knife and gold purse were tethered. He tied it back around his waist.

Naked but for the belt, Rabbit started to swim again and was relieved at his speed. The blinking light danced out of sight as he began to round the bend. From here, he would have to trust his instincts, as the light and he would both be under the same straightaway of planks. He resolved to improve his swimming technique if he got out of this.

It seemed to take an eternity. With every stroke, he got colder. His limbs got less responsive. They felt like bags of cement. He was so sleepy. He considered pausing, just to rest for a few minutes.

A light.

Peeking through the boards, there was a light.

Rabbit drifted toward the outer edge of the pier awkwardly and gazed up.

A head and shoulders were silhouetted against the golden light coming from the oil lamp. Someone was lying on the dock, looking over. They gestured at the pier, indicating a ladder built into the wood.

Gratefully, Rabbit took hold of the lowest rung. It was slippery with seaweed and felt soft to his hand. He breathed deeply, trying to will his limbs to climb.

He blinked, realizing he had almost slipped into unconsciousness. He took a deep breath. *You're almost there.*

The person above was reaching for him but saying nothing. Sound carries a long way over water. Smart.

Rabbit strained his body and reached for the second rung. He got his hand to it but the fingers didn't want to close. He glared at them, forcing his muscles to perform the action from memory that they naturally did from nervous feedback. He couldn't feel it, but he saw them grip. He got his other hand on the rung and pulled his torso out of the water. To his dismay, the wind on his wet skin felt even colder than the harbor, but he forced himself to continue. Finally, his eyes broke the level of the planks. He could see the oil lamp mounted to a bracket set in the seawall, flickering away. Hands closed around his wrists, and he tried to slither up onto the pier like a snake. That was a mistake. The edge of the wood finished what water pressure had been doing for the last twenty minutes; the knot in his belt slipped free, and the leather strap fell to the water along with his purse and knife. Rabbit desperately reached for it, but he was too clumsy and too slow. They disappeared into the harbor.

Splayed on the dock, Rabbit laid his forehead on the wood and breathed.

"Andor?" Rabbit asked blearily.

It was not the young soldier's voice that answered, but a wry woman's alto he last heard six hundred years ago in Egypt. "Try again, handsome."

Rabbit was barely conscious of the walk to a little boardinghouse, wrapped only in the stringer's cloak to combat the chill that would not seem to leave him. She deftly steered him from street to alley and back again, avoiding the drunken revelers who spilled out of the taverns. When they passed a night watchman, she whispered in Rabbit's ear to play drunk. The guard was so sympathetic and respectful of a woman fetching her drunken man home through the dangerous night that he escorted them the rest of the way and even pressed her palm with a copper coin when he saw where they were staying.

Not that the place was so bad. Her room was on the second floor above the tavern and had its own brazier. She silently readied a fire of wood coals in the brass bowl, and, within a few minutes, they were both warming themselves by its smoky heat. She shivered as she rubbed her hands over the glowing embers.

"Do you want this back?" he said, plucking at her wool cloak.

"Yes," she admitted to his surprise. She traded it for the blanket on the bed, which she gave to him. The woman didn't seem the least bit fazed by his nudity, so he pretended not to be, either.

He sat warming himself for a few more minutes before he finally said, "Thank you."

"Can you feel your fingers and toes?" she asked.

"Coming back," he affirmed.

A few more silent moments stretched by, during which he looked at her closely for the first time. Even though her body was draped in cloth from neck to ankle, he could tell she was athletic. He could see it in her hands and wrists as they adjusted the coals in the brazier. Her face was wide, with a strong jaw and big brown eyes. It was her mouth that said the most about her, however. Obvious smile lines were set in her dimpled cheeks on either side of her lips, like parentheses around laughter. Even now when she looked so serious, it seemed like she was on the edge of mirth. The effect was undeniably attractive, which made him hate her all the more.

"What's your name?" He shook his head. "Never mind. You wouldn't tell me the truth. What do you want?" he asked.

"Same thing as you, obviously."

"I mean from me."

"I know what you mean," she said.

He got his hands a little closer to the fire. "You're going to have to do better than you did this morning."

Her eyebrows pinched in confusion. "What are you talking about?"

He snorted at her feigned innocence. "Hiring Bedouins was a nice touch; naturally hidden identities."

She got up and paced aimlessly to the window. Checked outside. Came back and warmed herself. She seemed genuinely agitated. She began to speak to him, thought better of it, and stopped. Instead, she just stared at him, searchingly. Finally, she said what was on her mind. "The Bedouins weren't your play?"

"Nice try."

She was looking at the coals and seemed to be speaking to herself as much as to him. "You pulled that trick in Athens after the fourth Olympics."

His jaw dropped and he tried to hide it. How the hell did she know that? That was only his fourth mission. Had he told anyone the story that it might have gotten back to her?

Her smile popped and was gone like a flashbulb.

He had to admit, now that she had brought it up, the cart job didn't seem like her style. On her two previous thefts from Rabbit, she had let him do all the dirty work and then swooped in at the last minute to capitalize off his labor. Which left Nazarian for the Bedouin grift. Did she know he was here, too? Rabbit certainly wasn't going to tell her.

She continued. "It would have worked, if we were in it together. We only have two days . . ."

"No, *we* don't have anything. *I* have two days, and I'd appreciate it if you'd stay out of my way while I work." He got up.

"Oh, don't be stupid. What's your average job time? Two weeks? Three? You don't have time to make this pretty, Ward. It's a simple smash-and-grab."

"That sounds like your style."

She smiled nastily. "You expect me to be insulted by that? I take your shit just fine."

He headed for the door, blanket wrapped around him.

"Come on. You wouldn't be here if I hadn't tipped you off about the mummy."

"I wouldn't need to be here if you hadn't robbed me."

"You're welcome."

Rabbit glared at her and jerked open the door.

"Did I say you could take my blanket?" she demanded.

"See how you like getting robbed."

She laughed, snorting slightly in the middle of the sound. He turned around in the open door to look at her again. She was grinning widely. "That's the spirit! Nothing like a little necessity to get you off your moral high horse, is there?" She got up. "Come on. If we work together, we have twice the chance of bagging this thing."

"And what happens then? There's only one menorah. We can't split it."

"What do you want, a written guarantee? Yeah, I'll probably steal it from you. But the way I see it, if we work together, we've each got a fifty-fifty shot of getting it at the other end. Which is a hell of a lot better than I put either of our odds working alone." She stood staring up at him, hands on her hips. She barely came up to his chin.

He glared back at her. "I'll get the menorah, and I'll keep it."

Rabbit made it back to Andor's house late but without incident. On his way, he itemized what he knew. One, the menorah was here in the city; the manifest had been accurate. Two, for some reason the customs official had created a copy of that same shipping manifest page and passed it along to (possibly) Germanius Thrax. Three of them were here to steal it—Rabbit, the stringer, and Nazarian. She obviously wasn't above trashing his career and, from what he knew of the man, Nazarian wasn't above violence to get what he was after. Four, there was an underground movement brewing in the Jewish community here in the city. Was it possible that they intended to liberate the temple artifacts? Five, the first triumph was tomorrow. Procopius was unclear about whether the spoils of war were displayed at the first triumph or only at the second, but at least Rabbit could count on the city being in disarray, which could only help his cause. Six, the stringer wanted to work with him to secure the menorah, leaving it as a race for the grab back in the present. He had to admit, he was tempted. If they worked together, he'd have eyes on her. But more than that, he didn't just want the menorah for itself, he really wanted to beat her to it.

When Andor met him in the entryway of the Psellos house, the sleep-tousled young soldier was horrified. "What in heaven happened to you?"

"I ran up against the Blues again," Rabbit answered. "They really seem to have it out for me." He thought about telling Andor that he had a rival in town but decided against it. Better to keep the lies he had to tell simple.

Andor took him straight to the kitchen and put him in front of the fire. Against Rabbit's protests, he roused the cooks, who tutted and fed him hot broth. If the women were scandalized by his attire, they didn't let on. Once they were satisfied that he was warm enough, Andor got him a clean set of clothes and they sat down in the triclinium.

"Did you learn anything about Germanius Thrax?"

Andor looked grim. "I did. And if half of what I heard was true, you should not only avoid him as a business contact, you shouldn't even speak his name on the streets."

"Go on."

"He's in the trade business like you, but at a massive scale. His operations run from Britannia to India. People say he is privately funding much of the reconstruction of Constantinople, and that's just the surface. He is vastly rich, but no one speaks of him willingly. When they do, they say kind things with fear in their eyes. I had to spread some coin to hear the real story. He has started wars to sell swords to both sides. Businesspeople pay him for the privilege of his custom. And if they don't, well, there are stories of disappearances. One man said, 'The emperor rules Rome but Thrax rules the world.'"

"Sounds like good advertising for a criminal," Rabbit said.

"Please, don't be so flippant, Antigonus. Tell me you won't pursue this any further. I'm concerned for your safety."

The soldier was so alarmed, Rabbit couldn't help but feel bad for him. "All right. I'll drop it. It sounds like Germanius Thrax doesn't need my business anyway."

Andor relaxed a little and sipped his wine. "What about you? Did you make any good contacts across the Horn today?"

"A few leads. Unfortunately, I won't be able to follow up on them."

"Why not?"

"I ended up in the harbor tonight and lost my purse to the depths."

Andor winced. "Oh, that's too bad. I wish I could help you, but my uncle insists I live on my military wages so long as I insist on remaining a soldier. He thinks it will teach me a lesson. I'll give you a few coppers, though." He reached for his belt.

"I'm not taking your money." He would have taken money from Uncle Helias. He clearly had it to spare. He wouldn't take the young man's hard-earned copper, however.

"Do the Blues have a personal dispute with you? Two attacks in two days are unusual, even for them."

"It was my fault, really. Curiosity got the better of me and I went snooping around one of your uncle's warehouses. Did you know he has hired the Blues to guard them?"

Andor rolled his eyes. "No, but it doesn't surprise me. He's never officially joined a deme himself, but he'll work with anyone if there's profit in it."

"Like this Thrax fellow."

Andor stiffened. "My uncle is a profiteer, not a gangster."

It was the first time the young man had said anything positive about Helias. Rabbit had forgotten the first truth every kid learns on the playground; people complain about their parents and guardians all the time, but nothing will make them do a one-eighty faster than you agreeing with them. "I'm sorry, that was a callous thing to say."

Andor nodded, mollified. "Did you see what was in the warehouse?"

Rabbit shook his head no. "I'm not much of a spy, apparently. I did hear one other worrisome thing, though. Do you know anything about tensions in the Jewish community?"

"There are always tensions with the Jews. I don't know what they have to complain about. Their faith isn't considered pagan; it's not illegal for them to practice it."

"They can't have houses of worship though, correct?"

"Churches are for Jesus," he said, as though explaining something to a child.

"And they can't hold public office."

"That's because they'd bribe their way into control like they did in Antioch."

"Antioch?" Rabbit was familiar with this story, but he wanted to hear Andor's version.

"Thirty years ago. The Jews in that city had bribed their way into power and were running everything. They had taken over a church and were using it as their own. Porphyrius . . ."

"The charioteer?"

"Who else? He wanted to go to mass and was turned away at the door. So, he assembled a militia and evicted them. It caused such a stir that the Jews were ousted from power and control of the city was returned to Rome."

Andor was a good kid, but he was also highly misinformed. There had been no Jewish power grab in Antioch. The famous athlete had simply decided he was offended by some slight on their part and had led a mob of Greens to massacre them during their services. It was a stamp of shame for the charioteer that had taken him years to recover from. Now Rabbit knew the vehicle of his recovery: propaganda.

Rabbit didn't say any of this. He wasn't here to change minds and hearts. He was here to steal a candlestick. So, he simply took it in as though all of this was highly informative. "And here in Constantinople?"

"I don't know. Why are you so interested in the Jews all of the sudden, Antigonus?"

He shrugged. "Business is business and people are people, Andor. Unrest is bad for everyone."

"Now you sound like my uncle," he responded a little sourly.

"I'll take that as a compliment."

CONSTANTINOPLE

535 CE

TWO DAYS REMAINING

Rabbit woke before sunrise the next morning. He opened the shutters and looked out at the street below. No one was stirring. Constantinople was sleeping off the first of their Belisarius hangovers, leaving the city tranquil. He breathed in the chilly air and allowed himself a few moments to appreciate where and when he was. Then he dressed and went downstairs.

The smell of baking bread reached him halfway down the stairway.

"Good morning, Antigonus." One of the cooks called him quietly into the kitchen as he descended the stairs.

The kitchen was warm and glowing from the hearth oven. "Good morning, Fillis. Good morning, Agnes." He had learned the night before that the two women were sisters, both widows who had found productive occupation together in the Psellos household after the death of their soldier husbands. They were parents to Andor and Portia as much as Helias was. "Don't you two ever sleep? I thought I was the first one up."

"You have to rise earlier than that to put bread on the table, my good man," said Fillis.

Agnes added, "And if you don't know different, you must have lazy cooks."

"I'll keep that in mind," he replied.

"The loaves will be out soon. You sit yourself there by the fire and get warm. Master Psellos keeps a chilly house and that's certain."

He parked himself and watched them efficiently moving about their work. He wondered what it would be like to have their lives. Every day the same, their world revolving around this one room. He thought he would go stir-crazy.

As he sat, the two of them planned their upcoming market visit. They talked about this banker, that government official. Names, facts, and speculations raced between them like static electricity. The more they talked, the more he amended his assessment of their lives. They might spend most of their time in this room, but they certainly weren't isolated. In fact, they sounded extremely well-connected to the best spy network in any ancient city: the domestics. They knew who was having affairs, whose children were out of control, and who was having money troubles. He doubted they would have had this conversation in front of the family. As a foreigner, they must have exempted Rabbit from their discretion.

"Excuse me?" he ventured. "Have you heard anything about unrest in the Chalkoprateia?"

Agnes tutted sadly. "Who hasn't? Those poor women. There's been an arrest nearly every day for weeks."

"The jails are brimming," added Fillis.

"And their poor wives are so worried for them."

"They cry and pray for their return."

"What will happen to the children?" Agnes bemoaned. "They'll clog the streets as beggars, that's what. Poor things."

"Do you know why they're being arrested?" Rabbit asked.

The two of them glanced at each other blankly, then Fillis admitted, "We never thought to ask."

"It's all right, I was just curious," he said, taking a sip of the watered wine in his cup. He realized that their network, though vast, was primarily concerned with the human drama behind the closed doors of the city. He would have to look elsewhere for the political side.

"Here you are, Master Antigonus." Agnes handed him a slice of warm, buttered bread that was delicious. "Can we pack you a midday meal or are you going to buy something from a stall like that one," she gestured at the ceiling, presumably indicating the still-sleeping Andor.

"A midday meal would be most welcome," he said. "When is the triumph supposed to take place today?"

"Noon," replied Fillis.

"It won't come down our street, more's the pity, or we could watch it from the roof. As it is, we'll have to cram in along the Mese with the mob."

"If we go to the forum early, we might be able to get a spot on a terrace," Fillis suggested, wrapping another thick slice of bread with a piece of cloth.

"Theodosius or Constantine?"

"Constantine. Better sight lines."

"More popular, though. We'll have to get there earlier . . ."

Rabbit bade them farewell as they debated about the best seating and left the kitchen.

According to Procopius, Belisarius would walk somberly from his home to the emperor's box at the Hippodrome with the defeated King Gelimer. The simplicity of the event was an innovation Rabbit didn't think would excite the crowd much. A big parade would come later, with soldiers, prisoners, and musicians, where gold would be handed out to the viewers. That was probably what the sisters were expecting today. He suspected Fillis and Agnes would be disappointed that they had wasted so much of their time for today's austere event.

Rabbit, on the other hand, was very excited. He knew the history of triumphal parades and why this one was so special. Before Emperor Augustus, triumphs were celebrated to honor victorious generals. It was a reflection of the martial spirit from which the empire had grown. From a practical standpoint, the allure of glory and adulation lured them back to Rome, ensuring they wouldn't turn their victorious armies against the state. That all changed with the first emperor. During his reign, the last triumph was celebrated in honor of a general in 19 BCE. So, when Justinian had offered Belisarius a triumph in his own name, it was no routine reward. The general would be the first in five hundred years to receive such an honor. Was it any wonder he came back from Africa?

While he should have been sleeping, Rabbit's mind had been dissecting the problem of the menorah and had arrived at a course of action that, if successful, would offer a clearer shot at the theft and also allow him to watch the triumph. So, yes, he was pretty excited.

He had toyed with the idea of making a raid on the Second Military Gate while the first triumph was in progress. The problem was, he didn't know whether the guard around the Carthage treasure trove would be any lighter. The spoils of an entire kingdom were piled up there, and they might suspect someone of doing exactly what Rabbit was planning. This was Rabbit's typical MO, watch for the moment of weakness and exploit it. The plan he settled on had many more facets that could go wrong but avoided a direct assault on a military encampment, which seemed prudent. The first step required him to make a little spending money.

He walked briskly through Andor's sleepy neighborhood to the Mese and followed it toward the palace district. While most of the city was beginning to rise, the wide thoroughfare was already alive with activity. An army of laborers was decorating the street with garlands of flowers and colorful banners, which they hung from the buildings on either side or strung across to supports in the center divider of the wide road.

Within a few minutes, he reached the western arch of the Forum of Constantine. The forum was perfectly round with a circumference longer than a football field. It was open to the sky but was ringed by an uninterrupted white colonnade two stories tall with columns framing regular archways all the way around. On the north side of the colonnade was the entrance to one of the city's two senate houses. Rabbit was looking up at the statue of the emperor when the sun broke over the sea and lit it up with such brilliance that he had to shield his eyes.

It's going to be a good day, he thought.

The decorating crew had already completed their work here, and it was spectacular. Every arch of the colonnade was hung with flowers and the column was ringed with them. No doubt the guards would clear this space before the triumphal walk but, in the meantime, city life was beginning as it did every day. People were starting to gather in the forum to talk, trade, and sell their services. Today, Rabbit was one of them. He found an unoccupied space near the shady side of the forum and began to hawk his services to passersby.

"Writing and translation! Need a letter written, sir? Copy something for you, madame?"

Over the next two hours, Rabbit transcribed a love letter to a soldier from a blushing young woman, translated a modest will from Latin to Greek, composed a terrible poem for a desperate young palace worker, and settled a dispute about an inventory list written in Germanic that included, among other things, "two cherubs, missing wings and penises."

Most importantly, the work had earned him the handful of bronze coins he needed for the next step in his morning plan.

As he was transcribing a prayer for a young domestic, several well-dressed men rode past on horseback, headed toward the palace.

Rabbit turned away one final customer and resumed his walk west.

The lavish decorations led him all the way to the Augustaion at the gates of the palace district. Laborers were still embellishing their work here, and the air was heavy with the sweet perfumes of a dozen types of bloom. *Glad I don't have allergies*, thought Rabbit. He ignored the people trying to sell him commemorative medals of Belisarius and the luxury food vendors equally.

With single purpose, he marched up the red marble steps of the Baths of Zeuxippus, paid his bronze, and entered. Rabbit had business in the bathhouse.

The famed baths were every bit as lavish as history described. Multi-colored marble surfaces, elaborate frescoes, and cunning use of light made the baths feel even more spacious and open than they were, which was saying something; the building's footprint would have occupied a modern city block.

Rabbit followed some other men through a short passageway of red marble to a changing room. Unlike Rome, which had men's, women's, and shared baths, Constantinople's baths were divided strictly by gender. But just like Rome, the baths were an economic equalizer. Bakers and princes, smiths and palace officials all bathed together at Zeuxippus and at other public baths spread around the city. If you could afford the reasonable fee, you were welcome.

Rabbit accepted a towel from one of the employees, stripped, and put his clothes in one of the cubbies provided for that function.

The next room was warmed by braziers set at regular intervals. Fragrant spices were tossed onto the coals to scent the air. There were chairs and couches arranged in circles around the room occupied by lounging, chatting bathers. It reminded Rabbit of a country club or a nineteenth-century smoking room. Here was a class divider. He noticed a direct correlation between one's pre-existing cleanliness and the amount of time one spent "warming." Tradesmen might be able to pay the entry fee, but few of them could afford the time to lounge for as long as wealthy bureaucrats or merchants.

Rabbit scanned the room carefully but didn't see who he was looking for. What he did see was two burly soldiers flanking the entry to the next room who questioned everyone before letting them enter. Excitement flared in his chest.

"What's your name?" asked one of the soldiers as Rabbit approached.

"Pothos."

"Where are you from?"

"Ravenna."

"Got any weapons on you, Pothos?"

"None." Rabbit spread his arms to emphasize the point.

"All right, go on in."

Rabbit entered the hot room. True to its name, the space was dimly lit and heavy with steam. He began to sweat almost at once. The mood here was more subdued. There were pockets of conversation here and there, but the heat made everyone languid.

Rabbit searched the room and spotted two men sitting opposite each other. There was something about their posture, more upright and alert, which told Rabbit they were the ones to watch. He casually walked as close as he could to the pair and sat down.

His angle allowed him to see the younger of the two men clearly. He was in his mid-thirties, sinewy and carpeted with curly body hair. He had dark brown curls and large eyes that looked half-asleep. Rabbit recognized him from his mosaic portrait in the Church of San Vitale as General Belisarius. He had assumed correctly the general would want to be cleansed before his big day and had hoped that he would come here to the grandest baths in the city. He was pleased to be right.

The man sitting opposite him had sandy blond hair going grey and pouchy skin that implied he had lost weight in a hurry. "Why didn't you stay in Africa?" the blond man was saying. "Carthage is beautiful right now."

The general narrowed his eyes. "We both know the answer to that." He had a rich voice and spoke patiently.

"How could he be threatened by that? He offered you the governorship."

"How well did that work out for you?"

"I was a king," he said haughtily. Holy crap, thought Rabbit, that's the defeated king of the Vandals, Gelimer. "Anyway, it could have been worse. I may have lost the war, but now I can retire in style in Galatia. All I had to give up was my pride and my honor."

"And are you looking forward to it?"

"As I said, it could be worse."

Belisarius smiled and stretched like a cat. "I don't understand you."

"Me?"

"Any of you who clamor after power. It's thankless if you ask me. Give me a problem to solve, some troops and a few ships and I'm happy. It's after the fighting stops that I'm at a loss. As far as I've seen, a man with a sword and an enemy is predictable. A man with a sword and no enemy is dangerous."

Rabbit smiled inside. The general didn't know it yet, but his hypothesis would be proven within the year. His victorious troops stationed in North Africa would mutiny soon, and he would have to return to bring them back in line.

Gelimer seemed to be enjoying this. "So, take away the sword."

Belisarius shook his head. "That's even worse! A man with no sword ends up at the end of one." The corners of his mouth turned up. "Or retiring in Galatia. No, it's inevitable. As soon as you run out of enemies, you turn on each other. That's why all empires fall."

"Except Rome," Gelimer said wistfully. "Just when the corpse of the empire appeared to be cooling, you turned up. Rome always finds her Caesar, it seems."

"I'm no Caesar. I have just been blessed with many enemies," the general said grimly.

"Let's say adversaries," replied the fallen king affably. "I find I like you too much to call you enemy."

"You've surrendered to the crown now. Why not say friends?"

"Even better. Friend to friend, then. What's next? Persia?"

"Persia, Bulgar, maybe Italy. The Goths seem to have given Justinian cause and he's far too confident in me at present."

"What cause? Who said so?"

"Some nobody spice merchant from Rome."

He couldn't help it, Rabbit felt starstruck to be mentioned, even in unflattering terms, by this historical figure.

The general continued, "I'll believe it when the spymaster confirms it and not until. Anyway, my immediate worry is the Jewish problem."

That phrase, which popped up over and over again in history, sent a chill down Rabbit's back. *Some things never change.*

"Problem?"

"Rumors of unrest." He glanced around to see who was listening. "Justinian's advisor has been arresting people daily."

"They wouldn't dare make a move. Not while you're in the city."

"Maybe not, but I can't stay in the city forever. I'm worried seeing the temple treasures paraded through the streets tomorrow will touch them off."

"Temple treasures?" asked Gelimer. "Did I have those?"

"Apparently." Belisarius groaned to himself. "Potential war on every front. The last thing the empire needs is dissent within."

This was the moment he'd been waiting for. Rabbit had never done anything like this but, if it worked, it could be his ticket to getting the menorah.

"Excuse me, your lordships," said Rabbit humbly.

"Just one lordship now," joked Gelimer.

"I couldn't help but overhear what you were saying."

"You could have," said the general. "What you mean to say is you didn't."

Rabbit nodded, making it almost a bow. "Quite right. My apologies."

"You've already inserted yourself, did you have something to say?" he asked, though not too harshly.

Rabbit mimed building up the courage before he spoke. "The treasures of the Jewish temple are cursed."

Belisarius raised his eyebrows.

"Everywhere they have resided has fallen. Jerusalem was sacked by Titus. Rome was pillaged by the Vandals. Now Carthage has fallen to you, your lordship."

"I know the history," the general said brusquely, but he was looking at Rabbit with growing interest. "What are you suggesting?"

"Everywhere the treasures go, violence follows. You should send them away."

"And where would you suggest?"

"Why not Jerusalem? Let the Jews inherit their own bad luck."

The general chuckled. "Gift them back? You don't know politics."

"You could display them, in a church perhaps." Rabbit wasn't really making any of this up. One of the many stories about the menorah was that it had been taken to the Nea Church in Jerusalem to avoid the bad luck it brought. Who's to say Rabbit hadn't always been the one to suggest it?

Belisarius was staring at him. He glanced at Gelimer, who shrugged amiably. "We did have atrocious luck," the deposed king allowed.

"I'll think about what you said."

"Very good, your lordship. Only, not too much thinking. The parade is tomorrow." That made Belisarius stare in wonder. Rabbit was worrying that he might have overplayed the mysterious stranger card as he got to his feet, adjusted his towel, and started for the exit.

"Who are you?" the general asked.

Rabbit turned back to the general and again made a discreet bow. "Just some nobody spice merchant from Rome."

CONSTANTINOPLE

535 CE

Some minutes later, feeling pleased with having completed step one, Rabbit stood on the steps of the baths and looked at the crowd that had built up around the Augustaion market in the last hour. Yesterday, he had felt invisible in the bustling city, but last night had changed that. The Blues had said there was a price on his head and had even referred to a picture of him. How widely had that picture been circulated? He was anxious to get over to the Jewish quarter before the triumph, but first he needed to do something to change his appearance.

Keeping his head down, he walked into the crowded market. If the Augustaion was ancient Constantinople's Whole Foods, then today was Thanksgiving. The place was teeming. Servants haggled over partridges and geese. Heads of wealthy households inspected honeyed dates and amphorae of sweet wine. Everyone seemed to be shouting and elbowing as they competed to set the best board for their triumph-day feasts.

Rabbit slipped through the crowd toward a far edge of the market where non-food items were being sold. He zeroed in on a lonely stall selling used clothing. The stall owner haggled with him for a few minutes, and Rabbit walked out with a Greek-style brimmed hat. He crammed it on his head and adjusted the brim low to cover as much of his eyes as he could.

A few stalls down, he found a barber who offered to trim his beard for the big day, but he demanded more than Rabbit had left from his translation efforts. As Rabbit stared at the razors the man was selling, a voice spoke softly beside him.

"Need an advance?"

He whipped around and there she was.

"Nice hat."

He adjusted it on his head. "What do you want?"

"I was going to see if you'd reconsidered my offer, but it seems like you're busy"—she took in the hat and the barber—"with your style."

He took her by the elbow and led her even further out of earshot of the crowd. "Somebody put a price on my head. I'm just trying to blend in a little."

"Well, A-plus on the hat then," she said dryly. He turned away from her but this time she caught his arm. "Come on. We're both flailing here."

"Speak for yourself."

She stared hard into his face. Up close in the daylight, he could see that her eyes weren't simply brown. They were laced with black and amber and seemed entirely too large. "You have a plan," she said, breaking him out of the spell.

"I told you I did."

"Yeah, but when you said it before, you were lying. What changed?"

He turned away.

"Antigonus of Rome," she said softly to his back.

Rabbit quickly looked back to see if anyone else had heard her. Two young men were only a few stalls away sporting blue ribbons in their hair. Another walked right past him, approaching the barber.

"I could shout it."

"You wouldn't," he growled.

"You don't know me."

He answered in a quiet, genial tone. "Be careful. There aren't a lot of protections for a woman in this era. The right word in the right tone and you could find yourself in a very sticky situation yourself." He got closer with each word, speaking softly so no one could hear him.

"You won't, though," she whispered back.

"How do you know?"

"Because I know you."

They were so close he could see the motes in her eyes.

"Nobody knows anybody," he breathed.

A passing priest tutted at what he perceived to be their public intimacy. They ignored him.

She laid out the terms, her voice so soft he had to watch her lips. "For the rest of the mission, we work together, even when we're not together. Full transparency of information until the artifact is safely stashed. Once it's hidden and we go home, all bets are off. Deal?"

Two parts of his brain were in a tug-of-war. On a purely emotional level, he recoiled from the idea. He didn't want to give her the satisfaction of thinking she'd beaten him or, worse, that her wide, full-lipped smile or the close warmth of her body was in any way influencing his decision. On an intellectual level, he knew this was the right move. The closer he kept her, the fewer chances she had to scheme against him. She might even be helpful. Once they made the jump, as she had said, all bets were off.

She was staring at him smugly.

What do you want to serve, he asked himself, *your pride, or your plan?* Inwardly, he sighed. *Fine, dammit. Use her like she wants to use you.* He imbued his next word with all the sullen gruffness of a man beaten and begrudgingly giving in. "Deal."

She grinned. "Great. So, what were you doing in the baths?"

"Getting clean."

"We have a bargain," she reminded him.

Rabbit grimaced. "All right, but let's talk on the way."

She waved at the barber. "I'd like that razor, please."

"Of course, my good lady. One follis, would you . . ."

She pretended to be horrified by the price and grabbed Rabbit's arm to steady herself from the shock. "A follis?! Come, my love, there is another barber down the row who isn't trying to slice his customers on his own wares."

"My lady, my lady! I misspoke that's all. I meant a semifollis of course."

"I'll give you a decanummium, no more," she said firmly.

Rabbit stared at her. She was dickering him down to a quarter of his asking price when Rabbit knew damn well her purse was full of gold coins just like his had been.

"There's more metal in the blade, my lady, please!" he whined.

She tossed her hair. "Only because it's triumph day. I'll give you one decanummium and a half."

"A very fair price. An excellent price. Would you like it wrapped?"

"Then how could I defend myself from this brute?" she asked, wide-eyed.

The stall keeper handed over the razor. "God keep you, my lady."

As they walked away from the stall, she offered Rabbit the razor. "Unless you'd prefer to rely on that very mysterious hat."

He slipped it into his purse. It didn't look much like a modern safety razor, more like brass knuckles with the blade running along the outside edge. *Might come in handy for more than a shave*, he thought. "Thank you," he said grudgingly.

"I can't imagine why you aren't more successful with women," she mused. "Now, what about this bathhouse?"

"Nice try. You want this partnership so badly, you go first. How are you learning the details of my jumps? Who's tipping you off?"

"I don't know."

"Good talk." He started away from her, but she snagged his arm.

"I'm serious. That's not my part of the organization. I just go where they send me with the information they provide."

"But you are targeting me specifically."

"Yes."

"Why?"

"I don't know that either."

He shook his head. "You know my funders have washed their hands of me because of you. This is probably my last mission. The least you could do is tell me why you have it out for me."

A look passed over her face that was too complex to read. Pain? Sadness? Regret? She wiped it away with a half smile. "Despite what you might think, I don't have it out for you." She sighed. "But someone does. I'm just a pawn in this game. I did save your life, though. That has to count for something."

Rabbit scowled. "Just tell me what you know about the current situation."

"Something big is happening at the Hippodrome in the next two days."

"You mean the triumph? That's not news."

"No, not the triumph." She rolled her eyes. "Something, I don't know, violent. It's got something to do with this kingpin I've never even heard of called Germanius. He's rented a ton of warehouse space all over the city. That's what I was doing down at the harbor last night."

"Do you know what's in the warehouses?"

She shook her head. "I was going to investigate only I got distracted by this big pale fish."

Rabbit guided them toward the south side of the market.

"I talked with Belisarius."

She gaped at him for a moment before gathering herself. "I'm . . . impressed. How did you get close enough? Never mind. I thought you were always so proper about your museum protocols or whatever. What did you tell him?"

"That the temple treasures are cursed. That he should send them to Jerusalem before the second triumph."

She squeezed his arm and leaned in close enough that he could feel her warmth through their clothes. "Holy shit! You're the shadowy 'advisor' to the crown? That's amazing. I'll say I knew him when."

Rabbit grabbed a handful of dates from a table and handed the rest of his copper to the stall owner. "We'll see if he listens. Anyway, the crown already has its advisor. Joseph ben Levi."

"I've heard the name a lot," she said.

"Really? Here, or before?" He popped a date into his mouth.

She shook her head. "Here. I don't recall him ever being mentioned by Procopius or anyone else."

"I met him. He's like Methuselah's older brother. I assumed he was the one behind that story, but I thought it couldn't hurt to nudge him in the right direction."

She plucked a date from his hand and flashed him her parenthetical grin. "Well, full marks for balls. How did Belisarius respond?"

They passed under the Million Arch, which was draped with garlands like everything else. Where the hell did they get so many flowers at this time of year?

"He seemed to take it seriously. He's already worried about Jewish unrest and thinks parading the temple artifacts through the city is asking for trouble."

She twisted the date and deftly popped out the pit. "There's nobody left to protest. Do you know how many people have been arrested in the past few weeks? At least a thousand, maybe more."

He whistled. "I heard it was a lot, but I assumed the empress was exaggerating."

"You spoke to the empress?"

"Only a little. I was keeping a promise to a friend."

"Oh yeah, your soldier pal. His uncle is in deep with Thrax."

He debated telling her the next part. There was no way she would know if he omitted it. Inwardly, he sighed, knowing he was kidding himself. He had made a deal and he would keep it. "I also witnessed a secret meeting of Jewish men in a church basement on the outskirts of town last night. They looked like they were planning something. My guess is that something is the theft of the temple treasures."

"Maybe the Hippodrome hubbub has something to do with that." She slid her arm through the crook in his elbow. "See, here we are planning to rob some thieves. Fun, right? So, where are we going now?"

"To see if we can get in on the heist."

Situated just outside the Byzantine walls, in view of the Hagia Sophia church, the Chalkoprateia neighborhood was commonly thought of as the Jewish quarter in sixth-century Constantinople. Chalk means bronze in Greek and the neighborhood was known, not surprisingly, for its copper-and bronze-smithing shops and the Jewish artisans who worked in them. The neighborhood boasted more economic diversity than that, however. They walked past shops selling all kinds of wares.

By all appearances, this neighborhood appeared to be thriving. The shops were well maintained and prosperous. The only difference Rabbit could see between it and other neighborhoods was the preponderance of men in hats, which were not otherwise a staple of Byzantine fashion. As they walked a little farther, they turned a corner and spied the Theotokos Chalkoprateia, a church built almost against the Byzantium Wall. It had been a synagogue until the laws changed and it was co-opted into the Christian fold.

"Some things never change," he murmured.

"What?"

Rabbit gazed up at the stone building. "First, they take over the buildings and refuse Jews the right to hold higher political office than a Christian. In twenty years, it'll be illegal to have a Jewish prayer service in Hebrew. In a hundred years, the Jews revolt and riot, only to get stamped down again."

She nodded. "And anyone who survives it is forced to convert to Christianity or be executed."

"History is made up mostly of oppression, resistance, and murder. Wash, rinse, and repeat," he said.

"The Christians will get theirs when the Turks invade."

Rabbit looked at her. "How is that any better?"

"Every bully gets it fed back to them eventually." Her voice dripped with venomous anticipation. Rabbit glanced and saw a matching expression on her face, which she immediately hid. "So, what's the plan, anyway?" she asked, concealing the hatred that had been there a moment before.

Rabbit looked around at the neighborhood. Locals and shoppers were mixing together casually. Nothing looked out of place. Even so, he swore he could sense building anticipation that had nothing to do with the triumph.

"The men I saw praying and planning last night, how did they get in so deep with an order of Christian monks? The monastery is too remote. It would have to be someone from the Christian establishment who was also a member of the Jewish community. Someone who was close enough to understand their struggles but removed enough to influence other circles."

She scowled for a moment and then her brow rose. She looked at the church in front of them. "The local priest."

He nodded and walked toward the entrance. "Come on."

It was dark inside. The windows, which were small and mostly close to ground level, were shaded by the defensive wall to the east of the building. Only one, set high in the eastern peak near the ceiling, allowed in the early morning light. It fell in a shaft so crisp it looked almost architectural. Motes of dust danced through the beam.

"God be with you," said a voice beyond that light.

"And also with you," said the stringer in a quiet, reflexive murmur.

Rabbit glanced at her, but her lips were pressed hard together. The wording of that phrase was only used in the United States in the late 1900s (Rabbit wasn't sure of the exact dates). Before and after that, the accepted translation of the Latin was "and also with your spirit." So she had been raised Catholic but no longer practiced; he would have bet his life on it. It wasn't much, but Rabbit reveled in the minor insight. She knew so much about him while remaining a complete mystery herself. *Well, you can't hide forever, lady.*

A man dressed in dark clothing stepped around the beam of light, reinforcing the illusion of its solidity.

The priest was young, but Rabbit expected him to be younger. A church in the middle of the Jewish quarter had to be a terrible placement; priests of the era became rich from the largesse of their wealthy parishioners, and those would be in short supply in the middle of a neighborhood with so few Christians. The man was fair-haired, bearded, and tall, with an air of calm stillness about him that didn't seem like an act.

"I am Father Lambert," he said.

"Gallus," Rabbit replied.

"Helen," the woman said, smoothly threading her arm through Rabbit's elbow in a gesture of intimate possession. Rabbit fought the urge to pull away.

Lambert smiled gently. "You're here for marriage rites?"

"No," said Rabbit, a little too quickly.

She squeezed his arm. "What he means is we're already married, Father."

He smiled and nodded. "Something else is on your mind, then."

"My husband would like to unburden himself of his sins."

"God absolves all. What is your sin?"

"Pride," said Helen. Rabbit squeezed her arm with something other than affection.

"Pride is a powerful force when used for good, but it must be tempered by humility in the face of the Lord."

"That's what I tell him, but my husband . . ."

"Dear lady, perhaps you could wait here while your husband and I talk."

Well played. Helen had just given him a private audience with the man. He didn't strictly need this conversation to be private from her, but it wouldn't hurt. It also showed a measure of trust in him that he would tell her about the conversation. Rabbit followed the young priest past the ray of light toward the eastern side of the church. Lambert didn't stop there, however, but led him through a door into a small back room. A woman was there, polishing a brass bowl with a piece of cloth.

She looked up with surprise as they entered. "My wife, Rachel," he explained. The woman smiled at Rabbit. Inside, he felt his suspicions validated. Not only did the young priest work in the Chalko-prateia, but he had a Jewish wife. It didn't surprise Rabbit that he was married, of course. Celibacy wouldn't be required of the Catholic priesthood for hundreds of years yet. But his wife's heritage might well factor into the priest's sympathies for Jewish oppression.

"Would you excuse us for a moment, wife?" Lambert said. She said nothing, but replaced the bowl on the shelf and left the room.

"Now, you had something to tell me about pride?"

Rabbit was mute for a moment. He was looking past the priest at the back wall of the stone room. Behind and partially obscured by the little table was an arc of Hebrew words carved into the stone.

He had prepared a script in the night. Something to convince the priest that he too was outraged by the treatment of the Jewish community in the empire. But suddenly his mind went elsewhere. His script was gone from his mind. He was in Rome, 455.

The night was punctuated by screams. The Vandal horde was pouring into the city from the north, working its way toward the forum. They would make a deal, Rabbit knew; the city wouldn't be burned. On the way to making that deal, however, the Vandals wanted to make sure no one would form an organized resistance. Casual and brutal violence would keep people in their homes. Rabbit was scared and angry, but it was nothing compared to Aaron. The young man jerked at every squeal and scream that drifted through the city of marble.

"They're not as close as they sound," Rabbit reassured him. He dropped the heavy stone smith's hammer on the iron warehouse lock. It shattered and fell in pieces to the ground.

A woman's cry, long and keening, was cut abruptly short.

To Rabbit's surprise, Aaron took an involuntary step toward it.

"Aaron." He said it calmly, just to bring him back, but when the young man turned, his face was a mask of fury. He wasn't scared, he was enraged.

"Those fuckers," he hissed.

He was coiled, ready to lunge away. Rabbit grabbed him by both elbows.

"Aaron. Listen to me. This happened sixteen hundred years ago. You can't change it."

"I can't stand here and do nothing."

"You're not doing nothing. We get the menorah. That's how we win." He opened the door of the warehouse. "Don't you want to deny them the prize they want? Don't you want to return the menorah to where it belongs?"

The young man's shoulders settled slightly.

"If we don't get it, they will. They'll gloat over it, put it on a shelf just like the Romans did. You don't want that."

He shook his head.

"This is how we win," Rabbit coached him.

Aaron let out a shuddering breath. "This is how we win," he repeated.

Rabbit realized that the tall priest was watching him patiently. He didn't know how long he had been silent. The memory had wiped Rabbit's carefully prepared script out of his mind. Instead, he said, "I want to ask you about it, actually. Pride, that is."

"All right."

"What makes a person walk into danger when they know it's

bad for them? When they know they could simply be silent and unharmed? Is that pride?"

Lambert took a long, slow breath, then said carefully, "Courage, perhaps? If the cause is just."

Rabbit was thinking of Aaron and of how that terrible day had ended. "But what if the action is futile?" Less than an hour later on that day, Aaron's screams would ring in his ears. They never stopped ringing.

"Action in service of a just cause is never futile."

"It is if you die," Rabbit replied harshly.

"The martyrs of our Lord would disagree. If one's death places a grain of sand on the scales of justice for others to build upon, then it is a fine death."

"Is that Psalms?"

"That's Lambert." He smiled, breaking the veil of saintliness with humor. "I, too, struggle with pride."

Rabbit pondered that. "But what if you knew that history was already written? That your sacrifice would change nothing. Isn't that futile?"

"You're talking about destiny? That's a metaphysical argument, not a moral one. God has a plan for us, but we may never lift the veil to see it. We must proceed with intention, otherwise we dishonor the gift of life."

Rabbit was silent.

The priest continued, "Let me tell you about a notion I have. I believe that we each contain more than one self. One of your selves inspires you clearly to action. It sees the true path and knows what must be done. But there is another self inside us all . . ."

"Like the devil on your shoulder?" Rabbit said, sneering a little.

"No," the man said firmly. "The other self is not evil, but it is also not correct. It tempts us with indecision. It is insidious in its misdirection, arguing that it is the voice of reason, while the other is merely the voice of the heart. One of the noblest endeavors a man can engage in is seeing past that insidious doubt to the clear voice of the first self. There is a question behind your question, I know, a specific injustice, which brought you to me." He held up his hand. "We don't need to name it. In fact, it might be better if we don't. What I would encourage you to do is quiet that voice of prevarication and listen here." He pointed at his own heart.

"Do you?" Rabbit asked genuinely.

"I try. Every day. Do you, Gallus?"

Rabbit set his jaw and looked up at him. "I try."

The priest considered him. "Why are you really here?"

Might as well go all in, Rabbit thought. "I have information you and your friends might find worthwhile. Related to the Hippodrome . . ."

"My friends? I don't know what you mean."

Rabbit stared at his guileless face. Had he misjudged the situation? "My mistake. I apologize."

"But I know someone who might." Lambert stared at him searchingly, then seemed to come to a decision. "I would like to introduce you to someone who might help you find clarity of purpose. He changed my life."

Rabbit felt a thrill run down his spine.

"If you and your wife will wait here, I will send word and arrange a meeting."

"We'll wait," he said, outwardly calm, inwardly giddy.

The priest squeezed his shoulder and started out of the room.

"Father, one more thing. I have found myself the object of some unwelcome attention in the city. I bought a razor. I thought a change in appearance would make me harder to recognize." He rubbed his beard. "But I have nowhere to use it."

"My wife will give you water," he said.

"Thank you."

Lambert returned Rabbit to the company of his wife and Helen in the sanctuary. The two were joking and laughing as they led a bemused Rabbit to a small annex at the side of the church where the Lamberts lived. The home was modest but comfortable, with textiles and art hung to warm up the chilly stone block walls.

The kitchen followed the design of the one in the Psellos household, only on a smaller scale. A clay and stone oven built into the wall was radiating heat. Bowls of bread dough were rising on a little wooden worktable.

Rachel fetched down another bowl and filled it from a ceramic amphora of water.

She also gave him a small container of olive oil, which he assumed was to soften his beard. He rubbed a few drops into the bristly hair and got out the new razor Helen had bought him.

As he tested the edge, Rachel looked concerned. "You're not going to let him shave himself, are you?"

Helen looked taken aback.

"Without a glass, he'll cut himself to ribbons," the priest's wife chided.

Helen took the razor from him. "He's just so stubborn. Always wants to do everything for himself, even when I could clearly help."

"Men. They're all the same. Think we'll respect them more if they don't need us and make everything more difficult trying." She wagged a finger at him. "You have a clever and capable wife, Gallus. You should lean on her more, so she feels safe to lean on you."

"I . . ." he began, but trailed off, realizing he had absolutely no argument.

"Don't skimp on the oil, Helen. I've seen grown men cry from a dry shave."

Rabbit reached for the olive oil container, but Helen slapped his hand. She poured some of the cloudy green liquid into her palm, smoothed it over her hands, and stepped close to his left side. Her legs pressed warmly against his as she leaned over him and gently caressed the oil into his beard. Her eyes wandered over his face while

Rabbit tried his best to stare at the spoons hanging on pegs on the opposite wall. It was no good, however; she was so close he couldn't help but look at her. Her skin was soft and tan, and she smelled faintly of cedar. The corner of her mouth crinkled with mirth as she caught him looking and he averted his eyes again, scowling.

Rachel, meanwhile, had fetched a thick strip of leather with a loop of rope on either end. "May I?" she asked, indicating the razor. "Even new, these things don't hold their edge well." She poked the toes of one sandaled foot through one loop and pulled on the other, drawing the leather taut. With quick and practiced strokes, she rasped the razor over the strop, honing the blade.

"I've never seen Lambert without a beard. He'd probably look like a boy."

"How did the two of you get together?" asked Helen. She gave Rabbit's cheek a pat bordering on a slap and stepped away.

Rachel blushed. "Here in the Chalk. When he replaced old Father Gnaeus, he used to stand outside on Sundays, waiting for someone, anyone, to come to mass. All the neighborhood girls admired him, but I was the only one bold enough to talk to him. Once I did, others did too. Gnaeus always stayed in the church, grumbling about being abandoned among the Hebrews. Not Lambert. He opened his kitchen up for volunteer days to make bread for the poor. He helped rebuild apartments and shops that burned down after the riots. Everyone in the Chalkoprateia respects my husband," she said proudly.

"But how did you . . ."

"Marry him? It was my idea. He never would have asked my father otherwise."

"Did your family approve?" Helen asked. Rabbit thought that surely she was being too invasive and the woman would kick them out, but Rachel kept talking.

"My father refused," she said sadly. "He respected Lambert, and liked him, but he was not one of us."

"You disobeyed him?"

At that, Rachel did look insulted. "Of course not. For seven years, I waited. There were other suitors, but I rejected them all. My brothers and sisters married and had children, but not me. My father was not so strict as to force me to marry someone else, knowing my love as he did."

"And did he change his mind?"

Rachel shook her head. "He died feeling very much the same. Two years ago."

"I'm sorry," said Rabbit.

She nodded, accepting his condolence. "My eldest brother Abraham practically grew up with Lambert, as I did. It wasn't easy for him either, but he granted us permission when my father died. I was accepted into the church then and we married last year."

"Are you happy?" Helen asked without apology.

"I love my husband very much," she said and handed Helen the razor. Rabbit felt the iceberg below the surface of that statement but said nothing. Helen accepted the razor without further question and turned to Rabbit.

"Are you ready for this?"

A deep, anxious breath was his only answer.

"Don't worry," she said. "I'll try not to kill you."

Helen stood close to him again, her warmth radiating through the layers of their clothes.

"Look at me," she said. He raised his face to give her a better angle.

She touched the blade to his cheek, starting in front of his ear. The bronze was warm from the friction of the leather. He heard the prickling scrape of the blade.

You can't stand this woman, he reminded himself. For the last year, all she had done was embarrass him and make his life more difficult. She put a finger to his chin and gently guided him to turn his head. His breath was shallow. A little smirk crept onto her lips as the blade rasped over his throat. His heart was beating hard; he could feel the sharpened bronze pressing on his jugular. She was close enough that he could feel her breath warm on his cheek. He traced the line of her smile, her lips full and . . .

To his utter horror, he felt his body responding to her against his will.

"You know . . ." he said loudly and felt the blade bite his skin.

"Stay still!" Helen and Rachel said in unison.

Rachel handed her a cloth for the nick, which she pressed to his neck.

"What about you two?" Rachel asked. "How did you meet?"

Helen transitioned to his other side.

"Gallus wasn't always a spice merchant," she began. The razor scraped over his other cheek. "He was a soldier when we met, in Antioch. He didn't need to shave then, I can tell you that."

"I'm sure he was a handsome youth."

"Not at all. He was a gangly thing with ears like jug handles. He was sweet, though. He used to make up excuses to walk by the public fountain when I was drawing water for my family. I wasn't even a woman yet, but I could see he had an eye for me."

"And you for him."

"Not at all. I didn't like soldiers. I thought they were coarse."

"What changed?"

"Did you ever hear how Porphyrius led the Greens and attacked . . ."

"I know the story," Rachel said, sadness and anger vying for her features. Andor might have swallowed the imperial propaganda, but this woman had not.

"I was out doing an errand for my mother when they marched through the streets. The legion was mostly away from the city. Only a small garrison was left, and they chose to be otherwise occupied. At the gate to the Jewish quarter, only one young soldier stood up against them, ordering them to disperse. One gangly, jug-eared boy.

They swept him aside, of course, and nearly trampled him to death, but he had stood his ground doing what was right. That's when I fell in love." Rabbit felt the softness of her words and, as much as it galled him, he felt a twinge inside. What would it be like, he wondered, to have someone you cared about talk about you like that? Suddenly he was jealous of his fictional self.

Helen stepped back and surveyed her work.

"What do you think? Will we start a new fashion?"

Rachel inspected him while Rabbit felt his face. Helen had shaved his cheeks but left a goatee.

"By spring, every man in the city will be lined up at the barbers asking for a 'Gallus shave,'" she predicted.

Rabbit washed his face and reapplied a little more oil to soothe the scraped skin. As they left the apartment and headed back into the church, Helen whispered to him, "What do you think? Did I lay it on too thick?"

Rabbit was still trying to eradicate the little longing in his chest for someone, anyone, to be that proud of him.

"It was good," he said gruffly.

A few minutes later, Father Lambert returned. He brought with him a man who walked with a cane, but it was due to injury, not age. He appeared to be about thirty-five, with a solid build and a broad face, curly red hair, and hands like hardened leather.

"This is the man you wanted me to meet?" Rabbit asked the priest.

He shook his head. "Teacher is detained at the moment. This is Judah, he's a leader in our community."

The man nodded. "Lambert tells me you sought him out."

"I merely had questions to which I wanted answers," Rabbit replied. The rebel leader was clearly suspicious of him and Helen and made no attempt to hide it. He took a step forward and Rabbit, sensing danger, reached for the razor in his belt.

Judah's cane flashed, and Rabbit's hand went instantly numb where it struck him. A knife blade was at his throat. Rabbit waited for the stab that would end his life. Instead, the man said, "Now we can talk."

He took two steps backward. He still held onto the knife but dropped his aggressive posture.

"What the hell was that all about," Rabbit growled, touching his neck.

"If you were a spy, you wouldn't have gone for a weapon. Neither would she," he pointed past Rabbit with his chin. Helen was holding a dagger with a deadly look in her eye.

"So, you trust us because we thought about killing you?" she asked.

"Spies care more about the job than they do about their husbands," he explained. "So, tell me, why are you here really?"

"Because I know something that might be useful to you," Rabbit said.

"Go on."

"Everyone in the palace is worried that your people are going to take up arms against the city."

The man's lips pressed together, but he made no other sign of acknowledgment.

Rabbit continued. "They think that if they arrest enough of your respected leaders as hostages in the palace jails that they can keep you in line."

"I know this, foreigner. Everyone knows it."

"Do you know this? Belisarius is concerned that the sight of the temple relics being paraded through the streets will incite a riot. He's going to try to convince the emperor to send the relics away in secret and hide them in the Nea Ekklesia, a Christian church in Jerusalem." Rabbit hoped he had done a good enough job convincing the general to do just that.

Judah chewed on Rabbit's words for a few moments. "When?" he finally said.

That was the tricky part. Rabbit suspected that Belisarius had gone from the baths to his home. It was unlikely that the general would have the opportunity to make his case to the emperor until after that event.

"I don't know for sure, but I would guess between the two triumphs."

"Two?"

Shit, thought Rabbit. Helen glanced at him, tight-lipped. Well, in for a penny . . . "Two. The first one is going to disappoint people and the palace will decide to allow a second to be held. Between them, I believe the treasures will be secreted from the city."

"If you're right, Teacher will tell us. We'll take everything back they've stolen from us. What's in this for you?"

"Nothing," Rabbit lied.

"Bullshit. Nobody cares about my people but us."

"Father Lambert does."

"I know Lambert. I don't know you. You don't make sense to me. I don't think you're a spy, which makes me wonder what you are."

To Rabbit's surprise, it was Helen who answered. "It's not as mysterious as you might think. My husband is a righteous man. Most men, having learned what we did, would have minded their own business. They would have regarded it as a curiosity and nothing more. My husband is not most men. Knowing what he does, this was the only path he could have followed."

Judah regarded her coolly. "You honor your husband. But we shall see what Teacher answers."

After some additional negotiation, Judah promised to send word to the Psellos house when and if Rabbit's story was confirmed. They would need all the help they could get, and Judah accepted his offer to join the assault team who would go after the treasures in transit. Even so, Rabbit had the distinct impression that inter-cepting the menorah was a minor consideration to the rebel leader. Which begged the question, if the temple relics didn't rise to the highest level of importance to this group, what did?

CONSTANTINOPLE

535 CE

Not bad, Ward," Helen acknowledged as they left the Chalko-prateia. "Not bad at all. It's contained, both sides are motivated to keep it private, and, in the melee, we have a better chance of not being noticed."

They walked past metal shops and clothiers. A couple of Blues walked past in the opposite direction but neither of them looked twice at him. Rabbit self-consciously ran his hand over his newly trimmed goatee.

"Relax. You're practically invisible in that hat," she said and looped an arm through his. "So, what's the verdict? Was I or was I not useful in there?"

He hesitated a long moment. "Yeah."

"Do they charge you by the word?"

"I'd be a lot more grateful if I didn't know you were just setting me up to rob me again."

She shrugged. "That's tomorrow. Today, we have a triumph to watch."

"Are you kidding? We have too much to do."

"Like what?"

"We have to plan the rest of the mission!"

She smiled beatifically to passersby and patted his arm. "Judah said he'd have a team of horses ready, and you know they'll have weapons. We don't know if your little hints to Belisarius worked or, if they did, the disposition of the treasures. Until we do, what do you propose we plan, exactly?"

Rabbit knew she was right but didn't want to admit it. "Contingencies," he said. "We can scope out the harbors and the road leaving the Military Gate. We can arrange for transportation back to our decay points . . ."

"Or we could wait for the information from the palace and just plan for the thing that's actually going to happen. And with the time we've saved, we could witness an incredibly significant moment in history and maybe figure out what this supposed 'event' is supposed to be."

Rabbit stewed, staring at the shop fronts as they passed.

"All right," he said at length. "We might pick up something useful."

"That's the spirit," she said.

As they walked toward the Mese, they passed a construction site that struck Rabbit as familiar. It was the Basilica Cistern, the underground water reservoir that served the palace district. Rabbit had visited it in modern day. Its heavy bronze door was open, and workmen were coming out in a stream. Apparently, they had been released to witness the triumph along with the rest of the city. The block leading to the main street was clogged with pedestrians; no one would be getting any closer from this approach.

Helen tugged his arm. "Come on." She led him into a narrow alley.

"Where are we . . ." he began but stopped as she grabbed a banner and jerked it off the walls where it hung covering the mouth of the alley.

"Cover me," she said, pointing to the street.

Confused, Rabbit stood between her and the street. "There are privies in the bathhouse if you need to . . ."

"Thanks, but that's not what I'm doing."

He glanced over his shoulder and saw her adjusting what suddenly appeared to be a very pregnant belly under her clothing. The wadded-up banner made a surprisingly good prop.

"Ready," she said and took his arm again.

They walked back into the crowded street. She leaned on him slightly, having completely adjusted her posture and gait to that of a woman about eight months along. She even breathed heavier. Damn, she was good.

The crowd slowed to a milling churn a block away from the Mese. Rabbit could see the Hippodrome over their heads, but there was no chance of seeing the general process from here. Despite the density of the crowd, however, Helen was still in motion. Repeatedly, she used the same couple of tricks to move ever closer to the road. She would rise on her tiptoes and scan the crowd as though she and Rabbit were searching for a missing child. Next, she would get very close to someone. When they inevitably bumped into her, she would clutch her "belly" and gasp. In both cases, she was shuttled ahead through the crowd, followed by encouragement or apologies. Rabbit trailed after her. Crowd reactions varied depending on the individual and the tactic. Rabbit was chided quietly or loudly for letting his wife leave the house in "her condition." Some generous souls offered to help find the lost tykes and had to be graciously brushed off. Others were blatantly irritated at having to let anyone get ahead of them. Through it all, Helen kept up the act and propelled them forward.

Musicians were playing somewhere, and food vendors hawked hot nuts, figs, and honeyed bread, weaving through the crowd. Helen gasped and searched her way forward until suddenly they were standing behind a row of excubitors, palace guards in full regalia, who were holding the crowd back from the broad main street.

"That's how you do it," Helen said, pleased with herself.

She scanned the crowd and peered down the street between the shoulders of two guards. "Did you ever see the Cammarano opera?" she asked, eyes on the street.

"Not a fan," Rabbit admitted.

"Of Cammarano?"

"Of opera."

"*Belisario*. Good piece, but the libretto owes more to Shakespeare than history. There's this whole plot about his son being . . ."

"No offense, but what's your point?" Rabbit glanced around to see if anyone was paying attention to what would no doubt sound like crazy talk, but their neighbors in the crowd were too excited to pay them any attention.

Helen paused for a moment as if retracing her mental steps. "I was thinking about his wife, Antonina. In the opera, she hates him and conspires to have him blinded and arrested."

"That didn't happen."

"I know, but that got me thinking about Procopius. In his *Secret History*, he depicts Belisarius as a needy cuckold to Antonina's narcissistic sex fiend."

"Yeah well, most of the 'secret history' was probably made up to amuse his friends."

"Still, I was just thinking how crappy history is to women. If we're not hysterical weaklings, we're sex addicts or power-hungry manipulators. I don't know this chick from Jane, maybe she's everything he said, but what we do know is they went together on most of his military campaigns."

"Because he was dependent on her, Procopius says."

"Why is it so bad to be dependent on one another, though?"

"I didn't write it."

She punched his arm. "I'm serious. History loves this image of a man being totally isolated and above everybody else. I don't get it. We became the dominant species on the planet literally because of our ability to work together. But history wants to pretend that everything happened at the individual will of a handful of dudes."

"Queen Elizabeth," he countered.

"Don't get me started. Also, not the point."

"So, there is a point?"

"I think people venerate independence over partnership."

"Wait, we were on gender a minute ago," he began. She glared at him, and he raised his hands in defense. "Again, I have no horse in this race."

"It's like you're trying to be stupid."

"It's a gift."

She rolled her eyes. "Independence is associated with masculinity, regardless of the chromosomes you were born with. Dependence is associated with femininity. Any straying from those roles gets you mocked, hated, and sometimes killed."

"Maybe you just spend too much time in the past."

"Maybe you don't look around enough in the present."

"I . . ." he started. "Yeah, that's probably true."

He was waiting for her to say something about how this related to their current circumstance. When, instead, she dropped it and began scanning the crowd, he realized that it wasn't. A little warning bell went off in his head. *You're chatting with your adversary. Getting comfortable with her. That's how she operates. Be careful.*

There was a shift in the crowd that they both felt. They leaned forward, craning their necks to see along with everyone else on the street.

There were no trumpets, no soldiers marching in procession. It was just Belisarius and Gelimer solemnly walking down the street. The crowd didn't know quite what to make of the un-spectacle and seemed paralyzed between reverent silence and cheering. The result was a rolling wave of polite golf claps that dwindled into embarrassed regret.

As the two men walked past, Helen murmured, "The good general is a bit of a dish." Rabbit snorted laughter, which he tried to play off as coughing to his disapproving neighbors.

In a traditional Roman triumph, the victorious general would wear an elaborate version of field armor, polished to gleaming, with a full cape. His face would be painted blood red as a mark of theatrical divinity. Today, Belisarius was dressed simply in street clothes, albeit of the finest quality. The deposed King Gelimer wore the traditional garb of the Vandals, a long shirt over trousers tucked into boots. Over it all, he wore a long purple cape that trailed behind him on the cobbled street. There was no trace of the affable, world-weary leader Rabbit had seen in the baths. Gelimer looked nervous. He kept his eyes fixed on the road ten feet in front of him, which made it all the more apparent that he was focused all around him on a crowd that despised him and could tear him to bloody shreds if they chose to.

The duo processed past them, headed for the Chalke Gate into the palace. Rabbit knew they would be going to the emperor's private box in the Hippodrome, which was only accessible from the palace side of the building.

In their wake, the crowd was moving in a solid river toward the audience entrances of the racetrack. Rabbit and Helen joined the flow. Thanks to their position, they would be guaranteed a seat. Not everyone would be so lucky. The Hippodrome only seated 150,000 of the city's half a million people, and that didn't account for inns bursting with tourists.

The crowd moved in that slow, inexorable, rocking pace that all crowds do. Helen and Rabbit lapsed into silence, taking in the monumental façade of the track. In classic Greco-Roman style, its second story was lined with white stone arched porticos, through which Rabbit could already see the first of the audience members proceeding to their seats.

They flowed toward the main gate, a massive entrance topped by a bronze statue of an oversized chariot being pulled by a team of four horses.

Once inside, the smell of cooking meat and spices was thick. The first floor of the building was lined with stalls selling food and trinkets just like any modern sports arena.

"Bad news," said Helen as they passed a wine-seller. "You remember mentioning the privies earlier?"

"You're kidding," he said.

"Sorry, no choice. You want to get us a seat?"

"You'll never find me," he sighed. "I'll wait around here."

She scurried off toward the bathroom while Rabbit looked at the nearest stalls. With his remaining coins, he bought them a couple of hand pies warm from the brazier. He declined a cloth wrapper, which cost extra, and strolled to the next stall.

"Welcome to my shop," said the stall owner, a deeply tanned man with a missing front tooth. He spoke with a thick, indefinable accent and was wearing something approximating nomadic Bedouin garb. The stall was bounded by three tables with the open side facing the flow of people. Draped in colorful cloths, the tables were built up to precarious heights with shelves displaying hundreds of little items. "What can I interest you in? We have curiosities from across the world. Tinctures from the remote east that will make you feel like a teenager. Your wife will marry you all over again."

But Rabbit wasn't paying attention to the sales pitch. Something had caught his eye in the corner of the stall, and he walked directly to it. "Tell me about these."

"Ahh, a man of taste. These are mummies from the desert heart of Egypt where the mystic arts of preserving the dead have . . ."

"Where do you get them?" The display rack was mounted with an array of small, mummified animals. Most were cats, but there were some snakes and others, too. They bore the same slipshod appearance as the rabbit mummy from London.

"As I said, across the Nile, there is a . . ."

Rabbit took a quick step toward the merchant and glowered at him. "I work for the tax office. Do you want to change that answer?"

The stall owner sagged visibly. "Come on, I'm just trying to earn a living," he said without a trace of an accent.

"Where?" Rabbit pressed.

"There's a guy sells them out of a warehouse up on the north side by the wall."

"Let me guess, is it a Psellos warehouse?"

"Yeah, the one by the Platea Gate. Look, give me a break, everybody sells these things. They're harmless junk for tourists."

"Ever seen one of a rabbit?'

He shook his head. "I mostly buy the cats. They move best. Are we done?"

"Sure," said Rabbit, his mind racing. "Nice getup, by the way." He turned and left the stall, sure that the merchant was making an obscene gesture at his back.

Helen was back sooner than he feared she'd be, and they climbed the steps with the crowd. He told her about the mummy salesman.

"You think that's where your mummy came from?"

"More than likely," he said. "I'd like to check it out after the race."

As they ascended the steps, Rabbit could feel a deep rhythmic throb in his stomach. The crowd was stamping their feet in unison, creating what felt like a cross between a drum and thunder. The higher they went, the more he could hear the Blues chanting their slogans. If the other demes were chanting back, they were overwhelmed.

They emerged from the stone stairwell under a roof that sheltered the nosebleed seats. At the very top of the stadium, they managed to find a couple spots with a decent view of the emperor's box, directly across the track.

The building was shaped like an elongated horseshoe, with tiered seating on three sides. The flat end of the horseshoe housed the stables, tack rooms, and the starting gates for the races. Beyond it, the unfinished dome of the Hagia Sophia rose like the eighth hill of the city.

The emperor's "box" was an open-faced palace the size of a small hotel from which the noble retinue could watch the festivities in luxurious comfort. Its only entrance was connected to the walled palace grounds, which protected it from the masses. The box was both a grand display of the emperor's wealth and status and a defensive position from the crowd. It was the only reason Justinian hadn't been ripped limb from limb during the Nika Riots. It was empty now.

The center of the racetrack looked like a yard sale of precious antiquity. Statues, columns, and obelisks stolen from across the empire were arrayed without any attention to scale or proportion.

"Too bad we can't loot that, eh?" she said, following his eyes to the gaudy array.

"No kidding. I've only seen a couple of those pieces before."

"Did you look below us?"

"I'm trying not to." They were seated at the top of the Blues section of the track, trapped above tens of thousands of racing fans sporting their favorite color. He felt a little queasy. Someone in that sea of blue started one of their team chants again, and it rapidly spread through the crowd, accompanied by stomping feet.

He pointed to the right, and Helen followed his gaze to the Greens section. It didn't look very green anymore. There was just a knot of deme loyalists among the parti-colored clothes of the other attendants of the spectacle.

The famous Nika Riots had ended right here. For the first time, the Blues and Greens had united in an attempt to put their own man on the throne and punish Justinian for his oppressive taxes. They had made the Hippodrome their campsite and base of operations while rioting and burning half the city. It had all ended when the emperor offered the Blues a generous bribe. The deme accepted the gold and processed out of the stadium, abandoning the Greens to their fate. Halved in number, they were no longer a match for the army. Belisarius' troops locked the doors and slaughtered thirty thousand of them. The little knot shouting their slogans was all that was left

of them in Constantinople. Surrounded by acres of unrelated patrons, they looked petulant rather than fierce. The Blues, mighty
and dishonorable, ignored them.

Helen nodded and leaned in close to say something, but Rabbit
couldn't hear her over the shouting crowd. He could just feel her
breath on his ear, an uncomfortably pleasant sensation.

The crowd began to settle. He followed the collective attention
to the emperor's box, where a row of horn and drum players had
appeared. A moment later, they played a fanfare that silenced the
last murmurs in the audience.

The musicians stepped back, and Emperor Justinian took their
place at the front of the box. The audience made a show of elation
at the sight of him. It didn't strike Rabbit as particularly convincing.

He was speaking, but Rabbit could barely tell. The space was
simply too big for a person to be heard across it. Of course, the clever
Romans had solved that problem. One by one, a series of heralds
stationed throughout the crowd carried his words to the next like a
set of human antennae relaying a radio signal.

The speaker closest to them picked up the speech and began to
relay it, his voice strong and clear. "People of Rome," he boomed.
"Eighty years ago, the merciless barbarian Vandals attacked and pillaged the Eternal City. Their hatred and jealousy of Roman achievement brought them south out of their mud huts in their multitudes
to rape and kill and steal, defying all pacts, covenants, and other
natural boundaries of honor. Before the hammer of Roman might
could fall upon their heads, they fled back to Africa to gloat over
their plunder for eighty years. But Rome did not forget. When the
peninsula fell, Rome did not forget. And when the eternal peace
was made with Persia, Rome turned its eye south."

Rabbit made eye contact with Helen, and she mouthed "eternal
peace." They both knew it wouldn't last much longer.

"Rome never forgot this insult. Today it has been repaid a hun-
dredfold."

Belisarius came forward from the shadows of the box, leading Gelimer by the arm. He was distinctive at a distance by his purple cape.

"I give you King Gelimer of Carthage, leader of the Vandal nation that is no more!"

This time the crowd expressed some genuine excitement. As they jeered, Justinian stepped forward and ripped the purple cape off the man's back and threw it over the edge of the box. It fluttered on the wind, drifting down to the crowd, where they tore it to shreds with zeal. When the crowd grew quiet again, he continued.

"Rome does not forget. But let us, as our Lord Jesus Christ taught us, forgive. Gelimer, your kingdom is forfeit. Let that be enough without forfeiting your life. Instead, let you be banished."

"To Galatia, with more land than anyone here has ever conceived of," whispered Rabbit.

The crowd responded positively but soberly. If anyone noted that deposed kings got sent off to a rich retirement while petty criminals had their noses cut off in the public square, they didn't mention it loudly.

"General Belisarius," Justinian continued. The general prostrated himself next to Gelimer, placing his forehead on the floor of the box. "You have been the sword in my hand, carrying out my righteous vengeance. It has been five hundred years since a citizen of Rome has been honored with the imperial triumph. May this day live in the memories of Rome down through the generations. For as long as the empire stands, there will be valor, and the empire will stand forever!"

Helen shrugged. "Ballpark."

A Roman below them hushed her.

The crowd applauded wildly as Belisarius got to his feet and raised his arms to the people. Then the notables from the box settled into their chairs, including Gelimer.

The applause slowly died down and settled into chattering. Rabbit listened to the conversations around him.

"Was that it?"

"I thought it was going to be a triumph."

"He said it *was* a triumph."

"If you call walking to church a triumph."

"Bit of a snooze."

"Is there anything else?"

Rabbit leaned toward Helen and said quietly, "And that's how you get a second triumph."

The horns and drums played again, and the crowd settled. One of the gates had opened at the north end of the Hippodrome. Rabbit didn't know what was going on, but he was admittedly caught up by the breathless anticipation of the crowd staring at that black cavern. The herald for their section shouted up the stands, "Romans, I give you the pride of Constantinople, the first and greatest, the hero of the Hippodrome, Porphyrius the Charioteer!"

The crowd lost their minds in a deafening roar as four white horses burst from the gatehouse pulling a gleaming chariot. Rabbit wasn't a big sports fan in his own era but this was different. He wouldn't have admitted it to anyone back home, but he craned his neck right along with everyone else to get a better look at the legend of the Hippodrome.

Porphyrius was famous for three things: his unmatched skills in a chariot, his skill and ferocity as a fighter off the track, and his good looks. Seeing him pass by, waving to the crowd, Rabbit had to admit the last point wasn't exaggerated. He looked like a movie star, square-jawed and rugged with a mane of salt and pepper hair tied up at the back of his head. He was dressed from neck to foot in leather armor to protect himself from potential crashes and the attacks of competitors, but he was obviously sinewy strong. It had to be close to the end of his career now. It was hard to tell from a distance, but he looked like he had to be in his fifties.

The legend completed his welcome lap and rode his chariot back into the starting gates. As he entered the gate, a series of horn blasts sounded from the imperial box. It seemed to be some kind of countdown because the Blues around him relaxed somewhat and started talking to each other animatedly. Vendors selling bags of nuts hawked their wares up and down the stands while acrobats sprinted out onto the track and performed a series of stunts.

"You want to go now?" Helen asked.

Rabbit shrugged, trying to play it casual. "Might as well stay for one race."

"What is it with guys and car racing?" But she settled in right along with him.

A few moments later, a horn blast announced the start. Twelve chariots erupted from the gatehouse, 192 hooves beating the packed-earth track with a sound like rolling thunder.

The chariots filled the track from side to side, but they wouldn't stay that way. Like car racing, Rabbit knew that they would all be angling to secure the inside track. Sure enough, before they reached the first bend, the riders on the outside attempted to cut across the leaders on the inside. What Rabbit hadn't envisioned was the savagery of their methods. Each rider carried a leather whip to keep their horses "encouraged." They used it liberally on each other, snapping and slashing at the other riders in an attempt to knock them out of the race. So, sure it was like car racing, if the cars slammed into each other and the drivers rode outside the vehicle and tried to kill each other in the straightaways. These guys were nuts. Rabbit could see why Porphyrius was one of the best-paid athletes of all time. Winning hundreds of races under these conditions was unbelievable. Hell, staying alive for forty years of this brutality was unbelievable.

The crowd was on their feet as the chariots rounded the first turn. The efforts of the outside leaders to unseat the inside track had been in vain, and now two chariots were clearly in the lead. One of them was the legendary Porphyrius. His white horses gave him away. The other appeared to be a challenger named Herakles. Rabbit knew the rider's name because the fan sitting, and sometimes standing, to his right was shouting his name loudly enough to be heard even over the overwhelming support of the legend. The upstart's horses were grey, but his chariot and helmet were decorated in white, marking him as a racer for that team. Porphyrius was decked out in blue.

Herakles held the inside leader spot at the first turn with Porphyrius riding closely on his outside. The rider directly behind Herakles on the inside was a Blue, however, and he did something wildly reckless for the team. The moment they came around the bend, he drove his horses forward so that they nearly collided with the White leader's chariot. The front horse reared in fear, and Rabbit distinctly saw the back of Herakles' chariot bump off the ground as the Blue's horse kicked it. While he turned his attention back to his pursuer, Porphyrius made his move. His white horses poured on the speed, passed the White leader, and swung his chariot in front of him.

The maneuver made Rabbit understand how critical the team was to the win. He had imagined chariot racing to be a solo sport to see whose horses were the fastest on any given day. But individual speed and ferocity were only half the battle. Each color team had three chariots, and only one of them needed to cross the line to win. The rear riders spent their energy impeding the progress of the rest of the field to give their leader the best chance.

The next five laps were exciting but ultimately uneventful. There was jockeying for position in the back ranks, but the two leaders remained firmly fixed in place. Herakles didn't even attempt to make a pass, which drove Rabbit's neighbor to distraction. Apparently, he had money riding on the race; Rabbit thought he had gambled unwisely.

As the riders came around the turn heading into the sixth lap, the tenor of the race changed. The White team launched a planned, unified assault against the Blue rider pursuing Herakles. The plan was clearly to cut off team support for the Blue leader. As they did, Herakles veered to the outside of Porphyrius and pulled up alongside him. The legend sped up too, and the two of them were thundering down the track toward the final turn. The two riders were so close to each other that their chariots were knocking together. Herakles reached across into Porphyrius' chariot and grabbed for his opponent's ponytail. He missed but managed to rip the helmet off the legend's head. It tumbled back to be trampled by the pursuing teams. But Porphyrius didn't retaliate against Herakles. Instead, he lashed with his whip over and over again, not at his own horses, but at his competitor's. The grey team of four pulling Herakles sped up just as the white horses slowed slightly to take the turn. Realizing what was happening, Herakles broke off his assault on the other charioteer and tried to rein in his horses, but it was too late. His team thundered into the final turn at top speed. His cart wheels skidded, then teetered. The whole Hippodrome held its breath as Porphyrius, still close on the inside, kicked the top rail of his opponent's chariot and flipped it spectacularly. The chariot bounced through a full one-eighty, twisting the horses' leads and banging them together. Four horses, cart, and man went down in a cloud of dust.

The Blue who had been directly behind Herakles tried to veer around the wreck, went too wide, and smashed his chariot into the stone wall. His wheel shattered, and the horses dragged the broken cart careening around the corner, their rider lost in the dirt. The hapless charioteer tried to run for the edge but was trampled by the next team of four, one of whom tripped and went chest first into the ground, dragging his team with him.

Porphyrius left the wreckage behind him as two more chariots piled into the carnage and several others simply pulled up short, trying to find their way around. The racing great emerged from the wreckage to cross the finish line unchallenged.

The crowd went insane for it, reveling just as much in the wipe-out as they did in the victory. Workers poured onto the track to calm the spooked horses and attend to the riders. A few of the charioteers from the pileup miraculously walked away from it, but two others were carried away on stretchers, and Rabbit didn't think much of their chances. One of them was Herakles, the White leader.

Amid the crazed cheering of the crowd, Helen and Rabbit slipped out the back and left.

CONSTANTINOPLE

535 CE

Admit it, that was worth the side trip," Helen said as they left the Hippodrome. The Mese, lined as it was with flower garlands and banners, looked beautifully peaceful without its usual teeming crowds. The two of them walked unimpeded down the wide street.

"It was all right," said Rabbit, but he grinned.

She rolled her eyes. "So, where are we going now?"

"The mummy guy," he said.

"Oh, right. Why do you want to see this place again?"

"I don't know. I just have a hunch."

They walked in silence for a moment, which she finally broke. "You keep those cards pretty close, huh? No wonder you don't have a partner."

"I don't have a partner because I don't want a partner."

They stopped a young woman who was wheeling a food cart down the street and bought her last pieces of sweet bread for half price.

"Never met a price you didn't haggle, did you?"

"Oh! That reminds me, the strangest thing happened to me at the Hippodrome. They have these privies set up under the seats, right? I heard these two women talking about how you used to have to rent the pot, but for the last year, it was free."

"Okay."

"That's not the weird part. When I came out, three people, no kidding, three, started bartering with me to buy my pee. I got the equivalent of about seventy-five cents for it."

"Huh. I mean, it has a lot of commercial uses. Laundries use it to whiten clothes . . ."

"I know, I know. But the competition for it was way too fierce."

"So, what's the cause," Rabbit asked.

"There's just a crazy shortage right now."

"Somebody's buying up all the pee in Constantinople?"

"Yep."

"I don't suppose they knew who it was," he pressed.

"No, but apparently it's all going to Psellos warehouses."

"Last night when I was running from those Blues by the Psellos warehouse, one of them threw a chamber pot at me," Rabbit said. "Or at least I thought it was a chamber pot. It was definitely urine."

"You don't think that could be your pal Nazarian, do you? Up to something?"

"Something requiring thousands of gallons of pee? Unlikely. Too visible."

They walked for a little while in silence, but Rabbit was chewing over what she had said earlier. He picked up the thread of the conversation without missing a beat. "What do you mean I play it close to the vest? I told you where we're going."

"You said we were going to a warehouse."

"Right."

"You didn't say why. How does it relate to the plan?"

"I told you, a hunch."

"What hunch?"

Rabbit didn't want to say. Ever since he had seen that mummy in London, Rabbit hadn't been able to shake the feeling that someone was playing him. It made no sense, even to him, but he still couldn't shake the feeling. He knew this jaunt wasn't getting him any closer to the menorah, but he couldn't help it.

"Like I said, no wonder you don't have a partner."

Rabbit thought of Aaron but said nothing.

"What's your hard cutoff for leaving to get back to your decay point?"

"Tomorrow night. Anything later and I'd need to change horses along the way. I can't count on that kind of luck."

"Where do you want to hide the thing once we get it?"

"Nice try," he said, chewing bread. They were walking through the Forum of Constantine again.

She shrugged. "What's your plan if the palace decides not to move the treasures?"

"We'll have to get it from the encampment while the second triumph is being set up. Things will be in disarray; we can pose as porters."

"That's it? That's all you've got?"

His anger flared up. "You know what, if you don't like it, you do the planning. You're good at stealing from me. I'd like to see you plan and execute your own mission."

"What makes you think I haven't?"

"From everything I've seen, you're just a . . ."

"A what? Say it."

"A parasite."

"Parasite?"

"That's right. You rip me off, you rip off the museum, you rip off the taxpayers . . ."

"Taxpayers!? Are you kidding me? Look, go ahead and play the legal card all you want, but don't bullshit yourself that you're some kind of noble servant of the people. You collect old crap for rich people, same as me. You do it because you're good at it and you like it, and the only reason you don't like me getting in your way is because it might hurt your ability to do what you want. Same as anybody else."

People were staring. Rabbit tried to take her elbow to lead her away from curious eyes, but she jerked it away.

They walked in silence for a while, Rabbit curiously both fuming and regretting losing his temper. An hour ago, he had been basking in her kind words, even if they weren't really about him. Now he heard what she really thought of him and, frankly, it stung. He couldn't even deny it was true. Rabbit didn't do this job for some higher purpose. It was just like she said, he did it because he liked doing it. How had this gotten turned around on him? She was the thief after all.

As they passed under the Valens Aqueduct, he broke the silence. "I just don't understand you. You're as smart and capable as any legitimate chrono-archaeologist I've ever met. You could go after anything on your own merit. Why rob me?"

"You're right," she said. "You don't understand. Let's just leave it at that."

"You're not going to get the menorah."

"Why is that?"

The real reason came out of his mouth to his surprise. "Because I need it more than you."

She looked as though she was going to say something, then changed her mind. Instead, she muttered sourly, "So where is this warehouse of yours?"

"Near the Platea Gate, the merchant said."

They descended the edge of the Third Hill past churches and neighborhoods. From the elevation, they could see the waters of the Golden Horn, the narrow sea inlet on the north side of the peninsular city. Across the water was the Sycae, the trading port for foreign merchants. The Horn was protected by a sea chain one thousand yards long that could be raised to prevent hostile ships from entering the inlet. Rabbit looked out to the massive stone structures that supported the sea chain, but it was lowered now. Ships and boats were plying the waters of the Golden Horn back and forth to the Sycae.

"Psellos," she said, pointing. Rabbit followed her finger to a squat warehouse huddling among other buildings in the shadow of the seawall.

"Let's check it out," he said.

The building was old and bleached grey by the sea air. Inset in one of the two big barn doors was a smaller, person-sized door that was ajar. They went in.

The interior was dim, and it took a moment for Rabbit's eyes to adjust. His nose had no such delay, however, and he was immediately struck by the rotten egg smell of sulfur. As his eyes did adjust, he took in rows and rows of shelving crowded with animal mummies in various stages of completion. Beyond the shelving, he could see a few abandoned worktables.

"Hello?" he called.

A man stepped out from behind the shelves looking surprised. For a moment, he just stared at them, not moving, not speaking. Rabbit guessed the man to be in his twenties. He had a lean, wolfish look about him, and his hair was cut in a distinctive style Andor had told him the Blues had adopted from the Huns.

"We had some questions about . . ." Rabbit's words petered out as he realized what he was seeing. The young man was holding the mummy Rabbit had seen in London. He was sure it was the same one. The only difference was that this one was freshly painted white and stained with blood from the young man's hands.

Rabbit pointed at the mummy. "That's . . ."

Without a word, the young man turned and broke into a run.

Rabbit ran after him, chased by a cry from Helen to stop. He ignored her and sprinted through the racks and rounded the worktables, chasing a loud bang from the back of the warehouse. He followed the sound to a door slowly swinging shut. He threw it open and burst into an alley bordering the seawall, but it was empty in both directions. The thief was gone.

"Dammit!" he growled.

Frustrated, Rabbit went back into the warehouse.

Helen was standing behind a table, staring down at the floor.

"He got away. Let's see if we can find the owner; we can let him know he's been robbed."

"I found him," Helen said.

"Really?"

"'Fraid so," she said.

He joined her. She was looking at the body of an elderly man sprawled on the floor. There was blood on his face and neck.

Rabbit squatted beside him and gently felt his neck for a pulse that wasn't there. A hammer lay on the floor under the table that was wet with blood.

"We ought to get out of here," she said. "Not a lot of due process in 535."

Rabbit got up and looked around the tables. There were several mummies on the table in different states of completeness. "Mummy" was a generous term, really. They were more like pinatas.

"Cats," he said.

"Pardon?" She was watching the front door.

"They're practically all cats," he said. "He was stealing the mummy I saw in London, I'm sure of it."

"Great, could we talk about it on the street?"

She took his hand with persuasive gentleness and led him from the warehouse. When they got a block away, she rounded on him.

"Okay, Ward, no more bullshit. What's going on?"

"I told you, that was the mummy . . ."

"You just chased a Blue half your age into a blind alley. Fine, say it is the same mummy. Why do you care?"

He started walking.

"Where are you going now?"

"I've got to talk to someone."

"Who?" When he didn't answer, she just swore and followed.

A fresh cool breeze blew in from the sea across the harbor on the other side of the city. The races were still going on in the Hippodrome. Rabbit had heard them as they crossed the Mese. He just hoped the man he wanted to see wasn't attending them.

The harbor was quiet. A few merchant ships were tied up at the pier, receiving lazy maintenance from the handful of sailors who either weren't racing fans or had been crowded out of the Hippodrome. Rabbit inquired about the customs house, and one of them pointed toward a building jutting from the base of a squat tower on the north side of the harbor.

The little stone tower that housed the customs house was no more than fifteen or twenty feet tall. Its stones and their mortar had been smoothed by years of salt air. It was probably an early defensive tower and may have even predated Roman occupation. It looked quaint compared to the contemporary city defenses.

Rabbit knocked on the door, a grey wooden slab on thick bronze hinges.

No response.

"I've got a bad feeling about this," she said.

"Me too . . ." Rabbit said. He tried the door. It was unlocked and swung open with a grating sound.

They stepped inside and waited a moment for their eyes to adjust to the gloomy interior. But just like the warehouse, there was no denying the immediacy of the smell. It reeked of blood in the little customs house. The air was thick with it.

"We should go," she said.

Rabbit crossed behind a counter. "Dammit," he breathed.

The customs official Rabbit had tracked last night lay on the ground in a heap. His face was a swollen, lumpy mass; it took Rabbit a moment to recognize him. His clothing was dark with dried, tacky blood and, by the smell of it, the contents of his intestines. Rabbit didn't have to check his pulse to know the man was dead.

"Let's get the hell out of here," Helen said.

"Cry," demanded Rabbit.

"What?"

"Cry!" he hissed. A well-dressed older man was walking toward the open door.

She burst into the short, hiccupping breath of someone in shock and threw her hands to her mouth. Rabbit was impressed.

He stumbled out the door and intercepted the approaching man before he could reach it. He grabbed him by the upper arms and said in a constricted voice, "A man is dead. Call the watch."

A pair of city guardsmen arrived fifteen minutes later.

Modern police techniques were a long way from being invented; while one of them talked to Rabbit and Helen, the other set about inadvertently destroying crime scene evidence. Rabbit cringed as the young soldier seemed to touch everything in the room.

"What are your names?" the older soldier of the pair asked them. They were standing in the mouth of the customs house. The man who had raised the alarm stood some way off, trying to avoid the smell.

"Varus of Alexandria. This is my wife."

"What happened here this morning?"

"We got here a few minutes ago and found him that way," Rabbit replied. "We asked a sailor for directions; he'd remember us." Acting defensive didn't take much effort. Law enforcement was swift and brutal in this era. Anyone would be defensive.

"What about you?" the guard shouted to the well-dressed man. "What's your story?"

"I'm from the palace. The man was due last night with official paperwork. He never showed up."

"Do you want to look for it?" he gestured at the customs house. He clearly thought this was a generous offer, but the palace representative cringed at the thought.

"No," he said in horror.

"I could look for you," offered Rabbit. "What is it?"

"A shipping manifest many pages long, probably on a board," he said, grateful to be spared getting near the corpse.

Rabbit looked to the guardsman for permission.

"Make it quick," he said.

Rabbit nodded and went to the little desk. The manifest was lying there in plain sight, but he took a moment to rifle through it and a few other pieces of paper. His bumbling gave him time to look for what he wanted. On the second page, he found "the Treasures of the Jews." This copy didn't list the menorah. So, the official record never mentioned it, but the copied page ended up in the mummy. What game was being played, here?

He picked up the board and was headed for the door when he stopped short. The younger officer was inspecting the body, peeling open the custom official's sticky tunic to reveal the man's injuries. He had been stabbed several times in the abdomen, once directly under the ribs, which was likely the killing blow. But that wasn't what had stopped Rabbit's breath and caused him to stare, wide-eyed, at the corpse.

The older soldier noticed him. "Take it outside."

He did. His mind buzzing, he handed the board to the palace rep.

"Can I go now?" he called to the guardsmen.

"Go on, we'll contact you if we need you," the soldier allowed, and the man hurried away.

Helen was staring at Rabbit's blanched face. "Is it that bad?"

He shook his head, not daring to speak. A moment later, the soldier returned to them. "What a mess," he said. "What were you two doing here this morning?"

Helen jumped in. "We heard about the fall of the Vandals and came to see if a family heirloom was among the spoils. We thought to buy it back." The words came out shakily.

He looked at Rabbit, clearly weighing how much he trusted him. Rabbit nodded, confirming Helen's story. Finally, the guard sighed and nodded. "You didn't know the man, I take it?"

They both shook their heads no.

"What do you think . . ." Helen's voice caught. "What do you think happened to him?"

The soldier shrugged. "Who knows? Why does anybody kill anybody?"

She shook her head and hid her eyes behind her hand.

"Do you need anything else?" Rabbit asked. He was desperately trying to hide the sheer panic that was gripping him.

The soldier looked at him hard again but gave it up. It was clear he didn't suspect them. "No, take her home. Don't leave town though, all right?"

"We won't," he assured the man.

A small crowd of longshoremen and sailors had gathered by now. One of them grabbed Rabbit's arm as he and Helen tried to exit the scene. "What happened?"

"A man died," said Helen and pulled Rabbit away from him.

Murmurs were going through the crowd, and several of them were trying to get inside. Of course, they would know the customs official. The soldiers were trying to hold them off.

"Let's clear out," said Helen and steered Rabbit away.

They left the harbor and made their way to a little park near the Hippodrome. The moment they had some privacy, Helen turned a concerned face on him. "What happened? What did you see?"

Rabbit swallowed hard. "They carved a rabbit in his chest."

CONSTANTINOPLE

535 CE

Are you sure?" Helen asked. "The guy was a mess, could you really make that out?"

They were sitting in a nearly deserted public house. Rabbit didn't remember how they got there. All he could think was that he was in shock. She was leaning across the table now, talking in hushed tones to avoid the notice of the barmaid across the room. Rabbit had a cup of warm wine in his hand.

"I'm sure."

"Can you draw it?"

The surface of the table was carved up with a hundred initials and bits of graffiti. It appeared to be a norm of the establishment, so Rabbit pulled out his razor and tried to reproduce the image he had seen carved into the custom official's pectoral.

She looked at it then looked at him.

Then back at it.

"You know what that looks like."

"I know."

"It's the Playboy bunny."

"I know."

"All it needs is the bow tie."

"I know," he growled. "It was Nazarian. It must have been. I knew he was cold, but this is beyond anything I'd heard."

"Do you think he'd really kill somebody?"

"I don't know. I suppose it's possible he marked the corpse after it was dead." Rabbit shook his head. "I'll tell you what I do know. He's trying very hard to warn us off, which means we must be close to what he's up to."

Rabbit ran his finger over the rabbit carving in the wood.

"Drink your wine," she said.

He did. It was warm and sweet and flavored with spices. He felt his heart rate begin to slow down. But it did nothing to erase his certainty of what he'd seen.

"Are you ready to tell me what's going on with you now?" she said.

"I wish I knew," he replied.

She sat back in her seat and considered him. "I'll trade you," she finally said.

"What do you mean?"

"For every secret you tell me, I'll tell you one of mine. What?"

"I've seen how well you lie."

"Ditto," she said in English and then reverted to Greek. "We both know how to lie; how else could we do this job?"

"So where does that leave us?"

"I'll trust you with mine if you trust me with yours."

Rabbit realized that he wanted to tell her very badly. He wanted to talk all of this out with someone, he just wasn't sure that someone should be his enemy.

"I'm not talking about your deepest darkest truths," she persisted. "But I know something is bothering you about this job and, as long as I don't know what that is, I'm operating at half capacity." She leaned in closer. "I'm just thinking about the job."

Rabbit finished his wine. "I don't exactly know. I just have this feeling. It started when I went to London to see the mummy. The scientist said there were millions of them that came back to England as souvenirs in the nineteenth century. What are the odds that the one with the information I needed most was in a mummy of a rabbit— the only rabbit he'd ever seen."

She nodded, for once not questioning his logic but just letting him speak.

"And since I came to the city, everything has felt . . . wrong. We're the ones with superior knowledge. You and me. No matter where we go, we always have a leg up." He shook his head. "I don't know, it feels like something, or somebody is a step ahead of me all the time on this job."

"It's usually me. I'm kidding," she responded to his glare. "Go on."

"If I didn't know better, I'd say it felt like I'd stepped into a splintered history. Like there's this whole undercurrent here that just doesn't belong."

She shrugged but responded seriously. "Maybe that's how it's always been. Maybe history always missed half of what was really going on."

"I get that. Sure, our knowledge is always incomplete. I just can't help feeling like . . ."

"Like what?"

"Like there's some larger force at work here, and it's toying with me."

Her eyebrows knitted. "Like . . . God?"

"No, well, I don't know. Fate, maybe. Sure, Nazarian is a factor, but he's just part of it." He shook his head.

"Do you think it's possible that you were primed to see it? You know that thing where you hear a word for the first time and then suddenly you start hearing it all the time?"

"The Baader-Meinhof effect," he offered helpfully.

"Nerd," she said, mimicking his helpful tone. "Maybe you are tuned right now to see signs that reinforce that feeling."

"I didn't make up the murders, the theft."

"Oh, don't get me wrong, there is some shady shit going on in this city but that doesn't necessarily mean, and don't take this the wrong way, that doesn't mean it's about you." She raised a hand to the barmaid and pointed to Rabbit's cup.

Rabbit wrestled down his defensiveness at her comment. What was more likely after all that some higher power had guided his steps, or that there was simply a series of coincidental events related to a part of undocumented history?

The barmaid came over with an amphora and refilled Rabbit's cup.

"Thanks," he said.

"I like your beard," she said.

"Uh, thank you," he replied awkwardly.

The maid smiled coquettishly and swayed back to the bar.

Helen stared after her in surprise. "Damn, right in front of me, too."

"What?"

"The flirting."

Rabbit looked at the young woman as she resumed her place at the bar. "She wasn't."

"She a hundred percent was. I take it you don't date much."

"Here and there," he said.

Helen snorted. "Does that make sense to you?"

"Does what make sense?"

"City, history, not about you," she recapped.

The suspicion was still lingering in his mind, but he couldn't refute her logic. "It does," he admitted.

"So, what's the story with this manifest?"

"Nice try," he said with a smile. "You owe me a secret."

Her lips pressed together. They were nice lips. "What do you want to know?"

"Who pays you?" He cut her off before she could refuse. "I trusted you with mine."

She took a deep breath, then washed it down with some wine. "I try not to know. Rich people have their own networks. Somebody talks to somebody else. 'Where did you get that amazing fill-in-the-blank? Well, I can't say but I'll connect you to them if there's something you're after.' Nothing is direct. The organization is contacted through intermediaries, nobody wants names. Names get you in trouble."

"What if you do the job and the money never comes?"

"The money always comes, one way or another. Nobody would dare risk their standing. Not with me, they don't care about stiffing contractors. I mean with the network. If they don't pay, someone might think they can't pay. Believe me, they always pay."

"Tell me about this organization."

She glanced into her wine cup, and, for a moment, it looked like a great weight settled on her. When she looked up and shook her head, however, it was gone. "One secret at a time. What about the manifest?" He was about to speak, but she raised her hand to stop him. "Just to be clear, this doesn't count as a secret."

"It counts," he said.

"Absolutely not. This falls under the previous umbrella of partnership. Tactical details related to the mission aren't a secret."

"Are you a lawyer?"

"The manifest," she insisted.

Well, there was no harm in getting a second brain working on the issue. "There were two copies. One of them listed the menorah as part of the treasures of Jerusalem, the other didn't. The one that includes it is wrapped around a mummy that will eventually surface in London. Beats the hell out of me what purpose it serves here and now. The one that excludes it is destined for the palace books."

"So, what does that tell you?"

"The customs officer was a member of the rebels. I suspect he omitted the menorah from the official copy to keep it out of the public record. Maybe that's to cover it up when the rebels steal it?

It's hard to justify an investigation if it doesn't look like anything was stolen."

"Reasonable, but what about the rest of the temple artifacts? Why not write them out of the list and steal them too?"

He thought for a moment. "Maybe there's just too much to steal and have it go unnoticed. Yeah, I agree, that's weak."

"Maybe the menorah has a specific importance to the rebels that doesn't extend to the rest of the artifacts."

Rabbit leaned back on his bench seat. "We can speculate, but does it have any impact on the mission?"

"No way to know. But I get you, guessing at it won't impact the work. So, what does?"

"What about this? We know that there is an uprising coming, right?"

She nodded.

"We also know that there is no record of an uprising for decades."

"True."

"Now it's possible that this rebellion just fizzles out and never rises to the attention of historians. Who knows, maybe the Justinian plague robs it of energy and person power."

She was nodding, her mind clearly racing parallel to his. "But right now, it feels like this powder keg could blow any second. We know it didn't happen in our past, which means if it happens now . . ."

"Then the timeline is about to splinter."

They both stared into their wine cups for a second.

"Did we do something?" she began, echoing what he was thinking.

"I didn't," he said.

"You think I did?"

"Not by accident." He wouldn't say it out loud, but he had grown to respect her work. If she had made a material change, she'd know it. "So, what does that tell you?"

"History doesn't change itself, which means . . ." She grimaced as the conclusion hit her. "Nazarian."

Rabbit nodded. "Presuming he's alone. So, secret number two." He stared at her hard. "Are you working with him, too?"

He watched her carefully. Her eyes widened, pupils dilated a little, and there was a pause before she sputtered "No!" Either she was a better actress than he realized, or she was telling the truth.

"Glad to hear it. But that doesn't change the fact that we have a complication. If the timeline splinters before we recover and hide the menorah, it won't matter what we do after that. We'll have saved it for some alternate universe we won't return to."

"I know how splinters work! So, now we might have even less time."

He nodded. "I think we should plan as if that's true."

They paid for their wine and left the tavern. It was a short walk to Andor's house where Judah had promised to send word if the menorah was going to be moved.

The races must have ended in the Hippodrome because the streets were teeming with people again. That's what saved them.

They were about to turn onto the Psellos block when Helen grabbed Rabbit and spun him around to face her.

"What are you doing?" he began, but she cut him off.

"Don't turn around. There's a group of young men on the corner I don't like the look of."

She was peering past his shoulder, using him as a screen.

"Blues?"

"They're not wearing blue, but one of them has that haircut they seem to like."

"What are they doing?"

"Nothing. That's what makes me suspicious. They're just looking around at the street."

"Dammit. They must have figured out I'm staying with Andor. I hope the kid's all right."

"Any alternative access points to the house?" she said.

"There's a back entrance. I used it last night when I came back so late."

A quick walk around the block revealed lookouts posted near every approach.

"All right, I'll tell you what, I'll go in and bring Andor to you. Don't argue, these guys don't know me from Eve. The shave isn't bad, but I wouldn't rely on it up close. Where do you want to meet? It's too dangerous for you to hang around here."

"The Forum of Constantine. South side in the middle portico." His next words surprised him as they tumbled out of his mouth. "Be careful."

She rolled her eyes. "I know what I'm doing."

"I didn't suggest you . . . didn't," he finished to her retreating back.

He watched her pass the group of Blues on the corner without drawing their attention. After a moment, he left it to her and went south on the Mese toward the forum.

The crowd on the main street was politely festive. The sedate, nontraditional triumph hadn't exactly sparked a fire in the people. The mood was closer to that of a minor religious holiday than a victory of arms. The adrenaline from the races had passed, and now the population seemed slightly confused about what they should be doing next. Some went back to work. Food stalls were once again hawking their wares to the crowd. Those without obvious occupation walked slowly and aimlessly, unclear of their purpose.

Rabbit went to the forum and loitered around the portico where earlier that day he had been translating and writing letters. To his surprise, one of his customers stopped by within a few minutes of his arrival and asked him to scribe something else for them. He was inclined to say no, assuming that Helen and Andor would be along shortly, but the customer was persuasive and so he set himself to the task. By the time they left, he had a small line of additional clients wanting to buy his services. To kill the time, he took the next job, and the next, each time apologizing to the following person in line saying that he might not be able to get to their task. Before he knew it, the sun had dipped below the wall of the forum with no sign of Helen.

At first, he was worried that something had happened to them but, as the shadows lengthened, that concern eroded into distrust. How could he be so stupid? She had played him again. She probably found out when the temple treasures were being moved and went after the menorah herself, while he was copying letters in the forum like an idiot. He'd be lucky if he ever saw her again. He'd just get one of those taunting notes back in the present.

He was about to leave, berating Helen and himself, when her breathless voice sounded beside him.

"Come on. Now."

She was behind him, her head draped, breathing hard.

Every bit of suspicion washed out of him as though a drain plug had been pulled. "What happened?"

"Not now, come on. Stay behind me."

He followed her into a portico and around the edge of the forum to the gate at the east side where they rejoined the Mese. The crowds were thinning as the light faded. A few oil lamps were flickering to life in shops down the street. He desperately wanted to find out what was going on, but she stayed doggedly a few steps in front of him.

She wove a path through side streets, furtively checking to see if anyone was following every few moments. Finally, she stopped in a deserted alley.

She faced him, and he could see blood drying at the corner of her mouth.

"What the hell's going on?" he asked.

"Your friend Andor has been arrested."

"What? Why?"

She explained in a rush. "Those guys who were loitering around, they weren't looking for you, they were looking for him. They sicced the city guard on him almost as soon as he got there. I tried to help but . . ."

"Slow down," Rabbit interrupted. "Start from the top."

She took a deep breath. "When I got to the house, nobody was home except the servants. They let me wait in the garden, and I started talking to the old man who tends it. After a little prompting, he said that someone had come by earlier and dropped off a note for Andor's guest. How lucky, I say, I'm Andor's guest's wife. After that, they all took a lot more interest in me. You made an impression on those two cooks. They wanted to know how I'd gotten there, why I didn't come with you, etcetera. I don't even remember half the lies I made up before they seemed to believe me. I almost got them to hand over the note but then your friend showed up and started the whole thing over again, only he was a lot quicker to believe me."

"He's too trusting," said Rabbit, but she ignored him.

"I was about to tell him to bring the note and we'd meet you together but then there was this holy racket at the garden gate and a squad of city guards burst in and arrested Andor for colluding with the rebels. I tried to tell them they had the wrong guy and made such an annoyance of myself that they decided to arrest me, too. I was able to slip them and had to lose a couple of the younger ones who could keep up with me before I came to find you."

"What happened to your mouth? You're bleeding."

She shrugged. "One of them whacked me when I wouldn't shut up. Don't worry about it."

"I'm not worried. It . . . it just looks suspicious."

"Fine," she snapped and handed him a tiny handkerchief she produced from her purse.

She stuck out her chin and he awkwardly wiped at the blood. She winced a little but offered no word of complaint.

"Where did they take him?"

"The jail on the palace grounds, I assume."

"And you're sure you're okay?"

"I told you, I'm fine."

He handed her back the kerchief. She took one look at it and tossed it on a pile of garbage nearby.

"This is the last thing we need," he growled, possibly in an attempt to cover his tenderness for her injury. "I don't have time to add a jailbreak onto the agenda."

"I did get this by the way." She reached into her cloak and pulled out a crumpled piece of paper.

"Is that—"

"The letter from Judah, yeah. I swiped it in all the hubbub." She opened it. "All it says is 'meet at the church before dawn.'"

"Father Lambert's church in the Chalk. That means they're going to move the menorah. Belisarius convinced them."

"What do you think? You still want to meet them?"

"No. The cops busted Andor, which means they traced Judah to the Psellos house. Since you got the note, I'm hoping they don't have any evidence against him but, either way, Judah is under watch."

"So, they'll roust the meeting at the church too," she concluded.

He nodded. "And hopefully, they'll be preoccupied with that and ignore us while we're swiping the menorah."

She stared at him. "Was that your plan all along?" Rabbit relished her surprise and felt pretty proud of himself.

"It was one possibility," he said.

"You might have told me I was walking into a trap!" she hissed.

He was shocked at her venom. "I didn't know they would . . ."

"You just said it was one possibility." The anger on her face resolved into something worse. Hurt. "You wanted me to be arrested, too."

"That's not true."

But she was nodding. "Then you'd be free of me and could go after the menorah yourself. Let me ask you something. If I had been, would you have even gotten me out? Or would you have left me here to rot? On second thought, don't answer. I don't want to know."

Rabbit expected her to walk away but instead, she just stood there, glaring at him hatefully. No, not hatefully. Helen looked furiously validated, as though she had always suspected the worst of him, and he had just confirmed it. It was uncomfortable in its own right, more so because of how much it mirrored his own reaction to the Kahans' beliefs about him.

The truth was that he hadn't intended for her to be arrested. Far from it. If anything, he had been more worried about her safety than he ever expected. That unsettled him. Maybe it was better that she hated him. Yes. If she hated him, there was no risk of him getting any more comfortable with this arrangement. They weren't friends. They weren't partners. They were competitors. And she would betray him in the end. He could count on that.

"Hate me all you want but keep it to yourself."

"No problem." She dripped each word like acid.

"We should get some rest. We have to be at the Military Gate before dawn to stake it out."

"What about Andor?"

Andor. The Chalk rebels had set their own course. Andor was a different story. Rabbit had used Andor for his own convenience. Although he didn't want to admit it, his uncle had been right about that. But could he really leave him in jail? Byzantine justice was not based on incarceration but on swift punishment, the most common being death or mutilation. Criminals accused of lesser offenses than Andor had their hands or feet cut off. Eyes, noses, and tongues were also on the short list for state-sanctioned mutilation.

Rabbit started talking midway through his own thought process. "They have no physical evidence on him since you took the note. And breaking out of jail would either result in a worse punishment or a life on the lam."

"Are you serious? You want to leave him."

"I don't think they'll charge him. Plus, his uncle is rich, which will help his cause."

"He'll hate you forever, you know."

"He can get in line." His growl sounded forced, even to himself.

CONSTANTINOPLE

535 CE

ONE DAY REMAINING

They went back to the public house where Helen had been staying. Rabbit rented his own room using the translation fees he'd collected the day before. It was the size of a closet and had no windows, which only contributed to his feeling of being trapped. A few hours before dawn he rose, put on his sandals and cloak, and went into the hall where he found Helen waiting for him, looking no more rested than he was.

Without a word, the two of them traded the stuffy confines of the hotel for the chill of the streets. There was no hint of light on the horizon as they walked quietly through the deserted city, seeing no one but a dozing guard at the Constantinian Wall. They didn't talk, which was fine with Rabbit. He was busy thinking about all the ways this could go wrong.

As the outer walls came in sight, they settled themselves in an olive grove and observed the military encampment built up to guard the spoils of the short-lived Vandal war. There didn't appear to be any activity in the camp right now, but he could see that the spoils had been left on the wagons that brought them from the harbor. The combined volume of the treasure was staggering.

"Once the sun's up, they'll start uncrating it all for display."

She made no comment.

"The way I see it, we can do this a couple of different ways. One, we just stealth in, take it, and go. Pro, it's simple. Con, they probably have lookouts and watchdogs we'd have to slip past."

"And the gate is closed."

"Not a problem," he countered.

"Yeah? How do you propose we get it out of the city?"

"It's not leaving the city."

That got her attention. She gazed at him in confusion.

"And just where do you intend to hide it?"

"I have something in mind."

"Goddamn it, Ward. You agreed to be partners until we secure it. This isn't partnership."

"You're here, aren't you?" He didn't understand what she was so upset about.

"Asshole," she muttered. "Okay, what else?"

"We create a distraction and take it in the confusion. Mostly cons here. There's a lot of open land to cover before we'd be out of sight, so the distraction would have to be extreme and ongoing. Three, we walk in, announce ourselves, and ask them to hand it over."

"I assume the con for that is that it's so unlikely as to be impossible."

"Not really. In fact, it's my preferred option."

Helen was about to protest when the sound of plodding hoofbeats reached her ears. Moments later, a wagon slowly approached, pulled by a lone mule. A man slouched in the seat, looking barely awake in the dark before dawn.

"What is that?" she asked.

"Breakfast."

Rabbit didn't relish the next part. He stepped into the road out of the olive trees, making the mule startle. But he stepped forward and took the animal by the bridle and gentled it by rubbing its nose.

"Good morning, friend baker."

The man looked scared and disbelieving in equal measure. Rabbit disliked the idea of taking the man's cart and delivery for his own ends, but they had reached desperate times. Before he could make his move, however, Helen interrupted.

"How much for your cart?" she said, stepping into the road close to the driver.

"It's not for sale. Out of my way," he said with false bravado, "the soldiers are expecting me."

"Not for sale, or just not for a price you think I can pay?" She pulled out her purse and jingled it.

"It's worth more than your copper, that's for certain," he said.

"What about my gold? I'll give you a solidus each for the mule and cart."

"You don't have that kind of money."

She pulled out two heavy coins. "Don't I? How about a third for your cargo?" She pulled out one more.

He eyed the coins greedily, clearly already thinking of what he could buy with that money. "I don't want any trouble with the garrison."

"How much would ease your mind about that trouble?"

"Another solidus?" he said.

To Rabbit's surprise, she dumped the coins back in her purse with a jingle. "Too bad, friend." She started to walk away.

"Wait!" the baker said with a worried look toward the camp. "I can . . . work things out. Three solidi is a deal."

She shook her head sadly. "The deal is now two."

They negotiated their way back to two and a half solidi, and the man turned over to them the mule, the wagon, and the load of bread it carried. The baker disappeared back along the road, clutching his coins like a miser while Helen climbed into the driver's seat. The cart was lightweight, more like a chariot than a wagon, but it was plenty big enough to carry the stacked loaves for the guards' breakfast.

Rabbit walked alongside the cart, so as not to put too much strain on the mule. After a few moments, she asked.

"Were you going to rob him?"

Rabbit shrugged. "I didn't like it, but I didn't see an alternative."

"Happens sometimes, doesn't it?"

At first, Rabbit thought she was being flip. But when he looked up at her to retort, he saw that she was looking grimly ahead. He dropped what he'd been planning to say and instead asked, "Do you haggle over everything?"

"Sure, it makes people feel good."

"Are you kidding? I've seen you chisel people down to half their asking price over and over again, how does that feel good?" he asked.

"If someone gets their asking price without question, they instantly think they should have asked for more. If you haggle them down then come back up a little, they feel like they earned it. How do you not know this?"

He wasn't sure. Now that she said it, it made perfect sense.

As they approached the makeshift camp, Rabbit could see it wasn't set up in the traditional Roman fashion. There were no earthworks, no picket line. It was really little more than a ring of soldiers' tents set up in a square around the drift of crates and boxes from Carthage. They were inside their own mighty walls, and the Romans were feeling safe.

Rabbit and Helen rode up to two drowsy-looking sentries manning a gap in the tents where the road ran through to the gate. They perked up as the provisions arrived.

"Good morning, sirs," Rabbit chirruped solicitously to the guards. "Where should we unload?"

"There's a mess table by the captain's tent." He pointed directly across the camp.

"Would you like the first loaves?" Helen offered. "To honor your vigil?"

The guards hesitated for less than a heartbeat and then accepted the bread, which they gratefully broke as Rabbit and Helen proceeded into the camp. What had looked like a disorganized heap of booty from a distance was actually laid out in orderly quadrants with lanes between them, presumably for loading the parade carts that would soon proceed through the city.

The first glow of light was touching the sky as they wheeled the bread wagon through the unbelievable trove of riches.

"I have to hand it to you, you are fucking nuts," Helen murmured to him. "We are definitely going to die horrible deaths."

"We'll be fine," he said with confidence he didn't feel. Desperate times, he reminded himself.

At the far end of the camp, they spotted the mess table the guards had promised. It was just a few planks laid on top of what he would call sawhorses. Nearby was an informal fire pit surrounded by bricks, but the fire was out and the metal cookpot hung over it was cold.

Rabbit led the mule cart to the table. He and Helen glanced at each other and began to lay out the bread. It had been covered in the wagon by a piece of cloth, so they laid this out as a tablecloth to keep the food from getting dirty. They were just finishing the display when a man stepped out of the largest tent nearby. He was dressed like everyone else they saw in the city with the exception of his tunic, which was slit up the sides to the waist, presumably to allow him to sit a horse. He was tall and fierce looking, with deep-set eyes and a long scar that twisted up the corner of his mouth.

He glanced at the table and chuckled incongruously.

"Are you from the palace?" he asked.

Rabbit nodded affirmatively.

"Here for the . . . delivery?"

"That's right, sir."

The man gave Rabbit a quizzical look. *Shit*, Rabbit realized. He had been expecting someone who outranked him. Rabbit smiled as knowingly as he could. "Enjoy your breakfast, captain."

That seemed to soothe the man, and he indicated that they should follow him with an inclination of his head. "Leave the cart. It's already loaded for you. I thought there would be more of you. Do you need an escort?"

Rabbit shook his head. "Better not to draw too much attention."

Rabbit and Helen followed him to a row of wagons arrayed near the wall. One of them had a short, sturdy horse already in its traces. He walked them over to it. The wagon was piled with straw through which Rabbit could just make out the outline of a wooden crate.

"The bread was a nice touch," he said. "I don't know what my men are going to think about a board cloth though." He shrugged. "I'll tell them it's part of the triumph. Anyway, here you go. God bless you both."

Rabbit nodded to the man, trying to infuse it with as much respect as he could. As he had just reminded himself, speaking too much when you don't know enough about your role is a sure way to put your foot in it.

He and Helen climbed up onto the wagon seat. His heart was hammering in his chest as he braced for an attack.

The captain clapped the horse on the hindquarters, and it leaned into the traces, clopping placidly through the treasure trove. As they passed through, he caught her eyes surveying the stash.

"Don't even think about it," he said.

She said nothing, just huffed quietly to herself.

He held his breath as they passed through the exit. The two guards looked vaguely confused by their change in conveyance but offered no comment. One of them raised his half-eaten loaf in a grateful salute.

And then, unbelievably, they were out. Helen looked over her shoulder at the receding camp then stared ahead again, dumbfounded.

The anxiety of being discovered in the camp drained out of Rabbit, replaced by a warm glow of pride. "What do you think?" he asked.

"Did that seem too easy to you?"

"Not all plans have to go wrong," he said, annoyed.

"That seemed too easy to me," she said, frowning back at the camp.

As she said it, Rabbit saw the silhouette of another cart coming toward them in the early morning glow. The sun wouldn't break the horizon for at least another twenty minutes. Who else besides them would be out on the road already? As they slowly came into view, his worst suspicions were confirmed. The cart was pulled by two horses. Two men sat on the driver's bench and two more were in the wagon itself. They were hard-looking men with neatly trimmed hair and beards. They didn't need uniforms to mark them as military. Rabbit pulled his hat low over his face, burying it in shadow.

All four heads swiveled as the two wagons passed one another, unabashedly watching Rabbit and Helen.

Rabbit's breath caught in his throat as he recognized one of the faces.

The cart went by, their wagons bumping along the cobblestones. Helen looked back.

"What are they doing?" he asked.

"They're still moving. One of them in back is watching us. Do you think that's . . . ?"

"Nazarian? Yes, yes it is. He must have weaseled himself in with the real transport team."

"We should hurry. Once they find out what happened, they'll come after us."

"I can't while they're watching," he said. "I'm just praying the damn hat hid my face enough. You don't know him, right?"

She huffed. "I don't know him."

The gap between them opened. Rabbit fought the mounting instinct to speed up. "Now?"

"Still watching. We'll lose them in the crops soon."

"Now?" he asked.

"Almost. Alllllmost. Now!"

Rabbit snapped the reins. The mule launched into a canter. "Did you see any other horses at the camp? We might be able to put enough space between us and that wagon but not if they send riders. They'll catch us before we reach the Forum of the Ox. Which is convenient, because that's where they'll kill us."

"Where do you want to hide it?"

Rabbit hesitated. He really was holding out hope that somehow, he would shake her before hiding the menorah.

"We had a deal," she snarled. "I can't help you if you spend half your time trying to keep me in the dark. Are you honoring our bargain or not?"

They slowed down to pass through the inner walls then promptly sped up again. Rabbit gritted his teeth, picturing riders galloping out of the treasure camp, swords at the ready.

Against his better judgment, he told her his plan.

"That's good," she said. "Why don't we cut left, stay off the Mese, and slow down? The sun's almost up; pretty soon the city will be crawling with people. We'll blend right in."

She was right. Cantering down the main street would only draw unnecessary attention. He did as she suggested, veering left onto a side street at a trot. A group of women, arms loaded with laundry, jumped out of the way, cursing them to slow down. But Rabbit maintained speed until the angle of the road took them out of sight of the Mese. Only then did he ease up on the mule. The poor animal was sweating and steaming in the cool morning air.

Rabbit took the next right. Helen grabbed his arm. "Stop," she demanded.

She jumped out of the wagon while it was slowing down and ran into the shadowy lee of a roof overhanging an open-ended building. The smell of rotten eggs hung in the air.

A moment later, she burst out of the same door shouting, "Go go go!" Her arms were loaded with white cloth. A man was pursuing her, shouting and swearing.

Rabbit snapped the reins, and the beleaguered mule broke into a run. Helen threw the cloth into the wagon and scrambled into the bed as the wagon picked up speed. The shouting man was left impotently waving his fist at their retreat.

He glanced back to see her spread a couple of the cloths over the hay in the back and mound up the others on top of that, giving the illusion that their wagon was filled with a giant pile of multicolored cloth.

Hitching up her tunic, she clambered over the back of the seat and settled in beside him again. "Now we're a laundry truck," she explained.

They slowed down a block later and continued their circuitous route east through the city's minor streets. Twice they had to deny household servants who wanted to flag them down to send out the wash.

As predicted, the streets were beginning to fill up as Constantinople's population got about their morning routines. The foot traffic slowed them down somewhat, but Rabbit was grateful the first time he spotted another horse-drawn cart. Drifting among half a million people, there was very little chance of being spotted.

"You there. Stop your cart!"

Until they were.

Rabbit pretended he hadn't heard and steered the wagon into a narrow alley that barely accommodated the vehicle.

"Are you deaf?" There was a thudding on the back of the wagon. Sighing, Rabbit rotated in his seat. A city guard was walking behind the cart, glaring up at them. Helen glanced at him out of the corner of her eye.

"What's the problem, sir?" Rabbit asked innocently.

"I said stop your cart."

Rabbit complied, tugging on the reins. The guard hopped up on a footboard and looked into the wagon bed.

"Where did you get these clothes?"

He saw Helen make a face in his peripheral vision. *You win some, you lose some.*

"Well?"

"We're just local . . . aw, hell," Rabbit growled. He snapped the reins and the mule jumped into motion again. The guard lurched backward but managed to hold on.

The wagon bumped and bounced over the rough paving in the alley and occasionally bumped into the walls of the narrow lane. Amazingly, the guard managed to work his way over the back of the wagon and tumble ungracefully in, banging against the hidden menorah crate with a fresh round of cursing.

"Take the reins," Rabbit barked at Helen.

"Keep 'em," she said back, already climbing up from her seat.

"Do you know what you're doing?"

She fixed him with a tight-lipped glare and climbed over the back of the seat.

The wagon burst out of the lane onto a wider street, and Rabbit hauled on the reins to round the corner. Pedestrians leaped out of the way, cursing them. The guard was yelling something from the back and then abruptly ceased. Rabbit took one quick look and saw Helen standing over his fallen body, a sap gripped in one of her hands. She shot him a satisfied look.

Behind her, two horse-mounted guards were riding up, fast. One of them had a bow drawn. "Duck!" he shouted. She did, and the arrow intended for her slammed into the wooden back of his seat, quivering.

The second rider picked up speed and began to pull up on the left side of the cart. Rabbit returned his attention to the street, where the obvious commotion was clearing a path through the pedestrians. The horseman rode up next to him, his sword drawn. He was shouting something, but all Rabbit saw was the blade. He yanked on the reins, pulling the wagon to the left into the path of the horseman. The animal planted all four hooves and the guard was unseated, tumbling forward over the neck of his mount. Rabbit veered right again, just in time. The front left wheel bounced off something in front of one of the shops, and the whole vehicle went up on two wheels for a dizzying second.

Rabbit looked back. The archer had nocked another arrow and was drawing his bow. Helen was prone behind the cover of the wagon's back wall. This one was intended for him. He yanked on the reins. The mule slowed abruptly, and the archer's mount reacted too slowly. The animal banged into the back of the wagon, depositing the archer unceremoniously on top of Helen.

The cart-mule, frightened, had broken back into a canter without being told to. They burst out onto the Mese and its blur of colorful flowered garlands. Helen was grappling with the archer at the back of the cart. He was holding the wrist in which she held the sap. She was gripping his that held a dagger. The man was half again her size, however, and she was losing ground. She tried to knee him in the crotch, but the soldier deftly dodged. The knifepoint was approaching her side. Rabbit frantically debated jumping back to help when her eyes went wide. "Duck!" she shouted. Rabbit flattened himself over the back of the seat, feeling something yielding brush his back. The too-low garland caught the archer in the neck in an explosion of purple flowers. His arms locked with Helen's; she was dragged with him to the back wall of the cart where she hit the wood with a splintering crash. The soldier disappeared as he lost his hold on her.

Rabbit kept up the pace until the next turnoff where he turned and slowed. The street was clear, so he ventured a look back.

"Are you okay?"

She nodded, rubbing her wrist painfully.

The cart rolled crookedly the last few blocks to their destination. Glancing around cautiously, Rabbit drove the cart past the stone block entryway with its heavy bronze door onto the hill behind it. The weed-choked foundation blocks of the old basilica were still here; they would be long gone when Rabbit would see this location again in modern day. The gentle hill was largely unchanged, however, and it provided some visual shelter from the road. Rabbit stepped down from the wagon and patted the exhausted mule as it set about grazing on the weeds.

Helen came around the side of the cart and took in the scene with him.

He reached out his fist to her and she wordlessly gave him a bump.

When completed, the Basilica Cistern would be the largest reservoir of water in Constantinople, holding one hundred thousand tons. It would see the city through numerous sieges and was a crucial element in the city's defenses. But like much of the rest of the eastern half of the city, it had been damaged in the Nika Riots. Justinian had taken advantage of the opportunity to expand it while it was being repaired. Today, it was empty.

"Where are all the slaves?" she asked. "Weren't there supposed to be hundreds of slaves who worked on the expansion?"

Rabbit grinned. "When the foremen get a holiday, the workers get a holiday. Come on, let's get this thing off the wagon."

They dusted off the straw from the crate and slid it to the back of the cart bed.

"Where's the rest?" she asked.

Rabbit was thinking the same thing. The crate with the menorah was there, but that was all. The cart should be loaded with boxes, not just the one. Rabbit had a sinking feeling in the pit of his stomach. "Forget it," he said, uneasily. "Let's just count our blessings and hide the damn thing. How's your wrist?"

"Sore. But I don't think it's sprained. Come on, I'll be fine."

Together, they lifted the crate off the wagon. It was heavy, but not unmanageable. Side by side, they carried the crate over the crest of the hill to a hole in the earth where the workers had been going in and out of the underground building. A massive pile of soil and rocks from the hole was stacked nearby.

They descended into the dim confines of the cistern down a switchback ramp, passing under wooden scaffolds and timbers supporting the new roof construction.

Rabbit guided them to the edge of the old cistern floor, its stone blocks perfectly fitted together.

"Wow," she said. She had stopped walking and Rabbit followed her gaze to the interior.

"You've never taken the tour?"

She shook her head.

The cistern was like a cathedral inside. High, arched ceilings rested on a collection of mismatched but majestic columns looted from temples across the empire.

"Can you imagine the audacity to put so much history, so much beauty, where no one can see it?"

"Sure, I'd call it the Smithsonian Archives."

"You've got a real thing against the Academy."

"Oh my god." She put giant spaces between each word. "Did you just unironically refer to the pseudo-academic museum-industrial complex as 'the Academy'? What era did they salvage you from?"

"It's a term of art," he growled.

"Not helping your case."

"Forget it. Let's just get this thing in the ground."

It wasn't hard to find tools. There were shovels and picks lined up neatly against one wall. At the juncture where the original floor met the rocky dirt, Rabbit and Helen set to work. One of them would swing the pick to break up the packed earth, the other shoveled it out. They took turns, giving each other short breaks. Even so, Rabbit's shoulders and lower back were protesting by the time the hole was hip deep. He imagined the same was true for Helen, though she never uttered a word of complaint. It took another two hours after that before they agreed the hole was deep enough to hide the crate.

"I have new respect for gravediggers," she said.

He stretched, and every aching muscle agreed with her. "What do you think? Should we put this thing to bed?"

"Don't you want to check it first?"

He sighed and nodded. Together, they walked over to where they had laid the crate. It came up to his chest and was as wide as both of them together. The hasp that held the lid shut had no lock, just a metal pin that Rabbit slid out. They lifted the top on its hinges and looked inside. Wheat straw was packed in tightly. Rabbit pulled out a few handfuls and saw the burnished gold of the candlestick holders. Each was nearly the size of his palm and had a spike rising from an ornate cup. He reached out and touched his finger to the spike.

"Still sharp," Aaron murmured, drawing his finger away from the point.

Rabbit was shaking out the oversized cloth bag he'd had made for the theft. The warehouse was dim and musty, but that didn't concern him. What he was focused on was the faint whiff of smoke he had detected on the air as they entered. The Vandal horde had walked through the Roman walls unresisted an hour ago. The once-valiant people of Rome were cowering in their homes; even the garrison had folded without a fight. There was no one guarding the warehouse or Rabbit's planned escape route across the Tiber. He wasn't ready to celebrate yet, but he was feeling confident in his plan.

"It's hard to believe it's already one thousand years old," Aaron said reverently.

The menorah stood atop a wooden table among other artifacts. To its left stood a larger-than-life statue of Athena so realistic it looked like it might begin to speak. To its right was a large, ornate stone dais with a sun motif carved on its front. Its top was stained brown from years of sacrificial blood. To Rabbit's mind, the best thing to come from religion was the artistry it inspired. He didn't have much use for the rest of it.

"It's not going to get any older if we don't get it out of here."

Aaron nodded. *"Sorry."* He took one side of the cloth bag that Rabbit offered him and together they opened it up. *"I'm just really excited."*

"I know, I remember my first job."

"It's not just that. This is THE Menorah. I can't believe I'm really looking at it, touching it." He shook his head in wonder. *"I've just never felt so close to my people. You know what I mean? Like I have purpose."*

Rabbit stared at him.

The young man grinned in embarrassment. *"Sorry, I guess that's pretty cheesy."*

Rabbit shook his head. *"No, I don't think it's cheesy. Hold on to it."*

Back in the cistern, Helen was staring at him. "It's still sharp," he explained.

"Thinking about your old partner?"

"Let's just get this thing in the ground," he said brusquely and closed the lid.

Together they wrestled the crate into the hole and buried it, packing it tightly in sand and clay before laying in any of the rocks. Although the box was cedar, it would still decay in the moist ground under the cistern. Rabbit hoped the finer soil would slowly penetrate the air space when that happened and encase the gold firmly, protecting it from any sudden shifts in the weight above.

They stood looking at their work for a moment.

"We dug it deep enough, right?" she asked.

"I hope so."

She brushed the sand off her hands. "Let's get out of here. It's got to be close to dusk. You've got to hit the road if you're going to make your decay point."

"Yeah, I guess you're right." She started for the exit ramp, but he stopped her. "Hey, I know the deal's done and you're probably going to rob me back in the world."

"I'm a hundred percent going to rob you back in the world."

"Even so. I didn't entirely hate working with you."

She smiled warmly. "Yeah, well, I didn't entirely hate working with you, either."

They walked up the ramp together. Helen was right; dusk was settling over the city. To the west, the sky was a warm amber. To the east, the moon was already overhead in the still-blue sky. It could have been any night in his own time. Some things never change.

"Rabbit," Helen whispered.

He caught her warning tone and followed her eyes. A soldier stood by the wagon, petting the horse and gazing at them with dark glee. One of his arms was in a splint. There was no doubt it was one of their pursuers from earlier. *Stupid*, Rabbit thought. *We should have driven the horse away.*

He scanned around them, looking for an escape path, but everywhere he looked there was another city guard closing in on them. He considered trying for one of the gaps between the sentinels, but their bows were loaded and drawn. They wouldn't make it five paces.

One of the soldiers who stepped into sight was terribly familiar.

Yeshua Nazarian smiled at him and Helen. With a shrug, he mouthed silently, "Thank you."

CONSTANTINOPLE

535 CE

OUT OF TIME

Rabbit dropped to his hands and knees. A kick drove the air from his lungs and flipped him onto his back.

The jail cell door slammed shut.

During the arrest, there had been no mention of the menorah. It was the laundry heist, compounded by their flight from the law, that had earned their pursuit by the injured and wrathful city guards. Two of them had stood by grimly while one of their more able-bodied compatriots had worked Rabbit over like a heavy bag. He didn't think any ribs had broken, but that was the best he could say for his condition. Terrified of what they might do to Helen, Rabbit had sworn and cursed them throughout the beating, hoping they might exhaust their rage on him and leave her alone. They had been pretty thorough.

He sucked in air as his diaphragm finally relaxed.

Rabbit had been too scared when they brought him in to pay much attention to his surroundings beyond the broad strokes. He was in a crowded cell, one of many that lined both sides of a long hallway.

He took his eyes off the ceiling and found himself looking upside down at a man sitting on the floor behind him. His body protested as he rolled himself onto his stomach and gently eased himself up off the floor. It took him a moment but then he recognized his red-haired, taciturn cellmate, sitting among a dozen others.

"Hello, Judah."

"You didn't show up this morning. The city guard did instead."

"I'm sorry about that," Rabbit said. "Things haven't exactly gone to plan."

"I suppose I should kill you." He shrugged. "Eh, why bother? The city will punish you more than I would."

"Were you all arrested?" Rabbit asked.

"Wasn't that your intention? Never mind, don't answer. None of that matters anymore. Even the temple treasures don't matter." He put his head back against the wall and closed his eyes.

Rabbit got painfully to his feet and checked the door. It was made of heavy timbers with a small window at eye level. He pressed his face close to the opening, trying to see if he could reach the latch.

"You might as well rest. No one is getting out of here until it's time."

That caught Rabbit's attention. "Time for what?"

He cracked open one eye and closed it again without a word.

"Time for what, Judah?" But the man made no reply. To hell with him. To hell with this city. To hell with the rebellion and the murders and the Blues and the intrigue. Right now, only one thing mattered. He had to get the hell out of this cell and find a horse. The window for getting home was closing.

He pressed his face to the opening again. There wasn't even a handle on Rabbit's side.

"Antigonus?" came a surprised voice. Rabbit looked up and saw Andor peering through the window of the cell door across the hallway.

"Andor! I heard you were in here. What happened?"

Behind Rabbit, Judah was chuckling. "Antigonus, is it?" Judah said in a voice that would easily carry to the opposite cell. "I thought you were Gallus."

Andor was trying to peer past Rabbit to see the speaker.

"Who is that? What did they arrest you for, Antigonus?"

"Yes, Antigonus Gallus, what did they arrest you for?" Judah asked.

"Why does he keep calling you that?" Suspicion was creeping across the young soldier's face.

Rabbit felt pinned between the two of them. "Andor, it's hard to explain."

"Is it?" asked Judah, his voice dripping with feigned innocence. "It seems easy enough to me." He raised his voice to better reach Andor. "Your friend called himself Gallus when he cajoled me and mine into unlawful assembly so we could be picked off by the night watch."

"That's not true," said Andor, but he seemed uncertain.

"He led me to your door, which got you arrested as one of us."

"I didn't know that was going to happen," Rabbit insisted.

"Ask yourself this," Judah continued, "did he come to help you? This man is a spy, a criminal, or both. But he's not your friend. He's not anyone's friend."

Andor was trying to cover his hurt with anger and doing a poor job of it. "Is that true?"

"It's not the whole truth," Rabbit said.

"What does that mean? A thing is either true or not true. Which is it?"

"It's true . . . enough. I didn't mean for you to get arrested though," Rabbit said lamely.

"You didn't help me."

"What could I have done?" Rabbit asked and hated himself for it.

Andor stared at him. There was no malice in his eyes. No anger. Just hurt. "I would have helped you."

"Andor . . ."

The young man stepped away from the window and disappeared. Rabbit stared at the vacant window in his cell door for a moment and then sank to the floor and leaned against the door miserably.

Judah closed his eyes again, looking satisfied.

Justifications and distractions rattled around Rabbit's head. Andor was too trusting; it was really his fault. This would be a vital life lesson for the boy. Of course, Rabbit had screwed up by getting involved. He knew better than to make friends in the past. Andor wasn't really even a person anyway, just a shadow out of the past, long dead. As he had said to Helen, the boy's family was rich; he'd get off with a slap on the wrist. Only Byzantine justice was harsh, and maybe he wouldn't. For all Rabbit knew, the boy was supposed to reach the end of his story now, and Rabbit had always been the reason.

None of it made him feel any better. He desperately tried to distract himself by thinking about what to do next. If Rabbit broke out of this jail this instant and had a change of horses waiting for him between here and Greece, he could still make it. If he had a way to escape. Which he didn't. The time slipped by as he sat helplessly on the floor. In the absence of anything practical to do, he simply calculated and recalculated time as it slipped by. Now he would need two changes of horses. Now three. Finally, in the darkest part of the night, Rabbit accepted the truth. He had run out of time. He was never going home again.

He was awakened in the morning by a distant clatter and the small amount of light that filtered through the chinks in the wooden walls. By habit, he immediately began to catalog what he had to do next only to remember that it was all over. The year 535 CE was his new home.

He heard guards making their way down the hallway, passing out food. As he listened, a memory suddenly lurched into his head from his childhood. He and Tommy James were ten years old. It was a warm summer evening and they had been playing all day. The sun was near setting, and they were on a swing set talking about Greek mythology.

Rabbit's mind had been so lulled by the rhythmic creaking of the swing chains and the visions of another world that he hadn't noticed the teenagers until it was too late. There were three of them, approaching with the gleeful silence of hyenas.

Tommy was talking about Medusa when Rabbit reached over and snagged his swing chain. The look on Rabbit's face must have told him everything because he stopped mid-sentence and followed Rabbit's eyes to find the teens.

The message in their slow, predator approach was crystal clear. They were daring Rabbit and Tommy to run. One of the boys pulled out a pack of Black Cats, firecrackers that looked like little sticks of dynamite. Toyingly, he lit one, watching them as the fuse burned down. Just before it did, he flicked it at Rabbit and Tommy. It exploded with a loud crack that made them both jump.

He pulled out another and lit it, and this time the tension was even worse, waiting for that jolt of panic when he flicked it at them. Rabbit's mother had forbidden him to buy them, saying kids had lost eyes to fireworks. The fuse burned down, and Rabbit thought of it hitting his eye, burning a hole in his cornea, the juice leaking out down his Batman T-shirt as it deflated like a sack and dripped out on his cheek. The boy had flicked the second one and it cracked between them. As scared as Rabbit was, Tommy must have had it worse. He launched himself off the swing and sprinted for his bike.

Tommy was a quick kid. He had managed to get one foot on the pedal before they dragged him off, held him, hit him. Rabbit never moved the entire time. He was too afraid. He didn't want the same thing to happen to him. Tommy was crying when the boy with the firecrackers came over to Rabbit. Only he wasn't called that yet. Back then he was Robert or sometimes Rob. The boy looked back at his friends, delighted by the sight of the boy, too petrified to move. "Look at this little shithead, he's shaking like a rabbit!" Every time they saw him after that, that's what they called him. His friends had told him to ignore it, only he couldn't. The nickname had spread like a virus and seemed to be waiting for him when he went to high school. Eventually, the sting of its origin passed. When he began to acquire a little bit of notoriety in his field, it served to make him memorable.

He hadn't thought about that awful night in years, and now he was cringing with shame and regret as though it were yesterday. Why had it come back now? The shame of being discovered by Andor for what he was, maybe. A thief and a liar. He had let Andor down, just as he had let Aaron down. This time, he would have to stay here to face up to his failure. He felt dismal.

Still, something tugged at the edges of his awareness. It wasn't just the emotion that had brought back that memory. It was those damn Black Cat firecrackers that popped into his mind first. That's what triggered it. The black powder smell of those awful little firecrackers.

Rabbit sniffed the air and realized he wasn't imagining it. He actually smelled fireworks. They must be for the second triumph. Right, except for the small complication that black powder wouldn't be invented for another five hundred years. So, what the hell was he smelling?

The guard appeared at the door. Rabbit accepted a small cup of cold porridge from him and offered it to Judah. His cellmate glared at him, got up, and accepted the cup directly from the guard. The other inmates did likewise, lining up in a rough queue. Rabbit imitated Judah, who downed his porridge in a gulp or two then held out the cup toward the door where it was refilled with water from an amphora. Then the guard offered through the door a cloth bag with a shoulder strap. Rabbit, not knowing what it was, reached to accept it. Judah shoved him roughly and he stumbled into the opposite wall. Glaring even more at Rabbit, he accepted the bag, which appeared to be quite full. He put the strap over his head and reclaimed his spot against the wall. The guard handed an identical bag to every other man in the cell. When Rabbit approached the door again, the guard looked past him at Judah, who shook his head. The guard moved on.

Rabbit was perplexed. The sharp smell of black powder was unmistakable now. He had no doubt it was coming from the bag.

He knew his cellmate wouldn't answer, but he still couldn't contain his curiosity. "What's in the bags?"

"Careful or you might find out," the man threatened.

They lapsed into silence, Rabbit's mind racing. What else smelled like gunpowder? The main ingredient was sulfur, so maybe it was just something sulfurous for which Rabbit had no frame of reference. Still, that didn't explain why a prisoner was getting a bag delivered in the first place. Wait, where else had he smelled sulfur recently? The mummy warehouse! That place reeked of it. He had assumed it was part of the manufacturing process, but now he wasn't so sure. What the hell was . . .

The cell door opened, and a guard stepped in, hand on his sword. "You." He pointed at Rabbit. "Come along."

Rabbit got to his feet, a little unsteadily.

"Where are we going?" he asked.

"We're going to keep your mouth shut and you can keep your teeth," the guard responded.

Rabbit followed the guard into the hallway where he was tied at the ankle to a line of three other prisoners. One of them was Andor, who turned his face away from Rabbit.

The prisoners were walked out of the building. Through the window of every cell door they passed, Rabbit saw men wearing the same shoulder bags that Judah had received.

The morning sun outside the jail made him squint. As his eyes adjusted, they took in the beauty of the palace district. The ornate buildings, the lush gardens, the wine-dark sea as Homer had called it, it was all crisp and sharp and colorful. So real it looked unreal.

The procession wound its way into an intricately decorated courthouse presided over by a grey-haired judge and a jury of twelve men. In most respects, it looked very much like a modern court. Despite the gravity of his situation, for a moment he thought the judge might be the famed Tribonian who codified the set of laws known as Justinian's code. Instead, the judge's name was unfamiliar, and Rabbit forgot it as soon as he had heard it. Sitting among the attendees, Rabbit spotted Andor's uncle, Helias Psellos. Good. He had no doubt paid the appropriate bribes to get his son exonerated.

Unlike a modern court, the proceedings were extremely swift. The man ahead of Rabbit was accused and found guilty of usury, for which he was fined. They cut him loose and a clerk led him from the room. Rabbit suddenly felt something he had been blind to his whole life. His privilege. Rabbit had always been resistant, glib even, in the face of authority. He had never realized how much of that confidence came from the modern justice system and his place in it. He was a highly educated, well-paid white man, and therefore was afforded the best the system could offer. None of that applied here. He would like to have said the epiphany filled him with righteous anger on behalf of those who experienced this every day. At the moment, however, he was too terrified to be righteous.

"Antigonus of Rome!"

Rabbit stood.

"You stand accused of theft, having unlawfully taken the property of John the Fuller. How do you plead?"

Rabbit glanced over his shoulder and saw the fuller glowering at him. There wasn't any point in arguing the case.

"Guilty, your honor."

The judge looked slightly shocked but recovered his wits quickly.

"Very well. In the Forum of the Ox, your hands shall be removed at the wrist. Sit down."

Rabbit sat, dumbstruck. He had expected to be fined, or perhaps to have to work for the fuller to pay off the debt. He stared at his hands. He had just gone from being a permanent resident of the past to a mutilated resident. How would he live? He paid no attention to the next case and was still reeling with shock when he heard.

"Andor Psellos of Constantinople!"

The young soldier stood up.

"You are charged with aiding and abetting insurrection against the emperor. How do you plead?"

"Not guilty, your honor."

A city guard gave testimony that a known member of a criminal Jewish cabal had come to the Psellos house explicitly looking for Andor and that he had given the young man written instructions. He went on to say that members of the same cabal had been arrested for unlawful assembly later that night. Rabbit waited for the refutation that surely would come, but when the guard sat, no one else rose. Andor was asked for his side of the story, but all he would say was that he did not know the man who had delivered the note, nor did he have any idea about the note's contents. Not once did he mention Rabbit or Helen. Rabbit looked back at Uncle Helias, who was red with anger at his nephew's stubborn silence.

Before he knew it, the jury was leaning their heads together and quickly reached a decision. The speaker for the jury rose.

"Your honor, we find the accused . . ."

"Wait!" Rabbit said.

All eyes turned to him.

Rabbit's heart was hammering. This poor kid had shown Rabbit nothing but kindness and generosity right to the end. There was no way Rabbit could let him take the blame for something he himself had orchestrated.

"What do you have to say?"

"I know Andor Psellos. I was a guest in his home. He had nothing to do with the rebels from the Chalkprateia. That note was for me."

There was a rumbling around the court that sounded so much like a TV show that Rabbit laughed giddily.

"Is there something funny about treason that this court is not aware of?" the judge asked.

"No, your honor."

"Then sit down while this court deliberates."

Rabbit sat. He hadn't realized that he had stood up.

Andor turned and looked at him, his expression too complex to read. "I'm sorry," Rabbit mouthed.

Within moments, the judge was speaking again. "Varrus, was the note itself recovered?"

"No, your honor. but I saw it clearly and it . . ."

The judge waved him to silence. "In that case, this court has little choice but to believe your plea. Andor Psellos, you are excused from this court. Antigonus of Rome, your prior sentence is overturned. Instead, you are hereby sentenced to death by beheading to be carried out immediately in the public forum. May God have mercy on your soul."

In Rabbit's era, a prisoner being marched down the street would cause most people to turn away in embarrassment or fear. In Constantinople, Rabbit was a welcome entertainment. People jeered, some spat at him. A small crowd gathered in his wake and trailed him and his guards down the Mese.

Last night, Rabbit had thought never going home was the worst fate. As he marched toward his death, he realized how wrong he was. Constantinople would have been a fine place to live out the rest of his life. He could have continued his translation business, perhaps, or used his superior knowledge to become an advisor to . . . Something stirred in his brain, but he was interrupted before he could grab hold of it.

"Antigonus!" It was Andor, pushing his way through the crowded Mese to get to him. His face was pale with distress. Rabbit could see his uncle behind him, demanding he stop immediately. Andor ignored him.

"Don't touch the condemned," the guard barked at him.

Andor put his hands up but kept in step with Rabbit. "You didn't have to do that."

The last thing Rabbit wanted now was for Andor to say something in front of the guards that might incriminate himself. "I just told the truth," Rabbit said, trying to infuse it with as much *shut-up* energy as he could.

The young man looked at him helplessly, clearly wanting to say something meaningful but lacking the words.

"Good luck in the wars, Andor."

"May you find your way to heaven, Antigonus."

And then the crowd swallowed him up.

In the blink of an eye, they arrived at the Forum of the Ox. The crowd already assembled there grew by the addition of the trail of followers Rabbit had picked up along the way.

A circle was cleared in the center of the forum to accommodate a stout-legged platform bearing a thick block of wood, chipped and stained black. A barrel of a man stood beside the block wearing a mask over his face. *Curious,* Rabbit thought. *I didn't know the executioner's mask was a cultural norm in the sixth century.* His guard shoved him forward, breaking his reverie.

The executioner was leaning on a heavy, single-bladed ax.

Rabbit was walked to the platform. Both guards kept a hand on his elbows, which he found funny. *Where would I run?* he thought. The crowd around the clearing was celebratory, eating street food and talking animatedly among themselves. *They would turn savage if I tried to deprive them of their entertainment.*

He mounted the three steps onto the platform and the noisy crowd settled into silence.

Another man hustled up onto the platform, adjusting his colorful outer cloak. "Sorry, sorry," he apologized to the guards.

The soldiers rolled their eyes at the priest.

"My son, may I ease your passing?"

To his own surprise, Rabbit nodded.

"What is your name?"

He was about to say his pseudonym but what came quietly from his mouth instead was the truth. "Robert Ward."

The priest spoke quietly in Latin over a small cup, then held it out to Rabbit. He sipped a little watered wine from the cup. "Robert Ward, may the Lord Jesus Christ protect you and lead you to eternal life."

The priest backed away.

The guards shoved Rabbit to his knees. One of them pressed his head to the block and advised in a surprisingly cordial voice, "Stay still, yeah? If you stay still, it'll be quick and clean. You won't even feel it."

He and the other guard backed away.

Rabbit closed his eyes. He could smell the dried blood on the block, the sweat of the guards and the executioner. He could even smell the redolent garlands of flowers that decorated the street.

The platform creaked as the headman lifted his ax and raised it for the killing stroke.

It never came.

CONSTANTINOPLE

535 CE

Hold, hold!" an authoritative voice rang out across the square. Rabbit opened his eyes and saw the executioner lower the ax to the platform. The crowds parted to admit a splendidly dressed guard, the source of the commanding voice. A black and gold litter carried by porters followed in his wake.

The porters set down the litter gently.

The well-dressed guard bellowed, "By divine right of the emperor, I hereby order a stay of execution. Antigonus of Rome, you are hereby pardoned of your crimes and commanded to the palace of Justinian the Great."

Rabbit was so stunned that for a moment he stayed frozen to the executioner's block. Finally, one of the guards kicked his foot and hissed, "Get up, man!"

Rabbit climbed unsteadily to his feet.

The deprived crowd sullenly watched Rabbit descend the stairs and walk over to the leader of the procession. With a sweeping gesture, he motioned Rabbit toward the litter. The four bearers kept their eyes on the ground as he approached the elegant conveyance. Curtains hung from its open windows, and Rabbit held his breath as he approached, wondering who could be inside. But when he drew the fine cloth to one side, he discovered that it was empty. He climbed in and sat on a soft cushioned seat. At a bark from the guard, the litter rose from the ground and rotated, heading back to the palace district. Rabbit took a deep, shuddering breath. Remarkably, he was alive.

The litter ride was smoother than he would have guessed. The four bearers expertly moved together to create a swaying but gentle passage down the Mese. The cloth of the curtains was loose-woven linen that allowed him to see out while obscuring the view in. For much of the ride, he simply marveled at how quickly fate could turn. He had walked to the forum as a condemned prisoner, only to be carried back in the lap of luxury. His gratitude lasted as far as the Hippodrome, where his curiosity got the better of it. What the hell had just happened?

The litter passed through the Chalke Gate, past the open porticos of the senate house, through meticulously manicured gardens, and past a series of domed palaces and offices. At last, they passed under an aqueduct wall and arrived at a comparatively modest home set in a bright green lawn. The litter settled onto the ground and the guard lifted the curtain, inviting Rabbit to exit. He climbed out and looked up at the house. Comparatively was the operative word. The home would have been a lavish mansion in his own time.

"This way." The palace guard led him up the red marble steps and through a heavy wood door banded with hammered bronze.

The foyer of the mansion sported a colorful mosaic that traveled down one wall, across the floor, and up the other wall. It was abstract, semi-geometric, and looked like nothing Rabbit had seen anywhere else in the city. It reminded him slightly of Marc Chagall's stained-glass windows.

"Through here," the guard said, leading him toward a set of wood-framed glass doors. The glass was colorful and full of bubbles, letting through light but no image of what lay beyond. "I will be but a call away," he said warningly. "Don't do anything foolish."

He opened the door and admitted Rabbit to the solarium beyond. The first thing that struck Rabbit was the warmth. It was like a DC summer in the room. Sunlight poured in through the domed roof and tall side windows to illuminate potted trees and shrubs arrayed in concentric circles. Through the trees, he could just make out a ring of couches in the center. As he walked toward it, he realized that someone was already sitting there with his back to Rabbit. He rushed forward, eager to see the face of his rescuer.

She turned in her seat at his approach and, to his surprise, it was Helen. She took him in from top to bottom. Judging by her expression, he must have looked pretty bad. "Hi," she said. Her voice was shaky with worry.

She was clean and perfumed, her hair done in the style of the time. Her worn and dirty clothes had been replaced with a tunic and cloak of silk. Rabbit stared at her, trying to make sense of what he was seeing.

"Where are we?" he asked.

"I don't know. All I've seen are servants since I arrived last night."

"You're okay?" he asked.

She laughed, looking at his disheveled condition. Then she looked around furtively and whispered in a rush. "Listen, there's still a chance. I've got . . ."

She fell silent as a door opened and closed in the room. Shuffling footsteps approached. A moment later, the oldest man Rabbit had ever seen stepped out from between the shrubs. The man gently but confidently walked to the couch opposite them and lowered himself shakily to its plush upholstery, falling the last few inches as his strength failed.

"I know you," Rabbit said. "You're Joseph ben Levi. Justinian's advisor."

The old man was dressed in silk now and his cap was silk too. It was a far cry from the simple robe and leather cap he had worn in the presence of the emperor. Nonetheless, it was him.

The old man smiled, his eyes sparkling. "The wisest aunt, telling the saddest tale, sometime for a three-foot stool mistaketh me." There was something about the poem that bothered Rabbit, but he couldn't think what it was. "Sit, eat, Antigonus-Gallus whatever your name is."

Rabbit had been so stunned by seeing Helen that he hadn't even noticed the spread of food laid out on the round table before them. Fresh and dried fruits, dainty pastries, meat and egg pies, bowls of nuts, and urns of steaming beverages crowded the polished wood surface. It looked inviting, but Rabbit hesitated.

"Don't worry," the old man croaked dryly. "Do you think I'd rescue you from the block only to poison you now?"

Good point. Rabbit picked up a delicate plate holding a single pie.

"I don't have much appetite these days, so I like to indulge vicariously," the old man said. As Rabbit ate, he continued, "I apologize for holding you overnight but, well, I'm at my best in the morning. I have been looking forward to this meeting, oh, more than you could know."

"You were almost too late," Rabbit said.

"I am never late," he said. "I wanted to gift you with something that was given to me once."

Rabbit swallowed his bite of pie and picked up a fig from the table. "What's that?"

"Clarity. I firmly believe that no man knows what it is to be alive until he truly sees his death. I had the experience at a very young age, myself. It's what separates us from beasts. A rabbit, caught in a snare, knows the moment of death. But if it gets free, it shakes itself off and goes back to living as though nothing changed. They have an enviable lack of reflection, you see. Not that I would trade my sense of purpose for their sense of the moment, but I do enjoy the motif."

Something suddenly struck Rabbit. "You killed the customs official."

The old man shrugged.

"And the man who made the mummies."

"Both had played their parts. After that, their continued existence could only be detrimental."

"Their parts in what?" Helen asked bluntly.

"I'll answer your question with a question. What keeps a people down?" When neither of them replied, he urged, "It's not a riddle. What keeps a people down?"

"Taking away their rights. Oppress them," said Helen.

He pointed at her in agreement. "More specifically, just the right amount of oppression. Rome is a master of just the right amount. They say, you may live in our cities and practice your religion, but only under our watchful eye. Rome keeps her enemies close to her. That way, when the good people of the city buy their copper from us, they smile, they make small talk about the weather or the crops and we think, this is enough. When we sit with the Blues at the races, we forget that none of them raised a hand when the pogrom came to Antioch. We may not be wholly free to be who we are, but we are not reviled and murdered. The people of Rome subtly sweeten the bile of the state. You see? Just the right amount of oppression."

"You're behind the Jewish uprising," said Rabbit as he realized it.

He bowed with false humility.

"But you work for the emperor," Helen protested.

"As Joseph," he nodded, "I am the mystic advisor. I have saved Justinian from so many little traps. I have slowly built a following among the palace guards as well as the leaders of the Chalkoprateia, who call me Teacher. But Joseph couldn't do everything I needed, so I was forced to take on another persona, as well." He waited like an expectant schoolteacher.

Rabbit thought about it. "You said Rome keeps the pressure up just enough. You'd need someone to tip the scales, make the oppression too much."

"Enter Victor Vitensis," the old man smiled.

"The bishop?" Rabbit asked.

"He had a large following in the church. I picked up where he left off, assumed his writing style, and shifted the narrative to vilify the Jews." He suddenly transformed his whole persona in the blink of an eye into that of a fire and brimstone preacher. "They must not be allowed to read the Torah! They may not circumcise their sons! They must be forced to convert! If they do not meld with the Trinity, then they must be wiped out!" As suddenly as it appeared, he dropped the fanatic act. "The real Victor has been dead for twenty years, of course. I left his body to the sand crabs in Numidia myself. I made my 'Victor' a recluse. I wasn't about to waste my time in North Africa, so I sent him to the North African wastes, an ascetic who lives in a cave and releases his writings once a year to the only man who knows his whereabouts."

"You," Rabbit said.

Joseph smiled. "After decades of my vile writing, Justinian released the Corpus Juris Civilis earlier this year and tipped the scales. And now the oppression is just too much."

"All those men in jail," Rabbit realized. "You used the new code to arrest them."

"Where they now wait patiently inside the palace walls," agreed the old man.

"I wondered why Judah didn't seem worried."

"It won't matter." Helen looked genuinely saddened. "You'll never beat the Romans. This uprising of yours won't even be significant enough to reach the history books."

Rabbit thought she was being a little free and easy with the information, but he agreed. This old man had spent his life in vain. The visitors from the future knew it without question.

Joseph didn't appear fazed by her naysaying, however. "Yes, well, that was on my mind, too," he agreed, pointing to his temple. "And I thought, my people need something to turn the tide. Something that makes them mightier than their numbers, you see?"

Something was creeping into Rabbit's mind from the depths. Pieces were coming together. He held a grape in front of his open mouth, motionless. The old man smiled at him mischievously and continued. "I had an idea but making it real would take a fortune. A vast fortune. You must understand, all of this came to me after my first brush with death, all at once. Joseph, the man on the inside; Victor, the voice of oppression; and one more leg to the stool."

"Germanius Thrax," Rabbit finished the thought.

He clapped. "Yes! Thrax was my first and most valuable persona. I invented him in Carthage, a trader of unusual savvy and cunning. And in his name, I built the massive fortune I needed to do my work. He also has a vast network of spies and lackeys for carrying out any number of tasks quietly."

"The Blues," Helen said.

He nodded. "They have been useful. But they will be on the wrong side of history too, in the end."

"And just what is the product of all your work?" Helen asked.

Rabbit knew. He had smelled it. "You bought all the urine in the city for a year. All those warehouses were making saltpeter to mix with your sulfur and charcoal." He swallowed, and his throat was dry. "You were making gunpowder."

Helen looked at Rabbit in alarm. They both knew perfectly well that gunpowder shouldn't be here for hundreds of years. It couldn't be here. Its very existence flew in the face of history.

The old man grinned.

"Just how old are you, Joseph?" Rabbit said, dread creeping up on him.

"If I live to see it, I will celebrate my hundredth birthday this month."

"And all those personas of yours, you made them up in Carthage?"

"All part of the plan."

"And you had the extra manifest made and wrapped in a rabbit mummy."

Helen was looking back and forth between them.

The old man bobbed his head, he was so excited his whole body rocked with the force of it. "My invitation to you. I was beginning to worry you'd never come. And when that Israeli, Nazarian, was it? When he showed up, I worried you were dead. But in the end, he played his part, as well."

"What's going on?" Helen demanded.

"Sometime for three-foot stool mistaketh me . . ." Rabbit repeated the old man's words, numbly. "That's Shakespeare."

The old man's grin widened. "Puck. *Midsummer Night's Dream*. Good play. Too bad it won't be written for another thousand years."

"Oh my God," she whispered.

"Yeah," Rabbit sighed. "Helen, I'd like to introduce you to my old partner, Aaron Kahan."

CONSTANTINOPLE

535 CE

Y ou've aged, Rabbit."

Rabbit heard his response as though someone else was saying it. "Look who's talking."

Aaron chuckled softly. "How are my parents?"

The shift caught Rabbit by surprise. "They looked healthy the last time I saw them. We don't keep in touch."

"Pity. They liked you very much. There's no one else they would have trusted to take their golden boy back to the past."

"Explain," demanded Helen.

"I was Rabbit's ward." He chuckled at his joke. Aaron had made it when he was first assigned as his partner; he had been pleased with himself then, too. "The youngest person to jump through time. Barely twenty." Helen gaped. "I had a knack for knowing how to pull the levers of power. It's always served me well."

"But how are you alive? I saw you die." Rabbit felt like he was looking at a ghost.

"My moment of clarity?" He shook his head. "No, I didn't die, Rabbit. Twenty years I was a slave to old King Genseric in Carthage. Oh, it wasn't as bad as it sounds. I dribbled out little gems of knowledge to make myself valuable. Never anything so radical that it would tip the scales of history. Those I kept for myself. When the old king died, I was given my freedom. By then I knew what I wanted to do and how I would do it. Do you know what the hardest part was?"

Rabbit shook his head.

"Pride. I'm quite possibly the richest man on the entire planet at present. I have had my hand on the tiller of the greatest empire the Western world has ever known. I am about to launch an assault on the fabric of time itself. And no one knows. That's why I called you here, Rabbit." He abruptly turned his attention on Helen. "Rabbit taught me my most important lesson eighty years ago. Bury your pride. Do what you need to do and be what you need to be to get what you want. I have embraced that lesson to its end."

"I'm sorry, Aaron."

The old man looked shocked. "Sorry? No, haven't you been listening? When you left me behind, you created me. If I had gone back, I would be . . . you. Just another meaningless observer of history." He leaned forward and tapped his chest. "I am history."

"None of it matters. You know that, right? The moment the guns come out, time will splinter. There was no Jewish revolt in 535. This empire of Israel you've envisioned, it doesn't exist."

Aaron let out an exasperated growl, then raised his hands to the sky as though asking for heavenly patience. Rabbit was beginning to wonder if all of his fragments really had become their own identities. When he spoke, it was as though he was counseling himself. "It's okay. You just haven't had time to think." He looked back at Rabbit. "Yes, of course, time will splinter. That's the whole point. Our world was full of just the right amount of oppression too, you see? Just like Rome. Someone may salvage our world one day, but it won't be me. I'm making a new world, a better world."

"And you kept me here for what," Rabbit growled, "for spite?"

"No! It's not enough to launch the rebellion. I need history to know why and how it was possible. I needed someone to carry on where I leave off. I'm an old man, Rabbit. I won't get to enjoy the world I am making. You will. I leveled the playing field, now you can build the foundations for a more egalitarian future. Think about it. Abraham, Moses, Aaron, Rabbit. That's what I'm offering you."

"What if I refuse?"

"And do what instead? You can't go home. I know how long it takes to ride to Greece as well as you do. I will make you my sole heir. You will be the wealthiest couple in the ancient world."

"We're not a couple," they said in perfect unison.

"There's time," he said. "Rabbit, I am trusting you with my legacy. You can make this world better than our old one."

"It's just a splinter."

"Arrogant!" the old man barked. "What makes you think your world is so original? Hasn't that ever occurred to you? There may be hundreds of versions of our world for all you know. In some of them, time travel may not even exist! I can't reform all of them. Just this one. And you will help me. Because not everything is worth preserving."

A door opened somewhere in the solarium and a voice called out, "Sir. The triumph. We're expected at the emperor's box."

Aaron nodded. "I'll be right there, John," he called out to the guard. Then, to Rabbit and Helen, "I need to prepare myself. Rest. Eat as much as you'd like but don't think about leaving. I have men stationed at every exit. I'll return for you in a few moments." He rose painfully and left the same way he had arrived.

The moment the door closed in the distance, Helen turned to Rabbit intently. "We have to get out of here."

"He just said he's got guards stationed . . ."

"Not out of the building. Shut up and listen. You entered through Greece, but I didn't. We still have time to reach my decay point."

"What?!" Rabbit sat up straight. "Where is it?"

She shook her head. "I'll take you there."

Rabbit wanted to argue but realized he was only reaping what he had sown.

As though reading his mind, she said, "I trust you just as long as you need me."

Rabbit considered her. "Do you even know if I can return through your decay point?"

"Not at all, but I sure as hell know you can't return through yours."

She was staring at him, her eyes intense. Rabbit thought he'd never seen anyone more attractive. He extended his hand. "All right. Partners again for now."

She shook his hand. "I've seen what happens to your partners. Let's say friends instead." She looked in the direction Aaron had disappeared. "Secret for a secret?"

He looked at her quizzically.

"What happened to him on your mission?"

Rabbit too stared after Aaron. "We were in Rome for the menorah when the Vandals were pouring into the city. You know historians say they weren't as destructive as some other invaders, and that's true, but I can tell you they were bad enough. The legion guarding the city hadn't even put up a fight; people were barricading themselves in their homes or trying to flee to the countryside. It was ... perfect for the grab. We took advantage of the confusion, got the menorah into a donkey cart pretending to be refugees. We were driving it over the Tiber when one of their patrols caught us. They didn't care about us; they just wanted the cart to help haul loot to their boats on the Tiber. I took one look at them and wrote it off as a bad deal. The numbers didn't add up for a fight and I knew the moment they saw the menorah they wouldn't let us walk away with it. So, I backed off." Rabbit shook his head. "Not Aaron. He just kept trying to lead the donkey away like he hadn't heard them. When one of them shoved him, Aaron went after the guy. He was armed of course, and he managed to trade a little blood with the Vandal but then the rest of them circled him and cut him down."

"What did you do?"

"He was a dead man. They were all over him, kicking and stabbing him."

"What did you do?"

Rabbit took a long moment. He picked up a little pastry, considered eating it then put it back down. He was ashamed to admit the truth to her. But he had agreed. "I ran. I made it back to the decay point and came home without him." Rabbit stared at the food-laden table. It all looked suddenly nauseating. "I never told anyone the real story. Even to PJ, I embellished it."

"Why?"

"Because I let him die, Helen. I ran like a coward."

"You're ashamed?"

"Wouldn't you be?" He was exasperated with her.

"No," she responded simply.

He thought the question was rhetorical when he asked it and was stumped by her answer. "Really?"

"Hey man, I'm not going to tell you how to feel. I just think, you know, there are other ways to think about it."

He stared at her.

"If it was me, I'd be pissed off. It's a hunk of metal, it's not worth throwing your life away over, you know? He could have done what you did, back away, come back later in history, and try again. Instead, he picked an unwinnable fight. Over what? A thing."

"I could have defended him."

She sneered. "Yeah? How?" When he didn't answer, she went on. "It's kinda arrogant, isn't it? Thinking you have total responsibility for everything? But maybe it feels better to be ashamed than mad." At Rabbit's blank stare, she explained. "He did something irresponsible and stupid you had no control over, and he saddled your life and career with it. I think anger would be a pretty normal response!" There was a long silence between them. She picked up a pastry and imitated Rabbit's voice. "Thank you, Helen, you've offered me a valuable new perspective on my life." She took a bite and concluded more gently, "Nobody ever suffered less because you suffered more, Rabbit."

The fact was, Rabbit was considering what she had said, but he was too proud to admit it. Instead, what came out of his mouth was, "I didn't intend for you to be arrested. Back at the Psellos house."

"I'm not quite ready to let that go, but I'll let you know when I do."

"Fair enough."

"Secret for a secret," she said.

He was about to ask her when a door opened beyond the foliage and John's voice called to them. "Please come with me."

At the foot of the red marble stairs, Aaron awaited them in a little carriage and beckoned them to join him. The carriage had two plush seats that faced each other behind the driver's seat so that Rabbit and Helen could sit opposite the old man. Now that Rabbit knew Aaron's true identity, he couldn't believe it had taken him so long to figure it out. Sure, he was old, but the gestures and cadence to his voice were still familiar to Rabbit all these years later.

"I want you to pay special attention today, Rabbit," the old man said. "This is the day everything changes. I may not live to see the new empire shine, but at least I'll see the sun set on this one."

"What do you plan to do about the legions stationed in Thrace and Africa? Constantinople is highly defensible, but it's just one city."

Aaron smiled. "You underestimate me. This isn't the only board on which I have pieces. Forty cities and towns will hear my guns today. I own half the legions in Thrace. Belisarius' troops are eating rations laced with arsenic in Carthage as we speak. I have the ear of the church as well. I spent eighty years on this plan, Rabbit. Hell, I even got you here from another era to witness it for me. I'm not some trumped-up general with delusions of power."

They rode through the palace grounds as far as the carriage could carry them then dismounted and walked. The bearers who had carried Rabbit from the forum raised the old man in a tidy little sedan chair that was waiting for them. The walk through the halls of the interconnected buildings was long but luxurious. Rabbit, who had been in many of the modern world's great buildings, was still impressed by the sheer magnitude of the Byzantine palaces. When at last they got to a set of stairs the litter could not navigate, Aaron took to his feet. "Give me your arm, would you?" he asked Rabbit. He was slow on the stairs but still managed them better than many people Rabbit knew who were twenty years younger than he was.

"What do you think, then? Of my plan?"

"It seems you've been . . . thorough."

"I learned it all from you. You were such a hero to me back then. I was angry when you abandoned me, but it wasn't really your fault. I idolized you, thought you were infallible. Unconsciously, I think I must have believed that you chose this fate for me. Childish. Eventually, of course, I realized that, for all your skill, you were just a man after all. I knew that I could take what I'd learned from you and expand upon it, refine it."

"What did he teach you?" Helen asked. The question annoyed Rabbit. He didn't really want to know.

The old man grinned. As he spoke, he ticked his points off on his fingers. "One, anything can be accomplished with enough planning. Two, all contingencies can be uncovered with enough time. Three, be whatever the situation demands to keep your plan in motion. Four, everything not directly tied to the desired outcome is expendable. Without Rabbit, I would never have had the will to do what I have."

Rabbit felt his stomach drop. He thought about his brief, but obviously formative, time with Aaron and realized with sickening clarity that those were the exact lessons he had taught.

"Keep them close, John," Aaron said to his pet excubitor. They summited the stairs as a group and entered Emperor Justinian's private box. Mosaic designs vied with inset stone carvings on every wall. The floor was carpeted with a single Persian rug that spanned the entirety of the large room and down the three tiers of landings to a baroque stone railing. There were stacks of cushions on each of the tiers to make oneself comfortable while watching the races through the open front of the box. The overhanging roof ensured protection from too much sun or rain, while scattered braziers chased away the chill. The box was inaccessible from the stadium itself, its balcony dozens of feet above the closest seating for the masses; it was the pinnacle of comfort and personal security.

At present, there was a crowd in the room. In the middle of it was the emperor himself, wearing his crown again today for the public event. He was talking with a jowly, middle-aged man with unruly grey hair Rabbit identified as the quaestor, Tribonian. His bronze likeness hung in the halls of the US Supreme Court. It wasn't a particularly good match. Empress Theodora was across the room talking quietly with a well-dressed woman of similar age, probably Belisarius' wife, Antonina. Glaring at the two women over his wine glass was a fat man wearing a host of rings on his sausage-like fingers. That must be the praetorian prefect, John the Cappadocian, who would be fired and exiled soon. There were other courtiers Rabbit didn't recognize as well as a handful of excubitors who saluted Aaron's man John when he entered. Rabbit felt as though he'd just stepped into an episode of a salacious historical drama.

"Who are your guests, Joseph ben Levi?" asked a solicitous voice. The owner of the voice was a trim man in his mid-thirties with a rather large head and a beard that climbed high up his cheeks.

Aaron inclined his head. "Procopius. Antigonus, a merchant from Rome, and his wife, Helen."

"Dressed in the heights of Gothic fashion, I should have recognized your home city," the historian said sweetly. Rabbit glanced down at himself and remembered he was still in the dirty, sweaty clothes he'd been wearing for forty-eight hours. "To what do we owe the honor of such lofty guests in the box?"

"In selecting my guests, I knew I only had to outdo historians," Aaron replied with equal saccharine.

The young man's face hardened, and he fought to keep it civil. "If it's history you sneer at, Joseph, you needn't worry; it won't remember you."

Aaron smiled serenely back. "Oh, I don't know about that. Enjoy the triumph, Procopius." He guided Rabbit and Helen deeper into the box.

"I won't be sorry to see the last of that asshole," Aaron mumbled in English. "Oh look, they've opened up the track." He walked toward the open edge of the box with a spring in his step, looking across at the opposite seating. Streams of people were pouring in through every entrance.

The stands filled rapidly with people. With help from Rabbit and Helen, Aaron settled himself on one of the tiers of seating at the front of the box, cushioning his seat and back generously. Within moments, the sound of trumpets split the air in the Hippodrome. The heralds, dressed in bright, festive cloaks, entered the track to the applause of the crowd. They were followed by the prisoners, dozens of Gelimer's family chained together at the ankle. The fallen king himself was spared the humiliation of a second march through the streets. The musicians and captives led the way slowly around the track. Following them came the treasure. Cart after cart after cart rolled ponderously through the gates, laden with barrels of gold coins, paintings, statues, gleaming armor and weapons, heaps of jewelry, silver platters, rare animals—it went on and on. As the carts rounded the track, they stopped in a neat line on the outside of the track. When the outside ring was full, a second concentric line was formed. Rabbit had read of these spectacles before, but that hadn't prepared him for the sheer volume of wealth that poured through the doors. It was no wonder that no one had noticed the missing menorah.

"Most of that will be yours, of course," Aaron said. Rabbit looked at him, confused. He poked him in the chest with a bony finger. "Rabbit, I made this world possible, but someone will have to shape it, guide it. I'm entrusting you to write my story and to create your own. Use everything you know to make this world more just than the one that created us. Even if you didn't share my godlike knowledge of the future, you'd be perfect for the job. I never met anyone more moral in mind and amoral in deed than you. I know you'll do whatever it takes." He patted Rabbit's knee. "Thank you for coming back."

In spite of himself, Rabbit began to wonder what it would be like to set the course of an empire. He could create a new set of laws, one that was truly fair. He could revolutionize medicine, maybe even stop the plague from reaching Europe like the character in the L. Sprague de Camp novel, *Lest Darkness Fall*. He could eliminate hereditary wealth, establish a model for meritocracy in the government. With even his rudimentary knowledge of modern war technology, he could create a military that would be untouchable. It didn't need to be a conquering empire, of course. He could consolidate in a prosperous region and ensure a peace and vitality that might inspire other nations to follow suit. How would he prevent the corruption that seemed to creep into every long-standing government?

Helen was staring at him, a look of deep concern on her face. He averted his gaze back to the track, knowing his cheeks were burning but unable to stop it. *Jesus*, he thought, *that's how easy it is to become part of it.* Aaron was right about him.

The general's bodyguard was striding through the gates now, dressed in full armor with fresh white plums in their helmets. The applause and cheering began to increase like a wave that crested and crashed over Belisarius himself as he strode onto the track looking every inch the hero. Rabbit noted that his bodyguard numbered only a few hundred soldiers. Due to the limited space left on the treasure-laden racetrack, the soldiers were packed into tight formations.

Rabbit felt sick to his stomach as he saw their formation. They were easy pickings. "You could still call it off, Aaron," he said weakly.

Aaron snorted through his nose. Rabbit realized he wasn't laughing at his suggestion when he turned to him, a faraway look in his eye. "Todd Sliwinski."

Rabbit just shook his head.

Aaron gestured Rabbit closer so the old man didn't have to be heard over the crowd.

"I was just thinking about a schoolyard bully named Todd Sliwinski. It's funny how many old memories come back to you at the end. Todd was one of those kids who just seemed to be born mean. You know the type. Everyone was terrified of him. He was unpredictable, violent. Somehow never got caught. My grandfather always told me bullies got that way because no one ever stood up to them. So, one day when he was terrorizing a classmate of mine by the tetherball court, I walked right up to him and demanded he stop. He broke my nose." He seemed to come back to the present and shrugged at Rabbit. "My grandfather was wrong. Being right doesn't ensure anything. No." He looked out at the Hippodrome. "If history has taught us anything, it's that the strongest always win."

Belisarius raised his hands and received a wave of adulation from the crowd.

The old man didn't seem to hear. "Him, I'll miss. He's a good man, perhaps a little codependent but ethically unimpeachable. I was never able to sway him." He sighed, "Goodbye, general."

Rabbit didn't know where the source was. Under the track perhaps or maybe in a few of the statues arrayed on the center of the track. The blast shook the Hippodrome as the bombs went off. Sand and smoke and shrapnel exploded in a cloud. The crowd erupted in chaos. Bodies and parts of bodies were hurled into the air to land amid the treasures they had won. In one move, all significant armed opposition to Aaron's rebellion was gone.

In the box, there was screaming. Rabbit turned numbly and saw John pull a crude metal tube from a tall planter. Justinian's four personal bodyguards were surrounding the emperor, swords drawn. But they were looking at the source of the explosion and never saw John drop a paper packet into the tube and aim it at their backs. The primitive shotgun belched flame. Blood sprayed from the two nearest guards, and the five men fell in a writhing heap. One of the other excubitors descended on them with his sword, thrusting it into the pile of bodies. John loaded his gun again and stood his ground against the attendees trying to flee the box. Tribonian's head split open from a point-blank shot that also felled Antonina but didn't kill her. Her screams of agony and terror pealed through the box. As Rabbit watched, the empress ran down the steps to the edge of the box and hurled herself out into space sooner than face the bloody purge.

There was pain in Rabbit's wrist. He turned and saw Aaron clutching it. His face was contorted in a combination of agony and ecstasy. His right hand was clutching his chest. The old man was leaning back on Helen, who looked at Rabbit helplessly.

"Aaron?"

"My plan, Rabbit," he said through pain-clenched teeth. "What do you think of my plan?" Saliva was bubbling at the corners of his thin lips. Rabbit felt his pulse. His heartbeat was fluttering.

Rabbit didn't know how to respond. After everything he'd done, seeing it come to fruition appeared to have finally been too much excitement for his onetime mentee. He could see the desperate gleam in those dying eyes. For all his grandeur, audacity, and brutality, what was written across the ancient face was a childlike desire for approval. "There's never been anything like it in history," Rabbit said truthfully.

Aaron smiled and became still. Under Rabbit's fingers, the old man's pulse stopped.

He looked at Helen, who looked just as scared as he was. Another gunshot went off in the box, making them both jump. The people in the Hippodrome were trampling each other to escape and, on the track, the cart animals had panicked into motion, crashing into one another and churning the track into a cloud of dust that choked the air.

Rabbit was shoved roughly. He rolled down one tier of the seating and landed on a pile of cushions. Looking back, he saw John crouching on the tier above him, cradling Aaron in his arms. Tears streamed down his cheeks.

In the box above the soldier, there was nothing but carnage. Piles of bodies were strewn across the floor of the box. Blood ran in rivulets down the steps.

The excubitor wiped his eyes on a bloody sleeve, smearing his face with gore. He gently laid the old man down on the step, picked up his sword and gun again, and rose to his feet. He loomed over Rabbit, who still lay on the step below. Rabbit was sure the soldier would blame him for the old man's death. Instead, he settled his face back into a semblance of its customary calm. "Come. I'll get you to safety."

Numbly, Rabbit rose to his feet and offered his hand to Helen. She looked at him with fierce desperation. "John," Rabbit said, "Helen and I have somewhere we need to be."

In response, John dropped one of the paper-wrapped shotgun cartridges into his gun. "He told me you might say that. He said to tell you, 'You may choose how to spend your days, but not when.' You're staying here."

"What about her? Do your orders include her, or can she go?"

"Rabbit . . ." she protested, but he squeezed her hand.

The guard shook his head. "Only you. But if she tries to interfere, I won't hesitate to end her life."

Rabbit turned to Helen, reverting to rapid-fire English. "This is your chance. Go back to your decay point."

"You're coming with me," she insisted.

"I can't. We don't even know if it would work anyway."

"You can't stay here."

"I don't have any choice!"

"We'll figure something out. I'll . . ."

John interrupted in Greek, "Now, please."

Reluctantly, Rabbit and Helen preceded the soldier to the exit. The floor was slippery with blood, and the humid air clung to the meaty reek of entrails and the burn of gunpowder. John kept enough distance between them to prevent Rabbit from trying to disarm him. At the door, Helen abruptly folded at the waist and vomited.

Rabbit went to her side, supporting her and fighting the urge to follow suit. But John remained impassively at a distance.

"We should hurry," he said simply.

They gathered themselves and went back down the stairs into the palace. Distantly, Rabbit could hear the muffled cracks of gunfire, but the halls of the palace complex were otherwise eerily quiet. John guided them through the Byzantine labyrinth, always remaining far enough distant to avoid attack. For a giddy moment, Rabbit had the dim realization that there had never been a better opportunity to steal and hide the precious historical artifacts of the period. He also knew that none of those artifacts would be found in his own timeline. From the moment the bombs went off they had entered a splintered history, a past that was never the past of his own timeline. Then again, since this timeline was his new home, perhaps he should consider preservation for this new future. Ridiculously, he thought of leaving clues to its location in his history . . .

"Excubitor!" a shrill voice shattered the quiet of the hall as a man ran out of a doorway toward them. He was elegantly dressed, from his colorful robes to his jeweled hat. The panic in his voice evaporated with every step, replaced by an imperious haughtiness.

"What are your men doing about the . . ." His words cut off as John calmly ran him through with his longsword. Efficiently, he slipped the sword free and kept walking as though nothing had happened, leaving the palace official gasping in shock behind them. Rabbit heard the guard quietly whisper, "To God I commend your spirit."

They arrived at the building's exit unmolested. John ordered them to stand in a corner of the room while he carefully checked the grounds outside for danger.

"Go!" Rabbit hissed at Helen. "He said he won't stop you."

"I can't leave you here," she insisted.

"My decay point is gone. I'll never get to it."

"Use mine. There's still time!"

"We don't know if it would work for me, and if I run away now . . ."

She looked at him steadily. "If you run away, you'll lose your chance to take over what Aaron started."

"I could do so much good," Rabbit admitted.

She stared at him in disbelief.

John gestured them through the door. "This way," he said.

Outside, the sound of shooting was louder, and the breeze smelled of gunpowder. They saw in the distance a group of armed men walking into a building. One of them spotted their trio and paused, but John simply waved his gun in the air. The man seemed to recognize the symbol and followed his peers into the building, which Rabbit recognized as the courthouse where he was sentenced to death only a few hours ago. A moment later, one of its windows exploded outward.

They crossed the manicured garden, passed under the aqueduct, and were in sight of Aaron's mansion when Helen tugged at his sleeve. He followed her eyes across a lawn to a massive white stone structure. That would be the Palace of Boukoleon, Justinian's family home, built directly into the cliff overlooking the Marmara Sea. It boasted its own small harbor for the private pleasure cruising of the emperor. He got the message—if they were to escape, that was the way home.

Rabbit stopped.

"What is it," John asked.

Instead of addressing him, Rabbit turned to Helen. "It's now or never. I take it you need a boat to get where you're going."

She nodded.

John was searching the grass anxiously for danger.

"Do me a favor?" Rabbit asked.

Helen nodded again.

"Tell my boss . . . tell my friend PJ what happened to me. She deserves to know."

"Rabbit," Helen began, blinking away tears.

What the hell, Rabbit thought, and pulled her into an embrace. He hugged her for a long moment, punctuated it with a final squeeze, and released her. "It was nice working with you."

"It was, wasn't it?"

"Goodbye, Helen."

She smiled at him one last time, the parentheses of her dimples framing her lips. Then she turned and ran for the palace.

John escorted Rabbit back into Aaron's house. Now that he knew who lived there, Rabbit could see the modern influence in the design that must have come from his old partner. John led him through a library office that surely was well ahead of its time, past a privy with its own water source, and into a spacious bedroom.

"Open it please," John said, indicating a closet door. Closets. Another modern invention. Rabbit wondered what had become of this architectural curiosity in his own timeline.

The door of the closet was exceedingly thick and banded with bronze. Inside, it was empty but for a single comfortable chair, an urn of water, a bucket, and a body.

Nazarian was bound to the chair, head lolling, face blue. A noose was tight around his throat. "A gift from Teacher. He said you would be pleased to know that no one beat you."

Rabbit stared at the rigid face of his competitor.

"You'll be secure here until I return," John said.

"Where are you going?" Rabbit asked.

"I have work to do. I'll be back. Now, please."

Rabbit stepped inside. The air was cool and dry. He stood by the corpse in the armchair.

John nodded at him and began to swing the door shut.

As the gap narrowed, something flashed across the space, knocking John out of the frame. Rabbit was motionless for a fraction of a second before his brain registered who he had just seen.

It was Helen.

Rabbit threw the door open.

John was stumbling into a bedside table, his hand on the side of his helmeted head. His sword was sheathed, but the gun was out, and he was raising it even as he hit the piece of furniture. Rabbit caught sight of Helen, a heavy bronze rod in her hands. Rabbit closed the gap between him and John, sweeping the gun to the side with his left hand while firing an elbow hook with his right. It connected solidly, sending a shock wave down his arm. The gun went off with a sound like a cannon in the enclosed space. It shocked Rabbit just enough to let John regain his solid footing. His eyes were unfocused from the blow to the head, but he was drawing his sword. Worse, he was just out of reach. If Rabbit charged again, he would be slashed as the blade came free from the scabbard. He was forced to retreat out of range as John drew the longsword and stumbled to retrieve the gun. The soldier squatted unsteadily and reached for it. Rabbit looked around frantically. On a little dressing table, there were a few pieces of statuary and a small personal oil lamp. Rabbit snatched the lamp and hurled it at John. It bounced off him harmlessly but splashed oil on his face, partially blinding him. Rabbit chucked one of the statues, which missed wildly. The other connected with his forearm as he raised it in defense. The sword clattered to the floor. Rabbit picked up the little table itself and threw it at him. As John deflected it, Rabbit launched himself forward and crashed into the soldier. They tumbled backward onto the tiled floor. John was bigger than he was, but he was still reeling from the blows he'd received, and Rabbit had plenty of ground training. If he was able to ... pain exploded near his neck. The sonofabitch was biting him! Rabbit jerked himself free from the soldier's teeth and rolled, taking John with him so they were both on their sides, Rabbit behind him. He slid a blood-slicked arm around the soldier's neck and clamped it down, cutting off the blood to the man's head. He held him as the soldier bucked and fought and finally went limp. Once he was sure the man was out, he disentangled himself and staggered to his feet.

Panting, Rabbit touched his left trapezius and winced at the pain. The man had taken a chunk out of him.

"What are you doing?" he growled in frustration. "You could miss your ..."

Helen was lying on the floor in a pool of her own blood.

CONSTANTINOPLE

535 CE

Helen," he gasped and ran to her side. The wall to one side of the bedroom door was pitted from John's gunshot. Not all of it had hit her. He felt her neck. There was a pulse. Weak and fast, but she was alive.

Her clothes were bright red and steaming with blood. It was vivid, but on closer inspection probably wasn't more than a pint. She could live through this.

He began to assess her to see where she was hit when he heard a shifting sound behind him. Rabbit shot to his feet and ran to John's side. The soldier was still unconscious but was beginning to move slightly. With a snarl, Rabbit snatched up the man's longsword, raised it over his head, and stood there, trembling. Every fiber in his being insisted on bringing that sword down on the groaning soldier. It wasn't just to eliminate him as a threat; he wanted to punish someone, anyone, for the events of the day that had led up to this moment. Instead, with a shuddering exhale, he threw the sword across the room.

Hastily, he dumped the excubitor next to Nazarian's body, slammed the door, and latched it from the outside.

Back to Helen, he withdrew his razor and carefully began to

search for her injuries, cutting away the cloth of her silk gown as he found them. The first was a small hole in her left shoulder. It exited the other side and looked relatively clean. Blood was oozing from the wound, not flowing. He found a second laceration where a pellet had grazed off her lower ribs. That was superficial. Below that, however, he found something that made him wince. The third and last pellet had entered just below her ribs and was nowhere to be seen. Her back was unmarked. The small entry hole in her abdomen bled the least, which worried Rabbit the most.

He cut strips off his cloak and wrapped them snugly around her shoulder, pinning pads of additional fabric to the open wounds. The wool should be a good material to stanch the bleeding. He wrapped a third around her abdomen but knew he was kidding himself there. If there was damage to her internal organs, the bandage wouldn't help a thing.

As he tightened the binding around her stomach, she stirred for just a moment. "Kalonymos," she murmured.

"What did you say?" he demanded.

She had already lapsed back into unconsciousness.

"Dammit," he swore to himself. The odds of her surviving here were next to nothing. Byzantine doctors were unlikely to be able to perform the needed surgery successfully, let alone defend her against infection. And that was under the best of conditions. The city was in turmoil now. Given what he had heard, Helen would be lost among the tens of thousands who would die today. No one would notice or care.

Except for Rabbit. As it turned out, he cared very much.

"Helen," he said loudly. "Where's your decay point? I get that we need a boat, but where is it?"

He could take her to the harbor, steal a boat, and set out in hopes that she would wake up and tell him where to go. Or he could try to stabilize her before leaving and run the risk of missing his window. Whatever he did, he had to do it quickly.

He swore under his breath again. "You're a real pain in the ass, you know that?" He lifted her from the floor and carried her to the bed. "I'm going to bring help." He picked up John's gun and the bag of ammunition he had dropped on the floor. "Don't die," he called over his shoulder as he left the room.

Rabbit trotted through the palace grounds, fumbling one of the paper cartridges out of his bag. Loading the gun seemed to be as simple as dropping the cartridge into the barrel, which he did. At the back end of the tube was a simple hammer. It looked like the firing mechanism was simply to lever it up with a thumb and release it. Now that Constantinople had seen the terrifying effect of these weapons, just carrying the gun should make an effective deterrent.

Other than the occasional, muffled gunfire, the palace grounds were incongruously peaceful. It was a beautiful day; fluffy white cumulus clouds drifted through a blue sky. It somehow made the scattered corpses sporadically strewn across the lawns and steps more grotesque.

He ran through the senate house, through the Augustaion, whose open-air market was deserted, its carts and goods toppled in disarray. He could hear shots fired more loudly now to the east. The rebels appeared to be moving that way. If he was lucky, they would have already moved beyond Andor's neighborhood. If he was lucky, they would have left the family in peace on their way by. The events of the day hadn't left Rabbit feeling especially lucky.

He was passing the Million at a trot when something caught his ear. A whinny. Of course, the Hippodrome stables! He ran for the entrance. Looming over it was the painted face of Porphyrius the Charioteer, advertising a brand of olive oil. The likeness wasn't especially good, nor were the proportions. He wondered obliquely what the vain athlete thought of it.

One of the sets of double doors stood open. Rabbit darted in, checking his blind spots for trouble. He didn't see anyone, but there were several bodies strewn about the floor—charioteers, workers, and rebels by the looks of them.

The horses, thankfully, were mostly standing in their stalls. The blood in the air was making them restless, but they seemed otherwise unharmed.

Rabbit quickly picked out the calmest animal he could find, a tall brown mare who was eating hay rather than pacing the stall. "Hello, friend," Rabbit said smoothly. The horse looked up from its snack, took him in, and went back to eating. *Perfect*, he thought.

He grabbed a bridle from a wall of tack nearby and opened the stall door. The horse accepted the harness without complaint and Rabbit led it out of its stall.

"Hey!"

Rabbit turned toward the voice and saw the infamous charioteer himself coming out of a room at the end of the cavernous stable. Grey-black mane tied up in a topknot, Porphyrius was holding a jug of wine in one fist. He had the look of a man who had given up on the whole day as a lost cause. Well, that was until someone tried to steal a horse. He threw the jug to the floor where it shattered and pointed at Rabbit.

Eyes fixed, the man stalked toward him, pulling a whip from his belt as he did. Rabbit realized in horror that he had left his gun leaning against the stable door. *Too late now*, he thought and leaped onto the horse's back. As he was kicking the horse into motion, white light exploded across his vision and what sounded like an explosion went off in his right ear.

The horse reacted to the sound too and sprang into a gallop. As Rabbit's vision cleared, they were shooting out into the sunlight. Rabbit guided the animal to the left up the Mese. He touched the right side of his head, and his hand came away bloody. His ear was still ringing.

Galloping forward along the cobbled street, Rabbit could see the aftermath of the rebel wave. They hadn't burned as they had in Nika, but windows were shattered, and the bodies of animals and people littered the street.

Rabbit was almost on Andor's street when he heard the crack of the whip again. Glancing behind him, he saw Porphyrius riding up behind him on one of his white horses. Rabbit had chosen his mount for its quietude, and it was no match for the charioteer's prize stallion.

Rabbit looked back at where he was going just in time to make the turn, but he was chilled by what he had seen. Porphyrius' handsome face was alive with violent, ravenous delight.

Rabbit lashed on his mount along Andor's posh street. The problem was, once he dismounted, he'd be a sitting duck. *Time to do something stupid*, he thought. As he approached Andor's house, he gathered his feet under him so that he was precariously crouching on the animal's galloping back like a circus performer. As Andor's garden gate came into view, he launched himself onto it.

He was hoping for a graceful drop into the garden. What he got instead was a slide along the top of the wall and a collision with the stone arch over the entryway. The air went out of him, and he thought he heard a rib pop. To add injury to injury, the charioteer's whip lashed his back with a stinging crack. He felt his fingers scrabbling for a hold on the wall slip free and he tumbled into the street in a disordered heap.

Porphyrius rounded his horse elegantly and came around. Rabbit scrambled to his feet, barely feeling his countless scrapes and bruises through the adrenaline rush. He dropped into a low position, expecting to dodge. Instead of running him down, however, the charioteer snapped the whip at him as he rode by. It caught around his ankle and snapped taut. Rabbit was jerked off his feet and hit the stone street again. Luckily, the leather braid slipped free, taking a ring of skin with it instead of dragging him down the street.

"Try that again, bastard," he growled in English.

The white horse wheeled and came around. Sure enough, the rider snapped the whip again. This time Rabbit was ready. The moment it caught around his leg, he grabbed it with one hand, securing it in place. With the other hand, he grabbed hold of one of the stout bars on the Psellos front gate. As man and horse rode by, the whip drew taut again. Rabbit was yanked onto one leg in a grotesque arabesque. He squeezed the door with all his strength, feeling a yank from hand to foot that felt like every joint might break.

Porphyrius was jerked from the horse's bare back and fell to the cobbled street in a heap. Rabbit freed his ankle from the whip and gathered up coils of the leather braid as he closed in on the charioteer, who had yet to regain his feet. Rabbit jerked the whip out of his hands and threw it behind him. When he was almost upon the fallen athlete, Porphyrius suddenly sprang to his feet, a long dagger in his hands. He lunged at Rabbit, who tried to back away, throwing up both hands to deflect the blade. Lunge and dodge, lunge and dodge, he backed Rabbit up until his back hit the garden wall. The famous rider laughed, an ugly, angry sound. Then he abruptly jerked backward. Four inches of fletched arrow was suddenly sticking out from behind his collarbone as if it had sprouted there.

He touched the arrow, confused by it. The knife fell from his hand. He coughed and blood dribbled down his chin.

The garden gate opened. "Come in, master, come in at once!" said a terrified voice.

Rabbit heeded the invitation as the charioteer fell to the cobbled street.

Inside, Rabbit was met by a host of familiar faces. Phraates, the old gardener, checked the street then closed and barred the door. Behind him crowded Andor's sister, Portia, her fiancé, and, to Rabbit's immense relief, Brother Bautista, the family doctor. Andor called down from the balcony.

"Is anyone else following you?" He had another arrow drawn

tight in his bow. He was speaking to Rabbit, but his eyes were trained on the street outside.

"No," Rabbit croaked and winced. The simple action of using his voice hurt his ribs.

"You're hurt," said the doctor. Rabbit's relief chilled at the slurred words. He was holding a cup of wine. Rabbit extended his hand to Bautista, who offered him the wine cup. Rabbit dumped it out.

"I need you sober, brother." Andor bounded into the yard and extended his arms to embrace Rabbit. "Gently," he cautioned.

"I'm glad to see you alive," the soldier said, relief palpable on his face.

"He's been beside himself with worry," Portia added.

"Where have you been? The last thing I saw was when they took you out of the Forum of the Ox. When the fighting started, I tried to find you and . . . your wife!" he said in horror. "Is she . . . ?"

"That's why I came. She's hurt, badly, in the palace district. I couldn't move her. She needs a surgeon."

Everyone looked at the monk. He blanched. "I can't. I'm . . ."

"You're the best hope we have," Rabbit growled.

"I'll get the horses," Andor said and threw off the bolt from the door.

"Careful!" said Rabbit, afraid that his crazed pursuer might be waiting outside like a horror movie slasher. But the man lay dead on the stones.

Andor paused, glancing down at the man. "Did I really shoot Porphyrius the Charioteer?"

"You did. And thank you for it."

Andor shook off his wonder and went after the two horses, neither of which had gone far.

"I'm in no condition to . . ." Bautista was muttering behind him. Portia cut him off this time.

"Pull yourself together. This is what is needed. Get your bag,

Doctor." Her words weren't harsh exactly, but they invited no argument. Rabbit may not like Helias Psellos much, but he must have done something right in raising his niece and nephew. They were cut from the same cloth, honorable and no-nonsense.

Andor returned with the horses. "Do you think you can sit a mount?"

"Nothing's broken, I don't think . . ." Rabbit began.

"I meant him," interrupted the soldier, jabbing his thumb at the monk.

"Uh, I think so."

"You ride in front of me on the white. Antigonus, you take the brown." As Rabbit took the reins from him, Andor's face flashed with childlike excitement. "I can't believe I'm going to ride one of his horses."

They set off for the palace at a smooth canter. Rabbit's suspicions had been confirmed, the rebels had wiped out their opposition from east to west across the city and had last been seen heading for the walls. Those fortresses might offer some resistance, but the walls were intended to defend against outsiders, not insiders. Rabbit didn't hold out much hope for whatever garrison had not been turned to Aaron's side.

Helen lay where he left her. She looked ashen, and her pulse was reedy. Rabbit showed Bautista her wounds. The two superficial injuries were oozing bright blood, but the third, on her abdomen, was dry. Sickeningly, her belly was distended. She was bleeding internally.

"What made this wound?" Bautista pointed at Helen's stomach.

"A piece of metal, small." Rabbit showed him with his index finger and thumb. "It's still in there, I'm sure of it."

"It will have to come out."

"If it doesn't, how long will she live?"

"If it isn't removed, the wound will not heal on its own. Her humors will be unbalanced and . . ."

"How long," snapped Rabbit.

"A day? Three if she's very lucky. Unlucky."

Rabbit still had no idea how far away her decay point was. If it was close enough, he would prefer to leave her to the modern doctors he could take her to on the other side. But if the decay point was too far, she might die on the way. That was all if she ever came to and told him the location.

"What do you want to do?" the surgeon asked.

Rabbit walked in a quick circle, hoping for some new piece of evidence that would make the decision easier. None came.

"Okay. Remove it. Do the surgery." He turned to Andor. "I'm going to need a boat."

"What? Why?"

"I'll explain everything, but I need a boat. I think Helen found one in the royal harbor."

Andor looked horrified. "The royal . . ."

"The emperor is dead along with everyone else in his court, Andor. Get me a boat!"

Andor nodded, steeling himself. "Can you sail?" he asked.

"Only a bit," Rabbit confessed.

Andor grimaced, nodded, and left the room.

The doctor was lightly probing the skin around the entry wound. "Fetch me my supplies, would you?"

Rabbit retrieved his leather bag.

Bautista cut the cloth of her gown, exposing the rest of her stomach. She had a scar below the navel. A horizontal incision, long healed. Rabbit felt ashamed for invading her privacy.

"Open those curtains the rest of the way. You're going to need the light."

"Excuse me?"

Now it was the doctor's turn to look ashamed. "I can't do the surgery myself. I'll have to talk you through it."

Rabbit snarled.

"Do you want this woman to live? Then grit your teeth and follow my instructions! The instruments are in the rolled-up pouch. There's vinegar in that bottle to clean them with."

Rabbit unrolled the pouch. A collection of bronze scalpels and iron saws were neatly arrayed inside.

"That one," he indicated, pointing at a scalpel.

Rabbit swallowed hard. The blade on the thing was long enough to poke halfway through Helen's midsection. He picked it up. At least it was sharp.

"How do I start?" he asked the surgeon.

"Pull the skin taut," he said. "I'll hold this side and the lamp."

The doctor gently pulled the skin on one side of the entry wound while Rabbit pulled the other. Blood oozed sluggishly from the hole.

"Insert the tip of the blade into the wound. Just to the second line."

Rabbit doubled checked the side of the scalpel, seeing the crudely scratched depth guides in the bronze. His stomach twitching in sympathy, he slid the tip of the knife into the raw wound.

Even unconscious, Helen gasped.

"Keeping the same depth, cut down toward her feet, no more than a few fingers." He held up two of his own fingers to indicate the distance.

Rabbit started the cut. The skin parted easily, but the muscle underneath was like cutting thick rubber. The moment he parted it, blood gushed out around the blade, obscuring the incision point.

"I'm going to go too deep . . ." Rabbit protested.

"There was blood trapped inside, it's fine. You see, there are no bubbles, that's good. Now, keep the same angle on the knife. If you tip it, you'll go too shallow and have to cut again. One cut means one cut to heal."

Rabbit steeled himself and pulled on the knife again, rocking it slightly to keep it moving. He was reminded of opening a bag of chips, when someone pulls and pulls and suddenly the entire thing rips open all the way to the bottom. He was terrified the resistance would suddenly release and he would slash her open to the pubic bone.

Helen's arms shook uselessly, and she moaned and cried out as he cut.

After what felt like an hour, Bautista stopped him. "That's enough,"

Rabbit inspected his work. The incision was about two inches long. It bled, but not as freely as Rabbit would have expected.

"Well?" asked the doctor, expectantly.

Rabbit shook his head in confusion.

"Fish it out."

"With what?"

The doctor shook his head in irritation. "With this," he said, grabbing Rabbit's wrist.

Rabbit complied, despite his queasiness. Daintily, he inserted his index finger into her viscera. He expected it to feel like a bag of squishy ropes but, instead, his index finger encountered the underside of something firm. As she breathed, her lungs pushed down on the firm organ, making it rise and fall slightly.

He ran his finger over the surface. After a moment, he felt a small, hard protrusion on the surface. "I feel it!" The piece of shot felt like it was half-embedded. "Sorry," he said to Helen and shoved his thumb in as well. The abdominal muscle flexed, and it felt like his fingers were being squeezed by a powerful hand.

Finally, he got both digits on the bump. He had to dig at it with his fingernails for a moment but, finally, it came free. Rabbit carefully withdrew the thing. It was a small, not-quite-round pellet of iron. He heaved a sigh of relief.

"Well done," the doctor commended him.

"She was bleeding inside; do I need to find where it's coming from?"

"And do what?"

"I don't know, sew it up? Cauterize it? You're the doctor."

"Cauterize?" the surgeon rolled the word around in his mouth. He shook his head. "The blood system is too delicate and small for stitches. If the blood was coming from her liver, it should close on its own. If not . . ." he shrugged.

He fished around in his bag and came up with a small jar full of needles and a spool of thread.

Rabbit reluctantly reached for them. But the doctor smiled. "This much, I can manage."

He watched as the surgeon used a long, curved bone needle to sew her up with silk thread. When he finished, he tied off the knot and sat back on his heels, looking satisfied.

"Will she live?" Rabbit asked.

The doctor shrugged. "You did your part well. Now it's her turn. Tomorrow is in God's hands."

The monk left by foot, preferring to risk the dangers of the city than the likelihood of falling off the horse. Every few minutes, Rabbit sprinkled Helen's lips with a little watered wine, which, thankfully, she didn't appear to cough back up. Once, she rose from unconsciousness, murmured that word again, "Kalonymos," and sank back under.

Andor returned shortly after that. Between the two of them, they fashioned a makeshift stretcher for Helen and carried her to the little harbor attached to the emperor's mansion nearby. A sleek little sailboat waited for them.

"Where's the captain?" Rabbit asked.

He tapped himself on the chest.

"Can you sail it?"

"I was raised on a peninsula," he replied, as though it should be obvious.

Rabbit had a sudden but powerful contextual realization. A young man, raised Catholic, raised in privilege, who sailed as a hobby and felt drawn to serve his community through military service. Andor was Constantinople's equivalent of a Kennedy. In that light, Rabbit could almost envision him wearing a polo sweater. He laughed.

"What's funny?"

"I don't know what I'd do without you, Andor Psellos."

He grinned, proudly. "Let's get her in the boat."

As gently as they could, they lowered the stretcher onto the floor of the craft and pushed away from the dock. "Where are we headed?" Andor asked, readying the sail.

"I don't know," Rabbit admitted.

"What do you mean," Andor asked. "I thought you had some safe haven to go to."

"Does the word 'Kalonymos' mean anything to you?"

He nodded. "It's an island, almost due south across the Propontis." Andor was guiding the little boat through the serpentine breakwater expertly.

"Kalonymos . . . Kalonymos . . . Oh, shit," he realized with a sinking feeling. "Imrali. I know it as Imrali. That's where we're heading." In modern day, Imrali was the island site of a Turkish prison. It was forbidden to even sail near it let alone land on it. How did she have a decay point there?

"It's a quaint little island. Do you have a home in the fishing village?"

The boat exited the harbor and skimmed across the water, its sails full. Rabbit considered the young man. The timeline had already splintered. This Andor Psellos would have no more role in Rabbit's history than he ever had. He could tell him anything, and it would have no bearing on his own timeline. Lord knows this one had gotten pretty weird already, and Rabbit was tired of lying.

"I'm going to explain some things to you, Andor. It may sound like the inventions of a madman, but I guarantee you everything I tell you is true."

And so, Rabbit talked. He told him about time travel, about what he did for a living, and why he had come to 535. He told him about Helen and Aaron and how the rebels had been so miraculously armed. He told him about decay points, how he had missed his own and how he intended to get Helen back to hers. He told him about Aaron's plan for Rabbit, how he had lured him back to the past to trap him here to carry on his ambitious, insane plan. Rabbit talked for hours, while Andor guided them across the blue-black waters of the Propontis, which would one day be called the Marmara Sea.

"I suppose you think I've lost my mind," Rabbit concluded from Andor's prolonged silence. He was giving Helen watered wine again, her head resting on his lap.

Andor gazed straight ahead. He didn't speak for a moment and, when he did, his answer surprised Rabbit. "Why did you tell me all this?"

"What?"

"Why not do as Aaron asked you? He upset the world order. Without someone knowledgeable to guide it, our world may descend into chaos."

"Why do you think I told you all of this, Andor?"

The young man glanced at him in confusion.

"I can't do it alone. I don't want to do it alone. I'm going to need a partner."

Andor said nothing.

"You're a man of duty, honor, compassion, and virtue. I can't imagine anyone I'd want more to create a new world with. We'll need to work on your religious tolerance. Once we sort that out, I think you'll make a very fine leader."

Andor stared at the sea, too stunned to speak.

Kalonymos island came into view under the light of a bright moon hours later. They had been sailing for almost a full day. Rabbit had tried to impress upon Andor everything he could teach. He talked about equality, democracy, justice, and fairness. He also talked about the concepts of modern warfare and as much of Dale Carnegie's *How to Win Friends and Influence People* as he could pull from memory. By the time the boat was close enough to the island where they had to make a decision, he was exhausted and hoarse.

"Where do we land?" Andor asked.

Rabbit squeezed Helen's hand gently. "Helen?"

A slightly more forceful exhale was the only response.

"Helen, we're at Imrali island. I need you to show us where to land."

Blearily, her eyes fluttered open.

"Knew you needed me," her speech was sluggish and slurred.

"Where do we land, Helen?"

"Beach, northwest," she said and then drifted out of consciousness again.

Andor took the boat around the headland and was greeted by what looked like a mile-long, sandy beach just around the point. Inwardly, Rabbit groaned. That was still a lot of land to search.

Minutes later, the boat nosed up on the shore with a sandy hiss. Andor jumped out and pulled it a little farther up.

"She'll have left a sign, some kind of marker so that she can find it again." Rabbit hopped out of the boat and immediately fell to his knees. His legs were wobbly from hours of sitting in the boat.

Together, he and Andor searched the beach. Once they found her markers, they were both embarrassed that it had taken as long as it did. She had planted a trail of stones the size of bowling balls from the sand back into the fringe of scrub brush that lined the beach. At the end of it, she had assembled a ring of stones and built a fire within it. The fire pit was burned bare in exactly the size of a time dilation pad. *Clever woman*, he thought, with a little hitch in his chest.

Rabbit and Andor retrieved Helen from the boat and carried her on the stretcher to the decay point. They placed her inside the fire ring and Rabbit sat down beside her.

Andor perched on a fallen tree nearby. "When will it happen?"

"I don't know. Soon, I hope. Our water ran out hours ago."

Andor stood up. "I saw a little stream on the beach down that way. I'll fill the wineskin."

Rabbit watched him turn and opened his mouth to say thank you. Before the word came out, the beach blinked out of existence, and he was standing in a small, dark room.

Then the shouting started.

Five people stood around the portable dilator, not too different from the one Rabbit had used to jump. Two technicians, a man and a woman, sat behind the control panel gawking. The leader, a stylishly dressed woman wearing glasses, stood behind two guards, both men, dressed in black fatigues. They looked like they came straight from bad-guy central casting. Everyone was talking in what sounded like a Slavic language to Rabbit. The two mercs were jabbing evil-looking submachine guns at him and barking orders he couldn't understand. Oh, and of course Rabbit and Helen were naked.

Suddenly living as a rich world leader in the sixth century didn't sound like such a bad idea.

Based on the gestures from the machine guns, the guards wanted him to get up. He complied and was rewarded by being shoved against the wall.

The woman who appeared to be in charge looked him up and down curiously, as though he was an object in a museum. The mercs flanked her, fingers itchy on their triggers.

"Well, that's not supposed to happen. How did you get here?" She spoke in American-accented English. But it was an idle musing to herself, not communication to him.

"She needs a doctor."

The woman said something to the mercs, who grappled him to

the floor. Something struck him on the back of the head and he knew no more.

Rabbit awoke. His head ached. His back hurt. Every cut and scrape on his body sang a chorus of pain as he shifted. The smell of car exhaust, sewage, and unwashed bodies hung in the air.

He opened his eyes. A dirty, bearded face stared back at him.

There was warm air blowing on him. He sat up and took in his surroundings. He was in a dingy little park, nestled in among several other people atop a broad, grated duct venting warm air from the subway system below. At least he wasn't naked anymore. He was wearing black fatigue pants, presumably belonging to one of the mercs in the dilator. Rabbit wondered how that conversation had gone.

The man who had been facing Rabbit shooed him away. He dazedly rose, and his place was instantly taken by another poor soul trying to get warm.

It took him two hours, several blank stares, a few shoves, and a lot of repulsed swearing from the locals to learn that he was in Bursa, a city on the mainland, south of Imrali. Persistent inquiries of everyone he met eventually turned up an American tourist who, after much coercion, allowed him to use their phone.

It rang twice before a sweetly familiar voice answered, sounding tired and tense. "Good afternoon, this is Patty-Jo West. To whom am I speaking?"

"Hi PJ." The relief at hearing her voice was so profound a lump rose in his throat. "It's Rabbit."

WASHINGTON, DC

2018 CE

Thirty-six hours later, Rabbit walked out of Dulles Airport international arrivals and into PJ's perfumed embrace. She was so much shorter than him that her arms effectively pinned his elbows to his sides, and he could see over her head. When she released him at last, her first words seemed incongruous.

"GodDAMMIT, Rabbit Ward. You had us about scared to death."

"Wasn't my intention . . ."

"We don't have much time, so listen to me. The Feds are going to pick you up any minute and they'll want to know everything. You just tell them you had no choice but to go to that woman's decay point."

"I didn't have a . . ."

"And you had no idea you'd come through on Turkish soil."

"Technically, I had no . . ."

"And that woman was responsible for everything."

He put up a hand to stop her. "'That woman' saved my life. I'm not going to throw her under the bus to make myself look better."

She pulled him out of the flow of people closer to an unoccupied corner. "They took Ian into custody yesterday."

"What? Why?" Rabbit stammered.

"I couldn't tell you on the phone. I don't know why, but they frog-marched the poor man right out of the office. He was terrified, poor thing. You know how nervous he gets around authority figures. He couldn't stop talking."

Rabbit's mind was swimming. Ian? PJ jabbed him in the stomach.

"You don't understand how serious this has gotten. You say what you need to say. Believe you me, you don't owe that woman one damn thing."

Rabbit saw two men in unfashionable suits walking toward them, scanning the crowd. One had a photograph in his hand.

"Here they come."

PJ took his hand and squeezed it. "You have no idea what it was like when your jump decayed, and you didn't come through. I thought I'd lost you." There were tears in her eyes now. "Please just play along and don't give them anything to be suspicious of, doll. Can you do that? For a friend?"

The suits had ID'd him and walked over quickly.

"Dr. Robert Ward?" one of them asked.

To PJ he said, "I'll try."

"You willingly returned to a rendezvous point on an island . . ."

"Decay point." Rabbit corrected softly.

"What?"

"It's called a decay point."

The agent scowled at him. "You willingly went to the prison island Imrali Adasi."

"Yes."

They were sitting opposite each other in a featureless grey cube of a room. It looked like every interrogation room Rabbit had ever seen in a movie, which gave him the peculiar sensation that the world he had returned to felt less real than the one he had left, like a film imitating reality. He predicted that the bad cop, a clean-cut man in his thirties, would slam his palm down on the table next. Mercifully, he just leaned forward sharply to emphasize his words.

"That is a restricted area. If I told the Turkish police you were there without authorization, they would demand we turn you over to them. Do you realize that? What's so funny?"

Rabbit had tried to contain it, but the agent had spotted his smirk. "I guess I'm just a little surprised why you're not more interested in who gave a competing time traveler permission to jump from there. I told you before, I couldn't make it back to my own team. I didn't even think I was going to make the jump at all."

Bad Cop glared at him for a moment, then abruptly shifted topics. "When did you tell the lead technician, Ian March, about the planned mission?"

"I didn't. That's not my job. PJ told him when we arrived in Greece when she told the rest of the team."

"But you knew about it."

"I secured funding for it."

"So, you knew."

"Yes," Rabbit said patiently. "I knew."

"How long have you known Mr. March?"

"Eleven years. Since he joined the team."

"Did you know he was selling information to hostile parties about your missions?"

"Have you stopped beating your wife yet?"

"Excuse me?!" said the agent, rising half out of his seat.

Rabbit stared back. "It's a loaded question. I don't believe Ian did or would sell us out." Why was it that Rabbit could effortlessly maintain character in the past but was too damn proud to do so in the present?

The other agent put his hand on Bad Cop's shoulder. The man blinked and sat back down.

Good Cop took over. "Here's the thing, Dr. Ward. We don't think you did anything wrong. We're just having a hard time understanding how the sequence of events played out the way it did. Help me understand how this team learned about where you'd be."

The questioning went on for hours. The agents asked variations of the same questions over and over, trying to trip him up. Rabbit was exhausted from the jump and the plane flights after it, but he did his best to keep his cool and stick to the facts he knew. In the end, they sent him home.

"Suspended until further notice," PJ said, grimly.

"Saw that coming," he replied, staring into a gin and tonic.

"This isn't about you. Not really." She was similarly swirling a Manhattan, sitting on his couch.

"I'm still grounded though."

"They're convinced Ian was selling us out to a foreign power."

"Do you believe that?" he demanded.

She sighed and sat back further into the couch. "Oh, I don't know what to believe, honey. Everybody has their secrets. I shouldn't be surprised if Ian has some, too."

"He was my friend for eleven years."

"I know."

"You didn't even tell him about the location."

"I know."

Rabbit took a swig of his cocktail. "She's not working with a foreign power." Rabbit didn't know why, but he had not spoken her name to anyone since his return. It felt like a betrayal of her trust. Although why he should give a damn about that he couldn't say.

"What do you mean?" she asked, sitting up straighter.

He described the scene he had stepped into when Helen's jump decayed. "It had all the hallmarks of a criminal operation."

"Did you tell that to the Feds?"

He shook his head.

"Well, honey, maybe you should. They don't give a damn about the artifacts; they think they're on the verge of an international incident."

He shrugged and took another swig.

PJ's eyes widened. "Are you protecting that woman?"

"What? No!" he insisted.

"She's nearly ruined you."

"I'm not," he said with finality. "What's the plan for the retrieval operation?"

"The consulate is negotiating the permits with the mayor of Istanbul. It'll take some time, but we'll get it."

Rabbit snorted. "If they don't get it first."

Three weeks passed. The Turkish authorities permitted them to excavate under the floor of the Basilica Cistern, but they wanted to wait for the right time to close the facility to tourists. Rabbit had chosen the spot specifically because it was so public; the exposure should make it harder for Helen's people to get to it.

Although he was suspended from performing missions with the Institute, so much of Rabbit's work was about the acquisition of knowledge and skill that he should have been able to keep busy. A stack of books sat on his dining room table. They gathered dust.

The problem was not a lack of things to occupy his time. A dozen scientists had called and emailed once the rumor trickled out that Rabbit had successfully made a return jump from a different dilator. It opened up so many questions and potential for new possibilities. He wasn't sure what he could offer to any of them. He happened to be on the decay point; it worked. What else was there to say, really? He had no doubt this would have significant impacts on time travel theory, but he was equally sure they could do it without him. He ignored the requests.

He was restless. He flitted from one thing to the next, never accomplishing anything. When he sat down to study a book or a map, he found that he needed a drink. When he was getting the drink, he would notice a fly that needed swatting, etc. In three weeks, he accomplished nothing and was crawling the walls.

Updates about Ian were few and far between. He would be tried for espionage. Or maybe it was terrorism. Rabbit wasn't questioned again after the initial grilling, so he had no insight into the process. He still couldn't believe that his friend would knowingly sell secrets to anyone. If he was found responsible for selling out the team, it would ruin him professionally. It might even get him a minor criminal sentence, although Rabbit wasn't sure what law he had broken, exactly. On the other hand, tipping off the Turks to the presence of a portable thermonuclear device on their soil could bury him for the rest of his life in the kind of prison where they don't have visiting hours. No matter how much Rabbit might want an answer to the riddle, he just couldn't believe it was Ian.

Then of course there was Helen. She could potentially exonerate Ian and Rabbit both, but she hadn't come forward. That meant one of two things. One, she didn't give a damn. That stung. Two, she had died of the wounds she sustained in Constantinople. And, as much as he didn't want to admit it, that hurt worse. He was thinking about her when his phone rang.

"The dig team found the menorah," PJ said on the other end of the line.

That's it then, he thought. He should have been elated by the news. The treasure that had eluded him for all these years was finally his. Instead, his stomach was sinking. If she was alive, she would have stolen it. Wouldn't she?

PJ was still talking. "It's a fake."

Her words dropped on him like a bomb. "What?"

"The menorah is supposed to be solid gold, what we uncovered was gold-plated lead. It's old, all right, but it's not the real thing."

Rabbit's mind was racing. "Are you sure?"

"They've already run it through a battery of scans."

"No, I mean . . . it's possible the original texts may be wrong. The real piece might have been lead all along, just made grander in the descriptions . . ."

"There's more." She sounded hesitant.

"Okay . . ."

"You're not going to like this."

"Just . . . what is it, PJ?"

"The scans turned up an inscription in the lead. It's under the gold, completely hidden on the surface. It reads, 'We could have made history, Rabbit.' The inscription is in English."

Although he didn't remember sitting down, Rabbit found himself in a chair. Goddamn Aaron had delivered the last shot after all. In a flash, several puzzle pieces fell into place. The Bedouins who got tangled up in the procession weren't trying to steal the menorah. They were planting the fake among the spoils for Aaron. Rabbit had even helped them do it. The fake manifest had been used to lure Rabbit back; what a gamble that was. Meanwhile, the real manifest omitted the menorah, just in case it was ever discovered. Like everything else, it had been bait for Rabbit, to bring him back and to occupy him until he could be caught and convinced to stay. Aaron had even killed the mummy maker and the clerk to ensure Rabbit wouldn't clue into the plan. But Aaron had known Rabbit might get away, so he had left him a goodbye note. The old bastard knew his contingency planning.

"This doesn't look good."

"Of course, it's not good. Aaron ginned up this whole mission just to trap me. He didn't even have the real menorah."

"That's not what I mean. The FBI showed up at the secretary's office an hour ago."

"The . . . I thought the CIA was after this for the Turkish connection. What is the FBI . . ."

"I don't pretend to know what is going on between them. Maybe the FBI wants a piece of the case, maybe the CIA's case isn't coming together, I don't know. All I know is they are very interested in the fake menorah. They seem to think you were working with the stringer, that she double-crossed you and took the real menorah."

The same thought had occurred to Rabbit, but he didn't say so.

"Rabbit . . ." she continued.

"Hmm?"

She asked the next delicately. "You weren't working with her, were you? Because if you were, and I'm not saying you are, you could help the investigation."

He couldn't believe what he was hearing. Even PJ had lost faith in him now. Rabbit emitted a dry laugh of disbelief.

His doorbell rang.

"Don't get defensive. I'm only saying . . ."

He hung up on her and silenced his phone.

He crossed to the front window and peered through the tiniest opening in the window shade. There were two Feds on the doorstep. One he recognized. She had come to speak to Rabbit to set up the drop in Greece. Cook, he wanted to say. The partner was a new face.

Rabbit backed away from the window.

That inscription in the lead spelled more trouble for Rabbit than even Aaron could have predicted. What were they more likely to believe, that his hundred-year-old mentee had baited him back to the past with a fake menorah, or that he had partnered up with Helen and she had robbed him the same way she had twice already? He could be charged as an accomplice in the theft of a priceless artifact.

He didn't see any way this could go well. He needed time to think. To plan. He needed . . . he needed Helen. *If she's alive, she is the one who can set the record straight about me, about Ian, about all of this.*

While the FBI stood knocking on the front door with increasing intensity, Rabbit grabbed what he needed and slipped out the back door into the alley.

At the moment, Rabbit was simply hard to find. As soon as the Feds realized he was actively avoiding them, however, he would be a fugitive. It was safer to act as though he was already. Most modern conveniences were thinly disguised tracking devices, so they'd have to be discarded. He had left his cell phone at home where it wouldn't betray him. Happily, his emergency bag, a lightweight backpack small enough not to make him stand out, contained enough cash to sustain him for a few weeks.

Walking at a quick but measured pace away from his apartment, Rabbit shouldered his bag, his mental wheels turning.

Rideshares were just as traceable as a phone. Rabbit would stick to the Metro, or a yellow cab paid for with cash if he had to go somewhere that was an impractical walk. He didn't think he'd need it, but he also kept an unregistered motorcycle in a garage rented with cash a few blocks from his apartment. You couldn't do the kind of work Rabbit did and not have it affect the way you think. Call it paranoia if you want. Yesterday's "paranoid" is today's "prepared."

How could he find Helen? He didn't know her number, where she lived, or even her real name. *Start with how we connected*, he thought. She had learned about the rabbit mummy, which meant she might have spoken to the British archaeologist who had been working with it. He'd be the first stop.

A few minutes later, Rabbit walked into the sleek lobby of the Dupont Circle Hotel. He ignored everyone around him, trying to look like any other patron of the hotel as he walked past the tinkling wall fountain. It was over-air-conditioned, and the sweat on his skin chilled with an uncomfortable prickle. That was all right; he wasn't here for comfort. Among its many no-doubt impressive charms, the hotel also had a practical feature Rabbit had noted long ago—some of the last pay phones in America.

He beelined for the little bank of them and lifted a receiver.

A few moments later, the phone was emitting the distinctively foreign tone of the British phone system.

"This is Dr. Agrawal," the voice on the other end answered.

"Dr. Agrawal. This is Rabbit Ward, from America."

"Dr. Ward! What an unexpected pleasure. Is there any chance I could ring you back in the morning? I have a guest and . . ."

"This won't take long. Right around the time I visited you, was there anyone else asking about the mummy you were working with? A woman, perhaps?"

"Yes, as a matter of fact. From the Italian Archaeology Foundation."

"Do you remember what she looked like?" asked Rabbit.

"We never met in person, I'm afraid."

"Any chance you'd have her number?"

"Mm-no, she called the main office line, I think, and didn't leave it. Sorry to cut you short . . ."

"I understand. One more thing though. If she calls you again, would you tell her I'd like to talk to her?"

"Certainly. Good night, Dr. Ward."

Rabbit hung up. Dead end. Helen wouldn't call him again under the circumstances. Not wanting to linger anywhere too long, he left the hotel.

The Feds were convinced Ian was the leak. But Rabbit was sure he knew him better than that. Ian didn't live an overly extravagant lifestyle. He didn't drink more than average or do drugs as far as Rabbit knew, so it was unlikely that someone had used those levers to pressure him. His only major weakness was his big, dopey, romantic heart.

"Tourist," someone on the sidewalk mumbled under his breath as he weaved around Rabbit. He had stopped still as the thought had hit him. Ian's weakness. His romanticism. He might not sell information. He might not be blackmailed into giving up information. But might he talk too freely with someone he trusted? Someone like his boyfriend, Devon, perhaps? When did Devon come on the scene? It was more than a year; Ian had made a big deal about their anniversary and was disappointed because Devon had begged out of the date for work.

Ian's beau worked for a marketing firm in Georgetown, one of those small ones people annoyingly insisted on calling "boutique."

He checked his watch. Plenty of time to get across the river before quitting time. Rabbit picked up his pace.

"Hi, Devon," Rabbit said. He was leaning against Devon's car, a red hatchback, cancerous with rust.

The young man stopped in his tracks and glanced behind him. Seeing that he was alone, he assumed a terrible imitation of nonchalance. "Hi," he squeaked back, looking like a man who might bolt at any second. He cleared his throat. "What are you doing here?"

"I thought we should have a talk."

"That sounds great, only I have a lot on my plate tonight, so . . ."

"Clear your plate."

Devon's forced smile faltered.

"Let's go for a walk," Rabbit said. His tone made it clear that it wasn't a request.

Devon was in his mid-twenties, good-looking, and styled like a country-club kid. The disparity between his designer clothes and decaying car marked him as a guy with champagne taste on a beer budget. Now here was someone primed for bribery.

Rabbit led him away from the building where the little marketing business operated above an art gallery, in the direction of the river walk.

He let the silence hang between them for an uncomfortably long time. Devon's discomfort was palpable. When it seemed like Devon might run away to avoid another moment of it, Rabbit broke the ice. "Seen Ian lately?"

"You know I haven't. He's in some sort of trouble. Because of you," he added.

"What do you think that's about?"

"I have no idea. Ian and I don't talk about business."

"Of course you do. I mean, you're probably subtle about it. Encourage him not to bottle up his stress, that sort of thing, right? I'm sure you don't ask directly. Still, Ian loves to talk, and I bet you're a good listener."

"I don't know what you want from me. I've already spoken to the FBI, you know," he said.

The mention of the Feds made Rabbit twitchy. He scanned the passing tourists and professionals strolling on the river walk. Everyone who made eye contact with him was starting to look like an undercover agent. *Get a grip on yourself*, he thought.

"I want you to spill your guts to the Feds, tell them it was you who cajoled information out of Ian and sold it to criminals. I want you to be an adult, take responsibility for your actions, and exonerate my friend. Barring that, however, I'll accept this. Tell whoever it is that pays you I want to talk to them. Tell them I'll be waiting at the Lincoln Memorial tonight at nine."

"Whatever. Can I go now?" he said.

"Sure."

Devon turned around and headed back toward the parking lot. Rabbit called after him, "Hey, Devon?"

The young man turned without a word.

"When Ian is cleared, end it nicely."

Devon flashed his middle finger as he stalked off.

The classical stone edifice of the Lincoln memorial was lit up brightly, standing out against the twilight-blue sky. For half an hour before the meeting time, Rabbit sat between a few of the large, sculpted bushes that lay to the north of the building, watching. Tourists strolled in and out. An art student sat on the steps across the plaza, sketching the façade.

He didn't see anyone staking the place out, neither Helen's people nor the FBI. In all honesty, he didn't know who made him more nervous. Still, he had set this in motion. When the hour rolled around, he rose from the bushes and walked up across the front of the building and up the steps. No one immediately rushed him, and his heart began to settle down.

Rabbit felt a kinship with these buildings that were not comfortably at home in any era but loosely rooted in several. They were, to him, far more interesting and familiar than the monuments that reflected the aesthetic of his own age. These white stone columns reflected a national aspiration for democracy and justice. The fact that the ancients of Greece or Rome had been just as flawed, partisan, and bickering as the current government didn't detract from the noble goal.

He took in a deep breath, looking up at the seated bronze statue of the sixteenth president. "That hubris to eclipse the past keeps us locked in it," Rabbit said under his breath.

There was a sniff of laughter behind him and suddenly everything was all right. He felt his body relax in a way it hadn't since he had returned from Constantinople. The moment he had heard the laugh, he had also picked up her distinctive scent. Helen had lived. She had answered his call. "You're not an easy woman to get ahold of," he said as he turned.

It wasn't Helen.

Instead, the woman from her crew stood before him, the leader who wore glasses. Today she was dressed in blue jeans and a T-shirt, her hair under a baseball cap. Shit, she was the "art student." She'd been waiting for him.

"That's the whole point, isn't it?" she said. To Rabbit's blank stare, she reflected his statement. "Hard to get ahold of."

"What do you want?" he said. He couldn't help it. The disappointment when he had realized who it was had overwhelmed whatever manners he possessed.

"I thought it was the other way around, Dr. Ward. It seems to me you're the one who wants something again. Whatever could it be?"

He desperately wanted to demand that she take him to Helen, but his instincts told him to keep that to himself. He didn't want to give her the satisfaction of seeing how worried he was, but it was more than that. There was something about her that told Rabbit that she was one of those people who naturally cataloged the needs and fears of others to be used as carrots and sticks. His feelings for Helen were . . . complicated. But he sure as hell wasn't going to trust this woman with even a fraction of his worry. Instead, he shifted gears to safer territory.

"The menorah is a fake."

"The what?"

"Relax, I'm not wearing a wire. Is it your fake?"

"What do you think?" she smiled slyly.

He made a "wrong answer" buzzer sound. "Nice try. You don't know any details about it, do you? You couldn't have planted it. Right burial date, wrong object." To his satisfaction, he picked up a slight drop in her self-satisfied smirk. "That makes things easier. You asked me what I want. Here it is. Go to the Feds, tell them Ian March isn't working for the Turkish government. Also tell them that you don't have the real menorah, either."

Her self-assurance settled back on her like armor. "Who is Ian March?"

"Your source on the inside of my organization. I'm not asking you to confirm that, I know it. You guys played him well, but now it's over."

"Explain that to me," she said with mock innocence.

"He's burned now either way. If you don't help him, he'll either go to trial or be held indefinitely. If you come forward, it could clear his name, but he'd never work for the Institute again. As a source, he's spent." Rabbit tried to keep his cool as he described it. She was staring at him with cool detachment as he talked about her organization ruining his friend's life.

"That's a sad story, but I don't see what it has to do with me."

"Sure you do, you just don't care. What is he to you after all? That's why I'm prepared to make it worth your while."

He obviously had her interest, although she said nothing.

"There's no good evidence for the Turkish connection or the FBI wouldn't have bothered trying to pin the menorah 'theft' on him. It's thin, but it's all they've got. And with the right judge, they might make it stick. So, here's what I'm proposing."

He let that hang between them for a moment.

"I go get the real one. With your help."

She snorted laughter. Her hand fluttered to her face as if she could pull it back in. "Are you serious?"

"The real menorah never made it to Constantinople. Most likely, it never even made it to Carthage. The deposed king of the Vandals was surprised to hear they even had it. I'm just assuming here you know something about the business you're in and you're not just a petty little middle manager."

"I know the leading hypotheses," she said coldly. *Thank you,* thought Rabbit. *Now I know just a little more about you.*

"Then you know that if it never arrived in Carthage, it never left Rome with the Vandals. And if I know where it got lost, I can get it."

She shook her head. "I know *your* history, too. You've already been there. The law ..."

"Since when do you concern yourself with the law?"

"The capital *L* law. The physical law that says you can't return to a time you have already visited."

"I can't co-term the same moment. Which means you'd have to land me right after I left."

"It's not that precise. A few days here or there . . ."

"If you get it wrong, and drop me in the same time as my previous jump, who knows, maybe I cease to exist."

"Precisely," she said.

"One, it's a hypothesis that's never been proven. Two," he said grimly, "what the hell do you care whether I die or not?"

She stared at him for a long beat.

"You're wondering how I'm trying to play you. Let me break down how this goes. Scenario A, I go back, get the menorah, it saves my friend's life. Scenario B, you screw up my jump and kill me."

"Scenario C," she said, "you somehow falsely accuse me and my people of some kind of criminal action and divert attention from your friend."

"If you can figure out how that plan works, let me know. Believe me," he grinned evilly, "it would be my absolute pleasure. Unfortunately, I can't riddle it out, myself."

She considered him for a long moment.

"I'll have to make a call."

WASHINGTON, DC

2018 CE

The events of the next few days went by quickly.

Within half an hour, she had obliquely agreed to his request. A nondescript but comfortable car picked up Rabbit and the woman from the Memorial. The driver didn't say a word the entire trip, and she didn't instruct him.

They were dropped at an airport hotel an hour later, and she guided him to a room. On the bed was a change of clothes, a new wallet, and a passport that contained his photo under the name "Kent Meloy."

"How is this here already?"

"You said you wanted in."

He flipped through the passport, which contained multiple stamps. It was subtly curved, its corners soft and feathery as though it had been riding in his pocket for years. The creepiest part was, he didn't recognize the picture of himself on the lead page.

From the hotel, they drove to Baltimore/Washington International and were on a private plane in less than half an hour. Rabbit had never flown private. Security was less rigorous and much faster than flying commercial. No one batted an eye at his new passport.

Ten hours later, they were navigating the streets of Rome in another private car.

Throughout the day's travel, the woman said only what was needed to expedite their travel. Observing the smooth operation, Rabbit was no longer surprised by how Helen always beat him to the punch. Compared to official channels, this team was a frictionless machine of efficiency.

They arrived at a house in the middle of the night where a silent, grandmotherly type led him to a bedroom with its own attached half bath. He didn't think he'd be able to sleep under the circumstances and was surprised when he was awakened by a knock on the door the next morning. He opened it and discovered a little basket with coffee, pastries, and fresh fruit. Next to it lay a soft package wrapped in plastic.

As he tried to clear the cobwebs from his head, he drank the scalding espresso as quickly as he could manage. The package he unwrapped on the bed. Inside was a tunic with a double set of wide maroon stripes down the front, a heavy leather belt, and a pair of solid-looking sandals. This was the first area where the museum did better work. The costume pieces were amateurish compared to what he was used to. The fabric was too evenly woven, the stitching was clearly done with a machine and all they had done to wear it in was wash it in a little weak tea. As he donned the garments, he warmed himself in this brief moment of superiority, even though he knew it was primarily defensive. The machinelike speed of the criminal enterprise was humbling. He wondered what it must be like to operate like this all the time. No regulations, no months of preparation or desperate fundraising.

A second knock got him to his feet. This time there was a mercenary at the door. It was the man he remembered from Imrali, the one who had brained him. He was holding the offending submachine gun loosely in his hands and gesturing for Rabbit to follow.

He followed the man downstairs through the seemingly empty inn, through the kitchen, and out a small door into a malodorous alley lined with dumpsters. A faded food delivery van stood idling in the mouth of the alley, shielding the armed man and Rabbit from the sidewalk. It was painted with the red, white, and green branding of a company called "Consegna Puntuale." *On-time delivery*. Cute. The weather was already warm and humid, even though the sun hadn't quite risen.

The back of the truck rolled up as they approached, revealing the incongruous, high-tech interior. Around the dilator components idled another armed guard, the technicians who were already seated at their control bays, and the woman with the glasses. At the insistence of the armed man, Rabbit clambered up into the truck. The guard followed and rolled the door shut.

Everyone took seats, and the van lurched into motion, bumping and weaving over the rough streets at an alarming speed. *Drives like an Italian*, Rabbit thought.

He took in his surroundings more carefully.

Both guards sat opposite him, guns held loosely on their laps, their eyes fixed firmly on his chest. That's how they were positioned when he and Helen had come through last time. Noted. The techs had eyes only for their equipment. The woman in glasses sat closest to him. Maybe his senses were heightened by the approaching jump, but he looked at her clearly for the first time. Her dark blond hair was clipped short in the back but fell across her forehead in front. She had a strong jaw and cheekbones and big brown eyes behind the large, wire-rimmed glasses. She had replaced the casual artist costume with clothes that were stylish, comfortable, and monochromatic. The woman had the sleek, predatory appearance of a lobbyist.

During the whole trip from America, Rabbit had held out hope that Helen would appear to make the return trip with him. He was eager to get back to the past with her where they could speak freely. Through much of the plane flight, he had imagined what he would say to her. But she wasn't in the van, nor had the woman mentioned her. He had a sick feeling in his stomach about her but refused to give the lobbyist any leverage by showing her what he was thinking.

As if she was reading his mind, she smiled at him knowingly.

After a surprisingly short drive, the delivery van stopped. The interior lights of the cabin warmed, and the whole team sprang into motion. They must be at their destination.

"How long is the jump? The usual twenty days?" He had read an explanation as to why twenty days was the outside limit for a jump years ago, but the science had eluded him.

"You have six hours," she said.

Rabbit's jaw dropped. "I won't even be able to reach the city in that time. I don't know where you're dropping me . . ."

"It's a short commute," the woman said tersely. "How long?" she asked the techs.

"Twenty seconds," they stumbled over each other in answer.

"You'd better get in character," she said to Rabbit. Her tone of voice said everything. She didn't like the plan. She wanted him to fail.

Rabbit had no time to process what was going on. He could hear the telltale sound of the dilator warming up. He stepped onto the plate, still staring at the smug leader of this unsavory group.

"Five seconds."

She pointed past Rabbit and he followed her gaze. One of the armed guards was holding out a short sword in a scabbard. He reached out and took it by the hilt.

"Jump."

ROME

455 CE

The van was gone. Rabbit was standing on a paved street in the shade. Before him, a long stone span stretched out across a river, narrowing as it receded like a perspective drawing. The Mausoleum of Hadrian was at his back. That meant he was near the heart of Rome, staring across the Aelian Bridge. A few tendrils of black smoke rose over the ancient city. His stomach lurched. The smell of Rome, the long stone bridge, the sound of the Tiber. In an instant, they brought everything rushing back. This was where he had failed Aaron. Twenty years in his past, and now here it was, perfectly preserved. Waiting for him.

Rabbit took a deep breath and let it out shakily. He thought he might throw up.

Most people's terrible memories fade over time. Some people kept them alive by methodically revisiting them. Rabbit was one of those. Now, though, stepping back through history into the site of his shameful deeds, he realized that even the most painstakingly preserved memories were not the same as the real thing. They amplified certain aspects, while others were expunged. In Rabbit's case, he had been telling himself the story of his own guilt and shame for so long that he had actually made it worse. Looking now at the bridge where it had happened brought it back in clearer detail.

Helen had been right when she said he'd had no chance of saving Aaron that day. Nothing he could have done would have saved his partner. Rabbit would have died or been enslaved with him.

Although he could hear the sounds of voices in the distance, no one was in sight. Good thing, too. Those flagrant sons of bitches had stopped in the road with their blinkers on to execute the jump. Speaking of which . . . Rabbit slid his short sword out of its scabbard and hastily dug its point into the gap between the paving stones beneath his feet. With effort, he chiseled one up and removed it from the road. To be sure, he carried it to the edge of the river and tossed it over the side of the bridge. It landed with a splash. The decay point was now perfectly obvious from a dozen yards away.

He glanced at the sword Helen's people had provided him. Steel, too shiny to be accurate Noric steel. Not to mention the fact that gladii were decades out of fashion by 455 CE. Again, sloppy with the details. Still, it was sharp and pointy. That would do for now.

The first order of business was to figure out when he was. The smoke was a decent sign that the sack of the city was still in progress. It was reported to have lasted fourteen days. He hoped like hell he had arrived after his previous trip was over. The risks of overlapping oneself in time were the source of much debate, but he didn't want to become empirical evidence.

Aaron and he had tried to escape over this bridge as the Vandals were pouring into the city. What little evidence he had suggested that the sack was well underway. The sounds he heard from across the city were those of orderly pillaging, not the cacophony of an invading force. The citizenry was already terrified, and now the Vandals had turned their attention to the reason they had come in the first place: plunder. Rabbit decided it was safe to cross the bridge.

A fat raindrop landed on his face. More of them were beginning to darken the bridge stones. Ominous clouds were massed in the eastern sky.

The historical record of the Vandal attack was light on detail.

Rabbit didn't know what route they used to return to Carthage but assumed they must have docked their oceangoing vessels in Portus, near Ostia, where the Tiber met the sea. It was said the port could dock 350 ships. The logical thing to do would be to ferry the loot they were plundering from the city down the Tiber, which would put the center of activity at the Navalia, the shipyards just north of Agrippa's Bridge. The Navalia was no more than a half mile away.

He was about to set off when he remembered that he was holding a sword. If he ran into any pillaging Vandals, they might take him for an enemy combatant and cut him down. Dammit, why hadn't those idiots asked him what clothes he needed? A Vandal tunic and trousers would have helped him blend in. The sleeves of his Roman shirt were too short to hide the blade. He settled on strapping it to his thigh under his tunic, where most of it would be hidden.

Rabbit jogged awkwardly down the Via Tecta, a broad paved street that ran parallel to the Tiber a few hundred yards inland. He saw the Stadium of Domitian in the middle distance, the Baths of Nero and Agrippa poking their tiled heads above it.

He turned right on a side street and slowed to a walk. From here, he could see why the Vandals were quiet. Teams of them were carrying loads of spoils to the shipyards. When Rabbit had last seen them, they were in the frenzy of invasion. Now they looked tired, bored, and entirely unmenacing. The blond giants who had haunted his nightmares for twenty years were just people after all. In many ways, that made what they did worse. On the other hand, he felt at last that he could relax. The version of himself that had come here with Aaron was long gone.

There was nowhere to hide on the road, so Rabbit didn't try. Instead, he adopted the tried-and-true method of walking like he belonged there. It worked. The soldiers-turned-pack-mules returning from the river empty-handed regarded him as part of the landscape. They must be awfully confident in the passivity of the Roman people. The work teams, some with wagons, some with horses or actual mules, were mostly unarmed. Carrying a three-foot sword and a heavy shield would tend to limit one's ability to carry away loot. Two Vandals passed him, wheeling a cart groaning under the weight of amphorae filled with olive oil.

Rabbit skirted them all, walking quickly to the dock.

The rain was falling steadily now in drops the size of marbles. It hissed on the tiled roofs of the nearby buildings.

Much of the northeast side of the river was walled and fronted with a spacious walkway for loading rivercraft moored against the berth. The area was teeming with Vandals organizing plunder and loading it onto the boats. Much of this Rabbit would later see unloaded on the docks at Constantinople. *Enjoy it while you can; Belisarius will make you choke on it eventually,* he thought.

He approached a tall, wiry Vandal with a magnificent mustache who appeared to be in a position of authority. "Excuse me," Rabbit said.

"What do you need? Be quick."

"My master sent me."

"For what? No! Over there, on that pile, you steaming shit! Go on."

"My master is a wealthy man. His home is on the Esquiline Mount."

"You must be so proud." He blew rain out of his mustache.

"My master offers me as a slave if, in exchange, your men will spare the rest of his possessions." Rabbit had to raise his voice to be heard over the rain. He raised a hand to shield his eyes.

The man stared at Rabbit. "Your master sounds like a goat's asshole."

Rabbit shrugged, taking to his role.

The foreman considered, then shook his head. "Forget it. I wouldn't even know where to find your master's house."

"I could write it down."

"You can write?"

Rabbit nodded. "In Latin and Greek."

The man's mustache twitched as he calculated Rabbit's value as a slave. "If you leave that there, I swear to the Almighty I will gut you like a fish! Sorry, friend. I can't go making personal exceptions. Where are you from?"

"Athens." Athenians had a reputation as being the best educated, most valuable slaves. "If you won't accept me, you might as well throw me in the Tiber. My master said not to come home if I couldn't secure the deal."

"Put those jugs on that sow-bellied bucket. Not that one, the one with the oversized candlestick."

Rabbit snapped his head around. Sonofabitch. The menorah was sitting on the deck of a fishing boat twenty yards away. The rain dancing off its surface haloed it in angelic splendor.

"I feel bad for you, Greek, working for an elephant hemorrhoid of a master like that. Tell you what. If you stick around here and make yourself useful, I'll look the other way when we leave. You can make for the countryside, start fresh."

Rabbit grinned and nodded, legitimately surprised by the man's sense of mercy. "What would be useful? I could inventory the spoils if you have writing materials."

"In this rain? Don't bother. If that mule falls into the river due to your stupid handling, you'll follow him! What I really need is another body to keep these idiots in line. How much do you know about shipping?"

"My master is a merchant. I have some rudimentary . . ."

"Good enough. I can't afford to send these boats out half-full. Go up to the front of the line and make sure they're loaded as heavily as they can be without sinking the tubs."

Rabbit nodded and turned.

"Oh, and I hope it's understood that if you screw this up, you'll dine on your own acorns."

"I understand."

He pointed. "Front of the line. Hurry, or you'll miss it. What turnip-dicked idiot told you to collect all those sodden woolens? You'll stink up the boats!"

Rabbit left the foreman, shielding his eyes from the rain. It was coming down so hard he could barely see. He looked at the menorah as he passed. It was in the ship two back from the front of the line. Other goods were being packed in around it, securing it on the deck. Still, it stood out dramatically. Rabbit glanced back at the foulmouthed foreman. He was cursing his men, but still caught Rabbit's eye. He was a shrewd one. Rabbit wouldn't be able to simply board the wrong ship and get away with it.

He weaved through the workers in the blinding downpour until he reached the first boat in line. The gangplank was down, and he boldly marched onto a deck scattered with various piles of spoils.

"Who are you?" the Roman captain asked.

Rabbit jerked his thumb at the dock. "The foreman asked me to pitch in, check that the boats were loaded adequately." He was barely looking at the captain. His eyes were fixed on the menorah on the next boat, sure that if he looked away, he would lose track of it.

The captain was saying something, but the squall was carrying his words away. "What?" Rabbit half shouted.

"I said we can't take any more on deck. I've a belly full of captives, poor beggars."

Rabbit had been so fixated on the ship behind them that he hadn't noticed the stream of people descending into the hold. A few armed Vandals supervised the loading, their swords drawn and shining in the rain.

Rabbit's stomach dropped.

Supported by two other captives, a young man was stumbling toward the hold, his arms draped across their shoulders.

It was Aaron.

His face was swollen and purple, but the rain had washed away the blood. It was unmistakably him.

The captain poked Rabbit in the chest. "Hey! I said I'm fully loaded."

Rabbit nodded, barely hearing the man. His mind was racing. In Rabbit's history, Aaron lived as a captive in Carthage and would go on to become Germanius Thrax, Joseph ben Levi, and Victor of Vita. Rabbit had met him. That meant Rabbit couldn't save him. In his own history, he must have already failed. Right?

He glanced back at the menorah. It was the smart play. It wouldn't be easy, but he still had a chance to get it.

But what if he was wrong?

He had come back in Helen's decay point. What if he could rescue Aaron? Maybe that's why he didn't show up in anyone's history of the time. Some kind of inflection point? Rabbit knew he was justifying insanity.

He saw Aaron disappear into the hold.

Aaron would become a slave. He would lose his soul and murder countless people in his quest for a better world. This was the moment that would form him into the megalomaniac who would split history and attempt to drag Rabbit into his reality.

The damn menorah could wait.

With one last glance at the treasure, Rabbit saluted the captain and made his way slowly back to the gangplank. The captain immediately forgot about him and began shouting orders to his crew. Once he was sure the captain was occupied, he approached the Vandals who were closing the hatch on the hold.

"Excuse me," he said.

The two soldiers looked at him in surprise.

"I'm supposed to be down there, too."

They looked at each other, shrugged, and opened the hatch. Rabbit descended the narrow steps. It closed above him, and Rabbit took the last few steps in darkness.

He was cursed weakly by the people crowding the bottom of

the ladder. There was little room in the hold as it was. No one was happy about one more body joining the cargo.

If anything, it was louder in the hold than it had been above. The rain pounding the deck was joined by a boom of thunder. A moment later lightning flashed, revealing every gap in the wooden boat as a streak of white that left afterimages dancing across Rabbit's vision.

"Aaron?" Rabbit called out.

"Stop shouting, man!" someone whined in his face so close Rabbit could feel his breath.

The boat began to sway gently under his feet. They had unmoored and were floating down the Tiber.

"Aaron," he repeated. Ignoring the grumbling of the people around him, Rabbit pushed through the crowd. They swore and protested, but no one tried to stop him. As he made his way through the crowd, his eyes began to adjust to the dim light only to be blinded again by a flash of lightning.

"Aaron," he called every few steps with hushed insistence.

"Dr. Ward?" finally responded a voice from floor level.

Rabbit squatted low. "Aaron!"

Hands grasped for him, caught his arms. His mentee rose to his feet and wrapped his arms around Rabbit in a hug like a vise.

"I'm sorry!" the voice said over his shoulder. He spoke in English.

"You're sorry?" Rabbit asked, flabbergasted.

"You told me not to get involved. I was fucking stupid." He sounded ashamed and childlike. But his voice was light and clear. Rabbit thought of the ancient rasp of Aaron's voice at a hundred years old.

"I'm sorry I left you."

"You came back."

Rabbit's eyes were beginning to adjust to the light. He could see the misshapen lines of the young man's face, swollen from the beating he'd received.

"We're going to get out of here, okay, but we need to be quick. We only have a few hours to get to the decay point."

"A few hours? But it's a day's ride away!"

"I can't explain right now, just trust me. We can do it."

"But . . ."

"Aaron! We don't have time."

The young man steadied himself. "What do you need me to do?"

"First things first. We need to get off this boat. Follow me."

They shoved their way back through the crowd toward the ladder. The protests of the other captives morphed into curiosity as Rabbit put his foot on the first step.

"Shut up!" he hissed to the inquisitive crowd in Latin. "We're getting out of here."

That statement drew a mixture of vocal resistance and support. The captives seemed equally split between the fear of punishment and the call of freedom.

Enough of them were pushing in on Rabbit that he had no choice but to climb the ladder. Awkwardly, he drew the gladius from its scabbard and went to the top. Just as he was reaching for the hatch, lightning struck. The flash momentarily revealed through the gaps in the boards the silhouette of a man seated on top of the hatch. The boat was a commandeered shipping craft. Rabbit had noticed that none of the sailors onboard looked like Vandals. That meant a limited number of guards. The hatch probably didn't lock, and one of them had chosen to keep it closed with his own weight. *Sorry, pal,* Rabbit thought, as he placed the point of the short sword to a gap in the boards the afterglow identified as the guard's butt.

Squatting down on the rung, Rabbit braced his arms and rammed the sword up through the wood. A yelp of pain reached his ears and Rabbit threw open the hatch, yanking the sword free from the wood as it fell away.

The guard was holding his posterior in shock and pain. He

hadn't even drawn his sword. Rabbit launched at him and shoved him over the gunwale into the foaming river below.

He spun on his heel and saw across the deck another Vandal drawing his longsword. His eyes darted between Rabbit and the hatch. Aaron was out now, and several other captives were following.

Rabbit saw the burly soldier calculating the risk versus reward of attacking the armed man or the unarmed slaves. "Here!" yelled Rabbit, striding forward to draw his focus. He couldn't ignore the short sword once it was headed his way. The man shifted his feet on the rain-slick wood and put his longsword between them. Rabbit became highly conscious of the difference between their reaches. The Vandal was, as well. He grinned grimly and swung the sword in a tight, controlled arc. Rabbit backed out of reach. Again, the Vandal advanced, this time just with the point forward and aimed at Rabbit's midsection. He parried the careful stab, still retreating. Then the back of his legs hit the gunwale and he almost lost his footing. The Vandal feinted forward with the point of the longsword, laughing as Rabbit flinched and parried again, his gladius feeling as inadequate as a kitchen knife. He really wished he had a shield.

The soldier drew back his sword for a swing that could push past the short sword. Before the blow fell, the Vandal suddenly flopped over backward and crashed to the deck. Aaron stepped up beside him, holding a wooden pole as long as he was tall with a hook at the end. He had just used it to take out the Vandal at the knees.

In a blur of motion, Aaron raised the pole like an ax over the soldier. The soldier, who had lost his sword in the fall, rolled toward Aaron and grappled him to the deck. The pole clattered and rolled on the wood.

Rabbit leaped into the fray and managed to get a solid handful of the Vandal's hair, which he yanked on. Lightning flashed and an image froze in his retinas of a trail of blood between the soldier's teeth and Aaron's shoulder.

The three of them were a slippery pile of writhing fists and teeth. Rabbit used the hilt of his sword as a club, but the Vandal was still fighting like a cornered cat. The deck shifted dramatically on the waves of the river, and they slid across the planks and slammed into a wall of some kind. In the slide, the soldier got on top of Rabbit. He had managed to get hold of his sword arm and was gripping the wrist like a vise. Then he brought his head down like a rock. Rabbit saw stars as pain erupted in his face. He felt the gladius slip from his grip.

The man spasmed violently. Aaron's face appeared over his shoulder next to the Vandal's ear, a contorted mask of rage and elation. "You like that?!" he shrieked. He jerked forward, once, twice, in an obscene parody of sex. The Vandal opened his mouth. Lightning flashed and Rabbit's eyes captured an image that would haunt him for the rest of his life. The point of the Vandals' longsword was thrusting through his mouth into his hard palate, blood spilling freely around it onto Rabbit's face. Aaron loomed over his shoulder, the ecstasy of vengeance painted across it.

Rabbit blinked and the soldier rolled off onto the deck.

Aaron unsheathed the sword from the Vandal. His eyes were alight in his ecstatic, swollen mask of a face. He offered Rabbit a hand. For a fleeting moment, Rabbit didn't want to take it.

"Are you okay?" Aaron asked loudly to be heard over the rain. He was panting. The joy of hatred slid off the young man's face.

Rabbit wiped his face, winced at the pain in his nose, and nodded. "I'm okay," he answered and took his mentee's hand.

Rabbit got to his feet, and the two of them took in their surroundings. Twenty or more captives stood in scattered groups around the deck of the boat, vaguely menacing the craft's pilots, but taking no overt action. The Roman boatmen looked scared, not aggressive.

Rabbit retrieved his sword and sheathed it at his belt.

"What now?" shouted Aaron.

"Check to see who's on the river behind us. Where are we?" he asked the boatman at the rudder.

The man shrugged helplessly. "Nowhere. Farmland."

"How far from Rome?" Rabbit clarified.

"A few miles. More or less."

The wind was blowing hard upriver from the southwest. Rabbit looked out at the rocky shoreline and decided.

"Turn it around," he said, drawing a circle in the air with his index finger.

"What?" He looked terrified.

"Turn it around," Rabbit growled.

The pilot looked queasy at the thought. He glanced over his shoulder, clearly pondering who he feared more, the army at his back or the sword right in front of him.

"Raise sails!" he shouted to his fellows.

He steered the boat gently to one side of the river and then pulled hard on the rudder. The riverboat swung its nose around dramatically into the current as the sail filled with so much force, Rabbit through it would snap the ropes that held it in place.

Aaron was back at his side pointing. "Incoming."

The boat was a couple hundred yards away, a grey shape forming out of a grey background.

"Get everyone down. With luck, they'll think we're returning from port."

"The hatch?" he asked.

"No time." He told the nearest group to lie down on the rain-slicked deck of the craft. The directionless captives seemed pleased to have something to do. In no time, fifty or so people lay splayed on the boards. Rabbit hoped they would be obscured enough by the blinding rain not to arouse interest.

Aaron and Rabbit remained standing on the low quarterdeck near the captain, swords held at their sides.

The two craft faded to opposite sides of the river to avoid one another. Rabbit could make out figures on the deck of the approaching boat watching them. It was more heavily manned than their own craft had been. He made out five tall figures doing nothing other than keeping watch. Boxes were stacked on its deck. No surprise, the objects looted from Rome were guarded more heavily than the slaves.

The boats appeared to be approaching one another slowly. Rabbit felt as though he could see the eyes of the Vandals. One of them raised a hand in salute. Rabbit imitated the gesture. And then they were passing one another, and their relative positions made it clear how fast they were both moving, one screaming down the roiling river, the other pushed upriver by the gale winds.

Everyone heaved a sigh of relief as the treasure boat became obscured in the downpour.

"What do you intend?" asked the captain.

"South of the city walls, you let us out. Make up any story you like. Some of the captives may prefer to go to Carthage, but the ones who want to flee, you let go."

The captain crossed himself but did not object.

"Incoming," Aaron said again.

Another boat had just come into view around a bend in the river. Just like the prior craft, it was hard to make out in the rain. Rabbit was glad for Aaron's sharp eyes.

The captives dropped to the planks again. Fewer of them this time because some had chosen to take shelter from the rain below deck. The boat became clearer as it approached. When it was fifty yards away, lightning struck.

"Rabbit!" Aaron said. He was pointing at the approaching boat, his mouth wide. Rabbit had seen it too. The menorah was perched on the foredeck among piles of other spoils.

"I see it," said Rabbit.

"This is our shot! We can get it!"

Rabbit shook his head. How could he explain to Aaron that he had already lost him once; he had no intention of doing so again.

But Aaron moved with surprising speed for an injured man. He shoved the captain out of the way and grabbed the handle of the rudder. He leaned into it, and the boat tilted sharply to one side as it turned into the path of the approaching craft.

The captives slid across the deck to pile up against the gunwale. Aaron stumbled and barely caught himself on a rigging rope. The people on the approaching boat were moving rapidly, trying to steer out of the way, but it was too late. The prow of the slave boat rammed the side of the treasure hauler mid-maneuver and scraped the length of her hull as the boats passed one another. The stack of loot at the front of the hauler shifted and much of it spilled over the side. Rabbit couldn't tell if the menorah was among them.

"Hey!" The captain's shout got his attention. He was pointing frantically behind the boat.

Aaron had fallen in and was flailing in the water.

Without a thought, Rabbit sheathed his sword, ran to the back of the boat, and dove over the gunwale. He hit the water and swam after Aaron.

The river, swollen with rain, rose and fell unpredictably. One moment he could see his mentee fighting the current, the next he was obscured by water. A crate bobbed past Rabbit like a cork, barely missing him. He slashed the water with his strokes and then suddenly almost collided with Aaron, who was struggling to stay afloat against the power of the torrent.

Rabbit caught him under the arm. "Go with the current," he shouted. But Aaron's face was staring up behind him. Rabbit turned and saw the treasure ship loom up like a wall. Its wake caught Rabbit and Aaron and tumbled them across the side of the craft, beating them against the wood. In his flailing to get free of its pull, he caught a rope hanging in the water and snatched it. He slapped against the side of the boat and was dragged by it. His other arm was still wrapped around Aaron, but the young man was taking a face full of water and sputtering for breath. Rabbit tried to haul himself up higher on the boat, but no matter how he pulled, he seemed to be sinking. No, he realized. He wasn't sinking, the boat was. It had taken on water from the collision and wasn't going to make it much farther.

When a boat sinks, it creates suction as it displaces water. Rabbit looked up, saw the gunwale of the boat approaching them, and knew what was coming. He released the rope and tried to swim away, pulling with one arm. But sure enough, he felt the pull of the water drag him and Aaron back. It tossed them across the deck and banged them against its cargo. He tried to struggle to his feet, but it was no use in the waves. His back hit a mast, which knocked the air out of him, and he found himself looking at it. The menorah, lashed to the deck for safety, stood proudly on the boards of the sinking ship. It was a beautiful, horrible sight. Rabbit watched as the water rose to claim it.

He took a deep breath.

The water claimed him, too, rising above his head as the suction of the sinking boat seemed to pin him to the deck. Luckily, it was only for a moment and then the powerful hand of the river released him. A moment later he bobbed to the surface like a cork, floating amid wooden bits from the boat. He managed to get his arm over a crate and began to kick his way toward the river's edge, not fighting the current, but letting it carry him along like a serpent mount until finally, choking and sputtering, they washed up on shore.

They clawed their way up the bank, which was thankfully gentle in this stretch of the river. Aaron was the first to sit up. He gazed up and down the Tiber.

"We did it."

They followed the west bank of the river back toward Rome. Where the city walls touched the river's bank, they followed the road or slogged through the mud until they picked up the Triumphal Way. Aaron limped badly, slowed by exhaustion and his injuries, but he kept moving. The rain was finally beginning to let up as they slogged north on the flint-paved road. Across the Tiber, Rabbit could see the Vandals continuing their orderly plunder. He even picked out the foreman by his majestic, if sodden, mustache. The man was still directing workers, no doubt cursing them all. Rabbit smiled.

Then they met eyes. He stopped in place, staring at Rabbit for a moment. Then he glared. With a gesture and a shout Rabbit couldn't hear, the Vandal set several of his fellows into a run for the Aelian Bridge. So much for the barbarian with the heart of gold.

"We need to move," Rabbit told Aaron.

All of their muscles screaming from fatigue, the two men broke into a painful run.

When the road continued straight between the circuses of Nero and Hadrian, Rabbit veered off, hugging the river to cut the angle closer. The Mausoleum of Hadrian came into view as they broke free of the buildings along the walled shore. He looked behind them. No sign of the Vandals in the circuitous path through the buildings, but he didn't doubt they were close.

"Rabbit . . ." said Aaron.

"I know," Rabbit said.

Ahead, he could see another contingent stepping onto the far side of the bridge that ended at the decay point. Rabbit had no choice but to stay the course. He didn't know how much time they had left, and they couldn't miss the jump. He would just have to risk the soldiers to do it.

"Rabbit," the young man slurred. Then he collapsed.

Cursing, Rabbit hoisted Aaron onto his shoulder and winced at the pain from his not-quite-healed bite wound. He launched into a shuffling speed walk that carried him the last hundred yards. He spotted the missing paving stone and centered himself over it.

Three Vandals were loping toward them, almost across the

bridge. Gone were the human pack mules; these men had reclaimed their bloodlust and looked every bit as terrifying as Rabbit had remembered.

He stood his ground on the decay point. As the soldiers approached, the two leading Vandals raised their swords above their heads and broke into a full, mad charge.

Rabbit held up his sword to block the incoming blow. His sword arm shook with fatigue.

Then the world disappeared.

ROME

2018 CE

Rabbit blinked in the dim confines of the van. The Vandals had been replaced by the two mercs with their submachine guns. Not a big improvement. They were staring at him, mouths agape.

"Guida," a woman's voice said nearby. *Drive.* The van lurched into motion. He was unsettled by the sudden movement and stumbled to his knees trying to protect Aaron. He eased the young man off his shoulder. "Well, did you get what you wanted?" Rabbit could hear the woman's voice approaching as she spoke. She stepped around the technician's console. He watched her face as she looked at Rabbit then past him at Aaron. Confusion wiped away her self-assured expression, and then something else took its place. The blood drained from her face. "Portare in un ospedale." *Get to a hospital.*

"Ospedale? Perché?" asked a voice over unseen speakers in the van.

"Now!" she barked.

The van took a hard right. Rabbit dropped his gladius and braced himself on the floor. Aaron leaned on him heavily.

"Attentamente!" she ordered.

She took a step toward them but didn't get any closer.

"Why is everyone speaking Italian?" Aaron mumbled.

Rabbit carefully helped Aaron lie down on the dilator pad. His face was still almost unrecognizable from the swelling. The rain and dirt that had covered him were left in the past, but that made the scene almost more startling. His stark white tunic was dotted with fresh blood, expanding from his wounds into the cloth. At least none of the germs he had picked up in those wounds would have returned with him. Time travel was a great sterilizing agent. Two of the wounds were bleeding more freely than the others. Rabbit wadded up a handful of his tunic and pressed it to those spots. Aaron groaned.

"How did you do that?" said the woman behind him in a barely audible whisper.

"I don't know," Rabbit replied.

Rabbit waited in the hospital lounge for five hours. The van had dropped off Rabbit and Aaron at the emergency room and driven away, but not until the woman with the glasses had taken care of everything at the admissions desk and pointed out Rabbit to the medical staff as Aaron's contact.

"Everything is paid for," she said when she strode over to him a moment later. She handed him a duffel bag that contained his clothes, phone, and wallet.

"Thanks," he said lamely, accepting the bag.

"You could have told me this was your plan."

"Due to our great mutual trust?" he snarked. "It wasn't my plan."

She laughed through her nose. "There goes your reputation."

He shrugged.

She turned to leave.

"Wait," he stood up. To hell with it. He was too exhausted and too raw to be coy any longer. This might be his last opportunity to ask. "What about Helen?"

"What about her?"

"Is she all right?"

She looked at him curiously, as though he were an object in a museum. Rabbit swore he could see her file this moment away. "Goodbye, Dr. Ward," she said. Then she clicked away on the cold tile floor.

Rabbit spent the next twenty-four hours in the hospital waiting room, accepting each new update from the medical staff with the same glazed expression. His Italian was good enough for everything except the medical jargon. Aaron was out of surgery but was unstable. He was stable and had been moved out of the ICU but, no, Rabbit couldn't see him. Rabbit drifted in and out of shallow sleep where he dreamed of the two Aarons arguing with one another. The old man and the young were debating how to divide a cookie iced to look like planet Earth.

"Scusi, signore."

Rabbit jerked awake.

"Puoi visitarlo ora."

The nurse beckoned him forward, and Rabbit followed her numbly upstairs to Aaron's recovery room.

He was awake and smiled dopily when Rabbit entered.

"Hey, stranger," he said. Then he squinted at him, a look of confusion spreading across his face. "Why do you look so . . ."

"Old? Let me catch you up."

Rabbit explained that he had not suddenly aged twenty years, but that Aaron had missed those years and why. He carefully excluded Aaron's role in the past, what he had become and done, and how it had all unwittingly led to his own rescue. Aaron questioned him on every point, and Rabbit had to construct a series of half-truths to explain the sequence of events. There was no reason for the young man to have to live with the knowledge of what he might have been if Rabbit hadn't come back for him.

At last, when he was satisfied, Aaron settled back into his pillows. "Thank you," he said. "I owe you one."

Rabbit smiled. "Why don't we call it even?"

At Aaron's request, a nurse came and administered more pain medication through his IV. His eyes unfocused slightly, and his voice took on a dreamy, faraway note. "There was a moment, after the attack, when they were carrying me to the boat that it all came together. Everything, like inspiration painted on a canvas. Everything I had to do. A plan that would take me a lifetime. And I wasn't worried or scared. I knew with pure certainty that I could do it."

Rabbit knew exactly what he was talking about, and the thought chilled him.

"But I guess that was just dreaming, or maybe trying to make the best of it, maybe."

He drifted off for a moment, then opened his eyes again sharply. He looked at Rabbit, and those eyes burned with cold fire. Then, just as suddenly, his lids softened, and his gaze wandered away. "Oh, it's you," he said softly.

He slept again. No one insisted Rabbit leave, so he stayed in the room, talking to Aaron whenever he awoke, having to remind him again and again where he was through the narcotic haze. A few hours later, the nurse returned. This time, she was leading David and Sarah Kahan.

Rabbit got up and stepped away from the bedside. David rushed forward and embraced his bemused son, to whom he must look like a grandfather. David cried and hugged Aaron and had to be reminded by the nurse to be gentle.

Rabbit slunk out of the room.

"Where are you going?" a hoarse voice stopped him.

Sarah was standing in the doorway, her face unreadable. There were dark rings under her eyes, and her fashionable clothes were rumpled from the plane ride. She crossed the space between them in two steps and wrapped her arms around him. The relief he felt swept through him like warm water, weakening his knees. After a long moment, she released him and touched his cheek. The tired smile on her face was like the sun.

The next few weeks were an endless repetition of the same story. Rabbit was brought up on charges for breaking the Adams-Cortez Act, then the charges were dropped. The Social Security Administration and IRS tied themselves in knots trying to figure out how to record and penalize Aaron for his missed years of earning, and then they too dropped their efforts. Rabbit was reinstated with the Smithsonian, and sponsors came out of the woodwork. The charges against Ian were dropped, although he was slapped with a ban from entering the country of Turkey until further notice.

"I'll soldier on somehow" was his friend's only response.

A month and a half after Aaron's rescue, Rabbit and PJ stood side by side on the dredging platform. The retrieval of the menorah had been delayed a few times. First, a fresh corpse was found on the bottom of the river that had gotten the dig reclassified as a crime scene. Next, some Renaissance-era pottery was uncovered in a buried crate. The Tiber, like time, hid the glories and sins of the past in its many layers.

When the time finally came, Rabbit and PJ were called to observe. It was a beautiful day in Rome, and they were ferried out under the bright sunshine to the diving platform situated in the middle of the river.

The underside of the platform was loaded with imaging technology that helped the divers find what they were looking for. If land-based archaeological digs were delicate business, a dig in a moving river would be ten times more so. Nonetheless, as Rabbit and PJ watched, a stream of bubbles rose to the surface as two divers accompanied the rope reeling up from the water.

The rope was attached to a yellow plastic cage that rose out of the water. In it, the menorah stood proudly.

"You did it, honey," PJ said and rubbed his back.

"Yep," he muttered in return.

"Well, don't celebrate too hard. You did it!"

The plastic cage touched down on the deck. The menorah was worn and pocked with age but had held its shape.

"It looks smaller than I remember."

PJ rolled her eyes and huffed. "When you're ready to tell me why you're raining on your own parade, will you let me know?"

He just huffed in response. He had thought that raising the menorah would liberate him. It was the white whale he had been chasing for twenty years. It had come to represent so much to him. Now, looking at it, it was just a worn-out piece of metal after all. He had brought Aaron home, and that was the real victory, right?

As if she were reading his mind, PJ said, "It's funny, isn't it?"

"Hm?"

"These stories we tell ourselves about regrets and guilt, they become so much a dang part of us that it feels scary to let them go sometimes, doesn't it? Like it's a cornerstone in the foundation of your house or something. You just feel like you don't even know who you'd be without it."

He grunted.

"Well, honey." She patted his cheek. "It's high time you got to figuring that out."

The dig turned up a boatload of treasures that would need to be cataloged and tracked. It would be a huge win for the Institute. Given recent experience, security was tight and would remain so until all the artifacts were safely protected in facilities. There wasn't much for PJ and Rabbit to do. They stayed onboard a little while longer then were shuttled to the shore.

PJ suggested they go get a celebratory lunch. He agreed, but his heart wasn't in it. Not because of the menorah. He'd get over that. He hadn't heard from the woman with the glasses since Aaron's rescue, and he had no way of contacting her. He had probably seen the last of her. In all likelihood, he had seen the last of Helen as well. He just wanted closure. Even knowing if she were alive or dead would help. But it seemed that would be the final piece of the puzzle he might never get an answer to.

EPILOGUE

Macedonia, 335 BCE

Rabbit placed the last stone on top of the cairn and stretched his back. He had helped himself out on this mission, deciding to place the artifacts at the bottom of a mass grave near the decay point. He'd have half a day and no forced march this time. Just an easy meal under a blue sky before he made the jump back.

This was his first mission since his return to Rome. PJ had asked Aaron if he was interested in resuming as Rabbit's partner but, much to Rabbit's relief, his old mentee had decided that time travel might not be for him after all. Rabbit had done the mission alone as usual, and it had gone as smoothly as any in his career.

He washed his hands in the little stream that trickled through the base of the valley. A mass burial site was a great hiding place; grave robbers knew better than to look for treasure there. Still, he was second-guessing his selection. Rabbit wasn't one to feel disrespectful for disturbing a final resting place, but he hadn't considered just how revolting it would be to dig his way through a few hundred partially decayed corpses.

He used the gritty sand to scrub the grime from his hands, then splashed cold water on his face. As the disturbed surface of the water settled, its reflective surface revealed a second face, hovering over his shoulder behind him. Its wide smile seemed to be bracketed by parentheses.

Rabbit's breath caught in his chest, and he thought for a split second he might be hallucinating. He spun around and there she was.

Helen.

She grinned at him.

"Hello, handsome."

ACKNOWLEDGMENTS

I remember long car rides destined for summer destinations, cabins and lakesides observed obliquely, pale backdrops to those most magic of carpets: books. Thank you, Donaldson and de Larrabeiti, King and Clavell and McCullough and all the authors in between who made me want to tell stories. If even one person feels as transported by my stumbling in their footsteps as I did then, I will be satisfied.

Writing is a solitary process, but creating a book is eminently social. Thanks to my editor, Michael, for nudging me gently in better directions and letting me think they were my ideas; to Amy, who suffered through my atrociously inconsistent noun capitalization; and to the artists who made the book look like more than just a pile of pages. Thanks to Professor Pieter van der Horst, whose research connected the dots between the Jewish population of Constantinople and the racing demes.

Thanks to David, agent extraordinaire, for taking a chance on an old guy and his story no one quite knew where to shelve; to Naomi, the true chrono-archaeologist, who was the first professional to say those magic words, "I get it"; and to Susanna, the Great Connector, who made the match.

It was a match I would never have dared attempt if not for the support of my circle of fellow writers and readers. Thank you, Harry, Steve, and Jacob, for reading every scrappy word I write; the Smirking and Grinning gang for being the best cheer squad ever; and Uncle Joe, without whose deep knowledge of Catholic history I would have put my foot in it. But it truly would have been impossible without Daryl, my brother of the page. Your encouragement kept me going, your criticism made me better. Thanks for the beers and words, buddy.

Justin, the years we spent writing screenplays shoulder to shoulder in coffee shops and greasy diners gave me a sense of structure, both in writing and in life. My thanks to you and to Jason, who, for thirty years, have been so much more than brothers. And Andy-of-the-pants, you, Nicola, and the best west fam have shown me what truly living a life of creativity is all about.

Thanks also to my dad and stepmom, who instilled in me a love of reading; to my mom, who encouraged me to create; and to my big (but much younger) sister, Liz—there's still plenty of room up here on the pedestal you built for me. Climb on up, schwester.

Thank you, my sweet kids, Jo and August. You keep my eyes wide and my heart wider.

Finally, an enormous thank-you to my wife, Tess, shield-maiden of my soul, who implacably defended my writing time, listened to my every preposterous idea, and counseled me through the innumerable moments of human frailty that threatened to hold me back. You and me, all the way.

ABOUT THE AUTHOR

Jeremy Lawson

Andrew Ludington writes transportive adventure stories intended to make you forget your commute. He graduated from Kenyon College with a BA in English Literature and lives in Evanston, Illinois, where he moonlights as a technologist for Northwestern University. *Splinter Effect* is his first novel.